Thoroughly Modern People

The Long Way Home

Chima Njoku-Latty

MY DESTINY

A My Destiny paperback
First published in Great Britain in 2010
by My Destiny Ltd,
Copyright © 2010 by Chima Njoku-Latty

A CIP catalogue record for this book is available from the
British Library.

ISBN: 0956600107
ISBN-13: 9780956600103

Author Bio

Chima Njoku-Latty is a British author of Nigerian-Jamaican heritage. She lives in North London with her American husband and she is working on another novel.

Acknowledgements

A huge thank you to all my family – the best people in the world – who have never stopped supporting me in everything I do.

Mummy, thank you for being the best in every way. Sheila, without your discerning eye and *savoir faire*, I would not have got this book together, thank you. Ju, always there and always supporting me, thanks. Dee, the best mentor any pioneer could ever wish for, thanks for your strength and relentless support. Mark, my rock of all ages, always beavering away in the background, putting all the paperless pieces together and making them a reality, you're the best hubby ever, thanks. Jim, Jam and Kit – my readers – thanks for always being gentle with your criticism. Emmy, Isa, Liz and Luny, thanks for never stopping rooting for me.

Let's not forget Flossy Macpherson, Hugh O' Gara, Beckster Hallewell, Maria Tomas, Jadams, Shan Lee, Jackie Defoe, Gabriela Cogorno and all my friends who've never stopped believing in and supporting me. It ain't over yet peeps, so keep those prayers a-coming.

Chapter One

You say potatoes and I say patatas

Seven Buckley Gardens was a large, white detached building at the end of a leafy cul-de-sac near Muswell Hill Broadway in north London. In Flat 3, the first-floor apartment directly above the foyer, lived Arabella Winthrop.

To her neighbours, she was the hazel-eyed, cute little blond who always chirped 'hello' whenever she passed by on the carpeted staircase or on the street. Many of them liked her, even Old Grumpy Chops from Flat 7 with her pinched and mocking smile.

According to the elderly lady, 'that Arabella girl seems to live in constant Spring – bless her – skipping down the stairs as she does, like a lamb, or swinging her bag as she walks along like one keeping time with a gay ditty in her mind'.

The Arabella fan club, however, did not include moody Mary, the wizened red-haired copy writer from Flat 2, who reminded Arabella of a yam (but with hair) like those she'd seen displayed outside the row of Asian convenient stores. These shops aired their wares on Stroud Green Road mainly for the attention of an African and West Indian clientele, who strolled along with fingers poised to squeeze the items to find the best of the colourful but barely surviving produce that had been sourced from their home countries or near enough by.

For moody Mary, Arabella's gait was bad enough, but it was her perpetual smile –*urgh* – that was most irritating. Impatient and irascible, she didn't see how anybody could be that happy all the time, especially not in London. As far as she was concerned, 'Miss Skippidy-do', as she called Arabella, 'must be on something stronger than caffeine, if you know what I mean'. But none of the others wanted to know what she meant, and this intensified her dislike for Arabella, whom she often willed to fall, stub her toe, get shat on by a bird, anything to stop her smiling.

If only they could all see Arabella now as she was finishing off her packing. None of their opinions of her would change. It was six in the morning and she hadn't slept a wink, but you wouldn't have known it to watch her waltzing the clothes she'd decided to leave behind back to her jam-packed wardrobe. Inside, a higgledy-piggledly squeeze of haute couture, high street fashion and five-pound bargains that looked a million dollars after a touch of the Winthrop flair.

Arabella was a trendsetter who led with such ease and panache that many, including strangers on the street, tried to copy her effortless style but failed woefully. It would probably be the same when she got to America – Seattle, to be precise – where she would be heading in a few hours time, to be with Max.

'Max,' Arabella squealed with joy, as thoughts of him filled her mind: his smile, his walk, his voice, his name. 'Everything,' she announced aloud. She loved him in his entirety. Gentle, kind, loving, suave and distinguished-looking with his speckled grey low-cut afro, what was there not to love about the man?

Snatching up a long purple jersey dress from her Victorian four-poster bed, which was covered with a multicoloured patchwork spread of sewn-together antique tapestries that she'd inherited from her Nana, Arabella began to dance again, with the dress as her latest partner. It felt fabulous to be this happy and she didn't mind if the whole world knew it.

Well, not everyone and certainly not yet, she reconsidered with reference to her neighbours. What a nosey lot they were. *Most of them,* she clarified, not wanting to be unjust to Jeremy from Flat 5 by lumping him in with the rest. Like her, Jeremy, or Mr Stockbroker as the others called him, preferred to keep to himself, but he didn't guard his privacy effectively enough.

Poor lamb, Arabella giggled. He didn't do himself any favours forgetting his keys as often as he did. Nor by electing Gerard from Flat 1 as caretaker of his spares. Gerard was the lead gossip of the street and the one who kept everyone updated on Jeremy's penchant for 'fluffy little blonds whom he keeps rotating through the weeks, months, and years without sampling any particular one for longer than a few weeks'.

Poor, poor Jeremy, if only he knew. Arabella felt a pang of guilt for not having warned him that his confidant was his betrayer, but, she shrugged, she had no choice. He and Gerard seemed a bit too pally for her to have risked it. What if Jeremy disclosed that she was his source? *Oh dear,* she shuddered, not feeling much like dancing anymore.

Returning to the bed, Arabella began to fold the dress, her thoughts lingering on Gerard. As kingpin of the gossips, he wasn't someone to get on the wrong side of. He would have made her life hell by finding and dishing the proverbial dirt on her.

No, thank you very much, Arabella thought with a grimace. It wasn't that she'd done anything of which she was ashamed. No, she simply cherished her privacy and her right to have control over what to share with whom and when. And the only way she could do that was to stay off the gossips' radar by keeping quiet about Gerard's gossiping.

Arabella began to smile. What an irony it was to have the chief gossip as the unwitting safe keeper of her private life. She remembered back to two months ago when Max came round to beg her to return to him. She'd thought that his visit would have set the street abuzz with speculations and interest in her life, but it hadn't, thanks to Gerard.

Although moody Mary had tried to stir up suspicion about Max and what he'd come for, Gerard had overridden all speculation by convincing the nosey brigade to assume he could be 'Eleanor's dad'. And so, from then on, they disregarded Max with no more than their usual everyday smiles to show their lack of interest in him.

'Silly woman,' Gerard had hissed bitchily at the time, as he'd divulged all to Arabella at the main door, while listening and watching out for moody Mary or any of her allies. 'I mean, who else could the man have been?', he had twitched adamantly in his nervous way. Eleanor was the only black person that most of her neighbours had ever seen with Arabella, and as she had been introduced to them years earlier as 'my bestest friend in the world,' it stood to reason that Max must be her father.

'Come to stay?' moody Mary had allegedly quibbled suspiciously. But the others, now fully re-programmed by Gerard, were thinking nothing of it. Max's valise wasn't evidence enough that he'd stayed over, because he may have been collecting something for Eleanor. Had Max been younger, then yes, Gerard himself had readily admitted, maybe more suspicions would have been aroused. But he wasn't and they weren't. 'So rest assured that we're not with moody Mary on this,' he'd declared.

And thank God for that, Arabella reaffirmed with relief and finished folding the purple dress.

As she returned it to the fatigued-wood chest that was under the large bay window, which looked onto the lawn below, Arabella thought about the gossips of the street. Had they been more vigilant and suspicious of 'the benign-looking black gentleman' – as Gerard had referred to Max – they may have detected the little telltale signs and snippets of conversation that would have betrayed his identity as not only Eleanor's father-in-law, but Arabella's American boyfriend (well 'man-friend', seeing as he was twenty-six years her senior). But thank God they hadn't.

Shutting the chest, Arabella imagined what would happen if her neighbours were to discover the truth now. Oh, the gasps of horror and disappointment that would echo around certain properties on the street. She tittered at the thought. They'd be beside themselves: such juicy gossip in their midst all along and they never caught a whiff of it. How come?

'Gerard' would be the general and angry consensus. He'd always believed that Arabella was too ditsy to have any secrets and had convinced the others to ignore moody Mary's ranting that 'that smile of Arabella's hides many secrets –she's not as innocent as she's cracked up to be, mark my word'.

Oh how vindicated moody Mary would feel at the discovery of the truth about Max and Arabella. 'Huh, Eleanor's dad indeed', she'd scoff. 'Just because they're both black'.

Bless them, Arabella sympathised with a victorious smile, *especially Gerard*, without whose help Max would not have been disregarded by the Buckley Gardens gossips, who masqueraded as the street's neighbourhood watch team. Arabella could see them now in her mind's eye if they'd gone along with moody Mary's suspicions. What a stampede there would have been of residents armed with the best of British smiles knocking at her door throughout that weekend to welcome Max and smooth themselves into his confidence to get the how, when and wherefore of his relationship with her. She and Max would have been too inundated with unwanted attention to have had the time to begin discussing their plans for the future.

Sighing, Arabella rolled her eyes. God, it felt good to know that within the hour she'd be leaving this street and heading far away from her busybody neighbours and their small-minded shenanigans.

At once, Arabella began to daydream about getting on the plane and heading far away from London. *Oh what joy*, she purred at the thought and began to dance again around her modern bedroom that was quirkily, yet tastefully, punctuated with ancestral hand-me-downs from yesteryear. This latest little boogie was her happy lap of honour, she told herself. *And a well deserved one too*, a stray thought interjected, for not having brained her mother, Sophia Winthrop, thus far. 'Yes,' Arabella heard herself concur aloud. *It was quite an achievement.* She loved her mother dearly, but her vitriolic disapproval of Max had worn thin.

Meanwhile on Heath Drive in Hampstead, also in north London, Sophia Winthrop was beside herself with worry that her daughter, Arabella, would leave for America without saying goodbye. Arabella had never before hung up on her in the middle of an argument, no matter how heated, and neither had she ever switched off all her phones so that her mother couldn't reach her afterwards.

Who else could Sophia blame then for this change in her daughter but Max? 'The bastard,' she hissed. Not only had he turned Arabella's head so much that she was refusing to see any sense, but he was now coming between them.

Sophia's mind flipped back to the most important issue at hand –she didn't have a number. *Ow,* Sophia winced with frustration. As she did so, she glimpsed her reflection in the highly polished drinks cabinet at the far side of the large sitting room. Sophia turned on the reflection. 'You stupid, stupid woman,' she scolded it. 'You were supposed to get a number first.'

And that would have been some sort of consolation; she added silently and began to cry. Now how was she going to be able to occasionally check on her daughter to make sure that she was okay and not in need of anything? How was Oliver, her ex and Arabella's father, going to be able to mediate between her and their daughter if they didn't make up before Arabella left London? Sophia began to sob louder. It had all gone so wrong and it was all Max's fault. *That bloody man!*

Why couldn't he have just left Arabella alone? In time she would have gotten over him and found somebody more suitable. *And as for Arabella,* Sophia grizzled, *when did she become so stupid?* Maybe she, Sophia, could be silly at times, but Oliver wasn't –he'd never been

– and Arabella shouldn't be either. *She's daddy's girl, always has been.* Sophia's lips curved into an involuntary smile. She remembered Arabella as a child: crazy mop of curly blond hair, like her father, and always following him around. 'My little shadow,' he used to call her before she was promoted to 'princess'. *What a beauty she was,* her mother recalled, *and always laughing.*

Being a highly imaginative child, Arabella was low maintenance. She could entertain herself for hours with very little. Sophia remembered how entertained she herself used to be watching her daughter being kept amused by the most mundane of objects.

There was the time with the string, Sophia recalled. For more than an hour, she and Oliver had huddled together stifling their laughter as Arabella imagined the string into all sorts of flights of fancy, including a ladder which she held erect for angels to get back up to Heaven before their absence was noticed.

With a smile, Sophia also recalled how it didn't matter whether the books bought for Arabella as a child were targeted at boys or girls. All that mattered was that they had lots of pictures because no matter what the story, Arabella wasn't interested in it. She preferred making up her own and having new ones made up at bedtime for the same picture books.

Bedtime was never difficult like some friends had warned it would be. Once the story – which Arabella insisted must be read with the storyteller lying in bed with her – was over, Arabella would turn and stare into your eyes as if they were her door into the world of sleep. Within minutes, she'd be fast asleep and smiling. Her father often imagined that the stories came to life in her dreams with her as the main protagonist and that was probably why she smiled so much in her sleep. 'She's having the time of her life,' he'd often speculated.

Arabella was a treasured child. 'And still is,' Sophia added quietly, acknowledging her feelings for her daughter. So how could Sophia be expected to stand by and let the girl make a mess of her life with that man? *He's old enough to be her father, for God's sake. Ugh,* the thought of Arabella and someone that old made her skin crawl. Quickly pouring herself another large glass of wine, Sophia downed three-quarters of it in one prolonged mouthful. As she did so, she caught sight of a picture of Arabella aged five, walking hand in hand with her father through Highgate Woods.

Sophia began to smile through her tears. She remembered that Saturday very well. They'd been to Kenwood House, as they always did on a Saturday, and afterwards Arabella had insisted that it was teatime, even though it wasn't yet lunchtime. They had to go to Highgate Woods to her and Daddy's secret tearoom to have tea with the fairies. 'You know the one, Daddy,' she'd said to her father in her conspiratorial tone that was only ever used when speaking to Daddy.

'Am I allowed to come too?' Sophia remembered asking as she kept up the pretence that only Oliver and Arabella knew the enchanted café. It was their secret, one of many that she had to pretend not to know anything about. 'Yes, certainly,' Arabella had agreed, 'but only if you let us blindfold you first'. She was blindfolded until she momentarily sneaked it off, when neither father nor child were looking, to take this picture.

Gulping down the remainder of the wine in her glass, Sophia, who'd been sitting wedged between the dark wood Mexican chest and the cream-coloured corner unit sofa, heaved herself standing. Reeling slightly, she made her way to the chunky wooden beam ledge above the rustic stone fireplace and retrieved the photograph. Clutching it to her breast, she began to sob again. They'd been such a happy family until she'd spoiled it all when Arabella was six by insisting Oliver handle her father's death with the same grief that she was feeling.

It wasn't that this was exactly what she was demanding. She just wanted to feel that he understood what she was going through instead of being so damned happy around the place. *But how could he?* She smiled sadly. Oliver was one of life's troopers who just got on with things, one of the 'if-life-throws-you-lemons-you-make-lemonade' types like Arabella. Sophia kissed Oliver and Arabella's images in the picture in her hand.

That was all very well, she mused, if they went on indefinitely making the proverbial lemonade. But they didn't. Like everyone, there was a limit to how many of life's lemons they could bear being thrown at them. And the question was 'what was their limit?' With father and daughter not showing hurt in the way others did, it made it so bloody hard to know when they were close to their limit.

This was why she was so afraid for her daughter with this renewed relationship with Max. Unlike her, who would scream and shout all the way to her limit so that everybody knew about it, Arabella and Oliver just pootled on, seeming fine, until the day when they would suddenly react, leaving you wondering how, what, where, when and most importantly, why. She'd had that with Oliver when, unable to take the demands of her grief, he'd walked out of their marriage thirty-two years ago, and she'd almost had that with Arabella when she tried to kill herself after Max dumped her two years prior.

So how could she be expected to be reasonable, Sophia seethed, when her only child – and one with such a precarious and unpredictable state of mind – was moving halfway around the world to that _bloody America, of all places, to be with a man with no morals like Max?_ 'What mother would, or could, sit back and relax under such a circumstance?' she demanded aloud of her daughter's image.

Especially, she thought venomously to herself, _when the said man had not only cuckolded his wife with your daughter, but had also cuckolded his wife and your daughter with more than one floozy._

What if that happened again? she mused with dread. And even worse still, what if Max dumped Arabella again? Sophia was incandescent with fear and anger now, as she recalled how broken-hearted her daughter had been on her return from T.J.'s funeral two years ago. T.J. was Eleanor's husband and Max's son.

Glancing back at the picture, Sophia shook her head. _God forgive me_, she prayed, _but if anything happens to Arabella, he will be following his son to the grave._ She hated thinking this, but that was how she felt. Arabella was everything to her and she was going to fight tooth and nail to protect her. And if she didn't succeed, then she'd have to let Oliver know what was going on, so that he could step in.

And do what, though? she wondered. For starters, since Oliver moved out, Arabella seemed hell-bent on going against anything he wished, and that was if she gave him the opportunity to first express those wishes.

Her inexplicable tantrums at him meant that Oliver kept himself on the periphery of his daughter's life, so as not to cause her distress.

Then also there was the fact that Arabella, who was usually good at brushing aside heartache and moving onto fresh fields, was being particularly unreasonable and uncharacteristically adamant about this relationship. She was hell-bent on seeing it through, come what may. *But why?*

A thought suddenly occurred to Sophia. 'No!' she gasped. *She can't be.* In a panic, she ran back to the phone to call and find out if Arabella was pregnant for Max. As she pressed the speed dial button, Sophia glancing down at her watch, noted the time to be six thirty. Arabella would be leaving soon for the airport. Sophia's heart tensed up; she had to speak to her before she left and let her know that even if she was pregnant, she didn't need Max to bring up the child. They, her family, would support her through it all and if she felt trapped bringing up the child as a single mother, then she and Oliver, who were getting close and had been talking of getting back together again, could take the child and bring it up for their daughter. This offer could change everything, Sophia hoped. *Please God, let Arabella have switched back on her mobile,* she prayed.

As her mother prayed, Arabella turned on her mobile. She hated resorting to such extreme measures with her mother – like cutting off communications – but what other choice did she have? Her mother refused to see sense and as a result was making her life unbearable. She was in love with Max and that was it, end of topic. No amount of name calling or abuse of him was going to change that fact and that's what she'd been trying to get through to her mother. Amicably preferably. But if not, hey…

On cue, as Arabella was returning from putting back the last item of clothing that she hadn't packed, her mobile phone began to ring. 'Mater calling' flashed bright up on the screen. She smiled warily. *Talk of the devil,* she thought and answered the call.

At the same time downstairs, a black seven-seater people carrier turned off Colney Hatch Lane and into Buckley Gardens. As it edged up the street, its driver strained to see the numbers on the brick terrace houses that stood partially hidden behind a row of small trees.

Suddenly, above the manicured hedge at the end of the cul-de-sac, the top half of a large, white detached building loomed up in the hazy mist of the dawn light. It stood unassuming yet majestic, encircled by its well-kept lawn that was rimmed with a cobbled footpath and then a hedge.

As the driver pulled up at the pavement in front of the spacing in the hedge, he noticed that the heavy-looking black door of the property had the numeral seven clearly marked on it in silver. This was the building he'd been looking for.

The driver, an elderly grey-haired man in a crumpled light blue shirt and tan trousers, heaved himself out of his vehicle with a pant and shuffled his way across the pavement, through the opening in the hedge, down a couple of concrete steps, along the path, and up to the thick, round columns that were supporting the mausoleum-like entrance of the building.

Once there, he made his way to the video intercom on the right-hand side of the entry door. Getting close up to it, he found and pressed the button with the number three on it. The gadget began to fizzle. He leaned in expectantly and waited. Shortly afterwards the screen on the cream-and-silver transmitter box lit up.

'Hello,' an excited lady's voice crackled through. It was Arabella, thrilled at the thought that this could be her taxi.

The man moved in even closer to the gadget, this time with his lips. 'Cab,' he announced tentatively.

Hoorah. 'Thanks, I'll be down in a minute'.

The man thought of returning to his vehicle, but changed his mind. The job was to Heathrow and there'd been mention of lots of luggage when the cab was booked. His passenger would most likely need his help.

As he pondered this, the light in the foyer came on.

It must be 'er, he decided, and resuming his original position, the taxi driver peeped through the narrow, fortified pane of glass at the side to see if Arabella was about to make an appearance into the lobby with luggage.

But he could see nothing because his view was obscured and distorted by the partially frosted flower design of the chunky swirls of the carved glass that bent everything on the inside out of shape and into a giddying melange of blue and green mess.

Slightly dizzied by the jumbled vision beyond the grooves of the glass, the man stepped away from the window. He'd be better off buzzing the woman to see if she wanted help with her luggage, he decided.

As the buzzer began to go, Arabella, who was still on the phone with her mother, looked relieved at the interruption. The conversation, though begun well with an apology from Sophia, was now fast deteriorating and Arabella needed it to end.

She's just not hearing me, she concluded sadly.

'Arabella, Arabella,' her mother's voice rang out.

'Yes,' she sighed into the phone.

'Are you listening?' her mother demanded.

'Does it matter?' *You're not.*

'Oh darling,' her mother cried in apparent exasperation. 'Why won't you hear sense?'

Whose sense? Arabella thought silently. 'Oh, Mother, please,' she implored her. The buzzer sounded out once more, this time for longer. *And you can stop going on as well,* Arabella scowled at the intercom.

'I'm not saying you mustn't go ever,' her mother's voice intercepted, as if in negotiation.

'Mother!'

'But wait three more months before you do go'.

'What difference will that –'

Bzzz. It was the buzzer again.

Oh for Heaven's sake!

'In three months you'll have a bett –'

Oh stop, please! 'Mother,' Arabella snapped. 'The taxi's waiting, my buzzer's going, and I don't have the time to do this right now.'

'But –'

'I'll call you back in a few minutes, before I head off.' And with that she terminated the call, went to the buzzer, and answered it. Yes, she did need assistance with the luggage.

As Arabella waited for the cabbie to make his way up to her flat to help her, she remembered the nightmares she'd been having every night of the last three days. In her dreams she fell out for good with her mother. The thought made Arabella shudder: falling out with her mother was the last thing she wanted. Although her mother could be 'a royal pain in the behind', she was the only constant in Arabella's life since she was six. And Arabella didn't want to lose that. It was her grounding force, her compass through which she found meaning and direction for her life.

But with her mother's unrelenting insensitivity regarding the Max issue, could she hold on for much longer? No she couldn't, nor could she walk away either. Well, not just like that anyway. She had to try again to get her mother on side.

So one more call and that's it, Arabella decided. If her mother couldn't leave her disapproval aside to wish her well on her way, then that was going to be it for them, except for the odd note that she'd send to say she was well and okay.

Chapter Two

Morning blues.

On hearing the main entrance door slam shut, the taxi driver, who'd taken his place in the front of the now fully loaded people carrier, looked up. From the darkened expression on Arabella's face, it was plain to see that she was upset about something.

Appearing there as she did with that demeanour plus being dressed completely in black, Arabella looked more like she was heading to a funeral than to the start of a 'happily-ever-after' life with Max. The red cardigan draped over the black handbag that was dangling from her forearm did nothing to soften the solemnity of her appearance. She looked bereaved.

And it was due to her mother. Refusing to let the conversation with her daughter end on an impasse, Sophia had lashed out with a final *coup de grace*: 'Darling, never forget that when a mistress is promoted to the position of wife or main partner, she leaves behind the vacancy of a mistress. Who's taken your slot, I wonder?' What a blow.

Arabella was speechless. No tantrums, no retaliation, the conversation was over. Slowly she slid her mobile shut. It was a definite act of severance. Her nightmare had come true: she and her mother were no longer. There could be no going back, Arabella decided. Her mother's parting words were, to her, uttered for maximum hurt. *Family, eh,* she thought with a bitter smile, *who needs them?*

She did and she knew it, but what could Arabella do if, as she was so certain, her family didn't want her? *Nothing, absolutely nothing.* Arabella felt alone and vulnerable, but she wasn't going to cry, not externally, anyway. She didn't want to jinx her new life with Max with tears.

Start as you mean to go on, with a smile, she told herself as she shut the front door and headed towards the taxi. But the smile that she desperately tried to muster contorted into a quiver of a sob. Arabella bit hard on her bottom lip. *I must not cry. I must not cry,* she repeated silently. The walk to where the taxi was waiting seemed to Arabella to take longer than ever before, but she made it and without shedding visible tears.

As she got into the car and sat in the only free seat, which was directly behind the driver's, the cabbie watched Arabella in the rear-view mirror for a signal to head off. But she said nothing and instead gazed sadly out of the window beside her. As she did so, her mind boggled with hurt and anger at her mother. When did her mother start hating her and what right did she have to hate her, when she'd been the one who'd insisted on giving birth to her? Her thoughts paused momentarily.

Or am I simply unlovable? Arabella suddenly wondered. And was that what her mother was trying to warn her would be the outcome with Max too? Not even he would be able to love her? *Oh,* Arabella groaned. Her thoughts were too painful for her. She wanted them out of her mind. On cue Arabella's hands began to fidget in an indefinite manner with her forehead. It looked like a confused attempt to reach for the thoughts in her mind.

Oh, that she could curl up and die flashed through her mind. Arabella began to lean towards her vanity case that was on the seat next to her, in what looked like an attempt to curl up.

Just then the cabbie glanced at the clock on the dashboard. The time was quarter to seven. 'We can't just sit 'ere like this, love,' he told Arabella.

His voice sort of semi-registered in her mind. Sitting back up, Arabella cocked her head to one side.

'You all set?' the driver persisted.

I was, she mused in a distracted sort of way. *But …* 'I don't know anymore'. *Would Max be able to love me?* she wondered.

The driver gave her a puzzled look in the mirror, but Arabella, who was back to gazing out of the window, didn't see. 'Heafrow, wern it?' the man asked, trying a different tactic.

'Yes'.

'And which terminal?'

Arabella's mobile phone began to ring. It seemed to snap her out of her lulled state of mind. In a tizzy, she foraged in the handbag on her lap for it. It wasn't long until she found it. Quickly bringing it out, she examined its blue-lit screen. 'Max calling' flashed repeatedly. *Thank God.* She smiled apprehensively: his voice would tell her if he'd be able to love her or not. Arabella accepted the call.

'Hello, you,' she began uncertainly.

'Hey, pumpkin,' he chirped.

Hm, she purred. It felt good being special to someone, especially when that someone was Max. *The one.*

'Still arriving tomorrow?' his voice cut in.

Pardon? 'Of course,' she laughed nervously. 'I'm just about to set off for the airport. Why?' The phone began to crackle. He didn't respond. 'Hello?' Arabella called into the mouthpiece. Silence. 'Hello?' she tried again, but the line went dead. *Strange,* she frowned, as her insecurities began to prickle and become alert.

In no time, her mind was brimming with all kinds of imaginings surrounding his question. *'Still coming tomorrow?'* she repeated silently to herself. What an odd question for him to ask when he knew full well that she was from previous conversations.

So why did he ask it? her doubts demanded.

Arabella's mind began to race. She recalled the tone of Max's voice, as he asked the question. Was he hoping that she'd changed her mind? Was it his way of hinting that he didn't want her to come?

And then the line going dead suddenly like it had, she puzzled. *What was that all about?* Arabella tried to reason it through. *Did someone come into the room and he didn't want me to hear them?* she wondered. Arabella looked at her watch – it was late there – so it couldn't be someone at the office, and even if it was, why would he mind if she heard the person's voice?

Hm, Arabella frowned again. She remembered her mother's parting words to her. Had Max already found someone to fill the mistress vacancy? With his past track record, it wouldn't be such a surprise. *Yes, it would,* she countered immediately, almost starting to cry. He'd promised that things were and would stay different this time, there'd be no one else. And she'd believed him implicitly.

Fool, her beleaguered instinct sniped, just as Arabella recalled something that Bianca, Max's soon-to-be ex-wife, had once told her. 'Some men play golf, Max has affairs. It's his way of keeping fit,' Bianca had said.

Arabella had never forgotten those words and now their implication was again gnawing at her insecurity regarding Max. Arabella glanced heavenward. *Please don't let him be at it again,* she prayed, as she wondered where he was and why he'd hung up, so abruptly.

At that very moment, in Seattle, Max stepped into the garage in the basement of the building where he had offices. He looked at his watch. The time was quarter of eleven and there were still a lot of papers at home that he needed to look through before his meeting with his lawyers in the morning.

Max was feeling exasperated. Not only had his secretary been unable to reschedule some of his meetings for tomorrow, but his cell phone had just died, before he'd managed to ask Arabella to try to catch a later flight.

'Ugh,' he groaned aloud. When was he supposed to find the time to get everything done, especially now that Arabella was arriving earlier than they had originally discussed?

It was such bad timing for him. With the sale of his company yet to be completed, he really didn't have time for much else than back-to-back meetings with his lawyers, accountants and the prospective buyer.

Why couldn't Arabella have understood that? He sighed. Max paused. In all fairness, he reflected, maybe he hadn't explained clearly enough to her the magnitude of his workload.

And if he had? came to mind. Would it have made any difference?

Most probably not, he admitted with a smile. Not with Arabella convinced that he was going to meet and fall in love with someone else if she came later rather than sooner.

Meet someone else indeed, he scoffed. With a schedule like his, when was he supposed to find the time to do that? And besides, why would he want to when he had been given this second chance to see out the rest of his life with someone special like Arabella, who, thankfully, was as eager for a relaxed and laidback 'happily ever after' as he was.

Having arrived now at his car, Max opened the driver's door and got in. Before fastening his seatbelt he leant across to drop a bundle of folders onto the passenger seat beside him. As he did so, Max caught sight of his spare cell phone that was lying on the passenger seat beside him.

'Oh shucks!' he remembered. 'I haven't called Eleanor'. Reluctantly he picked it up and dialled her number in Tobago.

Eleanor was his daughter-in-law, whom he would have preferred to tell in person how he and her ex-best friend Arabella had reconciled and were now going to be living together. But however, thanks to Arabella's earlier than planned arrival, that wasn't going to be possible anymore. Eleanor would have to be informed by phone.

Holding the mobile to his ear, Max listened as his call was connected. After a few rings it was picked up. 'Hell —' Max began and then stopped. It was the answer machine that had clicked on. He slouched back in his seat and waited.

At the tone, he resumed speaking. 'Hey, you guys, it's Grandpa,' Max began with great cheer. 'I'm missing you all and I'm very excited about us all seeing each other again when you get here in two weeks time.

'The strawberries are ripe and ready to be picked, so hurry up and get here.' His voice developed a more serious edge. 'Hey, Eleanor, we need to talk urgently, so please call me back...Oh, and Paris,' Max interjected with a smile that lightened his tone. 'Thanks for the riddle you left on my voicemail. I hope to have figured it out by the time you guys get here or a new kite is yours. Take care and love you all.'

As he ended the call, Max sighed with relief. He hadn't been looking forward to having the 'Arabella' conversation with Eleanor, even it was just on the telephone.

Telling his sons, Lucas and Tevin, hadn't been easy, and although they weren't happy with the news, he knew that they would eventually come round to the idea if his and Arabella's few months' cohabitation trial was successful and they stayed together.

Ah, but Eleanor – 'ooh,' he groaned – that was going to be hard work. Even though it was two years since she found out about his affair with Arabella and he and Arabella had spent most of that time broken up, Eleanor had refused to have anything more to do with her ex-best friend.

Starting the engine of the car, Max set off home with his thoughts still on his daughter in law. He was unable to reconcile himself with the intensity of her continued anger at Arabella alone. He was as much to blame for their affair as she was, so why had Eleanor seemingly let him off the hook and not Arabella?

And even more puzzling to Max was how a usually soft-hearted person like Eleanor could despise so much and for so long, especially someone like Arabella, for whom she'd cared so dearly in the past. He'd often wondered if there was more to his daughter-in-law's anger at her ex-best friend. Not that Arabella could think of. 'Ask Eleanor,' she'd suggested. But that was out of the question. So rigidly had she steeled her heart against Arabella that Eleanor couldn't, it seemed, even bear to hear her name mentioned, let alone have a conversation about her.

So how was she going to react now to the news that the relationship between him and Arabella was back on?

Max groaned aloud. There were bound to be repercussions. At best, Eleanor would accuse him of having left Bianca to be with Arabella even though that wasn't the case. There would be no convincing her now that it had been Bianca's idea to separate in the first place and not because of any further indiscretions on his part.

With the way they'd drifted apart, of course Max had toyed with the idea of leaving Bianca many times before. He'd even considered it during his first dalliance with Arabella, but he'd never had the heart to go through with it. How could he? She was the love of his life and they'd been through so much together, including the race riots in the Sixties. Being white, it wasn't her fight, but she hated injustice too much to sit by and watch disapprovingly from the sidelines. No, Bianca was always a doer, and do she did. This was why he'd been attracted to her in the first place.

And then when he got to know her better? *Wow,* Max beamed. What an even more amazing human being Bianca turned out to be, one that he couldn't imagine not having in the rest of his life. With her admitting to feeling the same way too, there was no other way forward but to plan for the future and follow it through side-by-side.

That had been the plan anyway, Max interjected sadly.

He reviewed his life with Bianca. It was a good life to begin with, even though they had started with very little. But at least they were a team. Nothing fazed them. They trusted each other implicitly on every level, and that trust was never broken until after their three sons were born. Suddenly, Bianca took on the mantle of manager. Everything in their lives became like a military operation with fun and enjoyment (the two things they'd both promised would be the essence of their lives together) seemingly cast out.

'We can do all that later,' Bianca had insisted. 'Now's the time for getting serious about making it, for us and the kids,' she'd added sensibly. It wasn't such a bad idea, he'd thought, and followed through on their revised plans with thoughts of a great later life to ease the tension of never kicking back and relaxing.

It wouldn't have been so bad, Max recalled, if they could have laughed through the journey. It was what made them special: they laughed at life. But Bianca didn't feel much like laughing anymore, or so it seemed. She appeared to prefer her preoccupation with how their lives looked to the outside world. Were they giving the right impression? Would someone looking in think that they were doing good on all fronts?

What did he care? Bianca, he, and the boys were all that was supposed to matter and to hell with others and what they thought. Max shook his head. If only Bianca had remembered this fact.

The traffic lights in front of the car ahead of Max turned red, so he slowed down to a halt. As he waited for the lights to change, Max gazed idly at the trunk of the car in front of his. Thoughts of Bianca were still on his mind. *Why did she change?* he wondered.

He'd been wondering that all through their life together, but more so after they'd become successful. They were supposed to let up, start laughing again, but that didn't happen.

Suddenly Max remembered his sons. A smile spread across his face. *Thank God for them,* he thought, especially T.J. and the times they spent together doing all the things that they were supposed to have done when his boys were kids.

As he recalled those family weekends that T.J. had organised for all of them to hang out in his place in Seattle, Max's eyes began to well up with tears. Even though Bianca wouldn't let up on work and spent most of those times on the phone setting up some deal or other, he and the boys had great times.

Thank God, he thought, because it was memories of those times that had stopped him from breaking down and letting go of life when T.J. died.

Although Max regretted not having spent time with his sons when they were growing up, he was grateful to God for the chance they'd been given, to get to know each other better before T.J's death.

'Oh T.J.,' Max suddenly cried aloud. 'I miss you so much.' His sorrow was overwhelming. Bowing his head, Max began to weep. Why did his boy have to die, Max wondered? *Why? Why, God, why,* he demanded in his mind? There was so much good in him – in his life. Eleanor came to mind. *Poor kid,* Max sympathised. T.J.'s death hit her worst of all.

Max's thoughts rested on his daughter-in-law. It was thanks to those weekends that he and she had become close. Eleanor was like the daughter he'd never had and had always wanted. How sad it was going to be if their bond became strained and weakened by his renewed relationship with Arabella. *But it's bound to,* he feared.

When he gave her the news, Eleanor would probably accuse him of having moved from Connecticut to Seattle with the sole purpose of setting up home with Arabella. But this had not been the case. Bianca was the only woman he'd ever imagined or wanted or intended setting up home with. He'd always loved her, still loved her, and would probably love her forever, but they were different people now, wanting different things, and that had been the case for a while. Or so Max thought. The affairs had been his way of trying to figure out what was missing between him and his wife and how to fix it.

Max could see it now. There would be no persuading Eleanor that a year ago, when he and Bianca had finally decided to call it a day on their marriage after six months of trying to patch things up, Arabella wasn't in his plans. In fact, he'd been secretly hoping that the space would help him figure out how to get him and Bianca back to the way they had been when they were on the same wavelength, carefree and at their happiest. But that hadn't happened. Instead he realised that they'd both changed and no longer wanted the same things, so there was no point in being together, hurting each other.

He wouldn't like it, but Max felt that he could handle Eleanor believing whatever she chose to believe. His biggest fear concerned his grandsons, Paris and Malachi. Would Eleanor stop him from seeing them?

Oh that T.J. was still alive, Max sighed sadly. No matter how angry he may have been about the situation, he would never have let it get in the way of the relationship between his father and the boys.

Max winced at the thought of never seeing his grandsons ever again should Eleanor so decide. It was painful and he didn't want to imagine it happening. Steeling himself, he sighed again. No matter the consequences, Eleanor had to be informed. He owed her that much, especially after all she'd done to help make his move to Seattle as seamless and pain-free as possible.

When considering the options of which city to move to in order to give him and Bianca space to each make a fresh start, the fact that he already had a branch of his company here made Seattle an obvious choice. The logistical help from Eleanor allowing him to stay in T.J.'s first house was the deciding factor. Especially as it gave him a much-needed opportunity to grieve for T.J. on his own and in his own way, in a place that held memories of special times spent with his son.

Toot, toot, toot. The sound of the driver behind impatiently honking his horn jolted Max back to what was happening on the freeway. The car in front of his silver Mercedes had moved forward by about a foot.

Big deal, Max frowned, annoyed that his thoughts of T.J. had been so unceremoniously interrupted and for nothing of great importance.

Toot, toot.

'What?' he snapped, glaring in his rear-view mirror at the impatient driver of the red Honda saloon behind him. He could see the man wildly gesticulating for him to move forward, but Max refused to oblige. 'Relax,' he grizzled back and flicked on the radio.

Chapter Three

For old time's sake

Meanwhile back in the taxi in London and before Arabella could crumble into total insecurity, her phone began to ring again. The sound bolstered her optimism. It had to be Max ringing back, she concluded. *There,* she smiled, *of course he was to be believed.* He loved her and would continue to be faithful to her. There was no cause for paranoia, she chided herself. *He didn't hang up, he was cut off, so get a grip.*

With a cheered expression, she glanced down to accept the call that was alerting her with repeated vibrations as the phone rang in her hand. She caught sight of the flashing screen: 'Mater calling'.

No! Arabella recoiled. Her mother was the last person she wanted to speak to. Dropping the phone onto her lap, she left it to ring. With each ring, her insecurities regarding Max began to resurrect. Arabella needed to think things through. *In peace,* she screamed silently at the still ringing mobile as she attempted to block out its sound by plugging her ears with her fingers.

The driver, who was watching her with growing concern in his rear-view mirror, noticed the look of despair on her face. 'You orwight?' he called out.

With all her attention focused on the still ringing phone, she didn't hear him. *Stop ringing, please,* she willed it again, but it didn't stop. *Please,* she implored it. *I need to think.*

'We really need to get going, love'.

'I need to think!' she shouted out suddenly to the obvious surprise of the man, who was still watching her.

He turned his head to face her. 'What's going on?' he asked softly with unease.

The phone stopped ringing.

'Miss,' the driver pressed.

She looked up at him. 'Pardon?'

He gave her a quizzical smile.

'I'm sorry,' she apologised sheepishly. 'I was miles away. What did you say?'

'Nuffink, love,' he sighed. 'Only checking vat you're orwight,' he replied kindly in his strong Cockney accent.

'I'm great, thanks,' Arabella lied.

'Of course you are,' the cabbie quipped with a conciliatory smile. 'I mean, who wouldn't be, going away on 'oliday like you are,' he added in an obvious attempt to cheer Arabella up.

She forced a smile in response.

'I don't mean to rush ya, love, but you do 'ave a plane to catch,' he reminded her. 'So I need to know if we're all set'.

'Yes, of course,' came the empty reply, as the thought, *Kenwood House* popped into Arabella's mind. It was her favourite place in the whole world and one that was filled with her happiest memories, the only ones she could think of now. Arabella smiled broadly with her heart at the thought of them – she, Daddy, and Mummy – as the perfect family. The Winthrops…

'Miss,' the taxi driver butted in.

'Arabella Winthrop,' she confirmed.

'You what?' the man frowned.

Arabella couldn't help but smile. 'My name,' she explained, 'is Arabella'.

The man seemed taken aback. 'Right you are,' he replied. 'And I'm Arfur'.

'Pleased to meet you, Arthur'.

Arthur smiled back. 'Likewise, Miss, but,' he added, motioning to his watch.

'Yes, yes, I'm aware of the time,' Arabella riposted. 'But I just need to think some things through first'.

'You can do that on the way, love,' Arthur told her. 'Gawd knows wiv the morning rush hour traffic as bad as is expected, you'll 'ave plenty of finking time.'

'Hm,' Arabella grunted in a manner that seemed to suggest that she'd zoned out again and hadn't heard a word he'd said. And then suddenly, without warning, announced that, 'I need to go to Kenwood House'.

'You what?'

'We need to go via Hampstead, please.'

'Hampstead?' the man gawped. 'But we're going Heafrow, innit?'

'Yes, via Kenwood House on Hampstead Heath.'

'No, love,' the driver disagreed. 'We don't need to go fru there,' he explained. 'The quickest route from 'ere would be to go right. Then nip left unto the Norf Circular and –'

'I want to go via Hampstead.'

The cabbie looked perplexed. 'But vat's going out of our way. It'll costcha –'

'I've got enough money,' Arabella snapped and began to bring out her black patent leather wallet to show him.

'No, no,' the now flustered-looking man protested. 'I wasn't finking about you not being able to afford the journey,' he told her. 'No, I was just trying to save ya time and money.'

Arabella relaxed. 'Thank you'.

'Yeah,' the driver went on as he began to reverse the car. 'It's bad to waste money, y'know,' he insisted. 'Not wiv all them people starving in the world. I always say if you've got it and ya don't wanit, give it to charity. But don't waste it, no. Vat's sinful.'

'True,' Arabella agreed. 'I have a friend. No, sorry,' she corrected herself. 'I used to have a friend who believed exactly the same. She probably still does,' she added softly.

Arthur, who had by now fully reversed and driven the car back to the junction at the entrance of the cul-de-sac, glanced up at her in his rear-view mirror. 'You still wanna go via Kenwood House?' he asked.

'Yes, please.'

Clicking his indicator to signal that he was going to be turning left, he checked for oncoming traffic. With no cars coming in any direction, the cabbie turned his taxi left, out of Buckley Gardens and onto Colney Hatch Lane. They were now finally on their way.

'Begging your pardon Miss –'

'Arabella'.

'Sorry. Begging your pardon, Arabella,' he repeated. 'I couldn't help but notice,' he resumed in an unobtrusive manner. 'But ya looked sad when ya mentioned about y'mate. Did he die?'

Arabella looked puzzled. 'Which mate?'

'The one what used to say the same as me about wasting money'.

'Oh,' she laughed. 'That's Eleanor, and she's a she not a he.'

'Aw!'

'And she's still very much alive, as far as I'm aware'.

'Aw,' Arthur exclaimed again with an intrigued tone. 'So how come y'not mates anymore?'

'It's a long story'.

'It usually is, innit? Lucky we've got plenty of time till we get to the airport'.

'Yup. Lovely summer we've been having, isn't it?'

'You what?' Arthur looked up, as did Arabella.

'The weather,' she explained. 'It's been wonderful'.

'Right. Yeah, yeah, fank Gawd,' he added, quickly regaining his composure.

'Yes, thank God indeed,' she concurred and then paused. Moments later, she began to speak again, but this time as if to herself. 'I wonder what sort of summer it's going to be in Seattle.'

'Seattle,' Arthur piped up, clearly eager to know more. 'Izat where you're off to then, love?'

'Yes.'

'Just for the summer?'

'Or maybe longer.'

'Longer?'

'Yes, I hope, but that depends.'

'On?'

'On whether I prove everyone wrong and my relationship works out.'

Arthur smiled thoughtfully.

'What was that for?' Arabella intercepted.

'What was what for?'

'That smile.' she demanded.

'I'm always smiling.'

'Maybe, but that was more than a smile: it was very loaded.'

Arthur's face flushed crimson, like one who'd been caught in a lie. 'Don't mind me,' he told her. 'I dunno what I'm finking 'alf the time. Anyway, sorry to 'ave interrupted. You were saying?'

'Was I?'

'Yeah, about 'ow you're the only one who finks your relationship is going to work wiv the distance an' all vat when you're in Seattle.'

Arabella eyed him. 'What distance?'

'Between you and your *fella*, now you're off to Seattle'.

'What?' she puzzled, wondering where he'd got that idea. *If only that were the case,* she thought wistfully. With her newly acquired financial independence there was no need for there ever to be any distance between her and Max, which was what she'd finally got him to see a week ago.

Or forced him into agreeing that he could see, echoed in her mind. Those were more of her mother's choice words, which on reflection, after the strange call she'd just had from Max, now made Arabella begin to fidget with discomfort.

Was her mother right? she wondered. Was Max only going through the motions of them starting a life together to stop her from suspecting what he may be up to behind her back?

Oh, she shuddered at the possibility. *No way. Please, God.*

Lack of confidence took a foothold. *But then again,* Arabella mused sadly, it seemed pretty prob-able because why did it take so much convincing to get Max to agree to her going over to Seattle sooner than they'd originally discussed? Why had he kept on insisting that it would be a better idea for her to wait a few more months in London, instead of joining him immediately?

Yes, she understood that he was busy with the sale of his company, but if he *really* loved her as much as she loved him, wouldn't he want her to be around during such a difficult time? Even if it were just to have someone to talk to and to cuddle up to at the end of the day. *I would,* she decided.

So why doesn't he? Has he got someone…?

'It's lovely being in the park when it's like this, innit?' Arthur said.

Looking a little confused, Arabella lifted her head from against the window where she'd been resting it. 'Pardon?'

'It's a lovely morning, nice and crisp, but not cold.'

She looked out of the window. The risen sun stood ornate and blinding in the sky and its rays bounced off the leaves on the trees with jewel-like sprigs. 'Yah,' she replied. It was a morning full of beauty and hope.

'I don't like it when the mornings are clammy and 'ot, do you?'

'No, not particularly'.

Arthur purred with content. 'I love being in the park, on me own, on mornings like this.'

'Me too,' Arabella concurred. 'It helps me think more clearly'. And with that, she wound her window down slightly and greedily inhaled the fresh air from outside. As she did so, she began to smile. She wasn't sure which route they'd used to get there, but they were now driving across the gently unrolling tapestry of the north-west corner of Hampstead Heath that was unfolding its gentle green slopes around them.

Arabella's smile brightened. *There,* she beamed, was the pond that Daddy always swam in, no matter the weather. Arabella sighed. If only she'd dared to brave it on the day he'd last invited her in, how much richer the memories would be now. Arabella's expression began to cloud with regret. *If only…*

The panoply of trees caught her attention. The sadness in her eyes instantly brightened into child-like excitement. The open-armed trees were waving welcome, as her daddy had pointed out that first time. All this time and they still hadn't forgotten her. 'Wow!'

'Lavvly, innit?' Arthur chipped in. 'Nature, what a tonic!'

'Yah,' Arabella said, smiling dreamily as she noticed that they weren't now far off from Kenwood House. 'The happiest memories of my life are of here,' she revealed.

'Really?'

'Yes. I came here with my parents once a week in winter and practically every evening in summer until I was six.' The previously happy glint that had twinkled in Arabella's eyes at the glimpse of the familiar ground near Kenwood House now became shrouded by a film of tears. What she'd failed to tell Arthur was that the saddest memory of her life was also of here.

Oh, what a dreadful day that was, she recalled. Dropping her gaze to her lap, Arabella began to rub away at an imaginary mark on the screen of her phone as memories of the day her father walked out of her life filled her mind.

It was a Saturday, and unlike every other Saturday when she would come to the Heath and Kenwood

House with both parents, this time she and Daddy had come alone. Arabella smiled sadly. She should have guessed that something bad was in the offing. But how could she have, she shrugged, it had all seemed so exciting to be breaking the rules with Daddy, to be 'sneaking off for extra ice-cream' like he'd said.

I should have known, Arabella hissed silently at herself in accusation. Even though Daddy was smiling, his eyes were brimming with tears which he'd kept brushing aside whenever he thought she wasn't watching. But she had been watching and wondering until she could wonder no more. Arabella recalled asking him what was wrong. 'Nothing, darling,' he'd lied and fobbed her off with the excuse that they were tears of joy at being able to spend quality time on his own with his 'princess'.

What a lie, she hissed angrily.

The memory of that day was more than she could bear, so Arabella switched lanes with her thoughts. Without looking up at him, she addressed herself to Arthur. 'Do you have kids?' she asked him.

'Yes, a daughter'.

'Do you ever take her to the park?'

The man laughed. 'She's a bit old for that'.

Arabella laughed too, but sadly. She was thirty-eight years old and would have given anything for her daddy to take her to the park like he used to. She would have given anything to have memories of more recent years with her father. They could still try and climb trees. They could still race each other and maybe now she was older and he was not as nimble as before, she would win. They could have a swim together in the pond in winter, even if it were only once. They could –

'You forget how lovely it is, don'tcha?' Arthur's voice cut in. It was obvious that he'd been speaking, but Arabella didn't have a clue what about.

'Yah,' she agreed non-committally to whatever it was he was talking about.

'Well, until you go back, that is,' Arthur continued. 'Then y'wonder how the bleeding 'ell you could've ever forgotten somefing as pleasurable as that. It's mad, innit?'

'Yah,' Arabella chuckled sadly, wondering whether if her daddy were to come to Hampstead Heath, he would remember those times with her as fondly as she did. *Probably not,* she concluded. 'But that's us humans, I suppose'.

'Yeah, nitwits that we are.'

She couldn't help but to laugh out loud. *Nitwits indeed!*

'But it's true,' Arthur insisted. 'It takes us less than a second to get awl our priorities muddled up, dunnit?'

'I suppose'. *But not me, not anymore.*

'Why izat?'

Arabella shrugged. 'I'm not sure, really –'

'I'll tell ya why,' Arthur interposed. 'We're daft, that's why.'

'What d'you mean?'

'Well, we let the rat race take over our lives, don't we?'

'Not everybody'.

'Yes, everybody,' Arthur insisted. 'At some time or ovver, if not always for some,' he ranted on. 'We rush around like 'eadless chickens, chasing after the unnecessary and forgetting about the important fings in life like family –'

'That overrated nonsense.'

Arthur flashed her a glance in the mirror. 'Don't talk like that,' he rebuked her. 'They're the only ones who'll always be on your side and who'll ever love ya unconditionally –'

'Oh what tosh!'

'Oh ma days,' Arthur gasped aloud. Having arrived at Kenwood House, he slowed the car to a stop and turned his head to face his passenger. Softening his tone, he spoke. 'Don't be so cynical, love,' he told her. 'You probably just don't understand 'em, that's all.'

'Or I probably understand them too well.' And with that Arabella got out of the car and headed towards the magnificent building that was perched on the Heath. Standing in her usual spot, she admired this 'exceptional example of architecture at its finest,' as her father had taught her to.

As she stood staring at the building, recalling her father's voice raving about the building and one of its designers, Robert Adam, Arabella's eyes brimmed with tears. It was here at this very spot, on that fateful Saturday, that her daddy told her that he was leaving and wouldn't be back.

'I have to go,' he'd interjected suddenly, amidst a heartfelt explanation of why he'd chosen to become an architect himself. Arabella's lips quivered into a broken smile. She remembered her reply to her father. 'Wait a little longer please, Daddy,' she'd pleaded, without a thought to the fact that if he had meant it was time for them to go back home, he would have said 'we have to go' rather than 'I have to go'.

Looking at, but not seeing, the building in front of her, Arabella continued to remember that afternoon when she was six. *Poor man,* she thought as she recalled the look on her father's face as he'd knelt to explain himself. He was leaving to live apart from her and Mummy. 'Why?' the young Arabella had demanded, but Daddy didn't have a satisfactory answer. 'Because I have to,' was the best he could do.

That was the first and last time she's ever sensed anything resembling sadness in her father. But knowing what she knew now about him, and his reason for leaving her and her mother, Arabella convinced herself that what she'd seen in his eyes that day wasn't sadness at leaving her, but sadness at his marriage needlessly coming to an end because of her. Arabella smiled wryly. It was the last time she saw any glimmer of emotion except anger or irritation from her father.

This wasn't true, but Arabella had convinced herself that it was. She'd done so because shortly after that incident in the park, she'd overheard one side of a conversation between her mother and her maternal grandmother, Lucinda. Because of the snippet she'd heard, Arabella had (unbeknownst to her parents) been living her life since then wrongly believing that her father despised her for being born when he hadn't wanted a child.

'Oh, Daddy,' she now cried out softly, willing him to materialise before her, to tell her that everything was going to be alright, that she'd only imagined the conversation she'd overheard all those years ago. And if she hadn't, then to lie to her and tell her that he hadn't left because he didn't love her, couldn't love her.

But he didn't materialise.

Closing her eyes tightly, Arabella wished harder for her father. *Please call me now,* she prayed. *Call and say that I'm doing the right thing by going. Tell me that Max does genuinely love me and will never be unfaithful to me again.*

The call wouldn't be coming and Arabella knew it. (but not for the real reasons, which was that some years back, she'd ordered her father to stay out of her life and that's what he'd been pretending to do ever since, so as not to upset her).

Arabella began to weep. Oh, how her father had broken her heart. *But it's not his fault,* she added defensively on his behalf. How could it be when according to what she believed she'd overheard her Nana saying that day, her father had warned her mother that he wasn't ready to have children yet, but she hadn't listened. She'd chosen not to hear him, just as she was choosing not to hear Arabella's pleas for support of her decision to move to Seattle.

Why don't you ever think of anybody but yourself? she sobbed, suddenly remembering her anger at her mother.

Kneeling down on the grass, Arabella sobbed harder. If only her mother had heard her father's objections and not given birth to her, she wept. There would have been no cause for her mother's marriage to break down and she, Arabella, wouldn't have been alive to suffer with the pain of the knowledge that her father had walked out because he couldn't pretend anymore that he loved her and was happy that she was born.

Stupid, stupid woman, Arabella fumed. *You always think you know it all, that you've got all the answers. So tell me, what did you gain by giving birth to me?*

As the question passed unanswered, as usual, Arabella's anger began to wane into resigned determination. Oh, there were too many whys in her life and never any answers.

What's the point? she shrugged, rising to her feet. Asking herself these questions that forever plagued her, never changed anything except for the intensity of the pain they stirred up inside her, which seemed to only get worse with each passing day.

It was time for change: time to leave London and its unhappy memories behind for the last time. Pushing aside the sadness from her childhood and her gnawing insecurities about a future with Max, Arabella smiled hopefully through her tears. There was cause to be optimistic, she told herself, because if she played it right, by leaving the past in the past, as she'd promised Max that she would, sooner rather than later, she and Max may be blessed with a family of their own.

The possibility thrilled Arabella. Drying her tears, she smiled again, this time resiliently. Her insecurities and the past were back under arrest, somewhere inside, but closer to the fore than Arabella knew or than showed.

Glancing quickly at her watch and then closing her eyes, she counted back eight hours. *The time was seven thirty, time to get going. Seattle here I come, for good with any luck.*

And with that Arabella skipped back to the waiting taxi. 'Terminal 3, please,' she announced and fastened her seatbelt, as if in preparation for what lay ahead.

Chapter Four

Tomorrow begins with today, and what a nice day it is to start afresh

Exhausted from the sleepless night before, which she'd spent crying and worrying over what her mother had had to say about her decision to move to Seattle to join Max, Arabella slept right through the London to Copenhagen leg of her journey.

Now on the plane from Copenhagen to Seattle, she was trying to do the same, when suddenly a tetchy-sounding voice hijacked her sweet dreams of the future. It was the flight attendant.

'Is your seatbelt fastened, ma'am?' the stern-looking woman in the yellow and grey _crêpe de chine_ uniform demanded.

Arabella ignored her.

'Madam,' the woman's harsh tone growled.

But Arabella refused to be bullied awake. Sighing, she rolled over, away from the direction from which the voice was coming. Unfortunately, it was going to take more than that to silence the determined-looking air hostess.

'Is your seatbelt fastened?' she persisted with noticeable and growing impatience.

'Oh for Heaven's sake', Arabella grumbled under her breath and gave up the fight. Visibly agitated, she turned to face her adversary. Opening her bleary eyes a tad, Arabella squinted up at the unsmiling eyes of the stocky brunette who was hovering over her like a nemesis. 'What is it?' she demanded.

'Your seatbelt,' came the response, as if in accusation.

'Yes, it's fastened', Arabella grizzled back and shut her eyes again.

'Madame,' the flight attendant barked.

For the love of –'What is your problem?' Arabella growled back with equal ferocity.

'We are about to begin our descent into Seattle and I –'

'What?' Arabella cried with surprise and sprang bolt upright in her reclined seat. She looked at her watch. Five hours had passed since she'd last checked. 'Who'd have thought it,' she mused aloud and turned to look out of the window.

As she did so, her right hand sprang up instinctively to shield her sight from the bright sun whose rays were shooting rainbow-coloured daggers of light into her eyes and against the empty seat to her left.

Rainbows and sunshine, Arabella smiled. *What a great omen!* Leaning closer towards the window, she breathed in deeply, as if to inhale the good vibes from the warming arrows of sunlight. *What a beautiful day to be starting a new life.* All her worries about Max and their relationship seemed like a bad dream from yesterday. She looked down at the white, fluffy marshmallow clouds below. Fond thoughts of him wafted into her consciousness. She smiled again.

I wonder where Max is right now and what he's thinking.

Down below, somewhere on the Interstate 5 freeway (commonly known as the I-5), Max edged his way slowly forward in the bumper-to-bumper early evening traffic.

Looking down at his watch, Max's thoughts ran to Arabella. Her plane would be landing soon. After having managed to cancel one of his meetings, he had intended to be at the airport before it did, but that wasn't going to be possible now. He pulled a face: *argh.* His only hope now was going to be the customs check, if it took a while.

Remembering how much luggage she always travelled with, the corners of Max's almond-shaped eyes began to crinkle, as a fond smile traced its way across his lips.

Y*up,* he nodded, *that would work.* By the time they would have gone through all of Arabella's many bags, he should hopefully have arrived at the airport and be there waiting for her at baggage reclaim, as per arranged. He was looking forward to seeing her.

'Arabella, Arabella,' he whispered as he felt something tickle the side of his face. Leaning forward and to the right, Max surveyed his reflection in the mirror. Whatever it was that had been brushing against his face was gone. His thoughts went back to Arabella.

What does a beautiful lady like her see in a spent old man like me? he wondered.

He called to mind her face. Yes, Arabella was very pretty indeed, in an elf-like, anxious sort of way. It

45

never took much to have her bright and striking hazel eyes dancing about in their sockets, like balls of nervous energy, and her fingers fidgeting with her perfectly formed, slender little nose and delicate doll-like lips that always seemed ready to break into a smile, no matter how sad she was feeling at the time.

From the stories she'd shared with him about past relationships, it was obvious to Max that Arabella had done a lot of crying in her time, but you wouldn't know it to see her smile. It was as fresh as the first day of spring without a trace of regret for seasons passed or dreams run aground.

Max's thoughts rested momentarily on Arabella's lips. Oh, how he loved to kiss them, to hold her, to be with her. In short, he cared a lot about her and he was glad that he'd finally realised just how much. If he couldn't see life out with Bianca, he couldn't think of anyone better than Arabella to do it with instead. They were both looking for the same thing: happily ever after with someone like each other.

Max reviewed his feelings further. Yes, because she reminded him of how Bianca used to be, he'd always felt a special something for Arabella, but he'd also known that anything deep between them was out of the question and not worth considering, at least until now, that is, now that he was free.

In his own warped way, he'd been keeping true to Bianca by not allowing himself to get emotionally involved with any of his affairs. It had seemed the decent and only thing to do seeing as he hadn't been intending to replace her.

Without meaning to, Max's thoughts returned to Arabella. He began to smile again. *Arabella, Arabella,* it was hard to believe that she'd waited. Hard to believe that she still wanted to be with him even after all he'd put her through. What a special lady!

What a diva, something in him recalled. Never one to be knowingly under-dressed. That's my girl.

Talking of which, Max frowned, glancing at himself again in the mirror. 'What were you thinking of wearing this absurd turtleneck sweater today of all days?' he scolded his reflection and pulled the flat roll of cashmere as far away as he could from his dark neck. It was making him hot and bothered. Max's irritation turned to the radio. 'And you're not helping either,' he snarled at the affected drone of the DJ, who warned about the traffic jams in too smug a tone for Max's liking. Max flicked the radio off and turned up the air conditioner.

As he did so, he caught a glimpse of the time. *Five after six, damn.* With the traffic still not moving much, it was a sure thing now that he was going to be getting to the airport later than he'd been hoping.

Poor Arabella, he frowned, she wasn't very good at being kept waiting, even for the shortest of time. Max remembered an incident in Rome when he'd arrived ten minutes later than scheduled.

'Phew,' he exhaled. *The fuss, you'd have thought I'd abandoned her.* Max rolled his eyes in fake exasperation. Arabella could be quite high maintenance at times and although he didn't usually go for such women, there was something about her, something special that made her kooky, demanding ways more endearing than annoying.

Yes, many things about Arabella frustrated him, like the way she'd get so worked up over little things and throw what he saw as unnecessary tantrums. But Max found it hard to hold them against her. They seemed to him to be more like manifestations of deeper vulnerabilities and insecurities than merely acting up.

Sighing, he smiled pensively. Although she'd never said much about her family, he'd sensed that there were issues there, issues that were the root of an unnecessary needy streak he'd noticed in her character.

It was so incongruous seeing such a beautiful woman like her, with everything seemingly going for her, being so needy like someone who felt undeserving yet craving good things to come her way.

Max recalled Arabella's eyes, which were hazel and pure like those of a child. They guarded as well as betrayed the vulnerabilities of what, at first glance, appeared to be an unconquerable spirit. He liked these paradoxes about her. It was nice for a change being with someone who, like himself, wasn't always so damn perfect and capable. Just like him, Arabella was prone to mess up.

He remembered Bianca again. She used to be like this before she changed. She wasn't afraid of failing, so she tried everything and learnt a lot. It was hard for Max to imagine how having kids could change someone so completely, as he believed it had changed Bianca. Once again, Max tried to imagine why that had happened, but he couldn't.

How could he when he wasn't privy to all the snide comments from his wife's family about her marrying a black man and how he'd 'surely drag her down into the gutter with him'? He'd trusted her too much to ask if she was hiding anything from him and she'd loved him too much to open him to the potential hurt he may have felt if he knew how disdainful her family was of him and their children. And so Max had gone on, none the wiser that his wife hadn't changed and she remained unaware that his affairs could have been avoided by telling the truth.

And so divorce was the proposed solution. _It's a shame,_ Max sighed, but what other option was there when it didn't seem to matter to Bianca what the reality of their life was so long as it all looked good to the outside world?

It riled him to remember that anew. _That damned outside world,_ Max hissed. It contributed nothing to the basic nuts and bolts of their life and yet Bianca afforded it such importance. Something that Arabella would never do, he hoped.

The thought of her cheered him up. She was a godsend. And thank God for her: little messy Arabella with her random and at times irksome ways that made him happy to still be alive. Max nodded, yes it was great to be granted a second chance with someone like Arabella who was a healthy mix of mess and order.

And overly neurotic, something else in him added.

'And neurotic,' he chuckled aloud in agreement.

Pausing for a moment, he considered his feelings about this aspect of Arabella's character. If the truth was to be told, it was what he liked least about her.

But in her defence, he reasoned, maybe all that would change now that they were taking their relationship to the next level. _Maybe,_ he smiled hopefully. The car in front of his began to move and Max followed suit.

Chapter Five

To the victor, the spoils but oh, what a pyrrhic victory!

Back on the plane, Arabella's stomach knotted with excitement. It was hard to take it all in: Max was finally hers.

'Excuse me, madame'. It was the flight attendant again.

What now? 'Yes?'

'Your seat –'

Turning quickly to face the woman, Arabella yanked at her belt. 'I've already told you,' she hissed. 'It's fastened.' *Thank you very much.*

The flight attendant motioned towards Arabella's seat. 'It needs to be in the upright position for landing,' she declared abruptly.

'Oh,' Arabella exclaimed, as she finally realised what the woman had been trying to tell her all along. 'Sorry,' she smiled sheepishly and adjusted her seat.

As the flight attendant resumed her military style pre-landing inspection of the remaining passengers, Arabella took another peek at the sleek white gold watch that Max had brought for her when he came to visit her in London two months earlier. The time was five minutes past six, Seattle time (Arabella had kept it on Seattle time, to make her feel close to Max at all times).

Almost there, she thrilled silently. In less than an hour, she would have landed and soon after that she'd be in Max's arms. The thought set her heart aflutter.

Unlike during the early years of their relationship (which began seven-and-a-half years ago), when they couldn't risk waiting for each other at airports for fear of being spotted, today they were going to be like any other couple in love. Max would be there waiting like other expectant partners, while she would do her best to get through security and customs as quickly as possible to get into his arms.

'Mm,' she purred. How great life was going to be from now on, without the clandestine meetings in hotel rooms in different countries. From now on, they'd be flying together and checking into hotels together, instead of their usual *modus operandi* of one of them checking in first and the other sneaking in later, thus leaving no evidence that they'd ever been in the hotel at the same time.

They were a couple at last, a couple who would be getting married and having a child one day. *Soon,* she hoped. Arabella delighted silently at the image of their perfect little family unit that her daydreams had conjured in her imagination.

The thought of how far they'd come since those early days made Arabella's stomach begin to knot with butterflies of mixed emotions: joy and fear. On the one hand, it was great that she and Max were at last a couple, but what, she mused nervously, did that count for in the 'world of Arabella'?

Not a lot, she had to admit. Men had a habit of running out on her, no matter what. She hated to be so pessimistic, but her past didn't offer her much hope.

Take Kenneth, for instance, Arabella recalled. Together for ten years, he was the longest ever relationship she'd had. She was the girl for him, he'd always said. The one with whom he wanted to spend the rest of his life, meaning the bits when he wasn't cheating on her with Tina, Susannah, Maria, Rachel, and God knows who else.

She knew about the affairs and she forgave him each and every one of them. And she and Kenneth even went so far as to set a date for their wedding. *But,* Arabella smiled wryly, a week before the event Kenneth called to say he couldn't go through with it with a clear conscience.

Conscience, indeed, Arabella sniggered sardonically, as she now remembered that day. The irony wasn't lost on her. But according to Kenneth, he'd apparently found a conscience somewhere within him and it wouldn't let him go through with their wedding knowing that she wanted children and he didn't.

Before she could get her head round it all and tell him that she loved him so much that she wanted him with or without kids, he whispered a lame 'I'm sorry' and hung up, never to be seen nor heard from again.

And then at the other end of the spectrum lay Wilson, a six-week affair that got her up the duff. After initially making the right noises – 'Wow cool. If you want it, sure, I'm up for us having a baby' – he got cold feet and decided that having a baby would put too much pressure on a fresh and blossoming relationship such as theirs.

So blossoming was their romance that he didn't show up at the hospital on the day of the termination. How could he when he was busy getting better acquainted with a giggly raven-haired school teacher who was good for a two-week shag until she started wanting a boyfriend?

Yes, this was the pattern of the colourful and predictable embroidery of her life.

Past life, Arabella interjected quickly as she tried to brush aside these unhappy recollections of a history she wanted to rewrite with a happy present and happier still-to-come future.

She recalled all the opposition to this attempt for a happy ending with Max. Why didn't those who were supposed to care most about her want her to do this? Didn't they want her to be happy at last? And if they did, why not with Max?

Yes, he was twenty-six years her senior and still married – not for much longer, though – but what did that matter in the great scheme of things? Happiness was happiness in whatever shape or form it came, she concluded with great sadness. Her usually hazel-coloured eyes darkened to a murky brownish colour with the weight of the tears that were welling up in them. She was now thinking about Eleanor and Arielle, her two ex-best friends, whom she wrongly believed had dropped her because she'd inferred that she wouldn't give up Max.

Having lost her husband to a woman with whom he'd had an affair, Arielle's reaction hadn't been a surprise to Arabella, but the length of time she was spending in condemnation was unfathomable. That is, until now.

Looking back and recalling her friend's reaction to her last two relationships before Max, Arabella realised that it was to have been expected. If Arielle could ostracise her for two months respectively for having relationships with men who were officially separated from their wives when she met them, then what else but total banishment could be expected for a relationship with Max: a married man when they first met, who happened to be the father-in-law of their mutual best friend, Eleanor?

But Eleanor, Arabella cried silently. Her reaction was beyond Arabella's comprehension. Of all the friends she'd lost as a result of her relationship with Max, Eleanor was the most surprising to her.

Although Eleanor was Max's daughter-in-law, she was the one person – with the exception of Arabella's father who seemed to neither care nor mind what his daughter did – who never judged her. And so for that reason, Eleanor was someone whom Arabella had expected and hoped would have been on her side.

If not for that reason, then for all those hours they'd spent together discussing the unpredictability of love and how it struck when one was least expecting it to.

Yes, they'd been talking with regards to Eleanor and T.J.'s relationship, but they didn't limit the subject to them alone. Surely Eleanor could see that and accept the affair with Max on those grounds?

Obviously not.

Then for the sake of their relationship, Arabella mused. She and Eleanor were best friends, after all, and had been for a while, and that wasn't easily replaceable. Their friendship was supposed to be something special and important. Something that meant that even if, for T.J.'s sake, Eleanor could not openly condone Arabella's relationship with Max, she could have, at least, been a closet ally.

But Eleanor hadn't wanted that, either. She wanted nothing to do with Arabella.

Arabella covered her face with her hands. For as long as she lived, she would never forget that evening when Eleanor came to that decision: The time was about ten past nine on the night of T.J.'s funeral in Tobago. As she was feeling hot and sweaty, Arabella had retired upstairs to the room that had been allocated to her and Arielle to share for the duration of their stay.

While Arabella was running her bath, Max stormed in, in a temper. On his way back to the house from the beach that belonged to T.J. and Eleanor's property, he'd overheard Arielle as she stood by the kitchen door telling one of Eleanor's friend's about his affair with Arabella. 'Anyone else could just as easily have overheard her, Bianca, for instance,' he bellowed, demanding to know exactly what Arabella had told Arielle about their relationship.

'I didn't tell her anything, she guessed.'

'How?'

'How should I know?' Arabella fell silent. She thought she'd heard a noise in the bedroom and strained to listen.

'Well, know this, then,' Max interrupted. 'It's over'.

'What? Why?'

Storming out of the en suite bathroom, Max headed into the tastefully decorated brown and cream colour-schemed bedroom. Arabella ran out after him. 'You can't just end it like that,' she told him. As she did so, Arabella noticed something purple from the corner of her eye, but was too upset to pay it much mind.

Max swung round in anger. 'I can and I hav – Elea...nor.'

'What?' Arabella followed his gaze. 'Oh my God,' she gasped as she noticed her best friend standing there in her purple cocktail dress and matching suede mules with their space age heels in sculpted gold metal. So she was the flash of purple that Arabella had noticed but not registered. 'H-how –What are you doing here?' Arabella stammered.

But her friend did not reply.

Arabella began to panic. What was she to do? What could she say? What had Eleanor heard? What were she and Max going to do? What, what, what? She glanced over at Max. He looked as dumbfounded and shell-shocked as Eleanor did. *Someone has to say something or do something, but who and what?*

Unable to think constructively, Arabella frantically paced the room, like a bullet ricocheting from wall to wall, with repeated whimpers of 'I'm so sorry'. Suddenly Eleanor reacted by bursting into tears and making a dash towards the bedroom door, near to where Max was now standing, which she'd left ajar. Her distress was such that she soon began to hyperventilate and, aborting her retreat, made a pit stop at the bed. Slumping down on the edge of it, she seemed to regain some composure. She stared up at Arabella with pleading eyes. 'Tell me it's not true, please,' she murmured.

'Tell you what's not true?'

'That you're having an affair with each other.'

'Who told you that?' Arabella heard herself ask.

Eleanor erupted. 'What's that got to do with anything,' she shouted, and then lowering her tone to a brittle quiver, she demanded, 'Just tell me the truth: are you or are you not having an affair with my father-in-law?'

Arabella was thrown into a quandary. Should she or should she not lie?

If Eleanor had been standing there long enough, she must have heard their conversation, as could anyone passing by the room. God knows that she and Max had been shouting loud enough. So Eleanor would probably know that they were having an affair.

However, if Eleanor had only just come in, then she wouldn't know. But if she didn't know, why then was she reacting in the way she was and asking such questions?

'Yes, I am,' Arabella admitted, to her own surprise, and began to fidget nervously with her face and hair as she stood anxiously waiting and watching for what would ensue.

Eleanor took a deep breath and seemed to relax. 'Since when?' she asked quietly.

Arabella felt herself tensing up again. 'Um,' she stuttered as she tried to gauge the situation. It was hard to think straight with Eleanor's powerful stare seemingly boring into her head like a truth-seeking laser. Arabella tried to weasel out of answering the question for a moment longer. 'Since when what?' she asked, shifting her gaze to the bedroom door.

'Since when have you been shagging my father-in-law?' came the cold reply.

There was someone else standing outside the bedroom door, Arabella could sense it. Should she mention the fact?

'Since when?' Eleanor insisted in an angrier tone.

Arabella quickly refocused her attention on Eleanor. From the look on her best friend's face, it was evident that there could be no avoiding or further delaying answering her question and Arabella knew it. Immediately stopping fidgeting with her face, she wrapped both arms protectively about her stomach.

'We've been in contact since your wedding,' Arabella replied barely audibly.

'Pardon?'

'Your wedding.'

The bedroom door flung wide open. 'You started an affair at your son's wedding?' a voice shrieked from the other side of the threshold.

All three of them turned towards it.

'Bianca, honey,' Max gasped.

'Oh hell,' Eleanor sighed just as Arabella, who was scantily clad in an ivory-coloured silk camisole top and a matching thong, seemed to suddenly become aware of her inappropriate attire.

Shimmying behind a brown wicker chair, with a cream, orange, and red-checked blanket thrown over its backrest and a brown and tan Louis Vuitton holdall lying on its seat, Arabella shielded her lower half from sight.

Whatever she did was of no consequence. Both Bianca's and Eleanor's attention was focused on Max. 'Well, I'm waiting,' Bianca demanded of her husband.

Max straightened up. 'Honey, please,' he implored the stone-faced woman with steely blue eyes and short red hair that was streaked with auburn lowlights.

Something in the way he spoke to his wife stirred Arabella. 'Max,' she whined, but he ignored her.

He took the few steps up to Bianca. 'Let's go somewhere quiet and talk, please,' he beseeched her in a tone that clearly betrayed an incontestable bond between them.

But Bianca stood resilient. 'Did you start an affair with this girl at T.J. and Eleanor's wedding?' she asked.

'No.'

Bianca turned her attention to Arabella. 'Is that true?'

They'd met there, but the affair didn't start there. 'Yes, it started a few months later,' Arabella confessed.

'But it was nothing,' Max interjected. 'I promise you, Bianca.'

Arabella glared horrified at him. 'What?' she wheezed.

'It meant nothing to me,' he repeated without looking at her.

Arabella couldn't believe what she was hearing. 'But –'

'Ah,' Bianca cooed mockingly with feigned sympathy. 'Did he fool you like he did all the others?'

Eleanor jumped up. 'What?' she cried. 'There were others?'

'Yes, honey, before and during your friend there,' Bianca chirped bitterly. 'Some men play golf; Max has affairs. It's his way of keeping fit.'

The answer seemed too much for Eleanor, who dropped back down to the bed with a look of horror, disbelief, and disappointment, while a visibly shaken Arabella came out of hiding and plonked herself down onto the wicker chair without moving the bag.

Eyeing her with contempt, Bianca began to laugh. 'You thought you were special, huh, missy?' she sneered.

Arabella didn't like her tone. 'It was just a bit of fun,' she lied.

'Which doesn't have to end,' Bianca added. 'He's all yours, honey. Enjoy.'

'No,' Max protested. 'She and I are done.'

'Too bad,' Bianca shrugged, 'because I'm done too. I'm through with covering up your messes time after time.' And with that she breezed out of the room with her head held high and Max chasing after her, trying to convince her to change her mind.

Looking stunned and confused by what had just happened, Arabella and Eleanor sat in silence until Eleanor finally spoke.

'Why Max?' she asked.

Arabella stared blankly at her. 'It just happened.'

'How?'

'I don't know, it just did'.

'But he's T.J.'s father,' Eleanor shouted.

'I know.'

'So how could you go for him?'

'I didn't go for him, it just happened.'

'You're disgusting.'

Arabella didn't reply.

'Didn't you care about how T.J. would feel if he ever found out?' Eleanor resumed.

'It didn't occur to me at the beginning.'

'Of course it wouldn't,' she hissed. 'You don't care about anybody but yourself.'

'Eleanor,' Arabella protested.

'Don't fucking Eleanor me.'

Arabella looked away. 'I didn't intend for anybody to get hurt,' she explained.

'So you always say. But people do get hurt, don't they, Arabella?'

'Yes,' Arabella hit back. 'And most of the time, it's me.'

'And the wives,' Eleanor added coldly. 'But of course, you never care about them, do you?'

Arabella suddenly felt angry with her friend for the stance she was taking. 'They're not my responsibility,' she retorted. 'And besides, since when did you become Bianca's defender? You can't stand the woman.'

'I can stand her better than I can stand you right now.'

The words stung Arabella hard. *Eleanor can't possibly mean that,* she told herself. *She's got a lot on her plate right now, that's all. Too much, in fact, and definitely too much for one day, particularly a day like this. She needs a break, time for things to cool down, time for her to cool down.* Arabella got to her feet and walked over to a door that was a little further away along the wall running to the left of the wicker chair. Turning the handle, she opened the door and revealed an almost empty walk-in closet. She flicked on the light switch and leant inside. From a plain blue fabric hanger near the switch, she undraped a white knee-length kimono-style dressing gown with Japanese hieroglyphics all over it in black. Leaning back out, she shut the wardrobe door, put on the dressing gown, and then squatted down facing Eleanor.

'What now?' she asked her with a hapless smile.

Eleanor, who was looking drained, shrugged listlessly.

Arabella spoke again. 'I was just trying to find happiness,' she explained.

'I know,' Eleanor replied in a soft voice. 'But does it always have to be at other people's expense?'

'I wouldn't say it is,' Arabella refuted the accusation. 'If anything, I'm always the one who gets hurt, so I guess one could say it's always at my expense.' Pausing, she fixed her friend with a hurt stare. 'But that's okay, isn't it?'

'What is?'

'For me to be the one that gets hurt.'

'No.'

Arabella smiled sadly. 'So how come you're more angry about Bianca, whom you don't like, getting hurt, than you are about me, your friend, having been used and hurt by Max?'

Eleanor stared her square in the eyes. 'She's T.J.'s mother, Arabella,' she replied.

'So?'

'So, by hurting her, you hurt him, and I can't condone that.'

'But you can condone his father hurting them and me?'

'No.'

'You could have fooled me.' Arabella dropped her gaze. Yes, there could be no denying the fact that her track record for a while seemed to show a tendency to falling for married men, but as Eleanor knew, on two of those occasions she hadn't known that the men were still married until she'd already fallen for them. And on the occasions when she did know, as was the case with Max, she'd fallen for him without intending to. She didn't go in search of any of these men; they found her and went for her. Try as she may to resist them, she somehow always ended up believing their lies about there being a strong possibility of a 'happily-ever-after' future for them.

Should she have shown more care for their wives when she found out about them? Arabella pondered. Yes, maybe she should have, but weren't they more their husbands' responsibility than hers? Besides, it was hard to feel responsible for someone you didn't know, especially when the person's husband effectively convinced you that his wife was as unhappy as he was in the marriage and that they'd both agreed that reconciliation was no longer an option for them.

Arabella's mind ran to Bianca. She seemed far from the grieving wife. If anything, she'd seemed quite happy to find a reason to get out of her marriage. So obviously Max, unlike the others, hadn't lied at all on that front. Maybe he hadn't lied about anything he'd told her. Arabella's mind secretly began to fill with hopeful thoughts.

'Max and Bianca haven't been happy together for a while,' she found herself telling Eleanor.

'Well, that's hardly surprising, is it, if he's been cheating on her constantly'.

'True, but surely then that shows that he doesn't want to be with her,' Arabella remarked.

Eleanor's eyes flashed with irritation. 'That's no justification for your actions, Arabella,' she snapped. 'With all the single guys at my wedding, it was wrong of you to have made a play for T.J.'s father.'

'Oh, for God's sake,' Arabella retorted. 'Face facts, Eleanor, married or single, it makes no difference. They're still going to find a reason to walk out on us women, so we might as well grab whatever happiness we can, whenever we can.'

Eleanor looked incredulous. 'And that's your excuse for making a play for my father-in-law, is it?'

'I didn't make a play for him,' Arabella insisted. 'We were two lonely people who happened to get chatting at your wedding and later found that we were attracted to each other and it just happened.'

Thoughtfully, Arabella gazed out of the plane window. It was true: she and Max had never intended to have an affair. After they'd met at Eleanor and T.J.'s wedding, they'd bumped into each other first in Zurich and then a few months later in Berlin when they were both on business trips. It was nice being on a business trip and knowing someone visiting the same city also. And that was how it started. Innocently.

They would meet for dinner and concerts, but just as a way of getting out of their boring hotel rooms. And then one night after much wine and laughter, it happened. They kissed. It wasn't planned, it just happened midway through a good belly laugh. They'd both stopped laughing at the same time and...

Shocked by what had happened, they'd both retreated after that night and broke off contact. But try as they may to resist each other, they couldn't. As they'd exchanged emails and telephone numbers, Max called weeks later. They talked: it was to never happen again. "Never again," they'd both agreed. Then she emailed him weeks after that – she missed his friendship – they could keep in contact with each other via email, surely? Certainly, and so they did. Then Max wrote that he was going to be in Zurich again on business and was she going to be there too? She wasn't scheduled to be, but as the head office of the company, for which she was working in Singapore, was there, she could always find a justifiable reason to touch base with the mother ship. It would be a laugh hanging out again.

They met up in Zurich, as arranged, in separate rooms of course. They talked and talked and talked. They laughed even more. They drank some. They kissed. They slept together. They showered together. Max checked out of his room and into hers. The weekend turned into five days of unforgettable happiness (after respective calls home to say a flight was missed and there was no availability for a few days). The affair began.

Arabella's thoughts returned to her confrontation with Eleanor on the night of T.J.'s funeral. Eleanor didn't want to understand: the relationship with Max was a no-no and she wasn't going to accept it. 'No,' Eleanor snapped. 'Things like this don't just happen. You could have said no and that would have been the end of it.'

Arabella became irritated by her friend's apparent refusal to see her side of things. What was so hard to understand about the fact that she was in too deep, that 'happily-ever-after' seemed a strong future possibility for her and Max as a couple. She was in for the long haul like she had never been with other affairs before. 'Well, what can I tell you, Eleanor?' she hissed back. 'Maybe I'm the kind of girl who doesn't know how to say no or perhaps, even worse, doesn't want to say no.'

'My point exactly,' Eleanor screamed, violently waving her hands in the air. 'You could have said no, but you chose not to. It's your fault.'

'What?'

'If you knowingly put yourself in a situation that you can't say no to, then you are culpable.'

Arabella eyed her with disappointment. Maybe Eleanor was right, maybe she didn't do enough to steer clear from this sort of relationship, but that wasn't important now. What was important was that she was once again broken-hearted and confused about where to go from here. Of all the men Arabella thought she could trust, Max had been the one. What they had was so special, *or so I thought*. Arabella frowned as she recalled Bianca's delight when informing them that she was one of many.

Arabella began to cry. 'Why can't I ever find happiness?' she sobbed.

'Because you go looking for it in the all wrong places. It can never come out of someone else's sorrow.'

'You managed it.'

'Arabella,' Eleanor cried. 'I did no such thing.'

'Huh,' her friend scoffed. 'I seem to recall that T.J. was with someone else when you met him.'

'What?' Eleanor stared incredulous at Arabella, as if to say 'how could you say such a thing at a time like this?' But Arabella took no notice; she was angry and fighting back in the only way she could think of in the heat of the argument.

'Belinda,' she announced to Eleanor's apparent horror.

'Bel –' she froze. She was the ex who was hell-bent on breaking her and T.J. up, even after they were married. And she had almost succeeded too. Eleanor smiled bitterly. 'You acted like you didn't know a thing about the woman when I told you what she was trying to do to T.J. and me.'

Arabella nodded.

'But you knew about her before then?'

'Yes, Morgan told me from the very start.'

'And you didn't think to tell me?'

'And spoil your shot at happiness? No, I'm not that kind of person.'

'Of course not,' Eleanor laughed hollowly. 'You prefer to finish a person off when they're down.' Eleanor fell silent.

Had Arabella been paying closer attention to her friend's expression at that moment, it would have been clear that Eleanor was finding it hard to reconcile herself with what she'd just found out about T.J. And then Arabella would have remembered that fidelity was Eleanor's touchstone, that from the first day Eleanor and T.J. had met she'd pegged him as being different from all the others, that to Eleanor, he was the faithful, honourable kind of man, the sort who never overlapped relationships. Arabella would have realised that in that heated moment of thoughtless retaliation, she'd hurt her best friend far more than she'd intended or would have ever wanted to. But she hadn't and so was never going to realise why Eleanor forgave Max for their affair but not her and why she looked set to remain *persona non grata* indefinitely.

All Arabella saw was that Eleanor looked up defiantly at her and hit back with, 'At least he wasn't married.'

To which she countered with a further nail in the coffin of their friendship, 'It doesn't matter. He had a girlfriend whose happiness was sacrificed in order for you to get yours.'

Arabella saw Eleanor vanquished, as recognition registered in her eyes. 'I didn't know that, at the time.'

Arabella refused to back off. 'He did, and it worked out just fine for the pair of you which, to me, made not telling you worth it, as you would have probably done the noble deed by not following your heart. And then what?'

'Who knows,' Eleanor shrugged and fell silent again. She stared intently at her friend for a few moments before speaking again. 'So what are you going to do now that this relationship is over?' she asked eventually.

'Nothing,' Arabella retorted, also to her own surprise. 'I'm going to give him the space he needs to realise that what we had was special and doesn't come around everyday'.

Eleanor stared, wide-eyed, at her. 'He said it was over between you and him or weren't you listening?'

Arabella was resolute now. 'If he's the one, he'll be back, you'll see.'

Eleanor glared at her. 'Arabella,' she bellowed.

'What?'

'He's not coming back.'

'He will.'

'Like all the others?'

'That's low.'

'You asked for it.'

'Maybe, but you'll see, this relationship is different, Eleanor. Max and I have a connection and we really do make each other happy. And that's important to me.'

'But he's a married man who happens to be my father-in-law, and that's important to me.'

Arabella felt aggrieved. All Eleanor seemed to care about was the fact that Max was her father-in-law. 'Yes, and I'm sorry,' Arabella replied sadly. 'But you heard Bianca: she doesn't want him and I do. Is that so wrong?'

'That's neither here nor there, Arabella,' Eleanor sneered. 'He doesn't want you, he wants his wife.'

This irritated Arabella. 'Whatever,' she pouted. 'We'll see.'

At this Eleanor's gaze softened. 'Oh, Arabella,' she whispered. 'There's someone out there for you, you'll see, and it's not Max. You've got to understand that.'

Arabella was defiant. 'I love him and I know he loves me too,' she insisted.

'Arabella, please,' Eleanor implored. 'Let this go.'

'I can't.'

'You mean you won't.'

'I mean I can't.'

'There's no such thing as I can't.'

'There is with love, remember?'

'This isn't love, Arabella. This is T.J.'s family, *my* family that you're trying to tear apart.'

'I'm not trying to tear it apart.'

'Then walk away.'

Standing up, Arabella walked to the bed and sat down beside her friend. 'Please don't ask this of me,' she pleaded.

Eleanor shrugged off her attempted hug and stood up. 'Will you or won't you let this go?' she asked again.

'Ellie, please,' she begged her. 'You're my best friend and Bianca's daughter-in-law, I understand that, but you don't have to take sides.'

'Arabella,' Eleanor said, giving her an ironic smile. 'You just don't get it, do you?'

Arabella's eyes began to well up with tears. 'No, *you* just don't get it.'

Eleanor stared hard at her. 'This is not a question of my taking sides,' she explained. 'It's about you choosing to do the right thing for once.'

'The right thing by whom?' Arabella sniffed.

'By T.J.'

'But T.J.'s dead, so what does it matter to him?'

'It matters to me for him.' But Arabella didn't know to read between the lines of what she was being told.

Swiftly rising to her feet, she hastily approached her friend. 'Don't make me choose, please,' she begged her.

'Our friendship or Max,' Eleanor pressed, as she too began to cry.

'Please, Eleanor.'

'Choose.'

Arabella tried a last appeal. 'T.J. loved his Dad, and if he were alive, he would have understood.' *Like I was forced to when Daddy left.*

'No,' Eleanor cut in. 'This would have devastated him,' she added. 'So make your choice now.'

Arabella didn't respond.

'Then I'll do it for you,' Eleanor declared and began to make her way towards the door. Arriving at it, she turned the white knob once and the door opened slightly. With the knob still in her hand, Eleanor opened the door wider. Without looking back at a tearful Arabella who was watching her from beside the bed and willing her to come up with a compromise that would please them both, Eleanor announced, 'I want you packed and out of this house in five minutes.'

'But –' Arabella tried beseeching her friend, but it was too late. Eleanor had walked out of the door and out of Arabella's life, with Arabella's refusal to do the right thing regarding Max serving as fuel that would ensure that whenever Eleanor reviewed what had happened that night and Arabella's motivations for hurting her, she would see it all as a pattern of treachery rather than an accident.

Lowering her hands from her face, Arabella hugged her stomach protectively and stared sadly at the back of the blue leather seat in front. Even though all that had happened almost two years earlier, the pain still felt sharp and devastating like it was yesterday, especially given the knowledge that it was all so unnecessary.

Had Eleanor waited that bit longer, Arabella would have agreed to stay clear of Max for the sake of their friendship. With her disastrous love life, friendships mattered that much more to Arabella. And that was what she had tried so often to explain to Eleanor each time she'd called to reconcile. But Eleanor hadn't wanted to hear anything from her and always hung up after 'hello'.

Arabella's thoughts drifted to Max. How could he ever compare the mere geographic distance from his friends with her loss of Eleanor's friendship? Of course she could imagine how difficult things had been for him over the last year, alone and far away from his best friends – Matt, Rod and Eric – and their weekend softball games and barbecues. But at least he could call them and go to see them whenever he chose to do so.

Eleanor, on the other hand, was still refusing to take her calls, and as for Arabella jumping on a plane and going to Tobago to visit Eleanor, it wasn't even an option.

Suddenly Arabella felt the tyres of the plane bump onto the runway at Seattle Tacoma airport. She tried to look on the bright side of things. This was the beginning of the rest of her life: the beginning of a happily-ever-after life with Max.

If such a thing is possible, she wondered sadly as she found herself once again involuntarily recalling

Bianca's mocking words: 'Yes, honey, some men play golf; Max has affairs. It's his way of keeping fit.'

Was this really the case? Arabella mused. Or had Max's affairs been symptomatic of a bad marriage with Bianca?

She couldn't say, and that worried her.

Chapter Six

The great American welcome

After a harrowing forty-five minutes spent convincing a burly and unfriendly immigration officer that even though she didn't know exactly how long she'd be staying in the country, working illegally was not on the agenda thanks to the money left to her by her maternal grandmother. Arabella felt like crying.

Bastard, she cursed silently as, after all he'd put her through, he'd still only given her the standard three months' leave to stay in the country. What if Max didn't want to leave Seattle by then? What if they needed more time here before they moved elsewhere?

'Ooh,' she seethed. *And trust my luck, I've got a bloody broken trolley*. Things were definitely not going well.

Just then a bullish-looking customs officer beckoned her forward with a condescending nod and a growl of 'Over here, ma'am.'

'There's no need to be aggressive about it, you tosser,' she snarled back, almost audibly.

As he stood disdainfully watching her approach, Arabella felt an instant dislike for him, his country, and all things American.

'Land of hope and glory, my foot,' she hissed and cast a quick glance about her unimpressive-looking surroundings. 'And they reckon everyone's dying to come over here huh,' she sneered. 'That's what happens when people don't get abroad much.' For the first time since they decided it would be best for her to join him in his new life in Seattle, Arabella felt a surge of resentment towards Max. *He's selling the company anyway, so why couldn't we have moved straight to somewhere pleasant like the Caribbean? Why did I have to be the one coming over to this dump to take all this crap?*

It was your idea, her conscience reminded her.

Yah, she snapped at it. *But that was because he was dragging his feet and we were getting nowhere fast.*

Arabella was nearing the customs officer and her mental recounting of all the sacrifices she'd had to make for her relationship with Max had worked her into a rage. *Argh,* she fumed. *And all for the pleasure of what? Moving here? I don't think so. Thank God that moron only gave me three months.*

She was now in front of the burly officer in beige.

'Good evening, ma'am,' he begun sternly and then proceeded to spend the next thirty or so minutes ransacking her bags and cases without any due care or respect.

By the time it was over and Arabella had repacked and returned her luggage to the conveyor belt that would chug it to its final destination in the arrival hall, she was emotionally exhausted and even closer to tears than before this final encounter. *Why can't they be pleasant? It doesn't cost anything.*

Disenchanted with the harassed beginning of her new life, Arabella followed the directions to the second baggage claim that had been given to her by a kindly Somali immigrant worker, the only friendly face she'd so far encountered since her arrival in America.

As she surveyed the unsmiling faces bustling past in a hurry to get to whichever bully was waiting at an upcoming checkpoint, Arabella smiled wryly. 'And they call themselves free,' she murmured. *Huh, what a freedom,* she thought mockingly, *to choose to be cooped up in a country with bullies and thugs for protectors. God help the world.*

Catching sight of a clock on the wall, she remembered Max. The time was twenty past eight. *He should have arrived by now … and with a stonking great big bunch of flowers too, I hope.*

Within minutes, Arabella had arrived at the almost deserted and rundown baggage claim area that was designated for her flight. There was no initial sighting of Max, but she was thankful to spy all her baggage completing what she guessed must have been its umpteenth lap on the battered and scuffed steel and black rubber carousel. As she was about to make a dash to the opposite side of its bedraggled rotating belt to unload them, she remembered how heavy they were.

Hm, she reconsidered. *Not enough time.* And left them to go.

With her luggage now chugging out of sight on its way round back to her, Arabella's thoughts returned to Max. *Where is he when I need him?* She pouted as she noticed the sprinkling of remaining passengers getting help with their bags from people she assumed had come to meet them.

Unable to imagine that he would be late on such an important day for the both of them, Arabella scanned for him around the shabby baggage claim area that looked to her like it had been built in the Sixties.

Starting with the sparse grey and uncomforta-ble-looking seating that gave no room for personal space, her gaze darted from chair to chair in search of him. But he wasn't there. The only people sitting down were a nondescript ginger-haired man in jeans and a forest-green t-shirt and – Arabella paused – a thirtysomething blonde chap a couple of seats away from him. He reminded her of someone she knew, but Arabella couldn't think who.

Where's Max? Yah, she remembered and continued her scanning for him.

Immediately Arabella turned her attention to the heaving metallic escalator with years of black grime encrusted and engrained in its ridged steps. There were about ten people descending it, but none of them was Max. As she turned to check around the other conveyor belts behind her, a loud yet muffled announcement rang out from the loudspeakers that were fixed high up on the off-white walls. Her eyes continued their search, but Max was nowhere to be seen.

Arabella's face immediately clouded over with worry. *He wouldn't just not turn up, would he?* she won-dered, remembering their last conversation.

Of course not, the optimist in her intercepted. *Max not turn up, hah, that'll be the day.*

So where is he then? something else in her piped up.

Her confidence sagged. Yes, where was he?

She looked around again. He was definitely not where he'd said he'd be. Arabella began to worry.

What if he's not turning up? What if that's what he was trying to tell me with that strange call when I was in the taxi in London? Why didn't I call him back? Why –

The idea that maybe he'd left a message suddenly occurred to her. *Oh my God,* she thought, beginning to panic. *The coward. He couldn't say it to me directly, he had to leave it in a message.* She sighed heavily. *At least Kenneth had the balls to tell me the truth directly, albeit over the telephone.*

Quickly lunging into her bag, which was in the basket of the trolley beside her, Arabella grabbed her mobile phone and switched it on.

Come on, come on, she urged it as it took its time to activate. Its blue Nokia logo flashed up on the white background of the illuminating screen. *Come on,* she screamed at it in her head. But it seemed in no hurry. Up the logo flashed again… and again… and again… and –

Oh for Heaven's sake, she almost exploded. The wait was becoming too much for Arabella. Finally the battery level and time registered on the screen. Next the menu scrolled on, which was the sign that the phone was fully activated. Arabella couldn't relax. Shortly, the message he left would call her through its customary 121 mailbox channel and inform her that he'd changed his mind about them and wouldn't be coming.

Holding her breath, Arabella stared down hard at the screen of her phone, willing it not to ring. *No news is good news,* she told herself.

It didn't ring. She waited. It still didn't ring. Arabella exhaled tentatively. The phone still wasn't ringing. She began to relax. Dare she breathe?

No, not yet, in just a little bit longer, she decided.

A little bit longer went by and the phone still didn't ring. Arabella allowed herself to begin to breathe again, slowly at first because she didn't want to tempt fate. Then, after what she deemed to be sufficient time for the message to have come through, a slow smile of relief began to creep across her face. But it was too soon.

Brrr … brrr … brrr … It was her phone ringing.

Typical! Her heart sank.

Arabella stared at it in horror as its vibrations shook her hand. She gawped down at the number that kept flashing up. It wasn't familiar and it wasn't 121. *Relax, it's not a message,* she told herself and activated the call.

'Hel –'

'You have three voicemail messages…' the robotic voicemail interrupted.

What? Oh God, no.

'…Please telephone your messaging service with your pin number to access them.'

Messaging service, pin number, what the hell are you talking about? Arabella freaked out at the voice from her phone. She was in turmoil. Switching off her phone, she stared at it like it was contaminating her hand. What was she to do?

Call him.

But –

What else was there to do? Taking a few deep breaths, Arabella turned her phone back on and dialled Max. Ten rings later, his voicemail clicked on. *'I'm sorry I can't take your call at present, but –'* She ended the call.

I knew it, she concluded sadly. *He's refusing to take my call. Bloody coward!*

Just then her phone began to ring. It was a local number that she didn't recognise.

What now? Could it be the phone company calling to give her the pin number that the messaging service had mentioned?

Who cares! The worst had happened: Max wasn't coming She took the call.

'Hello?'

'Hey, pumpkin.' It was Max. With his phone having packed up, he was calling from his back up phone that was rarely used; hence why Arabella hadn't recognised the number.

Awe, her heart danced as she squealed with relief, 'Where are you?'

'I'm here.'

'Where?'

'At the airport – ' His phone began to crackle and then cut off.

With her mind fizzing with joy and anticipation, she looked excitedly around for him. How could she have doubted that he would come for her? How could she have –

On cue, a distressed squeaking sound interrupted her thoughts and caused Arabella to refocus her attention on the conveyor belt beside her. To her added glee, she spotted her largest case being precariously chugged towards where she stood. The baggage carousel was moving in such a strained manner that she gaily wondered whether the rest of her bags and cases would ever make it out of the hole in the wall before there was a system collapse.

She smiled carelessly. What did it matter, what did she care? Max was around here somewhere and life was great. She cast a quick glance around for him, but still couldn't see him. Three pieces of her luggage were now chugging past her. They caught her attention. She looked round. It seemed that everything else she'd checked in was out and processing past like a marching platoon on parade day.

Arabella decided to count them up to be sure. 'Large cases – one, two and … three – check. Holdalls – medium-with-broken-strap one – check. Intact smaller-sized one, check. Cabin bag, check. Vanity case … vanity case… ' She froze. It wasn't there.

'Check,' a mocking voice from nearby piped up.

Arabella swung round expectantly towards it. It wasn't Max messing about like she'd hoped. It was a young boy she hadn't noticed before and whose attention she'd obviously attracted by her tallying her luggage aloud, and who was now whiling away time by mimicking and making fun of her.

How embarrassing, she thought and cast a furtive glance about her. No one else seemed to be paying attention. *Thank God.* 'Thanks for that,' *you brat,* she smiled through gritted teeth, patting her vanity case, which she'd spotted on her trolley as she'd swung round. 'I wouldn't want to lose this baby,' she told him, as if he was remotely interested. With the final item checked off her mental list, it was time to set to work and get them off the carousel and onto the trolley.

Switching her attention to her clothes, Arabella quickly undid the five mother-of-pearl buttons that were fastening her tight-fitting red cardigan in place on her body. In preparation for the hard labour ahead of her, she whipped it off. Having never been fond of having things tied around her waist, she swished it about her shoulders so that it adorned the plunging neckline of her now much crushed black linen shift dress like a red scarf.

Slowly edging round and occasionally skipping to catch up with the pace of the slowly moving belt, whilst also dodging the odd remaining passengers still getting their luggage, the black slingback stiletto-shod Arabella wrestled and dragged her luggage down piece-by-piece. Single-handedly she managed to get them all onto the dark and grubby tarpaulin flooring before the last piece disappeared back into the second hole in the wall.

Now it was time to gather them closer together before loading them onto her trolley. It took less time than she'd anticipated. Panting slightly and with a delicate sheen of perspiration and an extra hue of red to her cheeks, Arabella smiled proudly down at her achievement. *Well done, ole gal,* she congratulated herself. Her luggage was set. But there was still no Max in sight.

Where is he? she wondered briefly. With her adrenalin still pumping, she psyched herself for loading her bags and cases onto the trolley. Whisking her now slightly damp abundance of shoulder-length dead straight hair into a makeshift bun at the crown of her head, Arabella fished out something that looked like a dark brown chopstick from her bag and used it to secure the bun.

Next she brought her trolley closer and busied herself with stacking and recounting her cases and bags. On her fifth turn to put something on the baggage cart, she became aware of someone picking up her final bag. Brushing aside a damp lock of hair from where it hung against the silhouette of her face, Arabella again looked round hopefully.

Instead of her debonair Max, with his twinkling eyes that creased roguishly at the outside corners and an ultra-low-cut afro with light speckles of grey, she was faced with the blonde thirtysomething guy she'd spotted earlier sitting near the ginger-haired man.

Up close, she noticed him to be of athletic build and quite handsome and –

Oh my God, she gasped on closer inspection. The man was the spitting image of Cort, Eleanor's off-and-on ex, before she met T.J. *That's why he looked familiar.*

Arabella's thoughts ran to Eleanor. How very besotted she'd been with Cort and what an absolute shit he was to her, forever breaking Eleanor's heart by leaving her and then always rocking up whenever she found someone new and was beginning to smile again.

Until T.J. came along and ended the cycle, Arabella and Arielle were beginning to worry about Eleanor and her seeming incapability to break free from Cort and their dysfunctional relationship. *How would things be now if Eleanor and Cort were to meet again?* Arabella wondered. She noticed the man in front of her smiling expectantly at her. The similarity between him and how she remembered Cort was too uncanny. *It's not him, is it,* she wondered apprehensively. 'Yes?' Arabella demanded with brittle disdain, as the dislike she used to feel for Cort all those years ago began to surface.

Stepping forward, the man plonked the lightest of her luggage on the top of the pile of bags and cases on the trolley in front of them. 'You're all set now,' he told her and came to a halt a bit too close for her liking.

Up that close, it was easier to notice that he wasn't Cort – *thank God* – but their similarities, which even extended to their German/Northern European accent tinged with a hint of American drawl, made Arabella uncomfortable. Stepping away from him, she smiled apprehensively. 'Thanks,' she said and, as if to say 'interaction over', she walked round to the other side of the trolley and began a purposeful search for nothing in particular in her bag.

But the stranger seemed to miss the hint. 'I take it you'll be staying in Seattle for a while,' he remarked.

'What?' Arabella scowled up at him, trying to deter him from further smalltalk.

'Your bags,' he pointed. 'There are many of them.'

You don't say, Sherlock!

'Are you here for long?'

'In the airport?'

'No,' the man laughed. 'I meant in Seattle.'

'No, just the weekend,' Arabella fibbed.

The man eyed her playfully. 'Are you expecting it to be a longer one than usual?' he teased.

Arabella burst out laughing. Unlike Cort, who was devoid of humour, this man was funny. And with such quick wit and repartee, it was hard to dislike him. She didn't mind chatting to him, so long as they both knew where they stood. Quickly and with an equally mischievous tone, she riposted, 'Are you trying to pick me up?'

'Would you like me to?'

'No.'

'Then you have nothing to fear.'

Although Arabella was not attracted to him in the slightest, his quick rebuff of the notion of fancying her stung a little. 'Why, what's wrong with me?' she retorted unintentionally aloud.

'Ah,' the man teased. 'You do want me to fancy you.'

Arabella flushed crimson. 'No,' she almost shouted. 'I, I –'

'You find it hard to believe that you are resistible?'

'No.'

'Then what?'

Arabella winced with shame. Even if she had intended to ask the question – which she hadn't – it would've been due to none of the above. It was just *oh God*, how was she going to explain it? 'I'm taken,' she blurted out.

'Good for you,' the man exclaimed, unable to stifle any longer the laughter he'd been holding back all the while. 'I'm sorry,' he apologised. 'It was unkind of me to tease you like this, but you made it so easy for me.'

Arabella blushed even redder: she was feeling very silly indeed. 'Yes, it was,' she confirmed without malice. 'Unkind of you, I mean,' she clarified.

'I know,' the Cort-lookalike concurred, reprimanding himself with a playful slap on the wrist. 'So we'll start again, ya?'

'If you insist.'

'Oh, I insist.'

'Well alright then,' Arabella conceded with feigned reluctance and shook his outstretched hand. 'Hello, my name is Arabella,' she said.

'And I am Thorsten,' he replied.

'Pleased to meet you.'

'Ditto,' he bowed slightly. 'And before I bid you adieu, may I be of any more assistance?'

'Actually you can,' Arabella suddenly thought aloud. 'I'd love to know the best place to wait to be picked up.'

'To be picked up,' he repeated with loaded tone.

'Yes, to be –' She suddenly realised. 'No, that's not … Stop it.' Smiling, she regarded him with interest. Sense of humour wise, he was just like Eleanor: sharp as a razor. They'd be good together, Arabella reckoned, but with Eleanor miles away and still not talking to her, *never the twain shall meet*, shame. 'So,' she interjected suddenly, 'do you or don't you?'

'*Nein, fraulein,*' he replied. 'This is my first time in Seattle.'

As he spoke, a gentle dragging sound could be heard approaching them. They both turned towards it. Just then a plump, middle-aged woman drew parallel to where they were standing. She was dressed in tapered cream slacks, a cream pair of what Arabella and her friends would call 'granny sandals,' and a white t-shirt with a brightly coloured drawing of a tropical island boldly embossed on the chest in green and bright orange. Behind her she was dragging a small lilac-coloured pulley case.

Smiling, Thorsten arched an eyebrow mischievously. 'She looks like a woman who has been picked up many times before, don't you think?'

'Don't be mean,' Arabella tittered.

'So we ask her?'

'We could.'

Immediately stepping forward, Thorsten intercepted the woman's path. 'Excuse me,' he said, stopping her in her tracks.

She faced them with a smile. 'Yes?'

'Sorry to bother you,' Arabella interjected.

'It's no bother,' the woman drawled in an American accent. 'How can I help you?'

Arabella stepped forward. 'I'm supposed to be meeting my boyfriend,' she began. 'But I think I've mixed up where.'

The woman, who'd been regarding her attentively as she spoke, broke into a charming laugh. 'I bet you haven't, honey,' she told Arabella. 'It's right here, but people always get confused.'

'Okay.'

'So you're not the first, nor will you be the last to ask this question, I dare say,' she added. 'Most airports these days barely allow non-passengers anywhere near the building let alone to walk right up to baggage claim to meetcha.'

'I know,' Arabella agreed. 'That did throw me a bit. So thanks for your help.'

'Oh, it's no bother,' the kindly woman told her, and before Arabella and Thorsten could take their leave of her, she asked, 'Is this your first time in Seattle?'

'Yes,' Arabella replied.

'Well, you're just gonna love it, honey. There are lots of fun things to see and do here.' The woman paused. 'Are you British?'

Arabella nodded.

'I thought so,' the woman chirped with delight. Turning to Thorsten, she patted him lightly on the arm. 'It's the accent, you know,' she whispered to him with a nod, as if she were divulging priceless insider information. She turned back to Arabella: 'You sound so cute when you talk. I could listen to that accent all day.'

'Thanks,' Arabella laughed shyly.

'I was in London last fall,' the woman continued. 'Are you from near there?'

Arabella nodded.

'Oh,' the woman cooed with even greater joy. 'I love London … it's a bit expensive though,' she added. 'But I love going there anyway. It's so much better than Paris.' She paused and flashed an uncomfortable glance at Thorsten. 'You're not from Paris, are you?'

'No, I'm from Germany.'

She turned and took a better look at him. 'German, huh?'

He and Arabella exchanged glances.

The woman scrutinized him some more and then, turning her attention to Arabella, spoke. 'He looks more Scandinavian,' she whispered, as if she still didn't believe that he could possibly be German. 'My grandparents were originally from Sweden,' she elaborated and turned back to Thorsten. 'I've still got some family there, you know.'

'Tha –'

'I go back to see them once a year,' the woman continued. 'You look like them.'

'Maybe we're related,' Thorsten quipped.

'Huh?'

'You and me, if I look like your family,' he teased on.

'No,' the woman hooted with laughter. 'You look nothing like my family.'

'Oh, what a pity.'

'But you look like the Scandinavians, though.'

'Or perhaps they look like me, maybe.'

'Oh stop,' the woman giggled coquettishly.

As she spoke, someone behind the woman caught Thorsten's attention. He acknowledged the person with a wave and turned to Arabella. 'That's the lost luggage lady,' he explained. 'I have to go now; maybe she has some news of my lost suitcase.'

'Oh,' the woman cried with a slight blush. 'Look at me taking up all your time. I do apologise.'

'No,' Arabella and Thorsten chorused.

'Well, I best be going now anyway. My flight was late and Jack and the boys must be at home wondering where I've got to.'

'Ok then,' Arabella accepted. 'And thanks again for your help.'

The woman was already on her way. 'My pleasure,' she called back to them. 'And say hello to London for me, when you get back home, y'hear?'

Ah, Arabella smiled, at last she'd come across a good old-fashioned pleasant American. Remembering Thorsten, she quickly turned to him. 'And thank you for all your help.'

'It's fine,' he told her with a reassuring wink. 'Take care of yourself and I hope you enjoy your *long* weekend here in Seattle.'

'Thanks.' Arabella blushed at his emphasis on 'long weekend'. She knew that he knew she'd been fibbing. *Too funny.* 'And I hope they find your lost luggage soon.'

'I hope so too,' he concurred and rushed off in the direction of the person to whom he had waved.

Turning for a final glance at each of her helpers, Arabella reviewed her first couple of hours in Seattle. Before she could conclude her train of thought, she suddenly felt a familiar tingling and a warm sensation rising from the pit of her stomach to her chest. Instinctively, she knew Max was nearby ... somewhere.

But where? she wondered excitedly as her eyes hungrily hunted through a crowd of new arrivals for a glimpse of him.

Moments later, a smile began to trace across her face. He hadn't spotted her yet, but there he was, to her left: the tall, confident, and distinguished-looking black gentleman in a maroon cashmere polo neck jumper and grey trousers who was purposefully striding towards her in the near distance. Her smile broadened. *My man.*

As she stood proudly watching him approach, a thought struck Arabella. *Yes,* she thought, *Arielle was right. He does look like a cross between Sydney Poitier and Denzel Washington. But much better looking than both,* she concluded.

With Max not too far away now, Arabella noticed how much younger and more relaxed he looked. Bianca's words came rushing back to mind. 'Yes, honey, some men play golf; Max has affairs. It's his way of keeping fit.'

Arabella's heart sank with the old familiar inse-curities that had been dogging her ever since her mother had made it clear that not only did she believe Bianca's words, but that she also believed that: 'Men like Max never change. Mark my word he'll cheat on you again, and who knows, it may even be with his wife this time.'

Arabella grimaced at her recollection of those words, but soon cheered up at the thought of Max sneaking around behind her back with Bianca. Arabella almost laughed aloud at the thought; that was definitely never going to happen, of that she was confident.

As she smiled complacently, Arabella remembered her mother's parting words: 'Darling, never forget that when a mistress is promoted to the position of wife or main partner, she leaves behind the vacancy of a mistress...' That wasn't so ludicrous a concept, especially as she could cite quite a few examples of friends' Dads who had run off with younger women, married them, and then left them a few years later for another younger woman. Her own father also came to mind. He hadn't run off with anyone, but since he'd left home, he hadn't managed to settle down with any one woman. *Was Max going to be the same?* Arabella wondered.

Just then Max spotted her. Their eyes locked, and his face brightened into the warmest smile she'd ever had from him, and she'd had many. He looked genuinely thrilled to see her. Arabella's heart gladdened. The look in his eyes, his smile, everything about the way he looked at her was all the proof she needed. There was no cause for worry or insecurity, she decided, and pushed her ever-present doubts to the back of her mind.

Chapter Seven

Layer by layer: getting to know you, getting to know all about you

Eager to be alone, Arabella and Max left the airport soon after their loving reunion and headed home via the back roads that bypassed the traffic jam. En route he stopped at the office to sign and pick up some papers.

After twenty more minutes of non-stop happy and optimistic chatter, interlaced with Arabella's unsuccessful attempts to elicit an acceptable justification from Max for his initial reservations about moving in together in Seattle, they pulled up at a white chest-high wooden fence. The fence corralled the back of the fourth in a row of fifteen identical white single-storey wooden townhouses, all part of a development eighteen minutes from downtown Seattle.

Still bursting with the excitement and determination to get their new life together off to a fabulous start that would eliminate all Max's prior reservations and any potential mistresses, Arabella hurriedly undid her seatbelt and scrambled out of the front seat of the car.

Rushing to the gate at the corner of the fence, she searched for the bolt.

'The latch's on the other side,' Max informed her and went to the back of the car to begin unloading the luggage. As he was opening the boot, he thought of asking her which would be the best bag to bring out for shower things and a change of clothes afterwards, but decided against it. If he did, he'd have to immediately break the news to her that her new home, for the time being, was going to be the Four Seasons Hotel in town.

Max glanced up at Arabella. *No,* he decided, now wasn't the right time to say anything about that. She was too excited, and judging from the many questions she was slyly casting his way throughout the journey, she was also distrustful of him. He'd be better off waiting until after dinner lest she assume that he was packing her off in a hurry before some other woman returned.

After dinner, she'd be relaxed, better rested, and would have had the chance to have checked everywhere out and seen the lack of evidence that there was another woman in his life or home, so there were no ulterior motives for him not having her stay in the house, except for the fact that it belonged to Eleanor and she wouldn't like it.

With this in mind, Max reviewed the amount of Arabella's luggage. *Phew,* it was extensive, but he'd have to brave it and unload the lot. It was worth the peace.

As he began to do so, Arabella, teetering up on the tips of her toes, peered over the top of the fence to find the bolt. Encountering it, she pulled a face. It wasn't a bolt but a complicated latch. *How on earth was she going to get past this?* she frowned. And then shrugging, she decided on the only option that came to mind.

Hearing the racket of her impatiently yanking, nudging, and bashing at the gate like a frustrated child with a complex new toy, Max looked up. It made him smile and reminded him of how much he cherished her fearless 'must-have-a-go-at-everything' approach to life and all its challenges. Nothing ever seemed too daunting or not worth the effort to Arabella.

She's similar, like that, to how Bianca used to be, he mused. Except that Bianca would always first work out a course of action before jumping in. Arabella simply dived in, like she was doing now.

Maybe not always the best approach, Max concluded, as he noticed the neighbours' adjoining fences begin to rattle under the pummelling.

'Whoa,' he called out. 'Take it easy, it's kinda tricky.'

'No kidding, Sherlock,' came the quick-as-a-flash reply that had Max smiling again.

That's my girl, ever ready with her quips. That was another thing he liked about Arabella.

Sensing that she was being watched, Arabella stopped brutalising the gate and turned round. Their eyes met in an exchange of tender emotions. With a flush of colour to her high cheekbones and a twinkle of shyness in her eyes, she smiled back. *I love you too.*

Mm, what a feeling! she purred silently. Dropping her gaze coyly, she savoured the moment. Yes, it definitely felt great. *Eat your heart out everyone, our love's here to stay.* Unable to contain her happiness, Arabella beamed back up at Max. He was still looking at her. 'What?' she demanded shyly.

'Nothing, just looking.'

She felt wonderfully overwhelmed. 'Stop it.'

'Stop it,' he mimicked her.

Rolling her eyes playfully and tutting with feigned exasperation, she turned back to the lock, but even her hands felt tingly, loved up and good for nothing. 'This bloody gate,' she complained happily. 'How does it work?'

'Like it's supposed to: pull the latch back with your thumb, then tap the gate forward with your hip.'

'Oh, is that all?' she scoffed in an attempt to veil her embarrassment at having become so rendered useless by her emotions. 'Lucky I'm not desperate for the loo, huh!'

'Real lucky,' Max mocked jokingly and returned his attention to the luggage that he was bringing out from the boot of the car.

After a few more tries with her thumb slipping off the latch before she had a chance to dislodge the gate with her hip, Arabella attempted the lock with her forefinger instead. It stayed. 'Looks like we're in business,' she shouted out excitedly and nudged the unpredictable gate open with her right knee. Before she could celebrate her success, the sudden jolt of the gate sent her reeling forward into the back garden.

Staggering to a halt a foot away from the entrance, Arabella beheld the garden in front of her. As she did, a feeling of calm engulfed her like she had entered a sanctuary. She recognised the feeling: it was the same as the one she recalled from her days in Asia when she, Eleanor and Arielle, wanting to get away from the busyness of life in Singapore, would retreat for a weekend of pampering at one of the spas that they frequented at least once a month in Indonesia and Malaysia.

Still marvelling at the potency of the aura of the garden, Arabella sensed Max approaching and turned to face him. 'I love it,' she announced.

'Mm, me too,' he agreed. 'It has a great feel when you step into it, doesn't it?'

'Yah. Who looks after it?'

Having now arrived beside her, Max relieved himself of the large case and the smaller of the two holdalls in his hands and paused briefly to proudly survey the garden. With his gaze still making its way around the horticultural masterpiece before them, he replied, 'I do.'

Arabella swung round as if she couldn't believe her ears. 'You do?' she echoed incredulously.

'Yes,' Max answered. 'I planted everything you see here.'

'You?'

He gave her a puzzled look. 'Yes. You seem surprised, why?'

'Because you don't look the type.'

'What type?'

'The gardening type.'

'And what is the gardening type?'

'Definitely not you,' she giggled as her frail but resilient late maternal grandmother came to mind. She was the only person Arabella had ever known who liked gardening. She smirked at Max. 'You're not doddery enough,' she told him.

'Doddery?'

'Yah. Unsteady on ye ole pins.'

'Unsteady on ye ole pins,' Max spluttered with laughter.

'Yup.'

He shook his head. What did gardening have to do with frailty? Max wondered. Or was that asking a dumb question? To Arabella's mind, seemingly full of irregularly juxtaposed thoughts and ideas, it probably was, he smiled. Max began to laugh again. What a mind! He admired her for it, though he'd never let on to the fact. It gave her a unique and refreshing take on even the most mundane of things and he liked that. For a moment, Max tried to imagine what life with Arabella was going to be like. He couldn't, she was too unpredictable. He smiled broadly. One thing was certain though: love it or hate it – he didn't know which it would be – but dull it was most certainly not going to be.

He caught her eye. 'I'm right though, aren't I?' she demanded with a look of mischief that he saw as goading him to defy her theory, which was exactly what he was going to do.

'No you're not,' he challenged her with a return gaze. 'No one in my family is doddery, yet they're all gardening types. Lucas, Tevin, Bianca ...'

Bianca, Arabella frowned. Why was she being brought into the conversation? And more importantly, why was Max still classing her as part of his family? Yes, she was the mother of his kids, but in about a month's time, she was also going to be his ex-wife and therefore technically no longer a member of the family. Or had Max forgotten? Arabella didn't like this and it showed on her face.

Max noticed. *What's with the look?* he wondered. It was clear to him that Arabella had something on her mind. 'What?' he asked.

'Nothing.'

He'd heard that word issued many times before and in the same tone and so knew better than to take it on face value. Max flashed a tentative smile. 'Do you mean nothing, as in nothing, or nothing as in something which you're not telling?'

Arabella forced a return smile. She so wanted to know why he was still calling Bianca family, but she didn't want to appear like an insecure nag. 'Nothing, as in nothing,' she lied breezily.

I don't believe that for a second, his eyes told her, but Arabella wasn't budging.

'There's nothing,' she insisted.

'So why the look?'

'What look?'

'That I've-got-something-on-my-mind look.'

'What?' Arabella giggled.

'It's still there,' Max pointed out.

'Oh please!'

'I see it.'

'No, it's nothing,' Arabella lied with genuine laughter. 'Nothing important anyway,' she added, as a viable lie came to mind. 'You didn't include T.J. in your list, that's all.'

Max dropped his gaze sadly. Leaving T.J. off the list wasn't intentional, but it wasn't such a bad thing, he told himself. It was a sign that he was at last coming to terms with the idea of his son being gone. It had taken a long time, but he was finally getting there. But back to the topic of gardening: 'Oh T.J.!' Max exclaimed loudly with a clear look of pride. 'Don't even start me on him,' he told Arabella. 'He was the best and keenest gardener of all of us.'

'Right!'

'You see this here garden,' Max said, gesticulating at the plants with great enthusiasm. 'It was him and me all the way.'

'Oh behave!'

'I'm serious,' he insisted.

'Sure and pigs fly.'

'Whatever!' And with that Max, picking up the case and bag by their sturdy beige leather handles, resumed lugging them towards the back door. A few steps away, he added, 'And we both – nondoddery father and son – had a lot of fun doing it too.'

Arabella smiled. She'd never noticed this about him, but it suddenly dawned on her that Max loved having the last word, but she didn't mind. He was funny with it.

And talking of learning new things about Max, she thought, shaking her head. *Him a keen gardener? Wow, who would have thought it!*

And T.J., she suddenly remembered. That was way beyond Arabella's wildest imaginings. Or was it?

Still wide-eyed with disbelief, she began to survey the full blooming plants around her in search of any telltale sign that would corroborate Max's claims. As she did so, it began to seem more and more plausible that Max may indeed have had a hand in the creation of this botanical treat before her. She nodded.

Yes, that was definitely possible, because there was something about this large rectangle of tranquillity that made her feel safe and protected just like he made her feel.

Her eyes began to scan around. Arabella liked the way the fern trees lined the fences on the left and right, blocking the neighbours' view, presuming they weren't standing on the tips of their toes and making a real effort to see over.

Max loves his privacy, she recalled, so it figured that he would choose such a layout.

Then there was the slate paving that ran down the middle of the well-kept lawn, from the gate to the end of the four slightly weatherbeaten grey wooden steps leading up to the back porch. For Arabella, it brought to mind *The Wizard of Oz.* 'Follow the yellow brick road,' she sang out suddenly as she hopped along the paving. Turning, Max regarded her with a contented smile of wonder. Arabella caught him watching her. She too smiled. It felt great to be catching Max so often sneaking her wonderful looks like these. Shyly dropping her gaze back to the paving, Arabella resumed her scrutiny of the yard.

Yes, knowing what she did of him, she could imagine Max coming up with something like this: a path of stepping stones to prevent his shoes from getting soggy and muddied by wet grass and soil on a rainy day. *Fussy dandy!*

She hopped off, into the grass to her left. Her eyes lit up on the fennel-like plants with large attractive yellow umbrella-shaped flower heads that marked the end of the line of fern trees a foot away from the house. Max's favourite colour was yellow, so that figured.

But talking about colours, Arabella mused. 'Wasn't purple T.J.'s favourite colour?' she shouted to Max.

Having deposited the baggage on the porch, he was now on his way back. He stopped beside her. 'Sure. Why?'

'Well, how come there's not a trace of it anywhere in this garden?' That would have been some evidence of his contribution.

'I did the back and he did the front and sides,' Max explained. 'So all the purple and red plants are around there.'

'Red?' Arabella retorted.

'Yes, that was T.J.'s second favourite colour.'

Moving further left, Arabella peered round the side of the building. *Wow!* Max wasn't kidding, the red and purple evidence was in full bloom all the way up to the other end.

She exhaled loudly. *T.J. a keen gardener? Who would have thought it?* Arabella was still finding it hard to reconcile herself with the idea of the biggest party animal she'd ever known having such a hobby.

Well, she shrugged. *I suppose this is how people who'd only known Eleanor as a non-stop partier felt whenever they found out that she was also a religious and devout Catholic who never missed Mass on a Sunday, no matter what.*

Arabella chuckled to herself at the recollection of people's faces during those Singapore days, when at five on a Sunday morning, Eleanor would say she'd have to stop her partying and go home 'to get some kip before Mass'.

'Mass?' someone within earshot who didn't know her well would inevitably cry out before demanding, 'You're not religious, are you?' To which Eleanor would proudly declare, 'Yes, very.' And would then head off home, leaving some other drunk friend or acquaintance to divulge her Sunday routine of 'Mass, brunch, shopping for shoes and bags, relax, more drinks, and then bed.'

With a smile, Arabella also recalled how on occasions she'd chipped in her proverbial two pence worth with a comeback of 'There's nothing in the Bible that says you can't be cool and religious, you know.'

Arabella smiled again at her memories. *What did she know about the Bible to have volunteered such a declaration?* she chuckled under her breath.

Something stirring in the undergrowth in front of where she stood returned Arabella's thoughts back to T.J. Just as being cool didn't mean that Eleanor couldn't be religious too, him having been a party animal didn't rule T.J. out of being a talented horticulturist.

As she stared up the alley of red and purple blooms, Arabella felt a twinge of a panic attack coming on, as flashbacks of her late Nana's house flitted through her mind's eye. Although her Nana's place was built with cement and painted in a slightly different shade of white, the side bit of her garden was very reminiscent of this one. It used to be Arabella's favourite part of her grandmother's home because it felt secluded and allowed her the privacy to play make believe without being seen by the adults. That is, until the day that was now struggling to be relived.

The memory won and began to replay in Arabella's mind. She was six and playing in Nana's side garden when she heard the telephone begin to ring. It was always kept on the landing of the mezzanine floor of the house, right by the side window above where Arabella always played. Her grandmother answered. It was Sophia calling to say she'd soon be coming to pick up her daughter. Somewhere in the conversation, Sophia must have started to cry, as she was prone to during this period, because Arabella recalled Nana trying to console her daughter. Shortly after this and typical of that time, the conversation between mother and daughter drifted to the marital separation.

Even now, as this painful recollection played back in her head, Arabella could recall nothing else of the snippets of the conversation that had drifted back into her mind, except the part when she heard Grandmother saying, 'But you do realise, darling, that part of the pressure he may be talking about could be the pressure of being a father. She did come rather soon after he'd told you he wasn't sure he was quite ready for fatherhood, didn't she?'

There it was, at last, the answer to Arabella's sole question in those days: 'why has Daddy gone?' It felt as awful then as it did now, being confronted by this dreadful fact that her Daddy, whom she adored and worshipped with all her heart and soul, hadn't and still didn't want her and that was why he'd left.

Arabella tried to breathe, but the air got trapped somewhere within a sob. Another sob came and another, but still no air. She could feel her chest begin to tighten. She inhaled and exhaled quickly, but to no avail. The breaths were shallow and ineffective, like a bicycle being pedalled in mid-air. She began to panic. 'I can't breathe,' she heard herself cry out without intending to. And before she knew what was happening, she was on the ground wheezing like someone having an asthma attack (which she'd never had in her life).

Max, who had reached the back gate on his second trip from the car, heard her. Dropping what he was carrying, he ran to see what was happening. He got to her in time to see her regaining the rhythm of her breathing.

'What's happening?' he demanded.

Arabella smiled apologetically. She hated seeing him so worried over 'nothing.'

'Oh come on,' he implored as he helped her back up on her feet. 'Something's wrong and I wanna know what it is. What happened? Are you sick? Did you fall? What?'

'None of the above,' she replied. 'It's nothing,' nothing that she ever wanted to share with him or anyone else.

But Max wasn't to be fobbed off. What he'd heard didn't sound like nothing and then finding her on the ground on her knees the way he had. 'No way, I'm not buying that.'

Playfully Arabella smiled ominously. 'If I tell you, I'll have to kill you,' she told him.

'Then die I must,' he quipped back.

Oh great! 'Promise you won't laugh?' she asked him in an attempt to play for time to come up with a good excuse.

'I promise.'

Arabella caught sight of the string of the tail of a kite lying by the side fence. 'I thought I saw a snake,' she fabricated on the spot with a guilty smile.

'A snake?'

'I have a phobia for snakes,' she confessed. It was the truth, and one of the things she and Eleanor had in common. So strong was her fear of them that she couldn't even touch a page with a picture or a drawing of a snake on it. 'And I thought I saw one, over there,' she said, pointing to the string.

Max took a peek. 'It's a string,' he told her.

'I know that now,' she said. 'And that's why I said there was nothing wrong. I mean, how embarrassing, hyperventilating because of a piece of string.'

Max laughed. Although nothing had registered in his mind in the heat of the moment when he was rushing to Arabella's rescue, he knew he'd expected worse. *Phew, what a relief!* And with that he happily led her towards the back porch.

As they passed by the yellow plant, Arabella pointed to it.

'Dill,' Max replied. People always asked him about it.

'Dill?'

'Uh huh, and that's oregano, thyme, parsley…' he said, turning to point out the different little potted plants that ran from the dill to the side of the bottom of the four steps leading up to the deck.

'And you grew those too?'

'Yup,' Max nodded.

'Why?'

'I like to cook with fresh 'erbs'.'

He likes to cook with fresh herbs, Arabella repeated to herself. 'Since when?'

'Since always, we've always done.'

Bianca included, I suppose? 'You never said.'

Max looked away, as if uncomfortable. 'It was our thing, something we did as a family in our special moments,' he explained. 'And, and …'

Arabella eyed him. 'And what?'

'And it was my rule never to discuss family times and special moments –'

'With your affairs?'

He nodded.

Arabella's heart dipped. She felt degraded to have him acknowledge her as merely one of his 'affairs.' And even worse still to know that he hadn't shared everything with her. 'Thanks a bunch', she pouted.

'I'm sorry.'

She glared at him.

'It would have been disrespectful,' he explained.

'To whom?'

'To Bianca and the boys.'

Arabella felt a hot rush of anger colour her cheeks. *Screw Bianca,* she screamed silently. 'What about respect for me?'

'I never disrespected you.'

She looked away.

'Hey,' Max cooed, reaching out and drawing her to him. 'It's the past,' he reminded her. 'And that's where we agreed to leave all of that. Remember?'

She nodded without making eye contact. How could she forget with him constantly reminding her of their agreement? Arabella gazed up sadly at him. Remembering that she'd promised to forget was one thing. Actually forgetting was another.

Besides, she sighed silently. How could she be expected to forget the past? It was where their happiest moments lay: those times that they'd spent – just the two of them –snuggled up in plush hotel rooms in different countries away from anyone who knew them.

How could she possibly let go of those memories of him sipping whisky and she wine, giggling non-stop at each other's idiosyncrasies? Those were special times – their special moments – hours and hours spent getting to know each other through sharing every detail of their lives with each other…or so she'd thought.

Arabella held Max's gaze. It was hard being confronted now with the reality that during those times he hadn't been sharing every detail of his life with her. For if he had, she would have known that he loved gardening and 'to cook with 'erbs'. But she didn't.

And like her mother had asked earlier that morning on the telephone, she too was now wondering what she really knew about this man.

As much as he knows about you, her conscience pricked her. *Nobody tells anybody everything.*

Dropping her gaze guiltily, Arabella recalled the panic attack she'd just had. She hadn't told him the truth about that, like she'd never told him or anyone else about what she believed was the reason why her father had left them.

With this in mind, it was hard for her to begrudge Max his special family moments and his wanting to keep them to himself. She looked back up at him with a sad smile. 'You're right,' she conceded. 'The past is best left in the past.' And with that, she followed him, against his wishes, back to the car to collect the rest of her luggage.

Chapter Eight

Refrigerated doubts

By the time Arabella followed Max to the porch with the last piece of her baggage, he had already opened the back door and was carrying two of her cases into the house. Curious to see what the inside looked like, she quickened her step and followed him through the light grey door that opened onto a small square that was overlaid with cream and terracotta splash-effect rugged stone tiles. As he came to the end of the tiles, to the right of the door, Max took off his shoes and then bore left in the direction of wherever it was he was intending to deposit her luggage.

Seeing him perform this little ritual with the shoes filled Arabella with nostalgia. Asia was the only place she'd seen people remove their shoes before they walked into the rest of a house, well apart from Eleanor's house after she and T.J. were married. Noticing Max do this and remembering how Eleanor used to forget to do it when they visited friends' places when they were both living in Singapore, Arabella assumed that it must have been something that Max and the rest of the Wilner clan had always done, which T.J. in turn had eventually passed on to Eleanor.

Instinctively, Arabella looked to the left of the door that she was closing behind her with the back of her foot. There, just as she had expected, was a small line-up of shoes: a pair of semi-formal black Calvin Klein lace-ups, a pair of grey and blue perforated fabric Gucci slippers with hard black leather soles, a pair of brown leather and suede shoes which were trendier than would have been expected for a man his age and looked like a cross between slip-ons and trainers. *They're nice, though*, Arabella acknowledged and added her slingbacks to the line-up.

Looking up from the shoes, she noticed a white door directly in front of the door through which she had entered the house and wondered what was behind it. With Max out of sight, she decided to have a nose around.

Opening the door, Arabella beheld a small, square room with white walls. Inside, on the left by the door, was a large washing machine, a large dryer and above them three pinewood cupboards. Walking to the cupboards, she opened the first of them and then, getting on tiptoes, peered inside.

The first one was neatly packed with Bold washing powder and three boxes of Bounce for freshening and removing static energy from clothes as they dried in a dryer. Noticing that, as in England, the Bounce came packaged in the same white and orange swirl boxes and the Bold in the same red boxes with white and black lettering, Arabella began to feel as if she were on more familiar territory. She opened the next cupboard.

'It's empty, as is the final one,' Max's voice confirmed from just behind her.

Startled and embarrassed by his sudden reappearance in the middle of her prying, Arabella slammed the cupboard door quickly shut and turned to confront Max with a guilty smile. 'I was just –'

'Snooping?'

'"Mhm, something like that,"' she volleyed back and began to take off her cardigan, which she had put back on in the car on their way from the airport.

'Waste of time; nothing to see.'

'I'll be the judge of that after a proper look when you're not around,' she smirked with distrust.

'As you wish,' he shrugged, and with that Max headed out of the utility room with Arabella following close behind him. Suddenly and without warning, he stopped, causing her to collide into his back.

'Ouch!' Arabella hollered and Max began to chuckle. 'Why did you stop like that?' she demanded.

'No particular reason.' He continued laughing.

'You can be so childish sometimes, d'you know that?'

'Mhm,' Max agreed, and bearing left continued on till the end of the rugged stone tiles. Veering a fraction right, he glanced round at Arabella who, after his prank, was keeping to his side while maintaining a watchful eye on his every move. 'This is the kitchen,' he announced, still tittering to himself as he did so.

Overtaking him, Arabella walked off the tiles and onto very clean and well-polished pine floorboards.

'The walls are so white and everything is so spotless,' she remarked, remembering her forest green lived-in kitchen that she'd left behind in London. This was the first kitchen she had ever seen with so many surfaces, and all of them empty and devoid of mess or utensils. Most kitchens she'd encountered looked operational with dishes, pots or other stuff lying around.

'Do you ever use this kitchen at all?' Arabella asked Max.

'Almost everyday.'

Yah, as a thoroughfare to the backdoor, Arabella thought, just as something on the counter ahead in the right-hand corner of the room caught her attention. *Oh, signs of life,* she declared silently and hastened towards the grey-speckled black marble surface that she'd spied. It was located to the left of the large window that looked out on the back garden from directly above the sink and on it were a kettle, a toaster, and a microwave. They were so neatly tucked away that one could quite easily have overlooked them.

Walking up to the counter with the utensils, Arabella stooped forward and ran her fingers across the top of the toaster. Not a crumb was brushed off. She jiggled it about a little and still no crumbs fell out. *It's never been used,* she decided.

She opened the door of the microwave. Inside was gleaming and new-looking and without a splash or whiff of food. *Also never been used.* So what was the point of having them, *unless* ...?

'Are these all new?' she asked, turning to face the baffled-looking Max, who was watching her every movement with increasing curiosity.

'Not since I've been here.'

'Which is how long?'

'About a year.'

Wow! 'And you use them?'

'Sure.'

Arabella knew that Max was a tidy person, but not to this extent. *Unreal!* Turning and closing the microwave door, she made her way back to the centre of the kitchen and began to twirl around with her arms fully outstretched at her sides. 'This house is bigger than it looks from the outside,' she announced and continued to spin around.

Max could stand by silently watching no more. 'What are you doing?' he asked her.

'Spinning around.'

'I can see that, but why?'

'I like to spin.'

'Okay.' He paused. 'And before?'

'Before when?'

'When you were shaking the toaster.'

'Oh then,' Arabella smiled. 'I was checking for crumbs.'

'Why?'

'It occurred to me to.' And with that she stopped spinning.

Shaking his head, Max laughed with bewilderment. 'You are one random lady, you know that,' he told her.

'Yep,' she nodded with a distracted air. 'Ah,' she gasped. Something else had caught her attention. 'I love these,' Arabella cried, pointing at the breakfast counter with the same marble top as the rest of the surfaces in the kitchen. 'My parents' house has got one. Well, my mother's house, now,' she clarified and raced across to the counter, over which one could see into the conventional-looking dining room. Hoisting herself up onto it, she tried twirling round on her bottom, but was stopped in mid-turn by Max, who caught her by the feet and pulled her gently towards the edge.

'And they never told you it was for food, plates and things like that, not butts?' he quipped, giving her a peck on the forehead.

'Ooh,' Arabella recoiled playfully. 'Is that a reprimand?'

'It will be if you don't stand up,' Max came back quickly at her.

'So I'd better, and quick sharpish too,' she riposted, and then pretending to have misunderstood what he'd meant, Arabella made as if to stand up on the counter. Before she could fully get on her knees, Max grabbed her.

'Don't even think about it,' he rebuked and whisked her off the counter without further ado.

'Oh, I like a strong man,' Arabella leered jokingly, groping at his biceps as he set her down on the floor.

'Stop that, it tickles.' Max squirmed and, quickly letting go of her, hurried to get out of her reach.

Arabella chased after him. 'Wuss!'

'Yes, now stop please,' he pleaded, gripping hold of her hands. 'I come from a long line of tickle-phobics,' he explained, jumping aside suddenly as she pretended to lurch forward. 'And there are more following me.'

'Of course, the twins,' Arabella recollected. She'd almost forgotten how Eleanor's sons would literally wet themselves at a single touch, the poor loves. 'Was T.J. ticklish too?' she wondered.

'No, not at all,' Max replied. 'On that front, he was completely Bianca –'

'Hard as old boots, then.'

'Stop that,' Max chided her with a frown.

Arabella flashed a glare at him. She didn't like him defending his ex so readily like that. And besides, she pouted. It wasn't as if the comment was unnecessarily bitchy or untrue. According to what Eleanor had said in the past, Bianca was a hard woman, so 'what's your story?' Arabella huffed.

'I'm famished and so must –'

'What?'

'Are you hungry?' Max was clearly trying to change the subject and Arabella realised this.

Fine, she conceded, but it didn't mean that the matter was closed. Bianca wasn't supposed to be featuring as often as she was in their conversations, and that needed to be addressed before it became an issue. 'I could eat something,' Arabella grudgingly admitted.

'Cool,' Max beamed as if he hadn't noticed her tone. 'I'll make us something.'

His smile did the trick and Arabella's anger subsided. 'May I please have a yoghurt or something first, though?' she chirped in a lightened tone.

'Sure,' he replied and headed to the fridge. Getting to it, Max opened its door. As he did so Arabella snuck up behind him, and then nudging him gently aside, she looked in.

'Double wow,' she exclaimed as she glimpsed its overall contents. 'Was this filled for my benefit or do you always have it like this?'

'It's usually like that,' he replied. 'I like a well-stocked fridge.'

Arabella cast him a suspicious glance. 'For you, or for you and whoever else?' she asked, resuming the interrogations that she'd begun in the car on their way from the airport.

Max shook his head. He knew where this was leading, but he was not going to be editing his answer. As far as he was concerned, if their relationship was to last, there could be no proverbial eggshells or touchy subjects, so the sooner Arabella realised that, the better it would be for them. 'For me predominantly, and then whoever else may stop by,' he replied.

Oh yah! 'Whoever else may stop by?'

He smiled with disappointment. 'Yup.'

'Like whom?'

'I don't know, whoever.' Max paused. He didn't want them fighting over silliness, especially today of all days, so he decided to give an answer which he believed would ease Arabella's mind. 'I work from home sometimes, so the company accountant for one,' he volunteered.

'And who else for two?'

Max sighed loudly with incredulity. 'Whoever, nobody specific.'

Turning, Arabella eyed him with even greater suspicion. 'I see.' From her tone it was evident that there was nothing Max could say to dissuade her from the route she was headed with her thoughts. But he tried anyway.

Please don't go there, he beseeched her with his eyes, but she was going to, even though neither of them wanted the row that it would probably lead to.

Arabella couldn't help herself, no matter how much she wanted to. Experience had taught her that there would always be that proverbial spanner in the works – in the form of whoever or whatever waiting at the ready to spoil things – whenever she got to a happy place. So she spent her life feeling constantly under siege from the fear of being let down.

Although these feelings lay subdued in her subconscious most of the time, once scratched up they took her over completely. It was almost like they forced out of her the questions that would elicit those answers that would sow deeper suspicions in her mind. And once that was done, all the hurt, betrayal, disappointments of every inch of her past came flooding back and filled her with a resentment that needed to be aired through bitchy little quips and questions, which got replies that made her feel vindicated for probing. It was one of the vicious circles of her life that she very much wanted to end.

So returning her attention to the contents of the fridge, Arabella fought against the resentment that was festering within her by changing the subject. 'Are these eggs washed?' she called behind her to Max in a lighter tone than she was feeling.

'Yes, I can't stand anything dirty in my fridge.'

She forced herself to smile. 'So I'm noticing, and everything's got to be in its correct section too, I see.'

'Yup … that's why the manufacturers make and clearly label them.'

Something in Max's tone irked her. 'Says who?' she heard herself challenge.

'Say I.'

Don't you always! Arabella gave him a look that betrayed her rising rancour. And then resuming her inspection of the fridge, she noticed that in the compartment marked cheese he had cheddar, smoked gouda and *hm* –

She paused, *here's more proof.* 'You don't like Emmental.'

'But you do.'

His response winded Arabella's resentment. 'Awe,' she cooed with an involuntary smile until she noticed the tier under the cheeses. There was orange juice, apple juice, mixed fruit juice, pineapple juice and 'guava juice?' Arabella's smile dropped. 'Who likes guava juice?'

Oh man! Max frowned. He'd thought they'd out-manoeuvred the emotional storm. 'Me, it's my favourite,' he almost snapped.

'Since when?'

'Since I can remember.'

Arabella's brows knitted suspiciously. *Bullshit.* 'I've never seen you drink a drop since I've known you.'

Max eyed her. He needed to get something straight. 'Am I under some kind of investigation?' he asked her.

Straightening up, she turned and faced him. 'Should you be?'

'I don't think so, but you seem to think that I should to be, so tell me: what are we trying to find out here?' he demanded sternly.

A look of uneasiness flashed across Arabella's face. Max's tone worried her. 'Oh, lighten up and stop being so paranoid,' she scoffed and turned back to the fridge. *Likes guava juice, indeed. Lying git.*

He knew what she'd be thinking. 'I really do,' he interjected to her surprise. 'But we've never been together in a country where they have it.'

'I know,' she lied, embarrassed at having been so accurately second-guessed.

But Max was on the offensive now. 'No, you don't,' he challenged her. Arabella cast him a questioning glance. 'You don't,' Max insisted, refusing to be cajoled out of his irritation.

Arabella recognised that tone. It was one, which usually came before a blazing row between them if she didn't stop needling him. She didn't feel much like that kind of argument today of all days, so a retreat was in order.

Quickly turning back to face the open fridge, Arabella resumed her search for some yoghurt. The transparent glass bottom drawer of the fridge caught her attention. The glass was so clean, so easily seen through, that there was no need for her to pull out the drawer in order to clearly identify its contents of eight or so plump tomatoes, a somewhat synthetic looking greener-than-normal lettuce, five much-too-orangey-to-be-real carrots, and three large onions that looked so white that Arabella assumed that they must have already been peeled.

'*Wow*', she marvelled again, but this time with concern. 'You're Obsessive compulsive.'

'And you're neurotic.' Max volley back and headed towards the sink.

What's that supposed to mean? Arabella wondered without looking up, but didn't ask. It was clear to her that Max was brewing for a row, which she wasn't prepared to give him on his terms. She continued her search. Seconds later she called out to him again. 'I still can't find the yoghurt.'

'There should be some there,' he replied.

'Where?'

'At the side, on the shelf after the juices.'

Arabella let her eyes wander up the inside of the door of the fridge. 'Juices and then two large cartons of skimmed milk.'

'Look behind the milk, there should be some tofu and then some small cartons of yoghurt.'

Bingo! 'Got it.'

Choosing peach yoghurt, Arabella shut the fridge door and moved back to the counter on which she'd been previously sitting. Soon after, Max, who'd been looking in a drawer under the counter on which were placed the microwave and toaster, approached her with a teaspoon in hand.

'There you go,' he said and handed it over to her.

As she was tearing the aluminium film from the top of the pot something occurred to Arabella. *Tofu.* 'When did you start eating tofu?' she enquired.

The question came out without her intending it to and Max knew that. 'I don't,' he smiled.

Arabella's eyes narrowed with suspicion. She was off again. 'So why've you got some in your fridge?' she probed.

'Tevin was here last weekend – he loves the stuff – don't ask me why.'

Arabella looked Max square in the eyes. *Yah, right!* 'How does he like it?' she smiled frostily.

He held her gaze. 'I don't know and I don't care to. He makes it himself.' Max's irritation was back up and the look in his eyes indicated so. 'What's all this about?' he demanded, even though he knew the answer.

Arabella's gaze dropped. 'What's what?' she asked defensively, beginning to blush and fidget. She hated having brought them right back to where she'd been avoiding.

'You're checking up on me.'

'What?' she cried indignantly with feigned innocence.

Max stood his ground. 'You are and I don't like it,' he told her.

'And I don't like you getting so defensive.'

Max looked incredulous of what he was hearing. 'Defensive, me?' he clarified.

'Yah.'

'You asked a question and I answered it and you call me defensive?'

'I – Look, why are we arguing?'

Catching her eye, Max held her gaze defiantly. 'I'm not arguing … are you?'

'I'm –' Arabella began and then stopped. She sighed deeply. 'I'm sorry. I think I'm just tired.'

So was he, he realised, and arguing wasn't going to benefit either of them. 'It's been a long day. For both of us,' he added with a thoughtful smile, and then pulling her to him, he hugged her tightly. As they embraced, he resumed speaking. 'I understand that with my track record trusting me isn't gonna be easy for you,' he said. 'But you've got to. Please,' he implored, leaning back so that he could see her face.

Arabella nodded.

'Please,' he stressed again. 'I really want us to work.'

Yay, she liked the sound of that. 'So do I.'

'And the only way we *can* work is with trust.'

Arabella's gaze dropped. 'I know, and I do trust you.'

Max wasn't so sure about that, but… 'Good, come on, I'll show you the rest of the place and then you can have a shower and something to eat and then we'll talk everything through, including the logistics of who's going where.'

And with that he took her by the hand and, steering her right after they'd passed the fridge, led her through the arch and into the dining room that she had previously glimpsed over the counter on which she had tried to twirl.

On entering the dining room, Max stopped, as if he had suddenly remembered something. Turning to face Arabella, he cupped her cheeks in his hands. 'And just in case the thought has crossed your mind at any time since we started up together again,' he began, 'I haven't, I'm not, and I don't intend to cheat on you.'

It was just what Arabella needed to hear. 'Thank you,' she said, beaming up at him. 'And same here.'

Too happy to eat anymore of the yoghurt, Arabella deposited the almost full carton and the teaspoon on the dining room table as they walked past it. As she looked up, her jaw dropped. 'Oh my God,' she shouted, startling Max as she did so.

'What?' he asked.

'The front garden.'

Max pulled a face. 'The front garden?'

'It's huge, it's a park.'

'It's not, it's a regular…' He broke off, and having noticed what she was pointing at, he began to smile. 'That's not the front garden,' he told her. 'That's the park. You can't see the garden from here.'

'Oh.'

'But it's pretty,' he added. 'It's got beautiful flowers and a strawberry patch and…' He caught a glimpse of the look on Arabella's face. It was obvious that she wasn't listening to him.

'My goodness,' she gasped. 'This place is going to be so awesome for entertaining.'

'Whoa!' Max flinched. 'I think we better talk through logistics before your shower,' he said. He knew that this conversation would most likely sour the mood – again – but from the looks of things, it was better had sooner rather than later, as he'd previously intended. Especially now that Arabella was already imagining the soirees and whatever else she could see herself organising there in Eleanor's house.

'Okay,' Arabella chirped and, disregarding the urgency in his tone, rushed off towards the rest of the house.

Dashing through the dining room and past the cream-carpeted staircase that led upstairs, Arabella stopped at the top of the three wooden steps that were beside a hip-level wall that marked the end of the dining room. She took a deep breath in, as if to inhale the sight in front of her.

Before Max could get to her, she'd hurried down the steps and into the sunken sitting room, past the red wall to her left, while dodging the purple sofa with three red cushions thrown against its stiff back rest.

In no time, she was standing in front of the four consecutive large floor-to-ceiling windows that took up nearly the entire front-facing wall of the lower ground floor. The sight before her was a beautifully framed view of a partially tree-lined park with a softball pitch in its middle and some woods to the right after a wire-fenced court that she assumed was for tennis. Arabella smiled broadly.

'Have you told Matt, Rod and Eric about this pitch?' she called out to Max who was now making his way down the three steps en route to her.

'Yup,' he replied. 'And even better still, we've played on it.'

Arabella giggled with content. 'I love this house,' she admitted as Max came up behind her.

'Me too,' he confessed. 'But –'

Arabella swung round to face him. 'What's upstairs like?' she asked.

'Nice. Would you like to see it?'

'Nah, not immediately,' she said, crinkling her nose. As far as she was concerned, seeing upstairs wouldn't convince her anymore than she already was that she was in love with the property.

Downstairs had sold it enough just as it was: mostly white-walled and spotless almost to the point of being sterile; spacious and open plan in layers that broke up the monotony of having too much room to roam; punctuated with a sprinkling of angular furnishings that, were it not for their rich depth of colours, could have justifiably been classed as Spartan. Yes, some would say that the house thus far could have done with some extra bits of furnishing and a warming woman's touch.

Which is just what I'll give it, Arabella mused, *but for now,* 'It's great.'

Max, who had been lovingly watching her, nodded his agreement. 'Yup, it's a great little place … but we can't stay.'

Arabella's eyes sprang wide open in wonder. 'What?'

'We're not going to be living here,' he announced.

Arabella looked deflated. 'Bianca wants it in the final settlement, doesn't she?' she asked.

'No.'

'Then why can't we live here?'

Max took a deep breath in. 'Because the house belongs to Eleanor and she lent it to me on a temporary basis only.'

'How come you never mentioned this?'

'It never occurred to me to,' Max fibbed. The truth of the matter was that he'd never mentioned it because he'd been hoping to have had time to move out before Arabella got there. That way she'd arrive at a place that was theirs instead of Eleanor's where she wouldn't be allowed to stay.

Arabella's shoulders slumped further.

'There'll be better places,' Max consoled her.

Arabella mustered a sad smile. 'Sure,' she replied. 'But tell me something.'

'What?'

'Us not being able to live here has nothing to do with a temporary lending of the property by Eleanor, has it?'

Max steeled himself. This was what he'd been trying to avoid. This was why he'd tried to put her off coming sooner.

'You can be honest with me,' Arabella pestered. 'You told Eleanor about us getting back together and she's angry and doesn't want me living in her house, does she?'

She wouldn't if she knew, but she doesn't know, so… 'No,' Max exclaimed a bit too suddenly and loudly, while taking her in his arms. 'It's nothing like that, pumpkin.'

'Max, please,' she beseeched him, drawing slightly away. 'No more lies, remember?'

'I'm not lying to you.'

'Max –'

'She doesn't even know we're back together again.' *There, now you know.*

'What?' Arabella cried. 'Bu –' Shaking her head with disappointment, she looked up into his eyes. 'I thought we agreed that there'd be no more secrets from each other or anyone else regarding our relationship.'

'We did and there are none.'

'Huh,' Arabella spluttered sadly. 'So what would you call not telling Eleanor about us, then?'

'Trying to do things in a proper and respectful manner.'

Arabella let out a hollow laugh. 'Crap,' she exclaimed.

'No, the truth.'

Visibly disappointed, Arabella broke free from his arms. 'Not so, Max,' she told him. 'You've had ages,' she reminded him. 'We've been back together for two months now.'

'I know, but I was waiting to tell her in person.'

'In person?' Arabella flashed him a glare. 'She lives in Tobago and you're in America for God's sake,' she snarled. 'So how were you proposing to tell her in person?'

'She's scheduled to be coming here in two weeks time.'

'In two weeks?' Arabella shouted.

Max nodded.

'How are we supposed to find a place to live in that time?'

'Exactly, and that's why I didn't want you coming over so soon.'

Arabella eyed him. 'Oh, so it's my fault now we're in this mess?'

'Frankly, yes.'

'What?'

'Yes, it is,' Max bristled.

Arabella held her breath for a second and then spoke. 'You could have told me about the *whole* situation,' she said more calmly than she was feeling. 'I would have understood.'

'No, you would so not have,' Max laughed impatiently.

'I would.'

'Oh, honey, please.'

'I would,' she insisted.

'Like you did regarding the sale of the company?'

'That's different,' Arabella pouted.

'How?'

'Because my being here doesn't interfere with your work, so saying I shouldn't come over because you're selling the company and will be very busy doesn't make sense.'

Max bit his bottom lip, as if to control himself.

'Well it doesn't,' she persisted. 'We're supposed to be together now, a team,' she stressed.

'Exactly, so let's work like a team, not adversaries trying to force each other's hands.' He eyed her with gentle reproach. 'You've gotta start trusting me and letting me take care of my business in my own constructive way. Look and learn now from this situation that forcing my hand only serves to muddy the waters.'

Arabella refused to agree. 'You could have stood your ground with me,' she protested.

'And start World War Three?'

She ignored the remark. 'So *you* look and learn from this that honesty is the best policy. If you'd only told me the truth about everything, I'd have been forced to wait.'

'Oh, now,' Max guffawed. 'And what a wait it would have been, full of accusations and suspicions! Phu,' he shuddered jokingly. 'Nope,' he disagreed. 'Letting you come was the best thing I could have done. This way, you see the mess it causes and why you should have trusted me to wait until I said the time was right.'

Arabella playfully squared up to him. 'I don't know what you're talking about. There's no mess.'

'No?'

'Nope.'

'Good, you keep posturing, lady,' he told her, feigning a sneer. 'Right up until you're all alone in your hotel room.'

'My hotel room, what hotel room?'

'The one you're gonna be sleeping in, as of tonight.'

'No way.'

'Yes way.'

Arabella scanned his eyes. He looked serious. 'That's not fair.'

'Oh?'

'Eleanor's not coming for another two weeks. I can stay here until then, surely?'

'Not without her permission, you can't.'

'But she doesn't have to know.'

'Yes, she does. Besides, she's been good to me by letting me stay here. I can't let her down by having you stay, when we both know that she wouldn't want that.'

'Bu –'

'Honesty all the way, remember?'

'This is so unfair.'

'That's life.'

Arabella gawped at him with disbelief. 'I might as well have stayed in London.'

'Really,' Max riposted mockingly. 'And leave me here, *alone,* with all those women that I could be falling in love with?'

'Oh bug off!'

Max tittered to himself and then, mimicking Arabella's voice and accent, added, 'Oh but it's going be such a hoot having you so close by.'

'I don't want to be close by. I want us in the same house, living together.'

'And we shall, m'lady, we shall. Once you find us a place. Talking of which, my secretary's booked you an appointment with a real estate guy for tomorrow morning.'

'But I've only just got here.'

'Honey,' Max cooed sarcastically. 'We're a team, remember? I'm gonna be working hard at finalising the sale of the company so that we can move somewhere exotic, to your liking, and seeing as how your early arrival will have me homeless in two weeks time and you're already homeless now, it's only fair that you work hard at finding us a place to live in the interim. Wouldn't you say?'

'Okay, but can't we move into the hotel together?'

'Nope, I've got too many papers and stuff here.'

Arabella began to pout again.

'And that means that I'll only be able to use our suite as a bedroom –'

'So you're coming too?'

'On the nights when I won't be working through the night, yes.'

'Yay,' Arabella squealed and hugged him tightly. 'That'll do me,' she thrilled. 'And I promise, from now on, to be cooperative –'

'Huh,' Max scoffed. If only he could believe that.

Chapter Nine

The warring Winthrops

At the end of a wonderful and welcome dinner of fresh sea bass and salad prepared by Max, a content Arabella picked up an almost empty champagne flute and, tilting her head back, drained the last droplets of lifeless fizz into her mouth.

Rising to his feet, Max took up his remaining half-full glass of water and walked to the side of the front deck where he leaned over and emptied the water into the strawberry patch below. Seeing this, Arabella also stood up and then, stretching across to the opposite side of the small garden table, she retrieved Max's white dinner plate. Bringing it just above hers she used his fork to drag particles of limp lettuce and a soggy cluster of tomato seeds from it and onto her plate. As she was finishing doing this, Max intercepted her.

'Why don't you call your mother and let her know you've arrived safely,' he suggested as he took both plates off her by their navy blue borders and placed them on top of the matching large oval platter with the bony remains of the sea bass that they'd eaten.

'Yah, maybe later when I've finished doing the washing up,' Arabella replied.

'That's okay,' Max smiled. 'I'll take care of that. You go call her.'

'No,' came the firm objection from Arabella. 'You cooked, so I should wash up.'

Seemingly taken aback by her tone, Max cast Arabella a puzzled glance that appeared to be asking *what was that all about?*

She smiled guiltily. 'I enjoy washing up.'

'Good for you,' he riposted, resuming his stacking of the dinner things. 'But there's a dishwasher here, so I'll load it while you make the call.'

'But –'

He looked up and held her gaze with a mixture of tender reproach and gentle appeal. 'You can cook and take care of the dishes another time, how about that?'

It was clear from his eyes that the discussion was over. The 'how about that' was merely punctuation. Acknowledging him with a resigned shake of the head, Arabella turned her attention to the chair from which she had recently risen.

'I don't see why I can't call her in the morning,' she complained, pulling a face as she unhinged and lowered the chair's wooden frame three notches, so that its one-piece green fabric back and bottom rest were flattened out like a hammock on trestle legs. With the seat now secured into that position, Arabella turned it to face the park. That way she had a great view of the breathtaking sky whose darker shade of rose pink mixed with its generous swirls of tangerine orange clung languidly to the contorting bubble clouds, which were now veiled in a haze of charcoal grey nightfall. Seemingly enraptured by the sight above, Arabella curled up on her seat in the foetal position and let her mind begin to wander until it rested on the thought of relationships.

Why are they always changing? she wondered.

Take for instance her and her mother. They used to be so close and enjoyed each other's company. *Like friends,* she recalled. It had been that way since after her father left them.

Flashbacks of how close she and her mother were filled Arabella's mind and her eyes began to brim with tears of longing for their past closeness.

Those days were sad times, she recalled. *Very sad times indeed.* But they got through them eventually, and together, she smiled dejectedly.

Arabella paused a moment. Who was she trying to kid? They never got over him leaving.

Not at all, she admitted. They merely learned to stem the tears and muddle through it all by getting on with life as best they could. They had to, or else there would have been no contact from her father.

He'd never actually said so, but Arabella recalled how he'd always become anxious whenever she cried on the phone to him. 'Scallywag,' he'd reproach her. 'Big girls don't cry,' and then he'd hurry to get off the line. Phone conversations with Daddy always lasted longer whenever she didn't cry and Arabella soon learnt this and soon stopped showing him her sadness.

She suspected that her mother couldn't play the game and that was why she and Daddy stopped talking altogether except for impassive 'hellos' whenever he called to speak to his daughter.

Arabella paused for deeper thought. Maybe her mother resented her duplicity. Maybe somewhere along the years she got fed up seeing it and that's why they drifted apart.

Does she feel betrayed? Arabella wondered. *That I let her down?* That would make sense. It would explain why her mother seemed unable to stop criticising everything that she did.

People have a tendency of snapping at everything and anything when there's something on their mind that they're not saying, she reasoned. Was this the case with her mother?

It must be, Arabella decided. *She despises me now for having been born, for being the cause of her losing Daddy while remaining the one in most contact with him.*

'She'll be worried if you don't call her,' Max's voice interrupted her thoughts with more talk about her mother.

I doubt it, the still dewy-eyed Arabella told herself, but remained silent as she began, once again, to reminisce about the way things used to be between her and her mother.

How great those days were when her mother cared enough about her to worry that she hadn't reported in with a call! How comforting it used to be to hear her mother's voice without the reproachful tone! How great –

But alas, Arabella sighed, steeling herself against an onslaught of fresh tears. It was time to face facts. Time had soured things between them and crying about it wouldn't alter a thing. Her mother was now all about 'I told you so' and criticising her every decision.

Urgh, Arabella grimaced at the thought. She was definitely not in the mood for any of that right now. Her reunion with Max was going better than she'd dared to imagine and she didn't want anything to spoil it by dampening her mood and making her over-sensitive.

'Arabella,' Max called out again as he walked over to where she was huddled up in the seat.

Blinking back the residue of tears until they were no more than a glint in her eyes, she rolled over onto her back and smiled weakly up at him.

'Did you hear me?' he asked her.

'Yes.'

'So come on.'

'No, I'll call her tomorrow.'

'Arabella.'

'I'm not in a phone mood right now.'

'Please,' Max urged her. 'You've got jet lag as an excuse to keep the conversation short and amicable.'

Amicable, Arabella thought, *wouldn't that be nice, but sadly …*

She noticed Max waiting, as if for a response from her. 'It's a bit late now,' she told him, squinting up at the large red leather-strapped Dolce and Gabbana watch he'd given her as her welcome gift. The time in Seattle was quarter past eleven at night, therefore quarter past seven in the morning in London. 'It's too early there.'

Max eyed her suspiciously. 'You know that's not true,' he coaxed with a smile. 'I remember you calling her at an earlier time than this on one of our travels, because you said she'd be up and fretting if you didn't.'

Arabella sat up with a huff. 'I'll call her in the morning, I promise.'

'Okay whatever.'

Oh God, she groaned, reluctantly rising to her feet. Why did he have to give her that look? It was her mother's 'I'm disappointed in you' look that always filled Arabella with the same guilt that was at present overcoming her. It was a guiltiness that she resented feeling, especially now, when she hadn't done anything to warrant it.

'She's fine with my not phoning on arrival these days,' she tried to explain, but Max, who was already making his way back into the house through the front door, didn't respond.

'Did you hear what I said,' Arabella called after him as she hurriedly stacked the empty champagne flutes into the tumblers. But he still didn't answer her.

Oh great, she grumbled. *Now he's got the hump.* Huffing and rolling her eyes with apparent exasperation, Arabella quickly grabbed the clattering glasses and hurried after him. Max was already in the kitchen by the time she caught up.

'She'll only spoil my mood,' she elaborated and placed the glasses down beside the plates on the counter by the sink.

Still saying nothing, Max took her by the hand and led her from the kitchen, back through the arch and into the dining room. Depositing her at the dining room side of the speckled marble-topped breakfast counter that she'd sat on when they'd first arrived, he unhitched the phone from its cradle on the wall and handed it to Arabella. '"Mom, I'm here safe and sound", that's all I'm asking you to call and say to her,' he said and headed back towards the front porch.

'Fine,' Arabella conceded quietly and took a deep breath as she dialled her mother's number.

'Double seven, double three, four, five, eight, six, Sophia Winthrop speaking,' a female voice at the other end of the line answered.

'Hello, Mother,' Arabella said at the sound of the familiar tone.

'Arabella,' the relieved, yet tired and guarded, voice responded. 'Where are you?'

Arabella rolled her eyes. 'Where do you think I am,' she replied.

Max was on his way back to the kitchen with the rest of the dirty crockery. Without stopping, he glanced across at Arabella and chided her with a scowl. 'Play nice, now,' he whispered.

'Well, I don't know, darling,' her mother's voice riposted at the same time as Max's reprimand. 'It takes eleven hours to fly from London to Seattle and you've been gone for almost twenty-four hours. So you tell me.'

'For God's sake, Mother,' Arabella snapped. 'The airlines don't run a door-to-door service, you know. It takes time to get through things like immigration and customs and then rush hour traffic back to the house.'

'Well, I'm glad you've arrived safely,' Sophia interjected with apparent sincerity.

Arabella felt bad for her prior tetchiness. 'Thanks,' she mumbled and then fell quiet.

Her mother didn't respond.

After a few seconds of awkward silence, Arabella spoke again. 'It's a bit early there, so I better let you get some more sleep.'

'No, I'm fine,' Sophia said quickly, as if to initiate further conversation. 'I haven't slept yet, but I will once I've heard all about your journey.'

Awe, Arabella smiled, glad at the thought that her mother wanted to chat further and that she had stayed awake while waiting to hear from her. But what were they going to talk about? The journey to Seattle was uneventful, so what else was there to report? No good idea sprang to mind, except 'the weather's great here'.

'That's good.'

Now what?

'But I do hope you packed some jackets and things, in case it gets chilly at night.'

'Yah.'

'Good.'

And then they both fell silent again. After a few moments they chorused.

'I –'

'I –'

'After you,' Sophia conceded.

'No, after you.'

'It was really nothing important,' her mother explained.

'Same here.'

They fell silent again.

Arabella looked saddened. *Surely we can do better than the weather?* she asked herself, but all that came to mind were contentious issues. *Best not,* she decided after each possible topic sprang to mind. In the end she settled for 'I only called to let you know that I got here okay.'

Oh God, she cringed at the utterance. It sounded awful, not at all how she'd intended it. *Damn! Damn! Damn!*

'Right … um' Sophia began to stutter 'Oh, yes … um, well, great. Urgh, may I have your number there … just for … in case of an emergency,' she added quickly.

Arabella bowed her head sadly. *She's hurt, but she's trying to hide it. She's using the same tactics that I use on Daddy.*

Anger began to seep in. *I'm nothing like him,* Arabella seethed. So why was her mother, who wouldn't pretend for her father, pretending for her sake? They'd have to discuss this.

But not tonight, she decided. It would have to keep for a more appropriate time, like all other contentious issues, which kept piling up not discussed and not resolved. *Ugh,* Arabella fumed as she decided to let go of her anger for the time being.

Fighting back her resentment, Arabella set her mind to redeeming the conversation, at least to a point where they could end the call amicably for a change. She mimicked Max's tactic of forcing a smile to lighten his tone. 'I'm moving to a hotel later on tonight so I'll give you the number when I get there, okay?'

'Fallen out already?'

Oh, here we go, Arabella frowned, but still forced another smile. 'No, Mother, we haven't.'

'So why are you moving to a hotel ... so soon?'

'This is Eleanor's place –'

'I see, and of course you're not welcome to stay, are you?'

Ooh, Arabella bristled silently with fury. *I must not retaliate, I will not retaliate.* 'No,' she lied. 'Max and I want to rent a flat downtown before we buy a place, so I just thought it would be easier for me to do the viewing if I'm staying downtown.'

'See, there you go again, trying to run before you can walk.'

What the – 'What's that supposed to mean?' Arabella barked.

'You've only just arrived there today,' her mother hit back. 'And you're already talking of buying a place together.'

'No, I'm not. I said we want to rent before we buy.'

'It's not what you said, Arabella, it's the way you said it.'

'Sorry?'

'Like it's a foregone conclusion, like it's all going to be plain sailing.'

'Maybe it will be.'

'Oh, darling,' her mother sighed with apparent exasperation. 'A lot can happen in a few months, so I wouldn't start counting my proverbial chickens just yet, if I were you –'

'Well, you're not me, are you,' her daughter snapped.

Max looked round from the sink and grimaced sympathetically. 'Calm down,' he advised.

Arabella shook her head defiantly in response. 'She started –'

'Shh,' he frowned.

'That's right, shush,' Sophia's voice cut in. 'Your temperament is getting as robust and disagreeable as your father's used to be whenever he was feeling up against it.'

'What?' Arabella yelped. *Used to be?* her eyes flashed with rage. *What planet is this woman living on? He's still as cantankerous as ever and, more importantly,* 'I'm nothing like him.'

'Damn right, you're not,' her mother hit back. 'He's smart, thoughtful, and sensitive.'

Arabella looked like she could scarcely believe what she was hearing. *Of course he is and that's why he dumped us.* 'Oh get real, Mother!'

'I wish you would, because then maybe you'll realise that we're on the same side.'

'Same side, huh,' Arabella sneered. 'You could have fooled me.'

'See what I mean?'

'No, I don't.'

Sophia sighed deeply. 'This is not getting us anywhere.'

'At last, she's realised it.'

'Why do you have to be so disagreeable?'

'Why do you have to be so mean?'

'Mean!' Sophia cried angrily. 'I'm trying to protect you, you silly girl.'

'From what or whom?'

'From getting hurt again.'

'I won't.'

'I pray not, but history is not in your favour,' Sophia began impatiently. 'Most married men who have affairs tend to go back to their wives in the end –'

'Except the ones like Daddy. They stay well away, don't they? I wonder why?'

'Your father didn't leave me for anyone else.'

'Sorry, I forgot, it was all my fault wasn't it?'

'What are you talking about?' It wasn't the first time Sophia had heard her daughter say this and she didn't understand it. Was Arabella having a sarcastic dig at her for messing up and causing Oliver to leave them or did she genuinely believe that her father had left because of her? Pondering on it briefly, Sophia decided on the former. Arabella knew how much her father adored her and so there was no way she could ever possibly believe that she was the reason why he'd walked out.

No, Sophia thought. Judging from her daughter's apparent disdain for her, it was most definitely intended as a dig at her. Sophia seemed to falter momentarily at her conclusion, but soldiered on. 'Was that necessary, darling?' her pained voice resumed.

'Yah.'

'Enjoy! Anyway, back to what we were talking about, it may do you good to remember,' her mother retorted, 'that since your father left, he hasn't stayed long with any other woman. Will Max be the same?'

'Ah, déjà vu. I wondered how long it would take you to get back to that. You can't bear to see me happy, can you, Mother?'

'Arabella,' Sophia rebuked her.

'It's true though, isn't it?'

'Of course not.'

'So why do you always say the things that you know will hurt me the most?'

'Don't be ridiculous,I don't!'

'So why can't you ever wish me well, then?'

'Arabella, I do, always,' Sophia cried softly.

'By criticising everything I do or say?'

'No, only when I see you heading for a disaster.'

'Which is all the time?'

'Oh, darling,' her mother's tone softened even more until it was almost a whisper. 'I'd be the first person to cheer you on a path if I could see good things ahead on your chosen horizon,' her mother told her, but Arabella wouldn't hear it. She was angry now and someone had to pay the price.

'What, like the abundance there is on yours?' she hissed.

Sophia could see no point in them continuing the conversation. It was evident that it was heading to more hurtful words and mindless tongue-lashings, which would inevitably lead to an increased distance between her and her daughter. It wasn't where she wanted to be, so it was best to bail out. 'Fine,' she conceded. 'I've had enough, so I'll bid you a good night and good lu –'

'Mummy, please don't go,' Arabella relented. 'I'm sorry.'

'I'm not the enemy,' her mother replied, almost as a plea.

'Then, I beg you, act like you're not.'

'I –' Sophia began, but was interrupted by her daughter.

'You are my mother, Mummy,' Arabella told her. 'You're meant to love me no matter what.'

'And I do.'

'But it doesn't feel like it anymore,' Arabella explained as tears began rolling down her cheeks in quick succession.

'I do love you, darling.'

'Then show it, like you used to,' her daughter implored. Just then, Arabella felt Max's soothing touch on her shoulder. She looked up at him with despair. Covering the mouthpiece with her hand, she spoke.

'I told you this would happen,' she sobbed. 'It always does, these days.'

'Ssh,' he whispered, cradling her by the shoulders. 'It's okay, babe, it's okay.'

'I'm sorry,' her mother's sad tone intercepted.

Arabella could tell that she too was now crying. *Oh no*, she sighed. That was the last thing she'd intended. Quickly drawing gently away from Max's hug, she moved her hand from covering the mouthpiece. 'Mummy, please don't cry,' she whispered.

'I'm not,' her mother fibbed, but her daughter knew otherwise.

'Good,' Arabella said, pretending to believe her. 'Cos I really didn't mean a word I said,' she too lied. 'I don't know what got into me. I think I'm tired –'

'I do love you no matter what,' her mother's teary voice interrupted.

'I know.'

'And I'm sorry that I've been making you feel that I don't.'

'You haven't.'

'I was just trying to protect you…'

'Yah.'

'…to stop you from getting your heart broken again and, oh Arabella,' she cried out in clear anguish. 'I don't want to lose you, like I nearly did the last time he hurt you. Remember, darling?'

Arabella didn't want to remember. This time was going to be different and that's all that she wanted to focus on. 'Things were different then,' she replied, purposely vague. Arabella had never told Max or anyone else about her attempted suicide and she didn't want him to know now.

'So you say, but what if –'

'Mummy, please,' Arabella interrupted her. 'We'll all be okay.'

Sniffing, Sophia paused, just as Arabella, also sniffing, wiped away the last of her tears with the back of her hand. Sophia resumed speaking. 'I pray so. And that you'll like me again.'

'Oh, I do like you,' Arabella spluttered with laughter. 'But just not when you're picking on me and finding fault with everything I do.'

'I wasn't finding faul –'

'I meant to say, when you're being protective –'

'In a manner that doesn't suit you,' her mother laughed in between more sniffs.

'No,' Arabella refuted kindly with a smile. 'Let's say when you're being protective in a manner that needs my getting better used to it.'

'So what you're effectively saying,' Sophia outlined cheerily, 'is that you don't like me often.'

'On the contrary,' Arabella corrected her, equally light-heartedly. 'As we talk less than we used to, it means that I like you more often than I don't.'

'So we're better off not speaking?'

'About certain things, yes,' Arabella interposed and then fell silent. Max, who was still gently massaging the base of her neck with one hand, tapped her.

'Okay now?' he asked quietly.

'Yah,' she whispered and so he left her to her conversation. With Max's soothing rub of her shoulders no more, Arabella took a deep breath, as if for courage, and fell pensive. Seconds later, she began to speak to her mother again. 'I know I make many mistakes in my life and you hate that –'

'I don't hate anything about you, darling,' Sophia cut in. 'I simply get frustrated when I see you heading down a path that I know will end in tears.'

'I understand that,' her daughter admitted. 'But you've got to respect the fact that you won't always be right and when you are, these are mistakes I need to make in order to learn, just like you have.'

'No, you don't need to make them to learn, darling,' Sophia disagreed. 'You're Daddy's girl; you're much too clever for that.'

'If only.'

Misunderstanding her daughter's 'if only', Sophia scoffed. 'Hm, you're probably even cleverer than he is.'

Bless you, Arabella smiled. 'But can we agree on no more pointing out.'

Sophia didn't respond.

'OK,' Arabella tried again. 'How about we say that you can warn me once per potential mistake?'

Her mother burst out laughing. 'Will you listen?'

'Probably not,' Arabella chuckled.

'Then how about two warnings.'

'Two,' Arabella cried, pretending to be horrified and then fell momentarily silent, as if reviewing the proposition. 'Without sounding like you're sniping?'

'No can do,' Sophia teased. 'That's the only enjoyable part of it all,' she joked on. She pretended to sigh. 'I'll tell you what,' she added. 'How about two warnings and one 'I told you so' when you ignore the warnings and things go belly up?'

'Nice try,' Arabella laughed. 'But no, definitely no "I told you so".'

'Oh, now that won't be easy,' her mother protested with a laugh.

'But you'll try?'

'Only because I love you.'

'I know,' Arabella replied warmly as her voice lightened to a childlike tone. 'And I love you too, Mummy.'

'Thanks,' Sophia whispered. 'I better let you go now.'

'Okay,' Arabella said. 'I'll speak to you tomorrow?'

'Yes please, darling. Call and give me the number and then I'll call you straight back. I know hotel phone charges can be pretty high.'

'Alrighty!'

'Oh, and do send my regards to Max,' Sophia added unexpectedly to Arabella's delight and hung up.

Arabella looked the happiest she had been in the last twenty-four hours. With the phone still in her hand and her lips curved into a broad contented smile, she glanced across the counter at Max, who, having returned to the kitchen, was now standing opposite and waving an unopened bottle of champagne to attract her attention.

How appropriate. 'Definitely, yes please,' she beamed. 'And while you're doing that, may I please call my father?'

As Max poured them fresh glasses of champagne, before mixing orange juice into his, Arabella dialled her father in Spain.

'*Digame,*' a young woman's voice echoed on the receiver being picked up.

It was Arabella's father's thirty-year-old and fourth mistress since he'd left her and Sophia.

'Hi, Constance,' Arabella said breezily.

'Arabella,' the woman's teary tone greeted her, but the bad line coupled with Arabella being too happy from the successful conclusion to her conversation with her mother meant that she didn't notice.

'I'm here,' she thrilled.

'Where?'

'In Seattle.'

'Seattle?' Constance cried with surprise. 'What are you doing there?'

'Didn't Daddy tell you I've moved here?'

'No!' she shouted. 'You know that he never tells me anything important. And besides, he wouldn't now, not with me having been given my marching orders.'

Having moved away from the receiver to take a sip of her drink, Arabella missed the second part of what Constance had said. 'He never tells anyone anything,' she tried to sympathise on her return, but Constance saw it differently. To her, Arabella didn't comment on the news of the break-up because she didn't want to get involved. So Constance changed the subject.

'How long have you been there?' she interjected quickly.

'I arrived today.'

'How do you like it so far?'

'I love it,' Arabella enthused.

'Awe,' Constance cooed. 'I'm really glad for you. Maybe I should come over there to find myself a man.'

Arabella stared down thoughtfully at the phone cord that she was winding around her little finger. 'Oh dear, is Daddy being an old fart again?' she asked.

Constance giggled evasively. 'That's one way of putting it, I suppose. Still I should have seen it coming, with him disappearing as often as he'd begun to.'

'Disappearing,' Arabella grimaced. *Not very promising at all.* That was her father's trademark sign that he would soon be bailing out of the relationship. If her memory served her rightly, shortly before her parents' separation her father had begun to stay away from home quite often. He'd also done the same to his three previous girlfriends. 'When did he start doing that to you?' she asked Constance.

'Doing what?'

'His disappearing act.'

'About six months ago.'

Oh dear! But who knows, this time. 'It's probably just a storm in ye ole proverbial teacup.'

'If you say so,' Constance hedged and terminated the conversation with a skilful 'I'll go and get your father for you.'

Catching Max's eyes as he headed to the fridge to store the remainder of the champagne, Arabella pulled a worried face. 'I think my Dad and Constance are having problems,' she whispered over the telephone mouthpiece she was covering with her left hand.

'She'll hear you, so tell me later,' Max frowned, gesturing towards the handset.

Complying with a nod, Arabella removed her hand from covering the phone and awaited her father's arrival.

'I swear he's deaf,' she heard Constance complain before resuming her loud shouting of 'Oliver, telephone.'

After a few moments, Arabella heard her father's voice in the distance.

'What is it?' he growled impatiently at Constance.

'Arabella's on the line.'

'Can I call her back?'

'She's in America,' Constance explained.

'So?' Oliver snapped. 'Don't they allow incoming calls there?'

After a muffled exchange of words that Arabella couldn't make out, her father came to the phone.

'Hello, scallywag,' he boomed joyfully.

'Daddy,' she cried with delight. 'I thought for a moment you weren't going to come to the phone.'

'Well, I nearly didn't,' he admitted.

'Oh,' Arabella retorted with disappointment.

Once again she and her father had begun on a misunderstanding. What he had meant by that was that Constance was packing up her stuff from near where the phone was and he didn't want to be in the same room as her, even for a second. But Arabella had understood him to mean that he simply hadn't wanted to come to the phone to speak to her.

'Scallywag, please,' her father rebuked her. 'You're not going to throw another of your tantrums, are you?'

Why does he always say that? Arabella bit hard on her bottom lip. 'No,' she replied in as bullish a voice as she could muster in her disheartened state. 'I can call back if you're still sleeping, or something else?'

But her father didn't respond, he was deliberating his next move. Her mother had mentioned her concern about Arabella's trip to America, so should he broach the subject now or was Arabella in too precarious a temperament? 'Oh,' Oliver groaned aloud.

Arabella heard him and it dampened her spirit further: she thought he was grumbling at the prospect of her calling again. 'Are you too busy to talk, Daddy?' she asked nervously.

Her tone came across to him as abrasive. *Oh no, she's in one of her moods again,* Oliver surmised and decided to end the conversation before Arabella flew off the handle, as she was prone to do whenever they spoke. 'I was rather,' he hurriedly replied.

'Working on the boat?'

'No, I've finished all that,' he explained and then fell silent. After an awkward few moments, he carried on speaking. 'I was in the middle of a game of chess with Tom Baintree.'

At eight o'clock in the morning with 'Tom Baintree?' Arabella wondered aloud. 'Is he that chap who was at Eton with you?'

'Which one?'

'The one I met last time I came sailing with you?'

'Yes, that's the one,' her father boomed enthusiastically. He remembered that summer with much happiness. It was like old times that he wished had never ended: him and his beloved daughter braving the elements and having a sterling time doing it. They'd laughed so much and gotten on so well that Tom had found it hard to reconcile the Arabella from that summer and the irascible rebel-without-a-cause who'd had Oliver beside himself with worry about her. 'They're coming sailing again with me this summer.'

'With just you?'

Oliver smiled wistfully. *I would have loved you there too, but you've rushed off to America.* 'And your mother too, I hope.'

What? 'My mummy?'

'Yes, hopefully it'll cheer her up and take her mind off things.'

'And Constance?' *What will it do to her mind?*

'What about her?' her father barked, irritated at the thought that Constance may have discussed their relationship with his daughter and she was now taking sides.

His sudden change of temperament upset Arabella. Although she would console herself that he didn't mean it in a bad way, what she saw as her father's constant testiness often disconcerted her and further confirmed in her mind that she was unwanted by him. 'Well, well, I'd better let you get back to your game of chess, then,' Arabella offered nervously.

'Yes, I'd better get back now,' Oliver agreed without hesitation. It was upsetting enough having the fragile relationship that he did with his daughter, but for it to get worse because of Constance, he couldn't handle it. He'd rather he and Arabella didn't speak for now. But then pausing for a moment, Oliver seemed to have a change of heart. 'So you're in America at last, I hear?'

'Yes,' Arabella replied expectantly.

'How's Max?'

Wow, he remembered his name! 'Great, we're both great,' she smiled excitedly. 'Would you like to speak to him?'

'What?' Oliver grizzled with discomfort at the thought.

'Would you like to speak to Max?' his daughter repeated.

'Heavens no, what would I say to the chap?' her father rudely declined at the same time as Arabella noticed Max frantically waving his disapproval of her suggestion. 'I'm in the middle of a chess game, remember,' Oliver added, almost as an afterthought.

'Well, um,' his daughter stuttered in confusion.

'How's the money situation?' Oliver cut in, in a parental manner, as if he were checking on her school grades. It was his tried and tested trump card that always got him out of awkward situations with his daughter.

Typical! 'I don't need any,' Arabella snapped in an angry huff. Her father had done it again and it hurt. Why did he only ever offer her money? Why did he seem to see it as his only fatherly responsibility towards her? Why couldn't he show as much interest in other aspects of her life like he had done for that split second when he asked about Max?

Fine, Arabella thought sadly, it was clear that he hadn't wanted for her to be born. But she was and it was time he started to accept the fact he had a daughter, one that loves him and would quite like for him to take some interest in her life. Or at least pretend to. *Lie to me, please,* she pined.

'Sure?' Oliver's voice cut in, to his daughter's further irritation.

'Money's not everything,' she growled.

'What was that?'

Oh, what's the bloody point? 'Grandma left me lots, remember?'

'Yes, of course she did,' he replied distractedly. 'So everything's okay, then?'

'Yes, everything financial.'

'So...' *What can I say next that won't upset you?*

'So what?'

'Is there anything in particular you called for us to talk about?'

'No, just to let you know I arrived safely.'

'Oh, jolly good,' came the relieved-sounding reply, as Oliver delighted in the thought that, for the first time, Arabella had actually wanted to check in with him on arrival somewhere. It felt great having her including him in her life this way. Oliver couldn't wait to share the grand development with Tom and Marjorie. 'I'll call you later on in the week,' he suggested.

'That would be fantastic.'

Oliver was beside himself with happiness. 'Right oh,' he boomed, and forgetting that she was now at a new number, he hung up.

Arabella was devastated. To her, her father had been in such a hurry to end their conversation and cared so little about her that he didn't even want to take a number on which he could reach her from time to time to check on her wellbeing. How sad was that!

Visibly upset, Arabella slowly replaced the handset and hurried out of the house.

Chapter Ten

Too old to play

A few minutes after she'd left the house, Max set off to the park in search of Arabella. As he couldn't see her sitting in the softball arena, he embarked on a walk around the periphery. Two corners later, he found her sitting on the ground by a small shrub beside the forest green gauze fence.

As he approached, Arabella spotted him and discreetly began to wipe away all evidence that she had been crying. Max saw what she was doing, so he slowed down and pretended not to notice.

After what he deemed to be enough time for her to adequately compose herself, he arrived beside her. 'Hey, babe,' he said breezily, and bending forward, kissed her on the forehead.

'Hello, you,' Arabella replied with a forced smile.

Walking round to her back, Max levelled the ground between her and the fence with his feet. Then pushing the sleeves of his sweater up to his elbows in uneven rumples before hitching his trousers slightly up from the knees, he spread his legs astride of her back and slowly eased himself down. Once seated behind her, Max wrapped his lean but manly arms around Arabella's waist and pulled her to him in a tight hug.

'Mm,' she purred, writhing into a comfortable position in his front. 'I needed that.'

As they sat silently watching the sporadic trickle of traffic to the sound of the sparring teens behind them, who were trying to outdo each other at shooting basketball, Max absentmindedly twiddled a lock of Arabella's hair round his fingers.

'Promise me something,' she suddenly piped up.

'What?'

'Promise me that we'll make better parents than mine.'

Max's body tensed up. *Parents?* This was the one thing he hadn't considered when he was coming to his decision about being with Arabella. He needed to think things through before getting into this sort of discussion.

'What's wrong with your Mom and Dad?' he asked in an attempt to keep the topic of the conversation neutral and away from their potential children, whom Arabella had apparently factored into their future.

'Wait until you meet them. You won't be asking that,' she replied.

'What's so bad about them?' Max persisted distractedly as his mind began to dabble with the 'kids' issue. Although he felt strongly for her and quite happily entertained the idea of spending forever with her, Max knew that there was no guarantee that things would work out between them. There was always the chance that Arabella could meet someone nearer her age and decide that she was better suited to him. Or maybe the cultural differences would drive them apart. Anything could happen.

But what if none of these happened and everything works out just fine, then what? Max asked himself. The issue of children would surely come up again. What did he want?

Max knew that he had to seriously think about it and come to his decision sooner rather than later and without pressure from Arabella.

'Max ... Max,' Arabella's voice seeped into his thoughts.

Not more baby talk, please. 'Yes, bab –pumpkin,' he replied too late.

Arabella looked put out. 'Nothing,' she said and fell silent. Seconds later, she glanced back over her right shoulder at him. 'You do want us to have kids, don't you?' she asked.

Oh hell! Max swallowed hard. How was he going to answer this question without causing offence? Arabella was young and without kids of her own, so it was only natural that she should be keen to have some.

But he, on the other hand, he couldn't say what he did or didn't want. With three children, whom he'd always assumed were his lot, he had to confess. 'The thought never crossed my mind.'

Arabella looked away with disappointment.

'But it's definitely something we need to think and talk about, sooner rather than later,' he added hastily.

Arabella's body tensed up and she frowned. 'But we can't not have kids,' she pouted.

She was half right. There was no way he would ever ask or expect her to sacrifice having children.

'I'm not saying that ... but... ' Max paused. 'It's kinda late in my life to be starting another family, don't you think?'

'No.'

'Come on, Arabella,' he coaxed. 'I'm sixty-four years old.'

'So what?'

'So it wouldn't be responsible of me to have anymore kids at this stage in my life.'

'Why not?'

'Arabella, because the average life expectancy for a man these days is early seventies. I'm almost there.'

'But you don't look it.'

'That's not the point,' he told her with a patient smile before reluctantly admitting, 'I'm beginning to feel my age these days. And that's the point. Even if we had a kid within the next twelve months, by the time he's seven, I'll be seventy-one going on seventy-two years old and maybe dead.'

Pulling a face Arabella shuddered. 'Don't talk like that,' she scolded him.

'I have to, babe. It's a strong possibility.'

'I don't want to talk about this anymore,' she declared and busied herself with watching the traffic.

But Max couldn't stop thinking about it now that his mind had been alerted to this. Not only was he feeling selfish for not having considered the fact that, due to her age, it was only natural that Arabella would want children of her own, but also he was having to face up to his mortality and the implications of their age difference. *I could be dead in a few years, damn!*

Would it be fair of him to ignore this fact and carry on regardless with their relationship? Or would it better for him to kill two proverbial birds with one stone by setting her free from becoming a young widow and free to meet someone younger with whom she could have as many children as her beautiful heart desired?

Max didn't like the latter thought, but he knew it was one he'd have to throw into the equation for further consideration.

Sighing heavily at the prospect, he began to rub the back of his neck. There was no more time for mistakes in his life, and in contrast to his past, it was high time he began to *fly right,* he told himself.

But what was that going to mean with regards to the dilemma in question?

Chapter Eleven

Soiled memories

A week after Arabella's move to America to be with Max, Eleanor and her two young sons boarded a taxi outside the Four Seasons Hotel in downtown Seattle. Although this was a journey she hated having to make, it was one she felt she had to. The news she'd heard when she was down on the East Coast with Bianca had angered her greatly and made her relationship with Max seem untenable.

Eleanor was still fuming even now, as she sat beside her sons in the taxi. As far as she was concerned, it was all Arabella's fault. Just as she had threatened, in Tobago the last time Eleanor saw her, Arabella had finally wormed her way back into Max's affection and life and was now shacked up with him in *her* house.

Bitch, Eleanor cursed silently as the taxi turned left and headed downhill towards the entrance to the southbound freeway. She was still finding it hard reconciling herself with this cold-hearted Arabella, who had not only destroyed all possibility of her ever having sweet memories of T.J., but had stolen her father-in-law off her mother-in-law and was now playing lady of the manor in her house. *Over my dead body,* Eleanor seethed.

Memories of Arabella's sweet face came to mind, but they didn't correlate with the person she'd become. *What happened?* Eleanor wondered for the umpteenth time in the past two years. If anyone had ever told her that she would one day be feeling about Arabella as she was now, she would have said 'never'.

Never say never, the cliché echoed in her mind. How true.

Thoughts of Arabella came back to mind – the old Arabella from the Singapore days – sweet, fun-loving, gullible and someone who definitely wouldn't intentionally hurt anybody or anything. The old Arabella needed protecting, Eleanor smiled.

Yes, it was occasionally hard work having to look out for and protect Arabella, Eleanor recalled, but it came with the territory and was what their friendship dictated they did for each other.

The three musketeers, she smiled. That was what T.J. nicknamed her, Arabella and Arielle. And what fun they had, no matter the situation. Others looking at their lives in those days may have categorized their experiences into good times and sad times, but to them they were simply the crazy, fun-filled never-giving-up times. Laughing or crying, they rolled with life's punches and lived on in hope because they were too thick-skinned to ever learn a lesson.

Eleanor remembered the night they met at a mutual friend's party. From then on, she, Arabella and Arielle became inseparable and had remained so even though Arabella and Arielle failed to understand her dysfunctional relationship with Cort. While she and Arabella rolled their eyes with frustration at each wasted potential romance that Arielle let slip by because she was too busy being once-bitten-twice-shy. And she and Arielle had disapproved of Arabella's seeming penchant for married men.

Ironically, Eleanor recalled, it was as a result of one of Arabella's affairs with a married man that she and T.J. met. It had been two years and two months since the conference company for which Eleanor had been working in London had posted her out to Singapore.

As she had done every Saturday night for the past year-and-a-half, Eleanor had arranged to meet Arabella and Arielle at Cascade's, the nightclub at the Falcon Hotel on Scott's Road. It was their regular Saturday night hangout because the great R & B music played there by visiting bands and the resident DJ guaranteed them a good boogie session.

With her skin glowing healthily from the humidity of the heat of the night, Eleanor shook her two hundred or so waist-length plaits into place and then hurried out of the blue 'Comfort' cab and onto the broad red carpet that led from the taxi rank all the way up to the tastefully lit hotel foyer, which was sparsely but opulently decorated with dark wood and marble. Halfway up towards the stairs that led to the entrance of the hotel, she veered right onto a thinner strip of carpet, and continued further along the pavement to where a long line of people stood waiting.

With her platinum hotel loyalty card in hand, and to the disapproving yet cowardly murmurs of 'there's a queue you know' of first-time comers who assumed that everyone was required to wait in line like them, Eleanor walked up the final runway of the carpet that was shielded overhead by a green canopy. At the red ropes with big golden clasps that were fastened onto the tops of the thin yet solid handrails that flanked the weather-beaten black metal steps leading down to the basement, she stopped and handed her card to Rajid, the bouncer.

'Good evening, Ms. Eleanor,' he smiled and began leafing through the sheets of paper on his bright blue plastic clipboard in his hand.

'Hi, sweetie,' Eleanor replied as her eyes followed his pen down the left-hand side of the page. 'There I am,' she chirped, helping the pen back up to the line on which was typed '*Nwachi Eleanor, Membership Number G77038105W*'.

'Any guests with you tonight?' Rajid asked without looking up from the page where he was now logging her arrival with a red line across her name and membership number.

With the entrance formalities concluding, Eleanor wasn't listening to him anymore. Her focus had shifted to the long queue behind her, which she was surveying for familiar faces of friends or friends of friends whom she could take in free as her guests. Standing five feet ten inches tall in her flat metallic gold toe-posted slippers that she was wearing, it was easy to see over the heads of the mainly shorter-than-average people in the queue.

Rajid looked up from his clipboard. 'Ms. Eleanor?'

'Mhm,' she responded distractedly and glanced down at the broad 'G' face of her watch. 'Ooh,' she winced. She was two hours later than she'd said she would be.

'Is everything okay?'

'What?' Eleanor frowned up at him.

'Is every –'

'Oh yeah, sorry,' she cut in with a strained smile. 'I'm later than I thought, that's all.'

'The night is still young, ma'am. You have another two and –'

Eleanor's eyes glazed over with disinterest. 'D'you know if –'

Someone roughly jostled her from behind and knocked her off balance.

Before she could react, a morose voice slurred dankly into the side of her neck. 'Do me a favour, will you?' it demanded in a thick Australian accent.

Taken by surprise, Eleanor swung round to confront her assailant but was disarmed by his hot, brandy-charged breath, which engulfed her face and hijacked all her air passages. Stifled and discreetly gasping for clean air, she recoiled.

'Watch it,' she snarled at the man who was having difficulty standing still.

'Pretend we're together,' the drunken man in a blue and white Hawaiian shirt continued indiscreetly as his jaw collided with Rajid's robust shoulder, which had been skilfully manoeuvred into position to shield Eleanor from a second blitz.

'Ouch! Fucking hell, mate.'

'Please stand back, sir,' Rajid ordered unapologetically.

'But I'm with –'

'Please stand back, sir.'

'That's not fair,' the drunken man whined. 'How come she gets to jump the queue?'

'I'm a member,' Eleanor interjected. 'And if you were with me, you'd know that, wouldn't you?'

'I would, wouldn't I,' the man agreed with a chuckle as he eyed her up with lustful approval. 'You're quite a looker, aren't you?' he leered. 'How about you get me in and we go downstairs and get better acquainted.'

Eleanor's reaction was instinctive. '*Get off,*' she barked, wriggling away from the clutch of his sweaty palm, which was groping for her waist.

Rajid fixed the man with an ominous stare.

'Come on, mate, you can't blame a man for trying,' the man smirked at an unimpressed-looking Rajid. 'Bet you wouldn't mind a go if you were allowed.'

Rajid fixed him with an even more disdainful glare.

'Oh it's like that, is it?' the man challenged.

Rajid stood menacingly silent.

'I can knock you out, you know,' the man threatened as he boldly advanced on Rajid.

The queue behind the man immediately retreated and fanned out into a large semi-circle of anxious but mesmerised eyes along the pavement as the people at the back of the queue shunted sideways and craned their necks to see what was going to happen next, while those who were originally at the front fell back in line with them at what they deemed to be a safe distance from the anticipated showdown.

'*Sir –*' Rajid warned.

'Don't fucking sir me, you condescending piece of shit.'

'Please step back, sir,' Rajid reiterated.

'Why don't you fucking make me,' the man snarled and hurled himself into Rajid's taut chest.

In a flash, Rajid had overcome the drunk, pinned him against the railings in an arm lock and was rasping into a walkie-talkie snatched from his hip, at some point between deflecting the man with his chest and the arm lock.

The stunned onlookers gasped then came back to their senses with a crescendo of cheers and applause that quickly died down at the rumble of heavy footsteps that were thundering up the sturdy iron stairs and heralding the approach of two more bouncers in black suits and shirts.

As Eleanor watched on agog, one of the bouncers quickly squeezed past her at the rope while the other gently pulled her towards him.

'I need you to go downstairs immediately, Ms. Eleanor,' he instructed her with an easy smile.

Without a thought, she nodded hurriedly and clonked her way down towards the dimly lit foyer below.

Safely downstairs inside the entrance door of the foyer, Eleanor exhaled with relief as she made a sharp left towards the music.

'Causing trouble again?' a male voice greeted her from the cloakroom window on her right.

Startled and still en route towards the claret-coloured heavy velvet curtains that separated the foyer and the club, Eleanor turned towards the voice. It was Guido, the manager.

'Hello, you,' she smiled feebly.

Guido's smile contorted into a grimace. 'Watch out,' he squirmed.

But he was too late: still walking fast, Eleanor had rushed straight into a figure that was slowly emerging from behind the velvet curtains.

'Whoa, easy!' a muffled American male voice scolded on impact.

Eleanor panicked and began flapping herself deeper into heavy folds of velvet, which immediately engulfed and disorientated her. After what seemed to her like an eternity of being smothered and feeling for the other side, she gracelessly tumbled out of the curtains and into the arms of her somewhat confused and highly irritated victim who was recovering on the club side of the curtains.

'Oh great, now take my eye out, why don'tcha?' the stranger snapped.

'Yeah, like you'd be any worse off without them,' Eleanor retorted.

'Pardon me?' the stranger challenged.

'There wouldn't be any need to if you used your eyes and stopped knocking people over.'

'What?'

'Oh stop whingeing,' Eleanor hissed and impatiently pushed free from his arms. She gave herself a quick once over and straightened up. Turning, she faced the man. 'You should –' she began and stopped as soon as their eyes met. Freezing in mid-speech, she swallowed hard. 'I, oh…' she bleated incoherently.

The stranger seemed equally flustered. 'I'm sorry … I –'

'No, I'm sorry –' Eleanor interrupted.

'No I'm sorry … I didn't mean to be rude.'

'You weren't. I … uh … I should've been looking where I was going … I…' Eleanor babbled on. 'Forgive me,' she finally declared, then hurrying past a doorway on her right that led into the club, she escaped through a second one that was directly in front of the velvet curtains. This one led into a side lounge: the cigar lounge that was partitioned off and secluded from the main body of the club by a large wooden wall at the side.

Once in the safety of the lounge, the flustered Eleanor stopped to catch her breath and compose herself.

Bloody hell, she thought. *Talk about gorgeous!*

She was referring to the man with whom she had collided. As she did so, she discreetly turned for a second look at him, but he was gone.

Typical, she frowned. *The good-looking ones always leave early.*

Resigned to the prospect of yet another night out at Cascade's with few, if any, good-looking men about to provide visual distraction for her and her two best friends, Eleanor cast a glance around to confirm her thoughts. As her gaze swept across the five slumped bodies at the small teak wood bar on her right, a middle-aged Western man with mocking, bloodshot eyes and a sneer for a smile caught her attention. Eleanor took an instant dislike to him and tried to outstare him with a glare.

'What're you looking at?' she muttered quietly. But he defied her with a broader sneer.

Losing her courage, Eleanor quickly looked away and headed to the middle part of the room that snaked between low coffee tables, which were corralled by comfortable-looking brown leather armless chairs. There she started to search for Arabella and Arielle.

A few steps later, as she made her way along, something blue to her left moved and attracted her attention. Turning, Eleanor spied a baby blue-coloured pashmina that was draped over the back of a chair. The tassels at the hem were blowing to the rhythm of the cold air that was wafting down from the air conditioner overhead. Eleanor stopped.

That looks like Arabella's pashmina, she thought, except that hers had a couple of singed tassels. Pausing, Eleanor strained to identify them. *It's hard to tell from here,* she decided and headed in for a closer look.

Moving nearer, Eleanor stretched forward to examine the tassels of the shawl. As she did so, a blonde in indigo jeans and a smart double-cuffed white shirt with a navy blue and gold Warner Bros logo cufflinks approached and snatched up the scarf. Eleanor flushed with embarrassment. *I hope she doesn't think I'm trying to nick it.*

Turning to the woman she began to explain. 'I'm trying to find where my friends are sitting and your pashmina looked similar to one of theirs.'

'Great,' came the reply accompanied by a vacant smile.

Eleanor smiled back, unsure. *Is she pissed or just patronising me? Whatever,* she shrugged and continued with her explanation that would exonerate her from all suspicion. 'Hers has a couple of singed tassels on one of the corners from a drunken night out,' she jabbered on. 'And I was trying to see if –'

Lurching forward suddenly like she was about to fall, the blonde distracted Eleanor from what she was saying. Eleanor started as if to catch her, but there was no need. Reaching out instinctively, the woman had already caught hold of the back of a chair and was now steadying herself. Still smiling and tittering mischievously to herself, like one with a secret that she was relishing not telling, the lady with the pashmina directed her wandering and unfocused glance at Eleanor. 'Sorry it wasn't hers,' she slurred. 'I hope you find her, though.' And with that she swished the shawl carelessly about her shoulders and staggered to a nearby floppy-haired and bookish-looking man who wrapped an arm around her waist and steered her in the direction from which Eleanor had come.

Making her way back to the walkway at the centre of the lounge, Eleanor resumed her search for Arabella and Arielle. The next table she came to, although unoccupied, had three half-empty flutes and an opened bottle of Tattinger that was chilling in a silvery-metal ice bucket.

It could be them, if they're with someone, she mused, but walked on anyway to inspect the remaining tables because she knew that the only reason both her friends would vacate the table at the same time would be to go to the dance floor in the main body of the club, which was the direction she was heading.

With this in mind, the rest of her search was perfunctory. Soon, Eleanor was standing at the end of the room, in front of a glass cabinet entombed in a stone bar where cigars from around the world lay showcased and waiting to be purchased. She could now hear the upbeat music drifting in through the entrance on her right and it lightened her mood.

Mm, Eleanor purred. She was really feeling up for a good workout on the dance floor. So, without further ado, she sashayed towards the music and in no time was across the threshold and on the club side where the music – and the voices that were competing to be heard over it – was loudest. Eleanor stopped. Now all she had to do was spot her girls.

Having taken the few steps that she needed to get closer to the overspill from the dance area, Eleanor stood silhouetted by the soft stream of light from the cigar lounge while trying to identify her friends from among the dense cluster of animated dancers and revellers in front of her.

To get a better view, she weaved and bobbed around on the spot, but it was futile. There were far too many people and too much activity for her to discern one face from another under such dim lighting. Frustrated, she lazily rubbed her eyes and tried to formulate a game plan in between being distracted by the music.

As she stood swaying on the spot to the rhythm of the beat and contemplating her next move, Eleanor became aware of someone, in the shadows to her left, watching her. Pretending to be still rubbing her eyes, she sneaked a glance. It was a tall, very fair-skinned black guy with shaved head. The little she could make out, his face seemed familiar but she couldn't be sure. Hoping he was known to her, Eleanor turned and leaning closer towards him, squinted to get a better look.

'Hey,' the stranger smiled. He'd caught her peering at him.

She smiled back. 'Hello.' *I do know him, but from where?* It suddenly dawned on her. S*hit,* she cursed under her breath and quickly looked away. It was the guy with whom she'd collided at the curtains. *How embarrassing, he'll think I'm following him,* and with that she scurried off in the opposite direction towards the bar in the middle of the club.

Once there, Eleanor stopped. 'What am I doing?' she asked herself and considered going back. But first she sneaked a glance back to see if the American was watching her. He was and with a bemused smile, like he too was wondering why she'd reacted in the way she had.

Oh great, she sighed. *You might as well go home now, Ms Loserville, he thinks you're a nutter,* she told herself and with that continued on her way. She wished she could bury herself six foot underground. Mindlessly tunnelling through the stagnant crowd that was tightly packed in the space that snaked in-between the teak wood wall that ran the length of the cigar lounge and the large oval-shaped cobbled-stone bar in the centre of the main body of the club, Eleanor soon found herself on the other side of the doorway she had earlier rushed past after her collision with the good-looking American.

Stopping to catch her breath, she pondered what to do next. Was it worth looking around the rest of the club for her friends or should she call it a night and go home before she made a further fool of herself in front of the Yank or anybody else?

What to do? What to do? she wondered as she began to look around.

Someone caught her eye. *Bingo,* she smiled with relief. It was Arielle, alone at a high table a few feet away to the left. At last, a much needed silver lining at the end of a very long and difficult day.

Dressed in a vivid turquoise Chinese silk strapless top and a tight pair of black hipster trousers, Arielle looked striking and mysterious as she sat alone, elegantly perched on a high stool, while clearly savouring the mellow taste of a Monte Cristo No 2 cigar. Her jet-black hair was pulled tightly back into a dramatic ponytail and her bottle green eyes were bordered with smudges of black kohl that gave a smoky-eyed rock chick look that Eleanor had never seen on her friend before.

'Ooh er, Mrs,' she crowed approvingly as she approached the lone lady.

Arielle was not so approving. 'You're late again,' she growled without looking at Eleanor who was now pulling up a high stool beside her. 'I know, darling, and I'm really sorry. Where's Ara –'

'That's just not good enough, Eleanor. You're always bloody late.'

Easy, tiger. 'No, I'm not.'

'Yes you are.'

' I'm n –'

'Oh, for God's sake, Eleanor, just drop it, will you.'

Eleanor eyed her friend. 'What's eating you?' she almost snapped.

'Nothing's eating me,' Arielle snarled. 'I've simply had enough of you and Arabella.'

Ah ha, Arabella, Eleanor smiled. They'd obviously had a falling out and that was why Arielle was in such a foul mood.

'Has she stormed off, then?'

'Who?' Arielle frowned.

'Arabella.'

'No such luck,' came the scathing reply.

'So where –' Eleanor began and then stopped abruptly. 'Shit,' she cried, ducking down. 'Hide me.'

'What?'

'Hide me,' she insisted as she kept a watchful eye on whomever it was she was trying to avoid.

Looking confused, Arielle anxiously surveyed the vicinity. 'What's going on?' she demanded.

'Nothing. I'll tell you later.'

'No,' she frowned. 'Tell me now.'

'Ssh, he'll hear you.'

'He, who's he?'

'No one.'

'Why are you hiding, then?'

'Oh, for God's sake, *shush*,' Eleanor ordered in a loud whisper as, turning slightly, she furtively tracked the person, who from the movement of her gaze, was at that moment apparently walking from behind

Arielle's right shoulder to the side of the bar that was nearest to their table.

'But no one can hear us like this,' Arielle explained, keeping her head perfectly still while rotating her eyes in the direction that Eleanor was focusing.

'*Stop looking*,' Eleanor scolded.

'Oh, com –'

'Quick, he's not looking now. Gently slide off your seat and head towards the dance floor,' Eleanor commanded as she cautiously slid off her stool and began edging towards her friend.

Arielle hesitated.

'Come on, Arielle, quickly...' Eleanor urged her. '...before he spots us.'

'Is he someone I know?'

'No, now get a move on.'

'Well, how's he going to spot me?' Arielle sighed. 'It doesn't matter if he sees me, so you go on ahead and I'll catch up with you in a minute.'

Eleanor frowned.

'Go on, quickly,' Arielle insisted as she made way for her friend's hasty escape.

Safely past her, Eleanor hesitated for a second.

'*Go on*,' Arielle almost shouted and hung back to see if she could pick up clues as to whom Eleanor was trying to avoid.

A couple of minutes or so later and from the safety of the edge of the designated dance floor, Eleanor had a better view of the jam-packed club. As usual, there was a selection of Indonesian, Thai and Chinese ladies, some of whom were prostitutes easily identified by their promise of 'me love you long time,' which they lasciviously drooled to lonely or drunk Western men.

Unable to spot Arabella and with Arielle having finally joined her, Eleanor swayed her way into a small clearing onto the dance floor.

As Usher's 'You make me wanna...' began booming from the powerful loudspeakers, which were overhead to her right and on the floor to the left, Eleanor closed her eyes and began to strut her funky stuff.

Unlike as usual, when she would dance for three or four tracks without opening her eyes, Eleanor opened them halfway through the song and turned towards the crowd to scan again for Arabella.

A shady-looking man with short, greasy brown hair at the corner of the dance floor was blocking her view of the nearest side of the bar to her. She leant slightly to the right to see past him. There was no sign of Arabella. Eleanor scanned to the left of the bar. As she did so, she caught the gaze of the man at the corner of the dance floor. His lips parted into a sleazy smile and his eyes beckoned her provocatively.

'Oh do me a favour,' Eleanor groaned dismissively with disgust and averted her eyes.

Turning towards the loudspeaker to her left, she spied the American.

When did he get there? Eleanor wondered, freezing to the spot. Realising that he was dancing with his eyes closed, she relaxed and watched him with a smile. He looked more handsome than she'd realised.

Arielle nudged her. 'Why are you looking so pleased with yourself all of a sudden?' she asked.

Eleanor nodded towards the handsome stranger.

'Well, hello,' her friend leered as her eyes widened appreciatively and she began to make more of an effort with her dancing.

Noticing this, Eleanor feigned a glare. 'Back off,' she playfully warned Arielle.

'D'you know him?'

'Nope.'

'Then may the best woman win,' came the challenge.

Eleanor flashed her friend an uncomfortable glance. 'Keep your voice down,' she scolded.

'What?'

'Shush, he'll hear you.'

Arielle's eyes narrowed suspiciously. 'He's the one from whom you were hiding before, isn't he?' she asked.

'Yes.'

'Ooh, the plot thickens! And he's the reason why you were late?'

'What?'

'Come on, 'fess up. You were getting in there before you came to join us.'

'Arielle!'

'No wonder you arrived in such a good mood.'

Eleanor looked on, amazed. 'What an imagination you've got, girl!'

'And what a player you're turning out to be. Good on you, beat the sods at their own game. But wait …' Arielle cut herself off. 'Why are you now hiding from him?' she wondered.

'Because I made a right royal tit of myself, that's why.'

Arielle tried unsuccessfully to stifle a giggle. 'Why, what did you do?' she tittered.

Eleanor looked mortified. 'Oh, where do I start?' And then she began to recount the tale. 'First I knocked him flying at the entrance, then before he could get over that, I almost blinded him as I floundered my way out of the fabric, and last, but certainly no less humiliating, when I saw him moments later and he said hi, yours truly scampered.'

'What?' her friend half-shouted. 'Why?'

'Because I'm an idiot, that's why.'

Casting a quick glance in the man's direction, Arielle spoke. 'Well, it seems that he's into idiots,' she noted with another discreet look at the man. 'He's watching you.'

'Ooh,' Eleanor whimpered nervously with glee. 'What shall I do now?'

'Go and ask him to dance.'

'I can't do that.'

'Why not?'

'Because ...'

'Oh, for Heaven's sake,' Arielle groaned. She'd never been able to understand how someone so seemingly fearless as Eleanor in everything else was such a 'scaredy cat' when it came to approaching men she liked. Had Eleanor not fancied the American and had just liked the way he danced; she'd have had no qualms approaching him for a dance herself.

Arielle decided to take the initiative. Unbeknownst to Eleanor, she was aware that the relationship with Cort was back on. Arielle couldn't stand him: 'the tosser' as she often referred to him. Anyone would be better for her best pal Elle than him. She cast another glance at the handsome stranger, who was still looking in their direction as he continued to dance at the edge of the dance floor. Arielle couldn't imagine him treating Elle badly the way Cort did. This was her chance to try to oust Cort. 'Then I'll go,' she decided and made as if to go.

Eleanor looked horrified. 'Where to?' she demanded.

'To ask him to dance with us.'

'What?'

'If he's with us, then you can talk to him and show him that you're not such a tit after all.'

Eleanor looked fit to faint at the mere suggestion. 'Don't you dare,' she shouted just as the tempo of the music dropped and Usher's voice began to fade to make way for the next track. To her apparent horror, everyone nearby having heard her was now watching her and Arielle, including the American. She gave him a sheepish smile. He smiled back.

'See, he likes you,' Arielle coaxed.

'Keep your voice down.'

At that moment, the crescendo of a female harmony of 'Doo wop' peaked. Both women seemed to recognise what was coming next.

'Now we're talking,' Arielle beamed and, dropping the conversation, began to gyrate her way towards the centre of the strobe-lit dance floor. Eleanor followed her as Lauryn Hill's words 'That thing, that thing, that thiiiiinnnnggggg' resounded around the club, awakening, as it did so, what seemed to be the entire female clientele.

Soon the dance floor was jam-packed with an army of women and a brave handful of their partners, who had shuffled onto the dance floor from all nooks and crannies. The sorority of dancing and singing women seemed to boost Eleanor's confidence and soon she was gyrating for all she was worth. She was a far better dancer than many on the floor, so it was her time to shine and shine she did.

With her newfound confidence, she danced Arielle nearer the loudspeaker where the American was still dancing. He was still watching and kept watching.

'I told you he likes you,' Arielle reiterated.

Eleanor smiled. 'Here's hoping,' she said, but refused to make eye contact with him.

Minutes later there was a diminuendo of Lauryn Hill's voice. The track was almost at an end and the sisterhood was beginning its retreat. Eleanor's courage too began to ebb.

'I need the loo,' she told her friend and motioned for them to join the mass exodus off the dance floor. Arielle complied, and as they were leaving, Eleanor turned for a final glance at the American. Their eyes met. He smiled broadly.

'Hey,' he mouthed.

'Hey,' she replied and headed back into the anonymity of the rest of the club with its crowded space and mellow lighting via the powder room with a hope in her heart that he would make contact when she reappeared.

After a quick assessment of Eleanor's chances with the American, the women emerged from 'the ladies.' He was nowhere in sight. 'Ah, there's Arabella,' Eleanor noted as she and Arielle turned the corner from the corridor and were making their way back towards their table in the seating area.

They had a clear view of a light brown-haired petite lady in a short-sleeved black cocktail dress as she was gracefully hoisting herself onto one of the high wooden stools around their table.

Arielle didn't react.

'She looks like she's lost weight, doesn't she?' Eleanor continued enthusiastically.

'Huh, in her dreams.'

'Easy, tiger!' Eleanor rebuked her friend and then, halting, turned to face her. 'What was –' she began, but Arielle breezed past before she could say more. Following her quickly, Eleanor caught her by the arm. 'Is there something you want to tell me?' she asked

'Yeah, black is slimming and scooped necklines work wonders for short-necked people.'

'Ha –' Eleanor began to laugh and then stopped. She'd remembered that teamed with her tight black pair of three-quarter length trousers was a black scooped-neck close-fitting top. She frowned at Arielle who was now en route to their seats. 'I hope you're not directing that at me,' she said.

Arielle turned slightly. 'I was talking about Arabella,' she explained and then with a mischievous smile added, 'But if the shoe fits, wear it.'

'Cow.'

'But an honest one, no less,' Arielle winked as she stopped beside a nearby table to allow a wackily-dressed Japanese girl with crazy red hair to get by.

As they stood waiting, Eleanor took the opportunity to loop arms with Arielle. 'So,' she demanded. 'What happened?'

'Where and to whom?'

'To you before I got here.'

'Nothing out of the ordinary.'

'So why the comments about Arabella and what she's wearing?'

'You commented too.'

'Not meanly.'

'But we were saying the same thing,' Arielle smiled bitchily. 'She picks the right clothes for her shortcomings.'

'Don't we all?'

'Yes, but shame she's not as good when it comes to picking men.'

'Who is?' Eleanor remarked, guiltily. She knew deep down that Cort was bad for her, yet she kept taking him back. How could she then take the moral high ground with Arabella over Arabella's penchant for the wrong men?

'True,' Arielle conceded, 'but at least some of us are once bitten, twice shy. Well, one of us is, anyway,' she added in a loaded tone before dragging Eleanor back into motion.

As they continued on their way, Eleanor wondered about Arielle's last comments. Was she implying that Arabella was embarking on yet another unsuitable relationship with a married man or was she inferring that she knew about Eleanor's reconciliation with Cort? Which was it?

Eleanor pondered the matter further. Seeing as how Arabella had recently been dumped and was still heartbroken, it was unlikely that Arielle was talking about her. So…

On cue, a blond and tanned man slid onto the stool beside Arabella and tenderly kissed her on the side of her feathery-effect cropped hair. Eleanor stopped dead in her tracks.

'I say,' she exclaimed, pulling Arielle to a halt beside her. 'Who is that?' she ogled.

'Another tosser.'

'You know him?'

'You don't need to know his sort to know what he is.'

Oh no, Eleanor frowned. 'He's not another married man, is he?'

'Yup.'

'Does she know?'

'More appropriately, does she care?'

'Of course she does, nobody likes to get hurt.'

'Then why does she always ignore the signs?' Arielle asked, rubbing her wedding ring finger with her left thumb for Eleanor to see.

Instinctively Eleanor's attention focused on the man's hands. 'But he's not wearing a ring.'

'Not at the moment he's not.'

'You saw him taking it off?'

'Nope.'

Eleanor looked confused. 'So how do you know, then?'

'Take a closer look,' her irritated friend ordered.

As they were now standing in front of the table where Arabella and her new friend sat oblivious to their arrival, Eleanor strained for a better look, but she could see nothing that condemned the man.

'Look more carefully,' she was told by Arielle.

Just then the mystery man, while tracing his left hand up and down one side of Arabella's pale face, slowly tilted her chin upwards with his right hand. She closed her eyes and puckered her cherry red lips expectantly.

As they kissed, Arielle nudged Eleanor. 'Quick, take a closer look now,' she ordered.

Eleanor shimmied slightly forward and scrutinised the man's left hand. Nothing struck her as unusual. She shrugged and pulled a face at Arielle.

'He's recently taken a ring off his wedding finger,' came the testy response.

'No, he hasn't.'

Arielle scowled.

'Has he?' Eleanor took another look and this time focused all her attention on the second to last finger on the well-tanned hand that was still stroking Arabella's cheek. There, for anyone who cared to strain to see, was the pale white strip of skin that confirmed the man's marital status. Eleanor winced. *Not again.* And then a thought occurred to her.

'Maybe he's recently divorced.'

'Do you know how long it takes for a divorce to go through?' Arielle snapped. 'He wouldn't still have the ring mark.'

'He may, if he was still in love with his wife and had kept wearing his ring; Lady Di did.'

'Oh behave.'

'Or maybe he was recently widowed.'

'Eleanor!'

'Well, we don't know, do we?'

'Yes, we do,' Arielle barked and alerted the lovebirds to their presence.

As Arabella and her new friend turned in tandem, a smile of recognition spread across her face.

'Elle darling, you're here at last,' Arabella purred in a manner which betrayed she was feeling happy, mushy and and loved up.

Oh, not again, Eleanor thought. It was good to see her friend happy after the previous weeks of sadness, but –

'When did you get here?' Arabella interrupted her thoughts.

'About twenty minutes ago, wasn't it, Arielle?' Eleanor smiled uneasily, as in an effort to not be caught looking at the man's wedding finger; she quickly turned to look at their mutual friend.

'That long ago?' Arabella pressed on carelessly.

'Yah.'

'So where've you –'

'We went to look for you on the dance floor, didn't we, Arielle?'

'No, we didn't.'

'I did.'

'Well, I didn't. I was glad of the peace without –'

'Let me introduce you…' Arabella interposed quickly. 'Morgan, this is Eleanor, my friend I was telling you about…'

'Pleased to meetcha,' he lilted in an American accent.

Ooh, it's a Yank fest tonight!

'And Eleanor, this is Morgan,' Arabella resumed. 'We met last night.'

'Last night, wow! That'll teach me for working late and not having come out to play,' Eleanor gushed with a fake smile as she pulled up a stool beside Arielle who was already seated next to Arabella and was looking all set to wreak havoc on the rest of the evening.

As they spent the following few minutes seated in strained silence, Eleanor wrestled with her conscience for the right thing to do.

Is it my place to let her know that he's married? she wondered. Outspoken as she usually was, this was the kind of situation in which Eleanor preferred not get involved, what with the idea of 'people in glass houses' and all that. How could she preach when her romantic house, so to speak, could hardly be deemed in order? And even if she could…

Surely Arabella must have seen the evidence of the missing wedding ring on his finger, Eleanor reasoned to herself.

Maybe not, her conscience pricked her. *You didn't without a good look and besides, it's not certain that he's still married.*

And that was reason enough to saying nothing until at least she had a better grasp of the situation. Happy to let herself off the hook of having to be the disapproving friend, Eleanor looked around the table with a broad smile. No one reciprocated. She looked back at Arabella and Morgan. They looked ill at ease and awkward.

What happened?

Arabella noticed Eleanor watching her. They uncomfortably exchanged reassuring smiles. Morgan began smiling too, Eleanor noticed without looking directly at him. She looked at Arielle. She wasn't smiling.

To be expected.

'So, Eleanor,' Morgan began suddenly. 'How's your evening, so far?'

'I was working for most of it,' she replied. 'But it hasn't been bad since I finished.'

'Working? On a Saturday?'

'I'm not supposed to, but hey,' she shrugged. 'When the going gets tough –'

'But on a Saturday night?'

'Why not?' Arielle cut in aggressively. 'She's a conscientious person and rightly so too.'

'Absolutely,' Morgan winced jokingly. 'Hey, there's T.J.,' he added almost immediately. The others glanced towards where he was now looking, but there was a crowd. 'He's a buddy of mine from Hong Kong and I haven't seen him in a while,' they were told. 'He's been touring the region on business.' And with that Morgan turned to Arabella. 'I'm gonna go say hi to him, d'you mind?'

'No,' Eleanor enthused before Arabella could respond. 'Sorry,' she smiled. 'You weren't asking me, were you?'

'I was asking all of you,' he winked.

'Ah, isn't he lovely,' Arabella cooed, to which Arielle replied.

'Bet his wife – Ouch, Eleanor!'

'Sorry,' Eleanor riposted innocently. 'I didn't realise your hand was there.'

'You –'

'Be nice, it was an accident.'

'On that note,' Morgan interjected and stood up. Kissing Arabella on the lips, he turned to the others with a smile. 'See you guys shortly,' he told them. And with that, he left to make his way through the crowd in the direction of the dance floor.

'You did that on purpose,' Arielle challenged Eleanor almost immediately.

'I had no choice,' came the whispered reply.

'He –'

Eleanor frowned. 'Come on, Arielle, let's not do this here or now, please.'

'Yah, Arielle, let's not,' Arabella joined in. 'You've stated your concern and I'm grateful for it, but please –'

'You've told her?' Eleanor asked incredulously.

'Yes, as any good friend should and would,' Arielle hissed.

Eleanor flinched secretly with guilt.

'But will she take any notice?' Arielle ranted on.

'I have, actually,' Arabella retorted. 'I asked him about it and, as I thought, there is a reasonable explanation –'

'There you go,' Eleanor piped up. 'There is a reasonable explanation.'

'Which is?'

'He and his wife recently separated.'

'That old chestnut,' Arielle sneered. 'And you believed him?'

'Why shouldn't I?'

'No reason. And I suppose he also told you that his wife doesn't understand him and that's why they've separated,' Arielle added sarcastically.

'All men aren't your ex, you know, Arielle,' Arabella sniped.

'Ladies,' a male voice loudly interrupted.

The three friends looked up with a start.

'You're back so soon,' Arabella cried guiltily.

'I said I wouldn't be long,' Morgan reminded them as he cast a questioning glance around the table.

'And you weren't,' Eleanor piped up with fake cheer. 'Good on you.' As she spoke, she caught sight of the person standing beside Morgan.

On cue the introductions began. 'Ladies,' Morgan announced. 'This is T.J., my friend from Hong Kong.' He was the American with whom Eleanor had earlier collided.

Immediately Arielle surveyed his fingers. There was no wedding ring, nor a trace of him ever having worn one. She smiled and playfully nudged Eleanor. 'Now we'll get to see up close how much he likes you.'

Eleanor sighed wistfully at her recollections of how she and T.J. had met. She'd never imagined that night that they would have ended up getting married a few years later. Let alone that their wedding would be the catalyst that would lead to this present fiasco in which she now found herself. She sighed again. And who would have thought that night that T.J. would be dead by now, leaving her to deal with all this nonsense by herself?

Oh, Eleanor groaned silently, bowing her head into her hands. *T.J. must be turning in his grave.* Suddenly another thought occurred to her, *and who would have believed that he was in a relationship the way he behaved with me that night?*

The thought upset Eleanor. *Once a cheat, always a cheat,* she hissed silently, which meant that he was probably copping off with other women when he went away on business after they were married. Eleanor's eyes welled up with tears at the possibility. She imagined what a laughing stock she must have been to him and his friends who would have been fully aware of his philandering.

She remembered the fact that Morgan was married and playing away with Arabella at the time. Arabella had been one of many, apparently from what she'd later learnt and told Eleanor. *Birds of a feather flock together* came to Eleanor's mind. Lifting her chin upward, she blinked most of her tears into the tops of the sockets of her eyes. What a fool she had been.

And what a bitch Arabella is. She'd known all along, but she'd never said. Why did she then have to when T.J. was dead and there could be no having it out with him? *But more importantly,* Eleanor wondered, even more angrily, *why did she have to tell me on that day of all days? It was his bloody funeral, for God's sake,* she sobbed silently. *Couldn't she have waited? Couldn't she have given me a chance to grieve first?*

A familiar thought crossed Eleanor's mind. Arabella must really have hated her to have told her about Belinda the way she did and on the day she did. *Well, the feeling's mutual now.*

'Are you okay, Mummy?' Malachi's little voice broke into Eleanor's thoughts.

Quickly and discreetly wiping away the dribbles of tears from her cheeks, she turned to face her concerned sons by her. Although at first glance they looked different, on closer inspection they looked very similar. Still looking at her sons, Eleanor marvelled at being a mother.

'Mummy,' Malachi pressed, beginning to look anxious.

Eleanor came to. 'Sorry, darling,' she said, forcing a smile. 'I'm fine, honestly.'

'Sure?' Paris interjected.

'Sure.'

The two little boys exchanged glances.

Eleanor couldn't help but to smile. They seemed like six-years-old going on fifty. 'I'm just a little tired,' she assured them.

'Maybe you should have a little sleep when we get to the house,' Paris advised his mother.

'No, I'll rest when we get back to the hotel.'

Although Eleanor's answer seemed to placate both boys, Malachi, who hadn't taken his eyes off his mother, became pensive. After a few seconds he leaned further forward, and stretching over his brother's darker-tanned legs, he tapped his mother gently on her left arm. As she looked round he asked, 'Why are we staying in a hotel when we have a house here?'

'Because Grandpa is staying there, remember?'

'But we have three bedrooms there,' he reminded his mother. 'Paris and I can share a room, you get one, and Grandpa gets the other.'

'True, but Grandpa needs some space right now,' his mother explained.

'Is it because of Aunty Arabella?'

Freezing at her son's words, Eleanor regarded him and his brother. As she looked from one child to the other, it dawned on her just how quickly they'd grown and were maturing, right under her nose.

And I haven't even noticed, she thought sadly.

Neither boy was a baby anymore, so she'd have to be more careful with what was said around them. Her eyes began to brim again with tears. Eleanor quickly looked away.

If only T.J. could see them now, he'd be so proud of them. Eleanor smiled. *So very proud indeed!*

Turning and leaning towards her sons, she gathered them into a group hug. 'Soon you'll be too old for this,' she teased as, with eyes shut, she held them tightly. Seconds later, she opened her eyes. Malachi was watching her.

'We'll never leave you,' he said.

'I know.'

'I mean it.'

Paris looked a little confused. 'What,' he demanded, breaking the hug to get a better look at his brother and mother.

'We'll never leave Mom, will we?' Malachi confirmed.

'To go where?'

'Anywhere.'

Paris frowned. 'What about school?'

'Not that kind of leaving, stupid,' his twin huffed.

'Hey.'

'Then –'

'Never mind,' Eleanor interrupted, playfully ruffling Paris' hair. 'So what were we talking about before,' she added quickly, in an attempt to change the subject before a scuffle broke out between the boys.

'About Aunt Arabella and Grandpa,' Paris recalled.

Oh no.

'Yes,' Malachi chipped in with great enthusiasm. 'Paris heard Grandma Bianca saying that Aunty Arabella was –'

Whoa, his mother panicked. 'What have I told you about eavesdropping on people's conversations?' she chided Paris.

'I wasn't,' he protested, but Eleanor already knew that anyway. For a while now, she had been increasingly noticing that, like T.J., Paris had an amazing ability to pick up people's conversations without intentionally listening to them, even in his sleep. She felt bad for having falsely accused him and made him sad.

'Hey you,' she winked, nudging him playfully to make up, but he didn't respond. 'Mister,' she persisted, still without success.

'He's mad at you,' Malachi confirmed.

'Are you?'

'Yes.'

'Why?'

'I wasn't eavesdropping on Grandma Bianca's conversation.'

'I know.'

The little boy turned to her with a bewildered frown. 'Then why did you accuse me of it?'

'It was a silly thing for me to do.'

'Yes, it was,' he eyed her. 'So why did you do it?'

Eleanor returned his gaze with an uncomfortable smile. 'Because Mummy's a silly woman?'

The little boy didn't reply.

'I'm sorry,' his mother apologized.

'And you won't do it again?'

Oh Lord. 'Mhm,' she nodded.

'Never, ever again?'

Eleanor crossed her fingers, *God willing.* 'Never again'. She hated ever breaking a promise, but especially one made to Paris because he wasn't one to take a broken promise lightly.

As the boys resumed their playing Eleanor drifted back into deep thought. How could Max be so insensitive to his dead son's memory by bringing his bit on the side to live with him in T.J.'s house?

Max must have known that, like his brothers, T.J. would never have approved of his father's relationship with Arabella of all people, let alone consider permitting them to use his house as their love nest.

And knowing this, Eleanor seethed. *How could Max then have gone ahead and shacked up with Arabella there in T.J.'s house?* This was his special house because it was the first one he ever bought, and the one in which he and his father had made up for lost times.

According to T.J., who disclosed this before his death, this house had also been where he'd realised that he was deeply in love with Eleanor and wanted her in his life for always. This epiphany had come to him when, during his first summer there, she'd visited for a month and proved herself to be quite the social hostess with the fun parties that she'd organised. Newly arrived on the Seattle social network, Eleanor's parties had apparently established him as a 'must know', which was something that was very important to T.J.

Eleanor's eyes narrowed and her lips pursed angrily. There could only be one explanation for Max's disrespectful behaviour to the memory of his son and it had to be...

Ara-bloody-bella, the home wrecking cow! I bet it was all her idea. In quickly decreasing circles of condensation that formed and disappeared as fast as she inhaled and exhaled, Eleanor's anger-charged breath steamed up the window through which she was glaring.

She doesn't care about anyone else's feelings but her own, Eleanor raged on. *And I bet she's living there just to spite the lot of us.*

Or maybe she thought I wouldn't find out, suddenly occurred to her.

No way. Eleanor refused to accept such a possibility with a shake of the head. As far as she was concerned, it was most likely done as a specific dig at her, another way for Arabella to hurt her. And even if it wasn't, *Arabella must have known that I'd find out, surely? With the rest knowing, it was only a matter of time before I did too.*

Eleanor shrugged. *But if she genuinely didn't expect me to,* she mused, as a malevolent smile began to trace across her face, *then it looks like I'll be having the last laugh after all.* Eleanor's eyes brightened at the thought and her mood began to lighten.

I can't wait to see her face when I get there and she realises that I know. Her smiled broadened. *Ooh,* she thrilled. *Imagine the shock she'll get when she sees me and then when I tell her why I'm there. Oh, I can't wait. 'Get packed and get out,'* Eleanor silently rehearsed with relish.

But there's Max to be factored into all of this, something in her suddenly remembered. He was her father-in-law – and a great one in every way apart from the Arabella issue – and a wonderfully devoted grandfather to her sons. And for both of these reasons he was worth keeping in their lives, surely?

Yes, of course, at all cost, but without Arabella. After all she had said and done on that evening of the funeral and was still doing to wreck the family, she was too bitter a proverbial pill for Eleanor to swallow.

So what to do and how? Eleanor pondered silently.

After a few seconds deliberating, her mind was made up. Arabella had to go no matter what and if Max so chose, then he too with her, but hopefully not with acrimony.

Eleanor mulled over the prospects in her mind. It would be possible to avoid any bad blood between her and Max, but only if she applied serious restraint. She would have to choose her words carefully so that although her feelings would be clearly communicated they would be done in a way that didn't cause too much offence to Max and in so doing sour things between him and her.

For the next ten minutes of the journey, Eleanor sat in agitated and fraught silence as she tried to formulate the best way to get across what she had to say. Finally she came up with what she deemed to be the perfect speech. Now all she had to do was to remember it.

She knew it wouldn't be easy, especially with how tense she was feeling, but it was doable if she kept silently repeating the words to herself.

She was managing fine until after the taxi, having turned left off the freeway, began driving along the winding suburban lane that ran past the park at the front of the house. Suddenly Eleanor caught sight of her house in the distance and her heart sank.

The last time she'd been back there was with T.J. and the boys shortly before he died. They'd had such a great time that trip. The thought of now returning without T.J., the thought of the memories, the thought of how she'd feel on stepping back in there –Eleanor felt like she was suffocating. She quickly wound down the window.

Would Max have made changes to the house? Eleanor certainly hoped so. It would make going back easier.

She remembered the speech for Max and Arabella that she'd been rehearsing. *Oh no,* she despaired, all the words were gone from her mind. She couldn't remember a thing. Immediately Eleanor tried frantically to remember them.

'*You've let me down, Max –*' No, that wasn't it. '*You've betrayed my trust,* Max –' *That wasn't it either.*

The taxi was weaving closer and closer to the house. Eleanor became even more agitated. She tried again and again to remember what she had intended to say. *'Does T.J.'s memory matter so little to you –*' Eleanor stopped herself. *That definitely wasn't it.* Starting off by questioning how much his son's memory mattered to him wouldn't be such a good idea. She tried a different approach. How about, *'I'm really hurt tha –*'

A short, sharp jab to the ribs knocked this latest sentence clean out of her mind too.

'Stop that, Paris,' Eleanor lashed out at the little boy closest to her whose arm had accidentally swung back at her during a tussle with his brother.

'But he started it,' the child protested.

'I don't care who started it, just stop it, this instant.'

Shrinking deeply back into the shabby torn grey seat of the taxi in an obvious attempt to evade the radar of his mother's attention, Malachi taunted his brother with a sly pinch and a stuck-out tongue.

Eleanor spotted him and stopped him in his tracks with a firm slap across the bare part of his legs, just below the suntan mark at the hem of his taupe-coloured shorts. 'And that goes for you too,' she bellowed.

He recoiled in silent pain and Eleanor winced with guilt that she could not contain. Leaning towards him with a sad smile, she apologised. 'I'm sorry for being so tetchy,' she whispered and gently massaged away the red handprint she'd left on his otherwise unblemished leg.

'It's okay,' he smiled patiently back at his mother. 'You just need to sleep, that's all.'

Eleanor couldn't help but to smile, even though she could feel her eyes beginning to prick with tears. T.J. used to say that to the boys whenever they apologised after doing something naughty. It was hard to believe that he'd been dead for almost two years now and they were still using his words just as he would have were he alive.

The taxi was now driving past the tennis and basketball courts and Eleanor could clearly see the house from the window beside Malachi. The stress and anxiety of the task ahead became too overwhelming for her. She needed more air – she had to get out into the open – immediately. Quickly leaning forward in her seat, she addressed the taxi driver. 'Pull up by that bus stop over there on the left,' she told him.

Almost instantly her sons began to fidget and to clear their throats loudly in an obvious attempt to attract their mother's attention.

'What?' Eleanor frowned.

Paris muttered something, but she didn't hear him. Then Malachi leant towards her and clearly mouthed the word 'please'.

'Please what?'

The little boy discreetly motioned his head towards the driver. 'To him.'

Eleanor pulled a face.

'You didn't say please to him,' Paris revealed.

'Oh,' Eleanor cried. 'Sorry. Please,' she quickly told the confused-looking driver who was watching them closely through his rear-view mirror as he slowed down and steered the car to a halt on the right.

'But we are not yet at your destination, ma'am,' the turbaned driver lilted in a heavy Punjabi accent.

Unable to mirror his pleasant disposition, Eleanor stared blankly back at his kind but questioning eyes in the mirror. 'Where we're going is just over there, across the park,' she told him as she pointed towards the neat row of white houses that were peeping through the gaps between the trees and their leaf-laden branches that could be seen on the opposite side of the park. 'It'll be quicker if we walk across from over there on the left.'

Without another word, the taxi driver checked for oncoming traffic behind and in front of him. Seeing that no vehicle was coming, he strained as he turned the steering wheel to the left until the car had completed its U-turn. Once done, the driver manoeuvred further right, so that he could park well out of the way of any traffic that may later come from behind and a little way ahead of the green bus shelter that Eleanor had pointed out.

With them all well out of harm's way, the turbaned man released the central locking so that his passengers could disembark once the bill had been settled.

As her sons ran on ahead towards the house, Eleanor reluctantly followed behind, a recollection from T.J.'s funeral running through her mind. It was halfway through the day of T.J.'s funeral and Eleanor could play brave and stoic no more. She felt the knot in her throat begin to tighten as she fought to hold her tears at bay. The dining room was empty, but she scurried for cover behind the long beige curtains that were pulled to the left corner of the wide-open glass sliding doors. The gay sound of laughter and chattering voices from the nearby sitting rooms was stinging her like sweat on heat rash. She felt overwhelmed.

'God, please make them stop,' she sobbed as she cowered against the metal frame of the door. Her grief had turned to anger. Convulsing with rage, she pressed her hands tightly over her ears.

Hadn't anyone told these noisemakers that her house was no longer a good time zone? Weren't they aware that laughter, fun and happiness had left the premises two weeks ago and were neither expected nor welcomed back? Without T.J., there was no point having them. Misery made a better companion for the loneliness she'd been feeling since she'd received the call telling her that T.J. would never be coming home again. Except in a coffin, as he had done today.

As her anger was beginning to give way to self-pity, the sound of approaching footsteps from the kitchen, followed by the swishing of the swing door into the dining room behind her, startled Eleanor into a state of high alert. With as little movement as possible, she mechanically patted her cheeks dry with a handful of curtain, clapped her eyes tightly shut, and then sucked her breath in to a halt and prayed to be passed by unnoticed.

Tense as an interrupted burglar impatiently waiting to exhale, Eleanor keenly monitored the purposeful male footsteps that were passing her by and heading in the direction of the two sitting rooms at the other end of the ground floor. To her horror, they stopped a little way past her, at the threshold of the pulled back sliding door. The owner appeared to be having a change of heart.

Keep going, please, she willed him on.

It didn't work. He had decided to turn back. She heard him swivel round on the balls of his feet, causing the sand on the soles of his shoes to be noisily ground to dust against the hard terrazzo floor underfoot.

'Enough room there for two, kiddo?' a familiar, playful voice rang out.

Busted. Eleanor exhaled with resignation as she recognised the voice to be that of her father-in-law, Max. She had no option but to open her eyes and turn around. With a look of apparent defeat, she stepped out of hiding.

'We're all gonna get through this just fine,' he told her.

'Will we?' Eleanor sighed, glancing up at his tired face that seemed to have aged overnight. Gone was the boyish twinkle in his eyes that used to give him the air of a loveable roué.

The power of grief, she concluded with a wry smile as she remembered the horrible lines of grief that she'd noticed on her own face that morning while she was getting herself ready for the funeral.

'I wish they'd all go away,' she murmured.

'Who?'

'All these happy people.'

Max smiled sadly. 'It's hard, I know,' he agreed. 'But it's just as T.J. would have liked it.'

'I know, but he's not here to see it or deal with them, is he?'

A flicker of devastation momentarily registered on her father-in-law's face, but he soon smiled it away. 'Wanna take a walk on the beach with me?' he asked Eleanor.

'They'll be there as well.'

'But not as many.'

'Hm.'

'And you know most of those out there.'

'It doesn't make it any better.'

'The boys are there too,' Max enthused.

'The boys,' Eleanor purred. 'How are they?'

'They're having the time of their lives entertaining everyone and keeping the party alive.'

'Bless 'em,' she smiled as her eyes welled up afresh with tears. 'I just wish I knew how they do it.'

'We've each gotta get by however best we can, I guess.'

'Yes.'

Max hugged her. 'Shall we go?'

'No,' she whispered, swallowing away the lump in her throat. 'No beach for me.'

Max cast a look of protest.

'Maybe a little later,' she added. 'A sad mummy will only dampen their spirits and spoil everything.'

'Aw –'

'And that wouldn't be fair, especially now that there's no daddy around to crack jokes and make things better.'

'They'll be just fine.'

'I pray.'

'And so will you.'

Eleanor's eyes began to well up anew as she remembered his words. She wasn't fine yet, as he'd predicted, but she was getting by. Sort of, no thanks to the effects of Arabella's disclosure later on that evening of T.J.'s funeral.

It was only thanks to Eleanor's family and Max that Arabella's words hadn't completely decimated her, as Arabella had probably intended. *Thank God for them,* Eleanor reiterated as she recalled how Max seemed to always call or visit her and the boys in Tobago whenever she was at her lowest and needed a shoulder to cry on. How he would remind her of the wonderful things about T.J. and get her thinking well of him again. Yes, Max was truly there for her, as he'd always been from the first day T.J. had introduced her to his family, she recollected.

From day one, Max had made it clear that he approved of her and was happy to have her in his family. And this took the sting out of his wife's unpleasantness, which could have wreaked havoc for T.J. and Eleanor's relationship.

Eleanor had also never underestimated her father-in-law's influence on her husband, nor had she ever failed to appreciate his contribution to the success of her marriage with the advice he'd given to both her and T.J. throughout, especially the one time when their marriage had hit a severely rocky patch over Belinda, who it appeared was out to break them up with insinuations that she and T.J. were having an affair.

Which knowing what she knew now, *no thanks to Arabella,* they probably were, Eleanor frowned. *The cheating bastard.*

But anyway, yes, she interjected, reverting to thoughts of her father-in-law. She owed a lot to Max and had always hoped to one day be able to repay the favour. *But alas,* she frowned, *now no thanks again to Arabella,* she was probably never going to get the opportunity if she said the wrong things and upset Max.

Oh, that bloody woman, Eleanor shouted silently in her mind, getting angrier as more thoughts of her ex-best friend engulfed her.

How could Arabella believe that they could ever be friends again after she'd sullied memories of T.J. by proclaiming him as having been no better than most other men, who were unfaithful shits?

Cheers for that, ole gal! Eleanor mused bitterly.

She shook her head in dismay. They were supposed to have been best friends, and best friends are meant to protect each other like they used to, or, more specifically, like she used to for Arabella. Never had she needed Arabella like she had on that day of T.J.'s funeral, and was she there for her?

Was she heck, Eleanor recalled bitterly. *What a best friend!*

Arabella's fateful words from that night came flooding back to Eleanor. 'Huh,' Arabella had scoffed. 'I seem to recall that T.J. was with someone else when you met him.'

Eleanor sighed. With friends like Arabella, who needed enemies? With that short sentence Arabella had not only denounced T.J. as a cheat – like all the others – but she had ensured that her best friend's grief and memories would always be laced with anger and resentment at a husband whom she was supposed to be mourning with happy recollections. A husband of whom she was supposed to be reminiscing with her sons without rancour.

Eleanor began to cry. How could she tell the boys that their dad was the best husband in the world when she no longer knew what to believe about him? How could she refer to him as an honourable gentleman when Arabella's words had proved him not to be?

Arabella had kept the secret of what she knew for all those years, why couldn't she have kept it permanently when T.J. was dead and couldn't defend himself?

Damn Arabella, Eleanor cursed. Damn her for sabotaging her memory of T.J. and damn her for not leaving Max alone.

Eleanor remembered the dreadful task ahead. Looking up to the sky, she softly cried, 'Oh, T.J., I miss you so much and I wish you were here to sort all this mess out like you used to.' No matter the problem or the issue, when T.J was alive, he was the man for the job. With his gentle approach, all troubles were calmed and all parties left feeling vindicated. With Eleanor's more tempestuous and emotional approach, God only knew how it was all going to turn out. She made the sign of the cross. Only God could help her say the right thing now to Max.

Chapter Twelve

United we mourn, divided we grieve

'Grandpa!' the excited voices rang out as Max opened the front door.

His face brightened instantly on seeing his guests. 'Paris, Malachi, hey champs,' he cried and embraced his grandsons who had wrapped themselves around his waist in a tight hug.

Looking back up, he smiled at Eleanor, who was coming up the final step and onto the front porch where they stood. 'Hey kiddo, what a pleasant surprise,' he told her. Returning his gaze to the two smiling faces that were beaming up at him with adoring eyes, he noted that, 'You boys are looking more and more like your Mom everyday, especially since she started wearing her hair so short.'

Although Malachi – whose Greek child-god-like looks because of his milky coffee colouring and soft dark brown curls that hung down to just above his eyebrows and the nape of his neck – had T.J.'s sharp nose and big brown lost-puppy-dog eyes and Paris had his maternal grandmother Clara's shorter curly afro, grey thoughtful eyes and unusually attractive bow-shaped lips, Eleanor was easily identifiable as their mother to any observer. Especially since she'd done away with her trademark headful of long thin plaits that T.J. had always loved and was now sporting such a short afro that one would be forgiven to think that her jet black hair was painted on. There was something in their expressive eyes and their smiles that was unmistakably her.

'Your mom looks sad and troubled about something,' Max interjected without looking at his daughter-in-law. 'Have you boys been upsetting her again?'

'Again?' Malachi enquired unhappily as he turned back to look at his mother. 'Did you hear what Grandpa just said?' he asked her.

Eleanor nodded. 'He's only teasing you,' she explained.

The little boy turned back to his grandfather. 'Are you, Grandpa?'

'Have you boys been good?'

'Yes,' the twins chorused.

'Then I'm joking,' their grandfather smiled. With eyes still focused on the twins, Max asked them, 'So why then is your mom looking like she's got the world's troubles on her shoulders and how come no one called to tell me you were coming earlier than expected?'

'Oh, she's just tired,' Paris explained with a casual backward glance at his mother. 'I guess that's also why she forgot to call and let you know that we were leaving Grandma Bianca's early.'

Releasing the boys and approaching Eleanor with outstretched arms, Max hugged her. 'So you switched schedule and went east first?' he whispered.

Eleanor tensed up. 'Yes.'

'So I guess you've heard?'

'Mhm,' she nodded, pulling away from him with a forced smile for her sons' benefit.

'I wanted –'

'Not in front of them.'

Max looked back at the two little boys, who were keeping a close watch on his interaction with their mother. 'What are you looking at,' he grizzled playfully and made as if to tickle them. As they gleefully sprang back to avoid his wiggling fingers, he whispered to their mother, 'I'll get them occupied and then we can talk.' And with that he turned back to his grandsons with a shout of 'Last one in the kitchen makes the smoothies.'

Without further ado, the boys raced into the house. Eleanor intercepted Max. 'Is she here?' she asked him.

'No,' he replied and then ran after the boys while their mother, who was making no effort to catch up with the three of them, brought up the rear.

Shaking her head, Eleanor couldn't help but smile with her heart at the sight of the three fast-moving figures in front that, having raced up the steps from the sitting room, were now slipping and sliding and almost falling to the floor as they sharply turned left into the kitchen once they were through the white arch.

Watching them brought back happy memories of when T.J. was alive. He also loved playing this game, which none of them ever seemed to tire of, no matter how often it was repeated on any given day or holiday. Max had apparently started it when T.J. and his brothers were kids. It was eventually resurrected on one of Max's many visits to Tobago when Paris and Malachi were two years old.

With her sons and their grandfather out of sight, Eleanor turned to shut the front door. As she did so, she glanced through the little window beside it. Her attention focused on the strawberry patch that lay to the right of the four wooden steps, up which she and her sons had come to get to the front door.

'The strawberries are doing very well this year,' she called out.

'I know. T.J. would be so proud of them. Hey, no going into the fridge before washing your hands,' Max's voice boomed from the kitchen.

'Paris,' Eleanor chided.

'It wasn't me, it was Malachi.'

'Malachi.'

'I'm washing them, but he hasn't washed his either.'

'I will, once you're done.'

Smiling, Eleanor shook her head again and turning began to make her way towards the happy chattering and laughter that could be heard coming from the kitchen. As she passed the red wall, a chill ran down her spine. Instinctively, she wrapped her arms about her and began rubbing at her shoulders and upper arms. It made no difference.

Having arrived at the bottom of the three steps leading up to the dining room, she made as if to begin her ascent, but her legs suddenly felt too heavy to move. She tried again, but it was in vain. Her soul wouldn't allow it.

I don't want to do this right now, she told herself, but it wasn't up to her mind. Her body was already turning and her soul was yearning to behold the room in which she stood and all its memories.

'Oh my God,' she gasped at the sight of the room before her that she'd been trying to avoid seeing. Contrary to her hopes, it looked exactly the same as how she and T.J. had left it the last time they'd been there together. Just as she'd been dreading that they would, the memories came flooding back and Eleanor began to cry.

'Oh T.J.,' she sobbed quietly. 'Why did you have to spoil it all by dying? Why?'

Feeling her legs begin to give way, Eleanor lowered herself until she was sitting on the bottom step. Taking a deep breath, she dared to have another look around the room with particular attention to the red wall this time. Its colour looked deep and vibrant.

'Did you repaint it?' she called out to Max.

'Repaint what, kiddo?'

'The red wall.'

'No, I'm sorry.' He paused. 'I didn't have the heart to.'

Eleanor looked back at the wall. 'I wasn't complaining,' she explained. 'The colour on it seems so fresh and new as if you did, that's all.'

She looked down at the floor. *It's just the way you like it, T.J.,* she thought, *clean, shining and spotless.*

But that's hardly surprising, she added, remembering how she and his brothers used to tease T.J. about how similar he was to his father regarding their near-obsession with cleanliness.

Eleanor cast a quick glance about her. *Yup,* she nodded. *He's certainly doing you proud with the way he seems to be keeping the place.*

And another thought struck her: *there's not even a trace of Arabella anywhere to be seen.*

Ooh, Eleanor grimaced. The mere thought of the woman rankled her spirit.

Agitated, Eleanor stood up and walked over to the purple L-shaped sofa. Once by it, she gently ran her fingers along its closest contours. It felt warm and familiar, it felt like home, it felt like T.J. She smiled at the thought of him.

I still can't understand what you ever saw in this couch, she told him in her mind. She sat on the sofa. It was firm and unyielding. Eleanor pulled a face. *It's still as uncomfortable as hell,* she remembered.

Just then, she caught sight of the vibrant green hanging plants whose leaves were running down both sides of the low dining room wall slightly to the left, in front of her.

Ah, she smiled. *They're still alive.*

Thanks to Max, something in her added.

Yes, thanks to him.

Rising to her feet, Eleanor took a few steps away from the sofa and began to survey the room in greater detail, recollecting as she did so the history of every item and its sentimental value to the family.

Halfway through this, she was interrupted. 'I haven't changed a thing,' she heard Max softly telling her as he rested a hand on her shoulder.

Flinching slightly at his sudden appearance beside her, Eleanor turned towards him with a smile. 'So I see,' she said, blinking back the tears that she'd only just become aware had returned. 'Part of me was hoping that you would have,' she added as she turned for another review of the room. She was now facing the floor-to-ceiling windows on the opposite side of the room. 'He loved having a park for his front garden,' Eleanor recalled out loud.

'Yes, it certainly is a unique feature for any house to have,' Max added as he joined his daughter-in-law to contemplate the park with its tree-lined borders and ball pitch in its centre. 'I taught him how to play soft-ball out there, two summers before you guys moved to Tobago, you know.'

'I know,' Eleanor replied. 'I was still living in London at the time and he called and told me all about it and about the painting of the red wall. It made him so happy.'

'I know.' Max's expression clouded with sadness. 'I was a bit late with certain things on the fatherhood side of things with him, wasn't I?'

'Better late than never,' Eleanor said, gently rubbing his back, as she was fond of doing to her sons whenever they were down about something. Cocking her head slightly to one side she looked up at him. 'It meant a lot to him that you made the effort to make up for the lost time not spent together,' she divulged.

'I know and I regret not having done so sooner.'

'Don't,' his daughter-in-law rebuked him. 'It was done at the right time for both of you, a time you could both appreciate and treasure.' She smiled thoughtfully. 'You should have heard him with the boys,' Eleanor continued. 'It was always "Grandpa Max taught me this. Grandpa Max taught me that." It made him so proud to be able to say that and to be able to pass on some of what you'd taught him.'

'Which wasn't much.'

'To you, maybe,' she interjected, 'but to him it was like the world and then some.'

'Really?'

'Na, I'm making it all up,' Eleanor quipped with a playful nudge. She noticed the glint of tears in her father-in-law's eyes. It was the first time she'd seen him this emotional since T.J.'s death. 'Of course it was,' she drawled. 'That's why, whenever you came to visit, he would insist that you and he play softball with Paris and Malachi, so he could show off some of the moves you taught him.'

Max smiled sadly.

'You meant the world to him, as did everything that came from you,' his daughter-in-law added. 'That's why he would never sell this house. He treasured the memories of you and him here.'

It seemed to be the tonic Max was in need of. His smile brightened.

Eleanor began to laugh.

'What?'

'Oh boy,' she sighed happily.

'What?'

'I was just remembering how excited he would get when the two of you would play this silly last-person-in-makes-the-smoothies game with the boys,' she giggled.

'Mm,' Max too recalled with a smile. After a moment's silence, he also began to laugh. 'Yes,' he remembered. 'He did kinda take those games seriously at times, didn't he?'

'Too seriously, if you ask me,' Eleanor frowned. 'Remember how sometimes he'd forget that the kids were supposed to be let to win?'

'Uh huh,' Max agreed, and they both laughed heartily.

'Oh,' Eleanor cringed. 'Do you also remember how he'd send you and the boys flying, in his quest to win and be first in the kitchen?'

'Hell, yes,' Max cried, shaking his head in playful dismay. 'That son of mine was one competitive S.O.B, wasn't he?'

'Like his father.'

'Hey –'

'Grandpa,' Malachi's voice suddenly interrupted them.

'Yes, sir,' Max replied, acknowledging the little boy who had hooked the fingers of one hand into his grandfather's jeans belt loop and was using the other hand to tug at the body of Max's grey long-sleeved tee shirt.

'What about the smoothies?' Malachi asked him.

'What about them?' Max riposted, bending to his grandson's eye level.

'Well, aren't you going to come and help us make them?'

'Yes, when you've got everything set and ready for me.'

The little boy said nothing and stood eyeing his grandfather with a puzzled expression.

'Is there a problem, champ?' his grandfather enquired.

'I'm not sure.'

'Meaning?'

'We couldn't find the strawberries.'

'What do you mean you couldn't find them? You walked right past them when you came up the front porch stairs.'

The little boy looked baffled.

'You boys need to go pick 'em and then wash 'em for me to be able to make the smoothies.'

The little boy's eyes lit up with delight. 'We can go and pick 'em ourselves?'

Mirroring his grandson's wide-eyed expression, Max nodded. 'That's the general idea,' he whispered back.

'You sure?'

'Of course I'm sure,' Max told him. 'You boys have gotta learn to pick your own strawberries one day, haven't cha?'

Malachi's beaming little face looked fit to explode with the thrill. 'I guess so.' As he turned to walk away, he seemed to remember something. Pausing, he glanced back to his grandfather. 'You coming?' he asked, still wide-eyed.

'And rob you boys of all that fun? Heck no,' Max declared. 'Your mom and I will watch from here.'

Running back to the kitchen, a highly excited Malachi broke the news to his brother, who, before anyone could change their mind, grabbed the first container he could find, then slipped and skidded his way through the dining room, down the three steps, into the sitting room, past his mother and grandfather, and out the front door before his twin had even made it to the dining room.

Clearly unhappy about having been left behind in such a manner, Malachi, who was loudly voicing his protest on his way, quickened his step and was soon outside nudging Paris out of the way so that he had equal access to pluck and snatch as many of the strawberries as his brother.

As they listened to Malachi complaining about not having enough room to work properly, Max fell solemn. 'He's so like his dad.'

'They both are.'

'Yes,' Max agreed and then fell silent. After a few moments, he turned to Eleanor. 'I miss him so much,' he confessed.

'Me too.'

Holding his daughter-in-law's gaze, Max spoke. 'I am so grateful to you for letting me have this place for the last twelve months,' he told her.

She looked away. 'It's okay.'

'I mean it from the bottom of my heart, Eleanor,' he insisted.

She flashed him a look of discomfort.

'You'll never know how much being here has helped me to start coming to terms with T.J.'s death.'

Eleanor looked surprised. 'I'm glad,' she replied. 'But how could it with all these reminders of him everywhere?'

'It is especially because of all these reminders that I'm becoming able to get past the grief.'

Dropping her gaze, Eleanor smiled wryly. 'It's because of the reminders of him everywhere in the house in Tobago that I've been finding it particularly hard to move on.' *And also thanks to what your girlfriend told me about him,* she added to herself.

'I'm sorry to hear that,' Max told her as he made as if to hug her.

'Don't,' she flinched and moved aside. 'Please,' she added with tear-logged eyes. 'It makes me cry more when people are nice,' she giggled dryly as the tears began to flow. 'See, I told you so.'

She took a few deep breaths, as if to compose herself, but the tears flowed on in torrents. 'I'm sorry,' she sobbed. 'But here's so full of happy memories that I've been trying to forget.'

Max looked deeply saddened. 'I'm so sorry,' he told her.

'Why?'

'I should have redecorated.'

'No.'

'But –'

'I haven't changed a thing in Tobago either.'

'But why not, if it makes you feel so bad?'

'I can't,' she confessed. 'Although I'd love to.' *At times, I want to wipe away all memories of him in order to stem my anger at him.* 'The memories are all I've got left of him, Max.' She turned. 'It's like this wretched sofa, for instance. I've never liked it and so I should be glad now to be able throw it away without any argument from T.J., but if I do, then what?'

'Then you can buy one you like, one that makes you happy.'

'That's what I thought before I arrived here today, but will another one really make me happy?' Eleanor retorted. 'A new sofa will merely be a seat. This one...' she began, but the tears cut her off. 'I'm sorry.'

'Stop apologising.'

'I'm sorry,' she spluttered through more tears. 'Anyway, as I was saying, this awful one here is T.J.: it's me and him, it's you and your family and him, it's him, me, and the kids and much more.'

Her father-in-law nodded as if he knew exactly what she was talking about.

'It's the history of a family,' she concluded. 'Our family.'

'I know.'

'Every time I touch it, it reminds me of him and how quick-witted and funny he really was,' Eleanor continued. 'I remember his trademark smart-alec quips when I whinged about how I detested it. I remember him bundling me onto it and nuzzling my head into its cushions until I wouldn't be able to breathe and would have to concede that I loved it just as much as he did, in order to be set free.'

'That's my boy,' Max chuckled sadly.

'Exactly, and I never want to forget the good times.'

'You won't.'

'I may if I change things.'

Max eyed her kindly. 'You won't,' he told her.

'But –'

'He's in there and always will be,' he said, motioning to the heart.

'Then how come it took you coming to this house with all its memories for you to start coming to terms with your grief?'

'All the memories from this house and every other house where I've spent time with T.J. have and always will be in me. But coming here was my first and only real opportunity to be on my own.'

'But you were on your own for the six months that you and Bianca were apart after the funeral.'

'No, we lived in separate houses, but we weren't really apart. I still spent a lot of time with her. She needed the familiarity of my being around.'

'And you also made quite a few trips to us in Tobago,' Eleanor recalled.

'Uh huh, exactly! I was constantly on the move and with others. Here was the first time I had no choice but to be still.'

'Oh, I can't bear to be still,' Eleanor confessed.

'Neither could I, because with stillness comes a lot of reflection and that brings back lots of memories, good and bad.'

You don't know the half of it.

'And boy, when those memories come!' Max exclaimed.

Eleanor nodded knowingly while Max looked around the room.

'In this house, I had nowhere to hide,' he resumed. 'As the memories flooded, so too did the feelings that came with them. They confronted me head on. I had no excuse not to face them, I had no one else's feelings to hide behind.'

Eleanor squinted questioningly.

'Here I didn't have to be strong for anybody,' her father-in-law explained.

'Oh, dear Max,' she cried. 'We didn't let you grieve, did we?'

'No,' he disagreed. 'I didn't let myself.'

'But only because we compelled you to stay strong for the rest of us.'

'No, you didn't, I forced myself.'

'But if we hadn –'

'You and Bianca were getting by as best you could. I on the other hand, well …' he shrugged. 'I guess I was doing the best I could to hide from my emotions and my grief. I denied facing the facts by playing the strong guy. We could have all cried together,' he said, as if with regret. 'It would have probably been better that way –everyone supporting each other – an opportunity at last for feeling something real together and without a care for what others might think.' He paused. 'And Bianca and I may possibly have stayed together.'

'Oh my God!' Eleanor exclaimed.

'What?'

'I'm doing exactly the same with the boys,' she realised.

'What do you mean?'

'I hide from them to cry. I avoid talking about T.J. in front of them for fear that I may break down. I'm –'

'Shutting them out,' Max concluded for her.

'Yes, but I don't mean to. I –'

'Think you're doing it for their good?'

'Yes.'

'Well, you're not, kiddo,' Max told her. 'You're a family. You should be grieving together and supporting each other through it.'

Covering her face with her hands, Eleanor began to cry again. 'Oh God,' she wept. *If only you knew everything, you'd understand that …* 'It's so difficult. I … I just, oh, I don't know. I can't. It wouldn't be right to let them see me falling apart like this.' *And it certainly wouldn't be right for them to hear me talking about him at the times when I'm hating him for what I found out from Arabella,* she concluded in her thoughts.

'It's not falling apart,' her father-in-law declared. Walking over to her, he cradled her as she sobbed. 'It's grieving.' As Eleanor searched her jeans pockets for the tissue she'd put there on her way up to the house, Max continued to speak. 'There's nothing wrong with them seeing how much their mother loved their father, how much she misses him and how it's okay for them to miss him too.'

Eleanor broke free from his arms. 'But I'm not stopping them from missing him,' she protested.

'I know that,' Max reassured. 'But sometimes our actions send out the wrong signals.'

'Meaning?'

'Well,' he said. 'Take Bianca for instance.'

'Ah ha.'

'And the reason why we finally broke up.'

Eleanor's eyes narrowed and her lips pursed. 'Which is?'

'She couldn't be with a man who didn't love their dead son enough to cry for him.'

'What?'

'I didn't cry for T.J..'

'I don't understand.'

'Because she never saw me crying for T.J., Bianca concluded that I couldn't have loved him enough.'

'But you did love him.'

'Of course I did and always will.'

'You should have let Bianca know this.'

Max regarded her kindly. 'Grief is never straight-forward and is always different for everybody,' he explained. 'For some it's a uniform emotion, they see it as one size fits all, so if you're not reacting in the same way as them, then you can't be feeling it as badly.'

'And that was Bianca?'

'Uh uh. For her, I needed to be crying in order to be considered as missing and having loved my son.'

'And you didn't cry?'

'No, not even half a tear, that is until I got here. Then I couldn't stop.'

Eleanor pulled a face. 'That can't have been healthy.'

'Exactly,' Max agreed. 'That's what I've been try-ing to tell you,' he explained. 'Crying is good, it's healing. Before I got to this house, I missed T.J. so much that it hurt. I couldn't bear the pain of knowing that he was dead, so I ran from it by shutting away all my feelings and emotions about it. I mentally blocked out anything that would make me sad. And then I got here and there was no one to hide behind when the memories leapt out at me from everything in the house. And then I cried and cried and cried until now that I've started to laugh again.'

'Does Bianca know about all this?'

'About the tears?'

'Yes.'

'Sure, we still share everything.'

Eleanor smiled hopefully. 'And?'

'And nothing.'

'She won't take you back?'

'I don't wanna go back.'

'Why not?'

'Things have changed.'

'Aunty Arabella,' Paris and Malachi's gleeful cries interrupted.

Eleanor's expression clouded and she turned to the window just as her sons were explaining that, 'We're helping Gran –'

'You're not going back to your marriage because of her, right?' Eleanor hissed on spying the blonde woman in jeans and a crisply laundered white sleeveless cotton shirt conversing with her sons.

'No, because of me.'

Eleanor wasn't listening anymore. 'I want her out of my house now,' she bristled in a low tone.

'She's not in your house.'

Eleanor flashed him a glare. 'I'm not in the mood for playing semantics, Max,' she hissed. 'I want her out now, so get her packing before I start throwing her things out.'

'What things?'

'Max, please,' his daughter-in-law snapped. 'Don't try to play me for a fool, it won't work.'

'Play you for a foo –' A glint of realisation dawned in his eyes. 'Eleanor, kiddo,' he cried softly. 'She's not staying here.'

'Since when?'

'She's never stayed here.

'What?'

'She comes to drop me off or pick me up, or –'

'How come?'

'We didn't think it was appropriate or fair on you for her to stay over.'

'Oh.'

'Mummy's inside,' Paris' voice rang out. 'Come in and say hi.'

'Oh no,' Eleanor winced. 'Paris, please no.' She turned to Max. 'I've got to get out of here now.'

'Eleanor, please,' Max implored.

'I can't, I'm sorry,' she told him and rushed up the three nearby steps and into the dining area.

Speeding after her, Max overtook Eleanor at the white arch that led from the dining room into the kitchen and intercepted her escape by grabbing hold of her right arm. 'She misses you so much,' he told her.

'I have to go,' Eleanor insisted.

'She was one of your closest friends, for Heaven's sake,' her father-in-law reminded.

With eyes flashing with disdain, Eleanor puckered her lips defiantly. 'A fact that should have deterred you both from sleeping together,' she hit back.

Just then Arabella's hesitant and nervous tone could be heard as she made small talk with the boys as they coaxed her towards the porch. Eleanor flashed an anxious glance in the direction of the front door. 'Oh, those boys will be the death of me one of these days,' she grumbled and then, returning her attention to Max, she spoke to him. 'I'll give the boys a few minutes to say goodbye to you,' she announced. 'And when you're done, please bring them to me at the pay phone around the corner.'

Before Max realised what was happening, Eleanor had wriggled her hand free from his previously firm grip. He sighed heavily with exasperation. 'You're gonna have to face her one day,' he told her.

'Be careful of what you wish for, it may not turn out pretty.'

Max looked sad. 'What if she and I end up together?'

'You already are, aren't you?' his daughter-in-law retorted mockingly.

'Will you be avoiding me soon too?'

'If I can't see you on your own, yes,' she volleyed back as, edging backwards; she strained her ears to ascertain the progress at the front end of the house.

Max shook his head in apparent dismay. 'That's ridiculous, Eleanor,' he scolded her.

'*C'est la vie,*' she shrugged just as the twins, who were still accompanied by Arabella, could be heard coming through the front door. Eleanor smiled sadly. 'I'm sorry, Max, I won't be changing my mind about this, ever,' she added and with that she escaped through the back door and went round the corner to wait for her sons.

Chapter Thirteen

You have every right to

'Hey, kiddo,' Max called out as he spotted Eleanor waiting on the plateau of square concrete at the top of the slope on the far left-hand side of the park near the pay phones.

She turned. 'Hey.' Her brows furrowing, suddenly, 'And the boys?' she asked.

'Inside making smoothies with 'Aunty Arabella',' he replied as he made his way up to join her.

As Max arrived beside her, his daughter-in-law scowled at him. 'Don't call her that,' she told him.

'Don't call who what?'

'She's not their aunty.'

'Neither's Arielle.'

'She's different.'

Max smiled.

'Anyway, I said five minutes to say goodbye,' Eleanor reminded him without a return smile.

'But I'd promised them smoothies first, remember?'

'That was before.'

'A promise is a promise.'

'So what am I supposed to do?'

'You and I could spend this time talking through a few things,' he suggested.

'I think we've said it all, don't you?' Eleanor hit back.

'No, but if you think we have,' her father-in-law shrugged. 'Your time is yours, do what you want.'

'I want to go back to my hotel.'

'So what's keeping you?'

'I can't leave the boys.'

'Why not? Now that Arabella's back with the car, I can drop them off later if you want.'

'No, I want them to leave with me now.'

'Fine, go get 'em. I'm not stopping you. I'll even drive you all back to town.'

Eleanor eyed him. 'This really isn't fair,' she protested.

'Tell me about it,' he agreed. 'You're the one calling the shots, so decide what you wanna do and I'll comply.'

'I just want to ...' she began and then stopped herself with a deep sigh of apparent frustration.

'You and me both, kiddo.'

'Okay,' Eleanor conceded.

'Okay what?'

'If you want to talk, let's talk, but only until the boys are ready.' As she spoke, she began to undo the three pink buttons on her jacket, revealing the white spaghetti-strap sun top underneath.

Noticing her doing this, Max, shielding his sight with his right hand, glanced up at the sun, which was blazing down from directly above the slab. 'It's kinda hot out here,' he noted, beginning to flap the hem of his long-sleeved t-shirt as if in confirmation. 'Shall we move to the shade?'

'No, I'm alright here.'

'Sure, but …' He paused and then, motioning his head suggestively towards the house, Max added, 'It's cooler back in there, you know.'

'I know, but I'm fine here, thanks.'

'Okay.' With that said, Max gazed thoughtfully into the distance at the busier than normal mid-afternoon traffic on the road below. 'This is a great spot, isn't it,' he remarked without looking at Eleanor.

'Yes, T.J. liked it, especially in the evenings and even more especially when he needed to think something through.'

'Is that what you were doing?'

'No, like I said before, my mind is made up, so I've got nothing to think through.'

'I see.'

Eleanor sighed again. 'So?' she demanded.

'So,' Max echoed emptily and they both fell silent.

After a few moments Eleanor spoke again, this time with a softened and saddened tone. 'He thought the world of you, you know,' she said.

'He was a good son,' Max replied, still staring ahead at the traffic.

After more thoughtful silence, his daughter-in-law changed the subject again. 'Did T.J. ever tell you how we met? About how it all began between us?' she added with a quick glance in Max's direction. The look in her eyes was loaded, but he pretended not to notice.

'I think he said it was in a nightclub in Singapore.'

'Yes,' she confirmed. 'I collided into him on my way into the club to meet Arabella and Arielle.'

'That's as good a way of meeting someone as any, I guess.'

'Then we were later introduced by Morgan, a friend of his from Hong Kong,' Eleanor resumed.

'You knew his friend Morgan?'

'No, Arabella did.'

Something in the way Eleanor replied made Max wish he'd never asked the question. Having already heard the story from Arabella, he could well imagine where his daughter-in-law was headed by bringing it up. It wasn't where he'd intended when he'd suggested they talk things through, but it was too late. He'd started the proverbial ball rolling, so now all he could do was to hope that it would all end amicably enough for him to still be allowed to see his grandsons.

'She'd met Morgan at a conference cocktail party the night before,' Eleanor was already continuing.

'Really!' he exclaimed, pretending to be surprised and to not know the story. 'Was T.J. at the same conference?'

'No, they didn't work in the same industry,' she explained. 'T.J., who was on a different business trip, just happened to be at the club at the same time as all of us when Morgan spotted him in the crowd.'

'How serendipitous!'

'Yes,' Eleanor smiled coldly at him. 'For all of us, wouldn't you say?'

Max willingly took the bait. 'Yup!'

'I mean for T.J. and me, and then later for you and Arabella,' she elucidated.

Oh boy, here's where it gets nasty! He could feel it from the tone of Eleanor's voice, but he wasn't going to shy away. When he and Arabella were no longer together there was no point riling his daughter-in-law with mention of her ex-friend. But now that Max and

Arabella were taking things to the next level, he felt that he needed to stand his ground, gently but firmly, to ensure that all concerned knew that the relationship was now serious. 'Yes, I guess you could say it was,' Max agreed.

There was an awkward pause as Eleanor kept an intense gaze on him. After a few seconds, she resumed speaking. 'Morgan was married too.'

Touchdown. 'Was he?'

Not answering, Eleanor looked away. Suddenly she exploded. 'For Heaven's sake, Max,' she beseeched him. 'Can't you see it?'

'See what, kiddo?' he asked, keeping his cool.

'She has form.'

'Meaning?'

Eleanor fell silent. She wanted to tell Max about how Arabella hurt people she was supposed to care about – about how she hurt her – but instead she answered, 'She only ever goes for married men.'

'Oh, Eleanor!'

'It's true,' his unrelenting daughter-in-law insisted. 'She's going to hurt you: she's going to leave you once you're no longer someone else's'

'Is that why her other relationships broke up?'

'No.'

'So how did they end?'

'The others came to their senses and left her.'

Max cast a questioning glance. 'So where's the 'form' you referred to?'

'What?' Eleanor eyed him with frustration. *Can't you read between the lines of what I'm trying to say here?*

'You said her form was to go after married guys and then leave them when they were no longer taken. How does them leaving her show this?'

Ignoring the question, Eleanor persisted with, 'She's going to hurt you.' *That's what you should be focusing on.*

'Maybe she will, maybe she won't.'

'She definitely will.'

Max smiled kindly. 'Then I'll face up to the situation when it occurs.'

'And boy, will it.' *You fool.*

Her father-in-law looked as if his patience was beginning to ebb. 'Eleanor, please,' he entreated. 'I'm an adult and I can take care of myself.'

So you think, but ... 'Fine.'

He seemed to relent. 'I know you mean well.'

She didn't respond.

'And I appreciate it.' Max paused. 'Look,' he said. 'If you really wanna do something for me, then please make it up with Arabella.'

'What!' Eleanor exclaimed aloud. 'No way! Never,' she cried adamantly.

'Why not?'

'Because I can't stand the woman.'

'Eleanor!'

'I hate her,' she added. 'And that's putting it lightly.'

'Eleanor, please,' her father-in-law rebuked her. 'You're a Catholic –you're not supposed to hate.'

I know, but I can't help it. 'I'll never forgive her.'

Max looked even more downhearted. 'That's wrong.'

'What she did was wrong.'

'What she and I both did was wrong.'

'She's a duplicitous cow.'

'I'm as much to blame for everything that's happened, if not more.'

'She was supposed to be my friend and T.J.'s, for that matter.'

'I was supposed to be T.J.'s father.'

'Yes, you were.' *And so you should have known better than to get involved with someone who hated him so much that she couldn't even wait for him to be cold in the grave before she began trashing his memory.*

Dropping his gaze, Max sighed heavily and then, linking his arm through Eleanor's, he leaned sideways towards her. 'And as such, I should have behaved better.'

Too right! 'Yes, you should have,' she agreed, unlinking arms.

'I know,' he concurred, and then pausing, he looked round at his daughter-in-law. 'But she makes me happy, kiddo,' he confessed.

'Until the day she hurts you.'

'Or not.'

'Oh, she will.' *Take it from me.*

'I'll take my chance.'

'Mug!'

'Maybe,' Max riposted, bursting into a slight chuckle. He paused. 'What is it with you British and this habit you seem to have of calling people names?' he asked.

Eleanor ignored him. And then after a few moments of what seemed like silent reflection, she began to speak again. 'Arabella can't even make herself happy,' she told her father-in-law. 'And as the saying goes "Misery loves company", so you better be careful.'

'She used to make you happy as your friend, didn't she?' Max asked her.

'Yes,' his daughter-in-law admitted. 'Used to being the operative words. She used to until she showed me her true colours. Arabella is a fake and a liar'. *Pretending all that time to be my friend, pretending that she cared a hoot about me and T.J.* 'She doesn't care about anybody but herself. She can't help it, it's how she is.'

'No,' Max declined. 'She lied to you, or rather she kept our relationship from you because she cared about you and didn't want you caught up in the politics of it all.'

That's not what I'm talking about, Eleanor thought, flashing him a glare. *But even if it were, you're still wrong because …* 'If she didn't want me caught up in the politics of it all, then she shouldn't have started seeing you in the first place.'

'I know,' her father-in-law agreed. 'But the whole thing just sort of happened.'

'Just sort of happened,' Eleanor hooted with derision.

'Yes, the feelings just sort of came up on us –'

'Oh, for the love of God,' Eleanor exploded. 'You're adults, Max, not kids, so do us all a favour and take responsibility for your actions.'

He looked as if he was about to say something, but Eleanor cut back in. 'I understand that feelings can begin to develop without our wanting them to,' she accepted. 'But what I will never agree with is that once they begin, there's nothing we can do about them. Like thoughts that we can choose to not turn into words, there's everything we can do about feelings.' Pausing briefly, she regarded him with sadness. 'You both had choices,' Eleanor told him. 'Stay and let the feelings grow or walk away while they were relatively benign and let them die down.'

'Not everybody can be so strong-willed,' Max interjected.

Eleanor shook her head. 'I disagree completely,' she said. 'Our will is the one thing that is truly ours to control.'

'That –'

'Please don't get me wrong,' she butted in again. 'I'm not trying to make out that it's all so easy, but as the saying goes "where there's a will, there's a way" and neither of you wanted to have the will.'

'We did,' Max countered. 'And that's why we broke it off.'

'Sorry, my mistake. Yes, you did,' his daughter-in-law corrected herself before stressing her belief that Max had been the one with the sense to break off the relationship with Arabella, 'On that night of T.J.'s funeral,' Eleanor recalled. Her mind began to recollect the events that took place that evening in Arabella and Arielle's allocated bedroom. 'Arabella neither had the will, nor the inclination to have the will, and that's why we're back at this point and having this conversation.'

'No,' Max refused to agree. 'She had more determination and a stronger will than I ever did.'

'Yes, to get you back, maybe,' Eleanor scoffed.

'What are you talking about?' her father-in-law frowned.

'I know that she refused to let you go.'

'Says who?'

'I know,' Eleanor insisted smugly.

Max gave her a puzzled look. 'How can you be so certain about something that's not real?' he asked her, almost mockingly.

'Because I know it to be real,' she replied. 'I got it straight from the horse's mouth, so to speak.'

Max shook his head. 'The wrong horse, I assure you, because Arabella broke off all contact with me after that night.

'What?'

'Mhm,' he nodded.

'But she made it clear that she wasn't going to let you go,' Eleanor half-mumbled.

Max shrugged. 'I don't know what to tell you, kiddo,' he said. 'Except that she obviously changed her mind sometime after your conversation because she did let me go. And without as much as a backward glance,' he added.

Eleanor's brows knitted into a quizzical frown. Why would Arabella refuse to give him up and then never make contact with him again? *It didn't make sense, unless she'd only got with him to upset me and T.J.* That still didn't make sense either, Eleanor decided, especially when she remembered the look on Arabella's face that evening when she was crying about never being able to find a lasting relationship. *And besides,* Eleanor reasoned, *if she did give him up, as Max alleged ...* 'Then how come you're back together again?' she enquired.

'Because I wanted it.'

'You?' She was now looking truly stunned. 'Why?'

'I care a lot about her.'

Eleanor shook her head sadly. She'd hoped that she'd be able to make Max see sense without letting him know the ins and outs of what Arabella had said to her that night about T.J., but it was plain to see that he was too smitten by Arabella to be able to see the truth about the kind of person she really was without it being spelled out to him, so Eleanor told him about what had happened that night after he and Bianca had left her and Arabella on their own.

Max listened intently as she spoke, and when she finished, he remained silent for a few moments more. And then moving closer to her, he hugged his daughter-in-law tightly. 'Oh, kiddo,' he sighed. 'She should never have told you that,' he agreed, 'especially on that day.'

'I know.'

'But I don't think she meant it badly.'

Eleanor's jaw dropped. Was Max that besotted with Arabella that he still couldn't see her for what she really was: a nasty piece of work? 'Yes, she did,' Eleanor shouted. 'She knew it would hurt me and that's why she said it.'

'It was probably a heat of the moment thing.'

'No.' Eleanor shook her head. Max couldn't have been listening to her when she was telling him the story. 'I'll never forget her tone,' she reiterated. 'It sounded like she'd been waiting to hit me with it for a while, like she hated T.J.' *There, I've said it, clear as crystal.*

Max looked torn. 'I wasn't there, but I know how much she cares about you and how unhappy losing you has made her that I can't see her ever having wanted to wilfully hurt you.'

Eleanor shrugged; maybe nothing was ever going to make her father-in-law see sense where Arabella was concerned. But she had. 'I know what I heard,' Eleanor insisted sadly.

'I guess you do,' Max accepted. 'But if she wanted you hurt,' he reasoned, 'why did she go to all that bother during the Belinda saga to make sure that things got sorted out between you and T.J. without you getting hurt?'

'She didn't.'

'She did, kiddo,' Max disclosed. 'She worked very hard for you behind the scenes, like one who truly cared about you.'

Eleanor looked baffled. What was he talking about? What was all this about Arabella working behind the scenes? 'Is that what she told you?'

'It's what I know,' Max replied, looking his daughter-in-law square in the eyes. 'It was Arabella who introduced me to the idea that you hadn't imagined Belinda's intentions of wanting to break you and T.J. up. She told me about T.J. and you, and how it all started when he was still with Belinda.'

'You knew too?'

'Yes, but that's not the point here,' he rebuffed her indignation. 'The point is that Arabella was the one who made it her business to find out what Belinda was saying behind the scenes and it was with that information that I convinced T.J. that even though nothing was happening between him and Belinda and he would have liked to be friends with her, it wasn't worth it because she may have only wanted to be friends with him so she could sow seeds of doubt in your mind about their relationship and in so doing break up your marriage, like she felt you had broken up her relationship with T.J..'

'Yeah, right,' Eleanor said, casting Max a distrustful glance. It was to be expected that he would try and cover up for his son and Arabella. Unfortunately for him, she was no longer the fool. Eleanor had always suspected that Belinda was out for some sort of revenge, but until Arabella's disclosure, she couldn't imagine what revenge and why. Now she did, it had changed things, but not for the better because it incriminated T.J. more, by proving that he was capable of what Belinda had implied. Like most other men, he'd turned out to be a love rat and this was the sticking point for Eleanor.

And as for Arabella, Max needn't have bothered trying to stick up for her. Her disclosure had shown Eleanor that she would no sooner look after Eleanor's interests as would Belinda. So Max could spin whatever yarn he wanted, but it won't work. *Not now, not ever,* especially since, like Arielle used to be, she too had become once-bitten-twice-shy. It had served Arielle well in weeding out the 'wrong 'uns' and it would also serve her well, starting with Arabella.

'She cares about you,' Max insisted, as if to counter what she was thinking.

Bless him, Eleanor thought with a patronising smile. Max genuinely seemed to believe what he was saying. But how could he when it was so obviously not the truth? 'True caring would have been letting what she knew about the ending of T.J. and Belinda's relationship go to the grave with T.J.,' Eleanor hit back.

'Yes.'

'But she chose to let out the secret, not only when T.J. could no longer defend himself, but when I least needed to hear it,' Eleanor almost shouted.

'And that was wrong of her,' Max confirmed.

I should say! 'So then, how can you stand here and tell me that she cares?' his daughter-in-law challenged him with eyes brimming with tears of anguish and rage.

Max hugged her again. He could because he knew it to be true: Arabella did and still cared very deeply for Eleanor, no matter what her actions of that day seemed to suggest.

And that was why he was not exonerating Arabella from blame. Her intentions may not have been deep-seated malice, but there was intent of spite, no matter how spur-of-the-moment it was. As far as Max was concerned, as one who cared as much as Arabella did for Eleanor, Arabella should have been more sensitive and refrained from letting her mouth run away with her on that day of all days.

'You have every right to be disappointed and angry at her,' he told his daughter-in-law.

Eleanor burst into tears. Her sobbing spoke volumes. 'Every right to be disappointed' was an understatement. The pain inside her was raw and intense. 'Disappointed' didn't come close.

The intensity of Eleanor's weeping showed just how devastated she had been by Arabella's revelation. Her deep wheezes of despair told of how badly she needed confirmation of T.J.'s deep love for her and yet how afraid she was to ask about it for fear of what other secrets she may learn.

Eleanor looked up at Max with vulnerable, bloodshot eyes. 'She was supposed to be my best friend, the last person I expected to hurt me.'

He held her gaze, his eyes pleading for forgiveness as he did so: forgiveness for not being able to ease her sorrow, forgiveness for the times he'd dismissed her anger at Arabella as being misplaced vitriol against a despised world that could move on without T.J.

Max was feeling bad for not having listened well enough to hear what she had been saying from the start. Arabella was the issue, not life carrying on. Had he taken the time to listen properly, he would have heard her, and he would have urged Arabella to make amends sooner, to do whatever she had to do to ease Eleanor's pain.

Poor child, he sighed sadly as he tried to banish his imagining of how bad the past two years must have been for his daughter-in-law, how betrayed and how alone she must have felt. There could be no more delaying now, things had to get sorted with immediate effect. *Yes,* Max decided. 'You and Arabella have to talk.'

'After what she's put me through,' Eleanor flinched back. 'If I never see her again, it'd be too soon, let alone speak to the woman.'

'I hear you, kiddo,' her father-in-law replied. He couldn't blame her for her feelings. 'But, she's the only one who can make you feel better, the only one who can answer some of the many questions I suspect you're still asking yourself day after day.'

Considering Max's logic, Eleanor reluctantly conceded that he may be right. Arabella, like Belinda, had been living in Hong Kong during most of the time that she and T.J. were married, and with the expat community being so close-knit, yes, there was a good chance that Arabella did probably know what, if anything, that T.J. may have been up to with Belinda or anybody else during his many business trips back to Hong Kong. 'But,' Eleanor sighed, 'what if he did cheat on me?'

Unlikely though he thought it was, Max knew that, like everything, there was always a small possibility. 'But what if he didn't?' he volleyed back. That was something he felt that his daughter-in-law had to also bear in mind.

With that said, there was nothing else Max could do about the situation but to understand and respect

Eleanor's wishes to no longer be pushed on the Arabella issue. Whatever the next steps were to be on the matter, they needed to be Eleanor's and in her own time, without any pushing from anybody. And he was going to let Arabella know so and why.

Chapter Fourteen

Music and daydreams: my favourite kind of summer evening

Standing on the corner of Third Avenue and Pine Street, Arabella looked down at her watch and deliberated her next move. The time was quarter to six on the evening after Eleanor's surprise arrival at the house. Having completed all her tasks for the day and with an hour to kill before Max came to the hotel to pick her up for dinner, she had two options. She could either turn left and go into Nordstrom, as intended, to buy the pair of Jimmy Choo shoes that had caught her eye earlier that day, or she could leisurely stroll back to the Four Seasons Hotel, where she'd been staying since her move to Seattle.

Arabella looked around her. *Hm, what happened?* she grimaced as she suddenly became aware of the change in ambience. Last time she'd taken in her surroundings was at Pike Place Market on First Avenue.

There, although the fresh fish and seafood stalls – usually lively and throbbing with activity and loud banter – had shut up for the day, the rest of the street-level part of the market with its muted tempo maintained a healthy pulse of activity.

The last throes of evening sun shun on valiantly, while music and the occasional punctuation of laughter could still be heard wafting out from the nearby cafés and patisseries, where last-minute customers were being treated like friends rather than customers. The world had felt a pleasant place to Arabella.

But in the here and now of Third and Pine, Yuk! Everything seemed so anxious and desperate, in particular the assortment of tired and sombre faces that were robotically rushing around in constant near-collision with each other as they hurried in and out of unexpected alleys, doorways, and nooks and crannies. The burgeoning throngs of people leaving work rushed for last-minute essentials or boarded taxis and buses to take them home where Arabella imagined that they would probably continue frowning until they dropped off to sleep.

You'd have thought at least some of them would be happy to be going home at last, Arabella mused as she took offence to the crowd's seeming lack of appreciation for the ending of yet another working day.

Before her inheritance, during the days of never-ending overdrafts, huge credit card bills, and long working hours to keep her debts on the right side of fifty-six thousand pounds, the best part of Arabella's day used to be when she stepped out of the office at between six and six thirty in the evening.

Oh what joy! she recalled. It was such a good feeling that she missed it now and sometimes wished she could go back to work just to be able to get that daily hit of euphoric adrenalin again.

But it wouldn't be the same now, though, she admitted to herself with a sigh. Unlike before, when she had to work to survive, now she could afford to walk out of a job on a whim and probably would at the slightest provocation.

Arabella was the type of person who needed to have the proverbial carrot and sometimes the stick dangling over her in order to keep at a job, or anything for that matter. She was a *raison d'être* kind of girl: the sort of person who needed a reason to get out of bed every morning. Right now, the hunt for a temporary home for her and Max was that reason, but what about in the further future?

Arabella paused to consider her options. *Charity work, perhaps?* immediately came to mind.

Hm, she liked the thought of that. But more on the fundraising side of things.

Immediately her thoughts ran to Eleanor. If only they were still on good terms.

Her reflections drifted to what Max had told her after his conversation with Eleanor yesterday.

What a waste of a great friendship, Arabella despaired. If only she could take it all back: those words that came out of nowhere because she was feeling under attack.

From what she remembered of that fateful evening, she'd grabbed at the first thought that had come to mind, which was about T.J. and Belinda. It was used more as a deflection from the reality that she was wrong to have become involved with Max, than as an implement with which to hurt Eleanor.

Hindsight, how great, she sighed wryly. If only she knew then what she knew now, how different it would all be! She would have taken all the words Eleanor chose to hurl at her without attempting to deflect them. God knows she deserved most of them for not having avoided what happened between her and Max, as she might well have if she had shown a lot more effort and restraint

Restraint, the word echoed in Arabella's mind. How often in her life had she been advised to exercise it in her actions? *Too many times to recall,* she sadly admitted. If only she'd for once taken the advice, there would have been none of these nasty repercussions: Eleanor's pain, her pain.

'Oh God,' Arabella groaned softly. Her pain had been bad enough, but now knowing about poor Eleanor whose world, according to Max, had been knocked off kilter; it didn't bear thinking about.

But then again, Arabella wondered, had she thought about her disclosure before voicing it, would she have refrained from making it?

Probably not, she had to admit. With Eleanor always having been strong and logical – except when it came to Cort – it would never have occurred to Arabella that Eleanor would have let such a meaningless revelation cause her to doubt T.J.'s obvious love for her. Especially knowing, as Eleanor did, that she too was involved with someone else – Cort – when she begun her relationship with T.J.?

Arabella would have thought that Eleanor would have dismissed it, at least on the grounds that as her infidelity didn't make her an inherently dishonest person and a serial cheat, it didn't have to make T.J. that either.

Arabella recalled her many drunken *tête-à-têtes* with Eleanor about love and how it came when least expected. She recollected Eleanor getting all mushy and doe-eyed at how she knew that T.J. was the one. So certain was she that she finished with Cort and never went back to him, no matter how often he attempted a comeback. Why couldn't she have realised or reasoned that it was or could be the same for T.J. regarding his relationship with Belinda?

Arabella shrugged. *Maybe Max was right, maybe it was the timing of the revelation. Grief is a strange thing, after all.* Arabella accepted this as she recalled how a couple of months after her maternal grandmother's death, her mother had begun talking about Arabella's father like she was back in contact with him and he was a changed man.

Arabella's thoughts returned to Eleanor. If only there was a way she could make her see sense that T.J.'s relationship with Belinda, like hers with Cort, ended within weeks of Eleanor and T.J.'s meeting in Singapore. And that like Eleanor, T.J. had seized the day – and thank God he had – because it had meant that they enjoyed eight of the happiest years of their lives together without infidelity or any other bullshit.

An idea came to mind. Arabella smiled. *Maybe there is a way,* she decided.

A few years back Eleanor had started a charity that focused on the education and health of underprivileged children in developing countries. And from what Max had told Arabella, it was now quite a successful and budding charity with partners and offices in Cambodia to look after Asian regions, Nigeria for the African region, and Venezuela for South and Latin America. What if she approached Eleanor through this avenue and asked to meet up to discuss a lucrative idea for the charity?

At the beginning she could make her suggestion that she, Arabella, using her own money, could launch an office for the charity here in Seattle or wherever she and Max finally ended up.

It could be a satellite office for fundraising, Arabella daydreamed. The scheme hit home. *That's not a bad idea,* she realised. It didn't have to be merely a ploy or wishful thinking, it could be a reality. *My future career.* The thought excited Arabella. 'The Seattle satellite office,' she voiced out loud, forgetting that she didn't want to be based in America.

How brilliant would that be! Arabella thrilled. Doing something she knew she'd be good at, and at the same time helping Eleanor to make a difference in parts of the world where that difference was so desperately needed.

And, she added, bringing herself back to the most important point of all: getting a nigh-on impossible opportunity to speak to Eleanor and tell her the truth about those careless words, and prove to her how inconsequential they were and why she has no cause to be so devastated.

Arabella couldn't resist further review of the charity idea. It was a brilliant one, even if she said so herself, an idea from which only good could come on all fronts for all concerned.

Wow! she exclaimed silently. *Frivolous Arabella becomes the charity woman, who would've thought it?*

She definitely liked the proposal very much, but would Eleanor?

Why not? Eleanor may hate her guts at the moment, but she was a bright girl and would be able to see the sense in it.

But just in case, Arabella decided to run the idea by Max first. He'd made her promise that she would give Eleanor all the time she needed to decide how she wanted to handle the situation between them. There would be no railroading her into a conversation.

As if I would.

But then again, Arabella pondered, what if she bumped into Eleanor before she had a chance to ask Max about the idea? What if the right situation presented itself, wouldn't it make sense to seize the opportunity and make Eleanor feel better sooner and at the same time pop the charity question, instead of waiting for Max's approval?

It sure did, she smiled. S*o here's hoping!*

With optimism in her heart, Arabella reviewed the charity matter further. Knowing the kind of person that she, Arabella, was, Eleanor would be a fool to turn the offer down. No charity, no matter how successful, could ever have too many rich supporters on their side. Especially ones like her who come from money on both sides of her family and knew exactly how to get cash from the old-moneyed classes.

Yes, like her, Eleanor also came from money, but unlike Arabella, Eleanor expected everyone with money to have a social conscience and not need to be appealed to in order to give to less fortunate people.

Although she agreed with Eleanor on that point, Arabella was more patient and accommodating of those rich who weren't naturally benevolent because she knew that the money could be gotten from them in the end if one took the time to try.

There we go, a unique niche for me: the limpet.

Arabella prided herself on not only having the required tenacity and time, but also the necessary thick skin. As far as she was concerned, when it came to begging for something that she really wanted, she was insurmountable. Rebuff her though others may try, she always hung on and got her own way. So that, coupled with her knowledge of what made the rich tick, what a force she would be in fundraising from that prospective sector!

Eleanor already had a taste of her potential from when the charity was first set up. As well as both her grandmothers – who were what Arabella called 'competitive givers', that is those who try to outdo their friends and peers in how much they donate to charities – Arabella had convinced other, not so naturally benevolent, contacts to support Eleanor's charity.

Apart from her maternal grandmother – who had died leaving a tidy sum to the charity – the others were still alive and donating. Surely Eleanor would be able to imagine how many more benefactors Arabella could attract to the charity, if it was her remit to do so.

Arabella was already mentally categorizing them: *the tax purposes givers, the competitive givers, the condescenders, the guilt givers* … the list was endless.

Wow, she delighted at the prospects. *This really could be mega.*

Suddenly she was overcome by a sense of guilt. Why hadn't she thought of this before?

Debts.

Yes, but that was a poor excuse. She'd been debt free for the past eight months. So what was her excuse for those wasted months?

There was none.

About to start mentally beating herself up for her past inertia, Arabella remembered Max. 'Leave the past in the past and focus on the future,' he would say.

And rightly so too, she agreed. For what was the point in wasting time and energy on things that are done and you can't change, when you can be working on an improved present and future? Eleanor came back to mind. If only she would see that and give Arabella a chance to explain things and make it up to her.

While on the subject of lost friendship, Arielle flashed into her consciousness. Arabella smiled sadly, _how I miss her too!_

Though harsher on first impressions, Arielle had a soft heart of gold. It was hard not to like her, and Arabella was pleased to have heard that she too was doing well. Like Eleanor, Arielle also had a passion for writing and was now by all accounts also a best-selling novelist like Eleanor. But unlike Eleanor, who chose to operate from sunnier climes, Arielle was keeping herself busy in the Cotswolds penning the constant flow of bestsellers that she did alongside a happy second marriage to an illustrator with whom she had a daughter.

For a second, Arabella tried to imagine herself as a best-selling author like her ex-friends, but was put off by the thought of all the pressures of deadlines and rejections entailed in writing for a living.

Next she tried to imagine herself travelling alongside Eleanor to sometimes dangerous locations to find out the needs of the world's poor and underprivileged, but the thought didn't appeal, either.

No thanks, she grimaced. She had definitely not been born with the constitution for all that palaver. Fundraising was more up her street, especially if the street in question was somewhere hot, safe and filled with all the necessary mod-cons.

Yes, she smiled, _somewhere exotic in the Caribbean would do me nicely_. She and Eleanor were definitely alike in their preference for hot countries.

And talking of sunnier climes, Arabella wondered, _what's happened here?_ Where had the lovely evening rays that had been warming her all the way up from First Avenue gone? She looked up with disappointment at the sun that seemed to be hiding behind a cloud.

It's all these bloody grumpy faces around, she decided. *They've scared it off.*

'I don't blame you,' she told it. 'I wouldn't want to shine on them either.'

With the sun and the devil-may-care attitude that it always inspired in her gone, Arabella lost all enthusiasm for any kind of shopping, especially the purchase of expensive shoes like the pair of Jimmy Choo's she'd seen and had been on her way back to go and buy.

For her, shopping was only enjoyable with a happy frame of mind and somewhere with an optimistic and decadent atmosphere. Hence why she'd never and still didn't understand all the hype about shopping being a great pick-me-up. 'Pick-me-up, my arse,' she'd always jeer. 'Pick yourself up first and then go shopping.'

Arabella believed that people bought better things when they were in a good mood. If you were sad or down, everything felt awful. So logically you'd pick up awful things, you'd look awful in them and then you'd get even sadder. So where was the 'pick-me-up' in all that? That was why all those who knew her knew better than to ask Arabella to come out shopping with them if she was down or if it was a rainy day or a miserable winter evening.

Christmas time was the only exception in winter because of the carols being played everywhere. They made Arabella feel hopeful, expectant and that all was grand in the world for everybody and, if not, would soon be. But that was only if none of the shops that she went into was playing Live Aid's 'Do They Know It's Christmas?'

For Arabella, that song was a shopping trip killer, every time. Once heard, she'd have to go home and reflect.

And that was exactly how she was now feeling amidst this sunless and depressing chaos of cars, buses and unhappy faces on Pine and Third, where the weight of the worries of the whole world seemed to have been piled high upon each passing shoulder.

Tomorrow's another day, Arabella decided and stepped forward to the curb in order to join the hand-waving battle for a taxi.

Having now become fully infected with the general feel of urgency and the impatient malaise of the crowd who were rushing to get home, Arabella, who'd just been beaten to the first vacant taxi she'd seen, rushed across Pine Street to get to a part of Third Avenue where there appeared to be less competition for cabs.

As she stood there in high alert, anxiously awaiting the familiar sight of the big and long sunflower yellow taxis, Arabella noticed a lone figure in jeans, a long, dark summer coat and a blue-coloured floppy velvet hat that would befit a jester. His whole demeanour intrigued her because unlike everybody else, he was stood stock-still, as if in a trance.

Seemingly unaffected and uncontaminated by the must-get-home-quickly buzz of passers-by, he seemed to have created a small clearing around him that inoculated him with a peacefulness that repelled the chaos of the jostling masses who mysteriously side-stepped this space to get to their destinations.

Arabella found herself relaxing as she watched him. After a short while he seemed to come out of the trance, and then like a magician plucking scarves out of an empty mouth or fluffy animals out of top hats, he slowly began to unpack paraphernalia from what looked like thin air, or at least that was what it looked like from where Arabella was standing.

First came a brass music sheet easel, which he erected to face the street, and then came sheets of paper, which were peppered with black hieroglyphics of music. These were carefully placed on the metallic book-shaped rest at the top of the stand and then held in place by clasps that he clicked into position. Next came a hard instrument case.

As Arabella marvelled at how she'd failed to notice all this equipment until they were being arranged into place, the jester-hat man unhurriedly opened the instrument case, revealing a saxophone with which he began to fiddle around. Having apparently achieved whatever it was he had been hoping to achieve with his fiddling, he drew up a small stool from behind him and sat down.

Fidgeting until his bottom slotted into what Arabella assumed to be the most comfortable position, he dragged the still-open instrument case scraping along the paved ground until it reached to just in front of his feet. He was all set now and proved this by unceremoniously drawing the saxophone up to his lips like someone who merely fancied having a go at an instrument that he'd found lying around a friend's place.

As his lips and the instrument met, the most captivating and alluring sound filled the air and hypnotized Arabella's senses. Like a tonic, she felt it gently exorcize the tension of the hustle and bustle around them. Rooted to the spot, she found herself slowly closing her eyes and inhaling the mesmerizing magic of the music, which seemed to caress her soul into total submission.

Suddenly the caress turned into a teasing staccato of highs and lows that brought an involuntary smile of mischief to her heart. Arabella opened her eyes to a glorious summer evening that seemed to promise a lot yet guarantee nothing. A rush of danger-charged excitement coursed through her body as the tiny needle-like rays of the now returned evening sun prickled her pores open and warmed her upwardly turned smiling face.

The hurly-burly of the rush hour had taken on a different feel and no longer affected her in the same way. Instead it appeared to provoke a feeling of recklessness and harmless irresponsibility in her and a nearby couple whom Arabella could have sworn that she had seen also begin to smile with mischief.

Arabella looked around without registering any particular thought other than the fizzes of impulse to start skipping, getting drunk and shopping until she dropped.

As the urge to shop overtook her, she remembered the Jimmy Choo shoes –aquamarine and frivolous – that would be a perfect buy for her present mood, not to mention for adding that certain *je ne sais quoi* to her new empire cut multicoloured chiffon dress. There was no time to waste: she had to get to Nordstrom and buy the shoes immediately before the shop closed.

With a skip in her step, she turned to cross back to the Nordstrom side of the street when she suddenly remembered the musician, the instigator of her happy state of mind. What was she thinking of running off like that without so much as a thank you of some sort? Spinning gaily round, she headed back towards the man and his music.

Before she got to him, he looked up in her direction with a look of recognition of a kindred spirit and a smile that seemed to suggest that he'd been expecting her.

He stopped playing for a second. 'Don't you just love summer evenings?' he remarked casually as she arrived, and with that continued with the piece that he was playing from heart.

'Yes,' she agreed. 'And especially when accompanied by beautiful music. Thank you.' She let drop two crisp twenty dollar bills that fell into his empty saxophone case without interrupting the vibe.

Still smiling and with a twinkle of insouciance in her eyes, Arabella turned to confront whatever else that evening had in store for her with a confidence in her stride that seemed to be challenging the world to *bring it on.*

Chapter Fifteen

It was bound to happen

Thirty minutes after Arabella's encounter with the musician, Eleanor and her two sons pulled up to the nearby Four Seasons Hotel in a taxi. As she hunted for her handbag, first under the white Nordstrom paper bag and then under the crispy thin blue Nordstrom Rack plastic one with its whitish grey writing. The driver clicked off the automatic lock so as to open the doors for his passengers.

To the delight of her sons, who loved crowds and a buzzing atmosphere, the full occupancy of the hotel, plus the time of day and season, meant that there was a rush of people, both in business and casual attire, hastening in and out of the countless taxis. The pavement that ran from the constantly sliding open entrance doors to the public road was abuzz with the commotion of uniformed porters and hotel guests identifying and retrieving luggage and shopping bags.

Still unable to find her handbag, Eleanor turned to Paris. 'Can you stand up a minute, please darling,' she asked him.

The little boy obliged but, unfortunately for his mother, as he did so his chunky dark blue sneakers, with Kickers emblazoned in white on the sides, caught her little toe.

'Ouch,' Eleanor winced, snatching her foot away.

Her sudden movement unbalanced the little boy and sent him reeling back onto the seat and onto his brother's hand, which was rummaging under more bags in search of the missing handbag.

'Watch what you're doing,' Malachi snapped.

Paris became impatient. 'I didn't do it on purpose and you know that,' he protested as his mother ushered him to stand up again. The bag was still nowhere to be found and the little boy was rapidly tiring of being nudged from both sides by his twin and their mother in their search. 'Can I please get out, Mummy,' he beseeched Eleanor.

Glad at the thought of one less body to obstruct her search, she nodded her consent and tilted her knees towards the open door on her right to allow him a freer passage through.

With what looked like more than enough room at his disposal, Paris began to scramble over his mother's uncovered toes to get to the freedom of the pavement. As he did so, he accidentally stepped on her left foot, grinding it into the tattered black rubber mat underfoot.

'Oh, Paris,' Eleanor whimpered and squirmed forward in pain to lift the little boy off her foot and onto the pavement.

Now out of the taxi and without taking into account the two taxis behind theirs and the impact the passengers from them would have on the chaotic hustle and bustle, Paris darted across the pavement, trying to get to the safety of the nearby wall, just as his mother called 'Watch out!'

Her warning had come too late, he had already hurtled into the side of a blonde woman who, having just disembarked from the taxi behind, was breezily weaving between oncoming people on her way towards the hotel entrance.

The impact of his body knocked the white Nordstrom bag from the woman's hand and onto the ground with a thud.

'Oh no,' Eleanor flinched with maternal anguish and lurched forward with open arms as if to catch her rebounding child.

'Don't worry, madame, it eez only a minor accident,' the taxi driver consoled her in a heavy Nigerian accident. 'He eez part Nigerian, after all, so it will take more dan dat to injure him.'

'But he's only a quarter Nigerian,' Malachi piped up, as if that meant less resilience to injury for his brother.

The taxi driver chuckled out loud. 'Don't worry.' He stopped and turned to Malachi, 'What woz your name again?'

'Malachi.'

'Eh hem, dat's it, Malachi. Yes, as I woz saying, Malachi, don't worry, even an eighth of Nigerian blood is enough to sorvive in life.'

As the talkative taxi driver continued his entertaining conversation with Malachi, Eleanor focused her attention on the blushing Paris who was still standing, looking both shocked and guilty as he gawped wide-eyed at the aquamarine shoe that lay peeping out of the bag on the floor.

'Hey, champ,' the blonde woman called out to the grey-eyed, light-skinned little boy who didn't seem to know what to do with himself.

Glancing up, he seemed to instantly recognise her.

'Oh my God, it's Arabella,' Eleanor gasped from the taxi, at the same time as the little boy in indigo-coloured jeans and a denim jacket cried out 'Aunty Arabella,' with relief.

She was the last person Eleanor expected or wanted to see at that moment in time. After her conversation with Max, yes, she was toying with the idea of talking things through with Arabella, but for the present, she was still too angry for it to be anytime soon, let alone this soon. So for now, Eleanor preferred to keep avoiding her ex-friend.

Malachi, who appeared to have been enjoying his banter with the taxi driver, had also been sporadically monitoring his brother's welfare. On hearing the mention of Arabella's name, he became overly excited and seemed to instantly lose interest in his chat with the driver. Before Eleanor had a chance to register what was happening, Malachi was halfway scrambling across her legs.

'Stop right there,' she ordered, catching him by the waist just before he made it out of the door and onto the pavement to join his brother and Arabella.

Aghast with the situation in which she found herself, Eleanor clutched tightly onto the little boy who, dressed in blue shorts, a red t-shirt and a red baseball cap, was dangling midway off her legs and out of the open taxi door, as she prayed that Arabella would walk on after a brief hello to Paris.

As she remained rooted in the same position, Eleanor frantically tried to think of a back-up course of action. It would have been okay if she had the option to refuse to acknowledge her ex-friend, but with Paris and Malachi present, that was out of the question. She didn't want them sensing any friction between her and Arabella because it would lead to far too many awkward questions from her sons, who were now at that age when they wanted to know the ins and outs of everything with their constant barrage of 'but why?'

As no great plan of action was coming to mind, Eleanor decided to bide her time, starting with getting Malachi back into the cab and out of sight. As she dragged him backwards into the taxi, his head brushed against the doorframe, knocking his cap off.

'My cap,' the little boy squealed suddenly to his mother's horror.

Oh God! 'Shush! I'll pick it up for you in a moment.'

'It's okay, I can reach it,' he told her loudly as he began to reach forward for the fallen cap.

Eleanor was mortified. With his wiggling body and mop of loose curls blocking her view of what was happening further away on the curb, all she could do was pray that Arabella hadn't been alerted to their whereabouts.

On cue and as if reading her thoughts, the taxi driver, who had also been following the activities on the pavement, turned to Eleanor with an update. 'Your son seems to know de woman very well. Is she a friend of yours?'

No, Eleanor hissed silently as she leaned back to let Malachi who, having retrieved his cap, was now scrambling back across her lap to his former seat.

'Yes, they're very good friends,' Malachi intercepted as he sat back down. 'My Daddy used to call them the three musketeers.'

'De musketeers,' the driver laughed loudly. 'I like dat. So where is de third one? Is she coming round de corner too?' he guffawed even louder, seemingly delighted by his own wit.

'That'd be so cool, wouldn't it!' the little boy thrilled back. 'But I think Aunty Arielle is back in England.'

'She didn't join de other two musketeers for dis trip?'

'We're not on a group trip,' the little boy informed him.

'I see, but like true musketeers they've ended up in de same hotel. So we can safely say dat great minds tink alike.'

'I don't know if Aunty Arabella is staying here at the hotel. I hope so, though…'

I jolly well hope not, Eleanor, who'd been keeping a watchful eye on what was happening on the sidewalk while trying to will Arabella on her way, huffed silently.

'… But I guess they must think a lot alike because Aunty Arabella's shoes that Paris knocked out of her hand are the same as a pair that my mum bought this afternoon.'

Big mouth, Eleanor thought and then peeped out to see for herself, but the bag that had been knocked to the sidewalk had already been picked up and was now being carried by Paris.

Oh God, Paris, Eleanor groaned. *Give her back the bloody bag.*

As if sensing his mother's attention, Paris looked round. Spying Arabella following her son's glance with her gaze, Eleanor ducked down and pretended to resume her search for her handbag under the shopping bags on the floor.

The taxi driver continued his conversation with Malachi. 'It seems dat ladies all over de world can never stop buying shoes,' he remarked.

'Expensive ones like my Mum's?'

'Malachi?'

'Yes, Mummy.'

'Will you please stop spreading my business about town.'

'But –'

Eleanor glared up at him. 'Please, stop.' The little boy fell silent to his mother's clearly visible relief. Exhaling loudly, she forced a smile. 'Now, please help me find my handbag.' And with that she resumed her forage.

No sooner had her search begun again than Arabella's voice rang out. 'Where's the other champ and your mother?'

Eleanor froze. *God please. God plea –*

'Over there in the taxi,' the little boy divulged.

'Shit,' Eleanor cursed out loud.

'Ah! Mummy,' Malachi gasped, swinging round quickly to regard his mother with shock and disapproval. 'That's naughty,' he chastised her loudly and in so doing unwittingly confirmed which taxi his brother had been referring to.

Eleanor clenched her eyes tightly shut in a futile last-ditch attempt to wish herself out of this nightmare of a situation, but there was no point, the nightmare was about to get worse and instinctively she knew it.

'Malachi,' Arabella's voice cried out in recognition.

Immediately and as if in reflex action, Eleanor grabbed hold of her son's foot.

'Ouch,' he cried out.

Eleanor quickly let go.

'You scratched me,' the child whined.

'Not on purpose.'

'I know, but it still hurt.'

'I'm sorry.'

'Awe,' Arabella cooed.

Oh shut up, Arabella! Eleanor had no choice now but to sit up and attend to her son. Pretending to be still oblivious of Arabella's presence in the vicinity, she began to fuss over Malachi. 'Did I scratch you badly, my love?' she asked him.

'Not too badly,' the good-natured little boy admitted. 'I think you startled me more than anything when you grabbed me instead of the bag.'

'Oh, I'm sorry,' Eleanor said genuinely. She hadn't meant to grab him so roughly and was now concerned that she may have actually hurt him. 'Let me take a look at it,' she told her son and leant over to inspect his foot.

Paris, who'd overheard what was being said as he and Arabella approached the cab, seemed to become concerned by the goings on in the taxi. 'Is he okay?' he asked his mother on his arrival at the cab door.

'Yes, he's fine,' she called out.

To which Arabella suggested, 'Why don't I help you bring out the bags and then you can bring him out to have a better look?'

With teeth clenched tightly, Eleanor sat up quickly. 'Thanks, but …' *Why don't you just get lost and leave us alone,* '… that won't be necessary.'

But Arabella wasn't listening, she was too excited. Since the day Max telephoned two-and-a-half months earlier asking for reconciliation, her mantra had become 'carpe diem.' And seize this day – and this opportunity – she most certainly was going to. How often was it that a daydream turned into reality in less than an hour? It had never for her, as far as she could recall. So this had to be a sign.

Quickly enlisting Paris' help, Arabella was soon reaching down by Eleanor's feet to get out the nearest bags to the door.

'No,' Eleanor ordered with a fixed smile that didn't mask the malice in her eyes. Paris flashed her a worried look.

Noticing him, Eleanor quickly softened her gaze. *Oh no, darling, it's not you,* she tried to tell him with her amended expression.

As well as being someone who was usually direct and often said what was on her mind, Eleanor was also one who communicated a lot with her eyes, especially with her inner circle, and her sons had learnt that.

Whenever they were out and confronted with an awkward situation, all they had to do was look at their mother's eyes. The instructions were always clear: 'yes, you may take the sweet or toy from that person' or 'no, you may not' or 'you're getting too boisterous now, sit still' or 'try and be friendlier.' Whatever she had to tell them, her eyes said it all.

Although this form of communication usually worked well, there were instances of misinterpretation, like now, when an innocent party would receive a message meant for another.

For that reason, Eleanor had no choice but to desist from her non-verbal communication while her son was in the line of fire. Her lips parted into a wide, disingenuous smile.

'Hi, Arabella.'

'Eleanor,' the blond woman cooed without malice. 'You look fab.'

'So do you.' Eleanor meant it: everything about Arabella looked so vibrant, fresh, and full of life. From her now dead straight, recently-dyed blonde hair, which stood out in stark contrast to the chic black trilby hat that she was wearing with an emerald green silk scarf wound stylishly around it, to her bright-as-a-button hazel eyes that seemed larger than Eleanor remembered them to be.

As the women exchanged harassed pleasantries, Arabella regarded her ex-friend with wide unblinking eyes that housed a mixture of terror, a steely will to overcome the terror and childlike delight at finally realising her recent daydream of coming face to face with Eleanor. Especially in a situation like this, that would hopefully deny Eleanor the ability to react in a manner that she may have were they on their own.

The look in Arabella's eyes seemed to demand a response. Eleanor held her gaze in a manner that seemed to say 'stop trying; you'll never win me over'. To which Arabella appeared defiant.

'I'm not giving up', her smile seemed to suggest.

The driver, who'd been watching them as well as sizing up other potential clients as they came out from the hotel, interrupted them suddenly. 'Oh no,' he grumbled loudly. 'Dat was an airport job dat should have been mine. Ladies, please, I don't mean to rush you, but man must wok.'

'Of course,' both women chorused as Arabella once again, without invitation, leant into the taxi and began taking control.

'Malachi, please grab the bags on the floor to your left. Paris, here, hang on to these,' she said, passing the little boy a couple of bags that she'd picked up off the floor of the cab by Eleanor's feet.

'My bag,' Eleanor cried with joy as it fell out of one of the bags that Arabella was in the process of retrieving before she moved onto clearing out more shopping bags from the front of the cab.

As his passengers busied themselves with gathering the rest of their belongings from the back of his cab, the taxi driver, having resumed his amiable disposition, occupied himself with overseeing Arabella's activities at the front, shepherding her with instructions. 'You've missed de green one, be careful, everyting is emptying out of de red one ...' Finally, he relaxed and announced, 'dat eez it, all done now.'

As she stepped away from the cab and back on to the pavement where Paris and Malachi now stood waiting with all the stuff from the taxi, a flushed-looking Arabella began to gather as many bags as she could carry in both hands. 'Wow, you've certainly been shopping, haven't you?' she chirped as she did so.

Eleanor stared at her in disbelief. *What are you doing?* she demanded with a flash of an eye. But Arabella carried on, undeterred.

Had Paris and Malachi not been present, Eleanor would definitely have snatched the bags off her and quickly put an end to the charade, but she couldn't. Her only option was to smile coldly and ask Arabella to 'please just leave the bags where they are.'

To which Arabella replied, 'It's okay, I don't mind helping.'

I do, Eleanor frowned. 'Don't, Arabella, please.'

'It's no bother.'

'Arabella,' Eleanor's tired but firm voice insisted.

'Oh, you sound tired.'

'What?'

'You sound tired.'

'Yes, I am,' *Of you, so now piss off.*

'Den allow your friend to assist you,' the taxi driver, who seemed in a rush to get going on his way, interjected in a loud voice as he counted out Eleanor's change. With such a public intervention from him, Eleanor had no choice but to desist from trying to stop Arabella from helping with the bags.

Looking Heaven-ward, she invoked divine intervention with a silent prayer: *Holy Spirit, please take control.*

Chapter Sixteen

Hey, is anybody up there?

Eleanor, who'd purposely been lagging behind to avoid getting into conversation with Arabella, looked up and noticed that, having arrived at the sliding doors, the leading trio were now waiting for her to catch up. Reluctantly she quickened her step and caught up with them. As she followed them through the doors and into the foyer, a porter intercepted them. It was the man who'd helped her and her sons take their bags up to their suite after they'd checked in on their arrival at the hotel a couple of days ago.

'May I take those to your room for you, ma'am?' he offered.

Casting a fleeting glance upward to the ceiling, Eleanor smiled. *Thank you God.* With the bags gone, Arabella would have no further excuse for hanging around. Unable to contain her delight, she turned, still smiling, to the porter. 'Yes, please,' she replied, eagerly handing him all the bags in her hands, except a small calico rucksack that she swung on top of her handbag that was on her shoulder. Retrieving a small card from her denim skirt pocket, she discreetly flashed the porter a reminder of her room number.

After this, turning to her sons, she pointed at the bags in their hands. 'And these too, please,' she told the beige-uniformed man, who had by now dragged up a nearby gold and black luggage wheeled carrier and was placing her bags onto it.

As he took the few bags that the little boys had been carrying, Eleanor relieved Arabella of those she was carrying for them. For the first time since their paths had crossed that evening, Eleanor flashed her ex-friend a genuine smile. 'Thanks for your help,' she told her. 'Good luck with everything.' *And may this be the last I see of you again.*

'Mummy,' Paris interrupted her. 'Remember you promised we could have those hamburgers we like from over there,' he concluded, pointing towards the slightly raised area in front to their right, where people could be seen sitting and having evening cocktails and snacks.

'Oh, those hamburgers,' Arabella drooled. 'They're fab, aren't they?'

What? Eleanor eyed her. 'How do you know?'

'I've had them a few times.'

'Oh,' Eleanor said, trying to sound more nonchalant than she was feeling. 'So you come here quite often then, do you?'

'You could say that.'

Eleanor tensed up even more. She knew Arabella too well. 'Meaning?'

'I'm staying here.'

Oh my God. Eleanor looked upwards. *I meant help me get rid of her, not move her in.* 'Since when?'

'Oh, since I got here, a week ago.'

'I see,' Eleanor frowned involuntarily. *And Max said nothing about that yesterday, when he brought us back.*

'What about the apartment? Max mentioned some-thing about you two renting one.'

'Yes, I've been looking for one for us,' Arabella confirmed. 'And I think I may have found it today.'

Yay. 'Thank God.'

'Mummy,' the twins frowned.

'What?' From the look on her sons' faces it was clear to Eleanor that she'd been a bit too enthusias-tic with her delight than was deemed polite. 'Thank God that her search is over,' she attempted to explain. 'House hunting is not a pleasant experience, is it?' she eyed Arabella.

'Noo,' her ex-friend exaggerated for the benefit of the boys. 'Some places? Ew!'

Alright, drama queen! Eleanor frowned. 'So you see, that's why I'm happy she's found somewhere nice that she likes.' *Not near here, or the house, I hope.* Keeping in mind that her sons' watchful eyes were monitoring her every expression, or so it seemed, Eleanor forced a larger-than-life smile. 'So, where's this lovely new home you've found?' she asked.

'I'm hungry,' Malachi suddenly interjected.

'Oh, darling, yes, of course, we better …' Eleanor began and then stopped. 'Arabella,' she shrugged with a well-feigned regretful expression. 'The kids have to eat, so…' *On your bike.* 'Once again, good to see you and –'

'Yes, of course.'

'But,' Malachi frowned. 'Aren't you coming with?'

'We mustn't impose on her any further.'

'Are we?' Paris cut in with a sad face.

'Never,' Arabella beamed down at him.

'Good,' he smiled back. 'So you'll have hamburg-ers with us?'

No, Eleanor almost barked out loud. *God, please, where are you? What happened to 'Seek and ye shall find. Knock and it shall be opened unto you'? I'm knocking, I'm seeking, I'm begging, help me. Sort this situation out for me, please? Once and for all.* She noticed that all eyes were focused on her. 'Yes?'

'Make Aunty Arabella come with us, please,' Malachi pleaded.

No, let her go away. 'Arabella?' Eleanor asked with eyes that seemed to be pleading for cooperation.

'Only if I won't be intruding.'

You will be and you know it ... 'No.' *So shove off.*

'Great, then I don't mind if I do, thank you.'

'What?'

'She said yes, yay,' the twins cried for joy in unison and hurried their mother ahead with them to secure a table for four.

What the ... bitch! 'Great,' an evidently bewildered Eleanor gawped back at Arabella with eyes that were clearly asking *why are you playing me like this?*

As Arabella followed behind the boys and their mother, she fell pensive. *What a stroke of luck, bumping into them like that,* she thought. *And now burgers and chips: result!* Remembering how hard and often she'd prayed for such an opportunity, she looked Heavenward. *Thank you,* she smiled. And with any luck, by the end of the evening, they'd be friends again, like she'd also been praying for. 'Remember?' she asked God, with another flash of a glance at the ceiling.

Chapter Seventeen

It's in the aura of a woman

In preparation for what was to come, Arabella made the sign of the cross. She wasn't a Catholic like Eleanor, but she'd seen her and other Catholic friends do it often enough in the past, whenever they were concerned about or hoping for something, so for Arabella it was worth a try. *Surely they wouldn't resort to it as often as they did if it didn't work?*

Also, as God seemed to be smiling on her at present, it was worth keeping Him on side by maintaining the prayers, she reasoned.

But just in case, Arabella reconsidered and brought out her mobile phone. *I'll call for back-up. Max seems to have a better way with Eleanor these days.*

With her eyes trained on the three ahead, who were now being escorted by a grumpy-looking waiter towards a table for four in the almost fully occupied bar and restaurant that stood centre stage in the foyer of the hotel, Arabella dialled Max's number, which to her dismay went straight to voicemail.

Typical, she grumbled, just as she noticed the other three stop en route. *Shit, they're waiting for me,* she assumed when she spied Paris looking around as if for her. Raising her hand, Arabella began to wave in the air until he spotted her. Pointing to the phone in her other hand, she implied that she was having a conversation on it.

The little boy acknowledged her with a nod, but did not say anything to his mother. Spotting Eleanor stuffing Malachi's red baseball cap into her bag then resume walking, Arabella realised that her absence hadn't been noticed by anyone except Paris and that may have probably only been because he'd turned round to take in his surroundings when they'd paused for his mother to put away the cap.

Looking a little dejected, Arabella pressed the mobile phone back to her ear and listened for Max's voice to finish speaking so she could leave him a message. As she was doing so, Arabella kept her eyes trained on Eleanor and the boys, watching as they weaved past the first table occupied by two business attired men who appeared deeply engrossed in what Arabella assumed to be a serious work conversation. Although she couldn't make his face out clearly because he was looking down at some papers on the table, the one facing towards her looked familiar for some reason.

Déjà vu, Arabella decided, dismissing the thought from her mind. She'd only been in Seattle for just over a week now and knew nobody here, so it was hardly likely that she knew this man. She shifted her gaze back to Eleanor and the boys.

They were now approaching a second table which was encircled by similarly patterned blue and white floral armchairs like the ones on which the two men were sitting at the previous table. At this second table, there was a man and a woman sharing a bottle of white wine. Casually dressed and looking on particularly familiar terms, Arabella labelled them as holidaying lovers or pre-date drinkers.

Eleanor and the boys had barely reached the table when the couple glanced up at them. Arabella assumed that Eleanor must have smiled because the woman flashed what looked like a reciprocal smile, as she followed Eleanor with her eyes.

Arabella noticed the man sitting with the woman doing the same, except that his look lingered that bit too long. *Hardly polite behaviour for someone in company of a date.*

Just then it became apparent to Arabella that he wasn't the only one. Other diners, too, were paying particular attention to Eleanor as she and the twins followed the waiter through the centre of the restaurant and towards a large navy blue and white sofa, which along with two similarly upholstered armchairs and a large coffee table, formed a semi-circle at the end of the seating area.

Arabella smiled to herself. She'd forgotten how often that happened whenever Eleanor came into a room. Now that she'd remembered, she couldn't help but to wonder again why that was. What was it about the woman that commanded such attention?

Yes, there could be no denying that Eleanor was nice looking, but how come she caused more of a stir than far better looking women? As she pondered this, Arabella's gaze drifted back to the first table with the two men in business attire. They were the only ones it seemed, not to have been affected by Eleanor. Why was that?

Just then the blonde man, who'd seemed familiar, looked up. Arabella instantly recognised him to be Thorsten, the Cort look-alike German from the airport.

Oh my word, she beamed, w*hat a small world.* As she considered the odds of her bumping into two of the only three people she knew in Seattle within minutes of each other, she remembered her thought at the airport: that, based on their similar wit and sense of humour, Eleanor and Thorsten would make a good couple if they were ever to meet. Her smile broadened with hope. Was today going to be that day? And if it was, what would they make of each other?

She didn't have to wonder for long with regards to Thorsten, because just then she noticed him notice Eleanor. *Down boy,* Arabella teased silently as his thoughts clearly registered in the expression on his face.

Wow, Thorsten thought to himself as he suddenly caught sight of the good-looking black woman just as she was turning back to face the direction in which she was walking. *When did she go by?* he wondered, but stopped suddenly on noticing that the man sitting opposite him was no longer speaking, but instead was casting him a questioning glance.

'Ja, absolutely,' Thorsten quickly interjected. 'I was wondering about that,' he added as if to sound more convincing.

'Yes, many of our customers do wonder, that's why I brought it up,' the man smiled, seemingly content that adequate attention was being paid to him and his spiel.

At that moment, Eleanor turned to answer a question Paris had just asked. With the man opposite him back on his sales pitch, Thorsten's attention returned to her. He saw her face fully for the first time.

Those eyes, Thorsten marvelled, s*o black and –* Eleanor's gaze swept past him *– powerful,* he concluded. Even though she hadn't looked directly at him, the power in her eyes felt such that Thorsten imagined she could read anyone's mind with a mere glance.

Not that it'd be hard to do in this room almost full of men, he smiled with a flash of a glance about. From the looks he could see on many of their faces, Thorsten was confident that most of the other men were thinking the same thing as him about this woman. *Nice package.* Returning his attention to her, Thorsten allowed his gaze to survey Eleanor from head to foot.

Ja, he nodded approvingly, *definitely a nice package. Very, very sensual, but not in a sluttish or overpowering sort of way. I bet women hate her, though,* he mused. Glancing round, he quickly reviewed the looks from the other three women he could see present. There was not a trace of bitchiness in the way any of them regarded Eleanor.

How unusual, he decided and resumed his observation of her. As Thorsten watched Eleanor speaking to the little boys behind her, he noticed her lips. Like her obvious and alluring sensuality that was incongruously as unintimidating as the girl next door, her lips also stirred up a paradox of emotions in him.

On the one hand, although they made Thorsten fantasize about ravaging them in that wildly lustful and passionate one-night-stand sort of way, he was at the same time sitting there daydreaming about kissing them tenderly in that longing and forever kind of manner one kisses someone you never want to let go.

Mm, Thorsten smiled, he could almost taste them. As he imagined their warmth, he noticed the man at the table beside his begin to lick his lips as he too eyed up Eleanor.

Hey, stop that, Thorsten frowned.

Seeming to become aware of being watched, the man looked round. Their eyes met. The man smiled. Thorsten smiled back reproachfully. *Ja, I see you,* he nodded, *so stop.*

The man with whom Thorsten was supposed to be engaged in a business meeting, spying this exchange of glances quickly took advantage of Thorsten's reduced attention to him and glanced at his watch. The time was thirty-five after six.

'Do you have any further questions on this matter before we move onto the next topic?' he asked Thorsten.

Pardon? Thorsten frowned.

'Any questions?'

Ah. 'No, none at all,' Thorsten blushed.

'And your previous objection has been adequately handled?'

'Ja, absolutely.'

'So now for the real business,' the man drawled enthusiastically in a strong southern accent.

Hm, interesting accent, Thorsten mused, *Texan maybe?* Prior to now, he hadn't noticed that the man with whom he'd been sitting for the past two hours and a half had an accent, let alone such a pronounced one. Thorsten realised that this meant that his interest in their conversation must have waned; otherwise he would never have noticed the man's accent, except maybe at the end when they would have been rounding off their discussion with a drink perhaps.

He tried to be courteous and refocus his mind on what they were there for. From what the man said, he had to be in the final lap of his presentation, so the end wouldn't be long now in coming. But Thorsten couldn't get Eleanor out of his mind. He wished he could meet her properly. But how?

Just then the two little boys with Eleanor caught his attention. *Are they her sons?* Thorsten wondered. There was a resemblance. Or was it his imagination? he mused as he momentarily regarded the man making the presentation.

Glancing in their direction again, Thorsten scrutinised the little boys, who at that moment seemed to be quibbling over something. *Ja, there's a strong resemblance, especially with the shorter-haired boy,* Thorsten noted. *She must be their mother,* he speculated unenthusiastically as the possibility that she was hence probably married and out of bounds dawned on him. He wasn't a practicing Catholic, but that was one part of his religion that he completely agreed with. *Thou shall not covet another man's wife.*

She may not be another man's wife, something in him piped up. She could be divorced. *Hm,* Thorsten frowned. The issue of divorce was something else on which he was totally in agreement with the Catholic ethos.

She could be widowed, another thought speculated.

No, Thorsten thought, rejecting both ideas. *She's too young to be a widow. And who would divorce a woman like that?*

No sane man, perhaps, but, Thorsten shrugged, *not every man is sane all the time,* he concluded with himself in mind for having gone against his friends' and family's better judgement and stayed with his now ex-fiancee, Nadine, for as long as he had. What had possessed him, he wondered. Firstly for not noticing how obviously mentally unbalanced she was and then for still proposing to her even after he was beginning to sense that all wasn't well with her?

Becoming aware of the silence around him, Thorsten turned back to the man who had been trying to make the presentation to him. He'd stopped speaking again.

Scheisse! 'I'm so sorry,' Thorsten apologised. 'But I have suddenly developed a big headache and I cannot concentrate.'

'Oh, I see.' The man didn't look impressed. 'Shall we try and get you some painkillers or something?'

'No, I'll get some later.'

'Are you okay for us to go on?'

Thorsten sneaked a peek at his watch. *Nein, it cannot be that late!* He looked at the time again. It was that late. 'No, I'm not okay to go on,' he announced. At the rate this man was going it would be a good few more hours before they concluded, and there was no way he could pretend to concentrate for that long.

Besides, Thorsten mused, he didn't have much free time left anyway. By six forty-five, some newly acquired friends were supposed to be coming here to meet him for the start of a night out that he was badly in need of after the terrible week of vicious arguments that he'd been having over the telephone with Nadine. He was still in the process of breaking up with her, even though he'd been making his feeling clear for the past two months that for him their relationship was over and there could be no reconciliation ever. 'Let's reschedule,' Thorsten decided finally.

The man looked disappointed.

'I'm sorry,' Thorsten said unapologetically. 'But if you had not postponed the meeting until so late in the day, we would have been okay. As it is, I've had a very busy and long day and I cannot do this anymore.'

A look of concern lodged in the man's expression. 'You're still interested in our possible collaboration, though, aren't you?' he asked.

'*Ja*, sure.'

The man looked unconvinced.

Beginning to smile, Thorsten tried to reassure him. 'Look, I'm German,' he told him. 'So I'm not in the habit of wasting my words. If I say interested, it means that I am definitely interested.'

The man leaned back in his seat with a look of relief. 'Your word is good enough for me, sir,' he told Thorsten. 'And I'm looking forward to doing business witcha.'

'Wait a minute!' Thorsten cried. 'I did not say that I am interested in doing business with you. I said I am interested in hearing more about your terms should my client decide to buy from you.'

'I hear you, sir.'

'*Gut*, so call me on Monday and we will talk schedules. *Ja?*' Thorsten smiled.

'Yes, sir.'

'Thank you for your time.' And with that Thorsten rose to his feet with his right handed extended for their goodbye handshake.

Taking the cue, the man gathered his papers and then, also rising to his feet, took hold of Thorsten's hand in a firm shake. 'Thank you again, sir, and I look forward to meeting witcha as early as possible next week.'

'Have a *gut* weekend,' Thorsten nodded.

With the man departing, Thorsten began to sit back down. As he did so, a burst of laughter attracted his attention. It was coming from the direction of Eleanor and the boys. Thorsten looked towards them. It was the waiter laughing and looking completely charmed by Eleanor.

She's funny too, he noted and resigned himself to admiring this great and seemingly well-rounded package from afar.

Chapter Eighteen

Watching you, watching her

During all of this, unbeknownst to Thorsten, Arabella was watching him watching Eleanor and wishing that she could be privy to his thoughts, so she could know exactly what had him so obviously captivated by Eleanor.

What was it about her looks that seemed to have him fascinated? Was it those oval-shaped eyes that she'd once heard described as sparkling like multi-faceted onyx?

Recalling Eleanor's eyes, Arabella smiled to herself. Yes, they were definitely 'multi-faceted' alright, in the way they would – depending on the thoughts flashing through Eleanor's mind – dazzle with euphoria, crinkle into warm and toasty empathy, or contort with rage. Or just simply stare at you, deep and unfathomable, making you feel vulnerable, as if she could read your innermost thoughts. There could be no denying that there was something enigmatic about Eleanor's eyes that compelled one's attention.

But what was it that made people look twice at her before they'd had a chance to notice her eyes or her cute, almost flat nose or her full, sensual lips?

It had to be something beyond the aesthetic allure of a pretty face and a great figure. But what?

Arabella scrutinised Eleanor, who at the moment appeared to be settling another minor dispute between her sons.

Maybe it's the confidence in her stride or her unique sense of style, Arabella wondered as her eyes surveyed Eleanor's clothes, from her exotic necklace of thickly entwined strings of chunky blue and brown wooden balls that perfectly followed the neckline of her short blue and brown caftan-style top.

So perfectly tailored to her shape was the caftan that it curved to an end at her hips, on which was balanced her long denim skirt, with its slits on either side that went as far up as her knees to where the brown laces of her soft leather sandals had been tied.

Hardly what I'd call a come-hither outfit, Arabella decided and ruled out Eleanor's outfit as the attraction today.

So what was it about then, she wondered, that gave Eleanor such presence, which got both men and women's eyes flashing with recognition of something that merited a prolonged glance?

Take the German, for instance, Arabella mused after having kept a watchful eye on him throughout his surveillance of her ex-friend. *Look at him. From the moment he clapped eyes on her, he's been unable to focus on anything else.*

Arabella analysed the way Thorsten was still looking at Eleanor. There was desire in his expression, but not lust. She watched him some more. *Hm!* He was looking at Eleanor like he genuinely wanted to get to know her better.

Arabella smiled mischievously. *But would she like to get to know you and will we ever find out?*

Just then the waiter with Eleanor and the boys laughed loudly, attracting Arabella's attention. She noticed that even the old sour-faced waiter had been charmed. Arabella marvelled at this: the man looked like he had never cracked a smile since the day he was born and never would until the day he died. Yet there he was now, all thirty-two pearls aglow. *How does she do it?*

Just then Arabella's phone began to ring. It was Max returning her call.

'Hello, you,' she answered.

'What's up?' he replied.

'I bumped into Eleanor and the kids,' she told him.

'Uh huh.'

'And I'm about to have hamburgers with them.'

'Great. Where?'

'Here at the hotel.' She glanced over at Eleanor and the kids. They were settling in at the table. 'Is this where you dropped them off yesterday?' Arabella asked Max.

'Yup.'

'So how come you didn't tell me that they were staying here too?'

'I thought it best to say nothing to either of you, lest she ran aground or you tried to ambush her.'

'Ambush her, indeed,' Arabella laughed.

'I know you,' Max accused. 'And so I thought it best to let life take its course and Eleanor get her space.'

Arabella laughed harder. 'Well, I'm happy to say it's taken its course right into my path, as I got out of the taxi not too long ago.'

'And all without you pushing.' Max sounded happy. 'How did the hamburgers come up?' he enquired.

'Well,' Arabella began to squirm.

'Oh no!'

'Calm down, I didn't have to push much.'

'Oh boy!' Max groaned. Pushing was pushing – be it much or not much – and that was what he'd specifically asked Arabella not to do with Eleanor. And exactly what he'd suspected she would do, hence why he'd refrained from telling her that Eleanor and the boys were staying at the same hotel.

From what he was beginning to remember about Arabella, she had a bad habit of never leaving things well alone. The word restraint didn't feature in her psyche. Whatever she wanted or felt like doing had to be addressed immediately, without due consideration of others' feelings or holding back for even a moment's calm assessment. Everything had to fall into place now if that was what Arabella so desired. She was always in a rush, it seemed.

Max sighed ominously. This was an aspect of her character that he'd forgotten about and which was already beginning to wear on him. It was bothersome, yet bearable enough at a distance, but up close as he'd been experiencing over the past week, at a time when his life was busy and tense and he could only accommodate easiness and calm: *I ain't digging it.*

Anyways, he exhaled noisily, *I'd better get over there right away.* 'I'm done here,' he told Arabella. 'So I'll see you guys shortly. Okay?'

'Okay.' Arabella could sense the tension in Max's voice and she didn't understand it. What had she done wrong, apart from maybe give things a little nudge in the right direction? And besides, Max would soon be here, so what on earth was he imagining that she could do wrong in the time left to her?

Chapter Nineteen

I remember you well

On spotting Arabella coming up the second of the two steps that led up into the dining and drinking arena, Eleanor watched her. She had to raise her hat to the woman for her persistence. Like always, she'd got her own way. But now what?

She knew what Arabella was hoping would happen, but how was she envisaging achieving it? Eleanor wondered. Had Arabella forgotten what she'd said about T.J. at his funeral? Had she forgotten about Eleanor's less than amicable feelings towards her since? Or did she just think that, by her mere presence, she could somehow bypass them or, better yet, make Eleanor forget about them?

Eleanor shook her head at the gall of the approaching woman. Nonetheless, she decided, a challenging smile beginning to creep across her face, whatever it was that Arabella had in mind should be entertaining. *Especially seeing as how she seems to have forgotten that I can be as wilful, if not more, than she is. I can be persistent when I want to be, like now.*

On thinking this, Eleanor regarded her sons lovingly. If only Arabella knew how much she owed to them. Paris and Malachi loved Arabella so much that Eleanor couldn't bring herself to deny them the enjoyment that they seemed to get out of being around her. And that was the only reason why Eleanor was going through with this charade of a supper.

Yes, Eleanor could have insisted that Arabella wouldn't be having hamburgers with them, but not only would it have brought on questions from her sons, but it would also have stirred up grumpiness, which was never a good thing just before bedtime.

On cue, Arabella arrived at the table. 'Sorry, but I needed to make an urgent call,' she lied unnecessarily as she struggled to pull back the armchair closest to Eleanor.

Neither of her fan club of two seemed particularly interested in her explanation; the game needed attention.

'You can't go again, it's my go,' Paris complained.

Eleanor intervened. 'Malachi,' she growled gently, rebuking the little boy who was sitting nearest to her.

'I'm not cheatin –'

'Malachi,' his mother repeated knowingly.

'Okay, okay,' the little boy conceded with a guilty grin that confirmed what he was up to. Grudgingly he pushed aside the napkin. 'I'm bored of playing this all the time anyhow,' he complained.

'So play something else,' his mother suggested.

'But Paris won't.' Catching sight of Arabella, Malachi stopped speaking and began to smile expectantly up at the newly arrived. 'You wanna play Connect 4 with me?' he asked her.

Arabella seemed unsure. 'Paris?' she checked.

'I don't like Connect 4,' he replied.

Arabella turned to Eleanor.

Yes, make yourself useful. 'Go ahead,' she told her. 'I'll continue this game with Paris.'

'Great,' Paris beamed and waited for his mother to have her go now that he'd had his. As she leaned over his twin to reach the napkin, a thought occurred to Paris.

'Why don't you switch places with Mummy?' he suggested to his brother.

'Good thinking, Batman,' Malachi agreed. Standing quickly, he hurried round the table to the other side of his mother who, delighted at an excuse not to have to sit so close to her ex-friend, had already grabbed her handbag and the cream-coloured rucksack from the floor and was sliding left to make room for him to sit in between her and Arabella.

As her child took his place on the other side of her, Eleanor began her search for the Connect 4, which she found in the first searched of the four outside pockets of the rucksack. Having been lodged in at an awkward angle, the game was proving difficult to retrieve. Eleanor focused on the job in hand. Wriggling her index finger into the pocket, she hooked it into one of the holes on the game and began to draw it out slowly.

The waiter returned. 'Ready to order?' he asked.

Eleanor glanced up absent-mindedly at him and they exchanged smiles of recognition.

'Ready to order?' he checked again with her, as finally easing the plastic stand of the game out of the pocket; she placed it on the table in front of Malachi.

Eleanor nodded and then flashed Arabella a questioning look.

'Yes, yes,' she replied hastily and then turned to look at the twins. 'Burgers all round?' she thrilled.

'Yeah,' came the rapturous response.

Her ex-friend's apparent ease with the boys softened Eleanor's resolve. *Arabella's a great mixer,* she had to admit, *the perfect partner in crime for all ages.*

As the thought crossed her mind, Eleanor noticed her sons do something they'd never done with anyone else: they included Arabella in their hand-holding ritual of fit-to-burst excitement at the anticipated yumminess of the burgers to come.

Since they were old enough to sit up, whenever the boys were excited about something, they'd reach out, hold each other's hands, close their eyes, and shudder with glee. No one else, not even their mother or father when he was alive, had ever been invited to join in, let alone been initiated in, as Malachi had just done with Arabella when he'd instinctively reached out and taken hold of her hand at the same time as Paris had stretched across his mother's lap and taken hold of Malachi's other hand.

The sight of this saddened Eleanor, not because she hadn't been included, but because she felt that her sons were choosing the wrong ally.

'Drinks?' the waiter interrupted, redirecting all attention back to him.

'Orange jui –'

'No, Paris, you know it doesn't agree with you,' his mother intercepted.

'It does,' the little boy fibbed.

Eleanor eyed him with a patient smile. 'It doesn't, darling,' she insisted. 'It gives you phlegm like it does me and Malachi.'

'Not anymore.'

'Come on, Paris, pick something else,' she urged him.

'But I like orange juice.'

'You also like apple juice,' his mother reminded him.

'Not as much.'

'Yes, you do,' Malachi intervened. 'Especially when Mummy adds sparkling water and it's all fizzy. We both do, remember?'

'Yes, that's true. Thank you, Malachi.'

Paris scowled at his brother.

'But you do,' Malachi cried in defence of his interference.

'So?' snapped Paris, ungratefully.

'So, you might as well get that cos she'll never let you have the orange juice.'

Ignoring her sons' bickering, Eleanor returned her attention to the waiter. 'Two apple juices, a bottle of sparkling water, and two empty glasses please.'

'Any –'

'Oh, and no ice, please.'

'And yourselves?' the waiter asked, looking from Eleanor to Arabella.

Eleanor paused for thought. Normally she would have had the same as the boys, but for some reason, for the first time in ages, she really fancied having some alcohol.

'Bolly?' Arabella interjected as if reading her thoughts.

Eleanor smiled involuntarily: it'd been ages since she'd heard that familiar word.

'Go on,' Arabella urged her. 'For old times' sake.'

It sounded like a good idea. 'Oh,' Eleanor deliberated, with the words *old times' sake* gnawing at the gut of her emotions for a reaction. The old times were definitely great and fun filled...*but they're gone now.*

She glanced over at Arabella, and to her surprise, her ex-friend had that mischievous smile on her face that Eleanor remembered oh so well. *Okay, so maybe not everything was gone from those days,* she conceded.

The expression on Arabella's face took Eleanor back years, to when they were living in Singapore. Eleanor felt her heart begin to relax into a smile – *the good old days* – when Arabella was adept at enlisting her as an accomplice in whatever mischief that had suddenly come to her mind. As Arielle was a harder conscript, Arabella would always begin with Eleanor. The temptation was usually started with that smile and then followed up with –

'Go on, be a devil.'

'Oh my God,' Eleanor laughed out loud. 'You never change, do you?' *Thank God,* an errant thought celebrated, causing Eleanor's heart to wince with guilt. She was supposed to be still feeling resentment towards this woman, but her naturally mischievous soul was finding it hard to resist the temptation of a like spirit. Eleanor felt torn.

'You know you want to,' Arabella tempted her further.

'I do, but –'

'She doesn't drink alcohol,' Malachi butted in, as if on behalf of his mother's better sense.

Arabella looked as if she'd been struck physically. 'What?' she cried. 'Since when?'

'Since them,' Eleanor informed her, trying to muster up her disenchantment with Arabella.

'That's a lie,' the blonde woman accused.

'A fib,' Paris corrected her. 'And no, she's not fibbing.'

'But you used to drink after they were born. I remember clearly all of us sitting on your beach drinking.'

Yes, Eleanor smiled as the memory of those times began to replay in her mind's eye. She could see it all now, clearly. *They were great times,* she recalled. And yes, she too was drinking. 'But only a glass or two.'

'Or three, or four, or five. You were knocking it back as much as the rest of us.'

'No, I wasn't,' Eleanor disagreed. She couldn't help but smile broader at the recollections playing back in her mind, now without prejudice. 'T.J. was, but I wasn't.'

'You were.'

'No,' she giggled with nostalgia. 'I never had more than a couple of glasses in a day.'

'You did,' Arabella persisted.

'No, I didn't.' The picture freeze-framed in Eleanor's mind: she was the only sober one of the lot at the time. 'It's no wonder that you didn't notice, being as drunk as you all were,' Eleanor jibed jokingly. 'If I'd had any more than two, I'd have had a hangover for the whole of the next day.'

'But you never get hangovers,' Arabella recalled.

'That's true about before the boys were born,' Eleanor agreed. 'But after, ooh,' she grimaced.

'So how come you never mentioned it?'

'For the same reason that you didn't notice: it made no difference.'

'Fair enough! Anyway,' Arabella interjected, 'how about we get a bottle and you have your two glasses and I'll drink the rest?'

'Hm,' Eleanor's resolve was returning. 'I really shouldn't.'

'Why not?' Arabella whined.

'It may not agree with me, seeing as I haven't touched a drop since T.J..'

'Yes, you did. At the funeral.'

'That's two years ago.'

'Even still, it'll be like riding a bike.'

'Goodness me,' Eleanor frowned. 'You're like having the devil on my back.'

To which the since silent waiter sniggered.

Arabella turned to him with a conspiratorial wink. 'A bottle of house champagne, please.'

'No,' Eleanor rejected. 'I need to be in a fit state to get them to bed later,' she reasoned.

'And you shall be.'

'Not if I drink, I won't.'

'Chill.'

'It's not only about getting them upstairs, you know,' came the retort.

'I believe you.'

But Eleanor wasn't taking her word for it. 'There's the teeth cleaning, there's bed time stories, there's –'

'Stop, please,' Arabella protested with a laugh. 'I'll help you, like I used to.'

The words 'used to' hit a raw note with Eleanor. Immediately she had a flashback of her prior anger and it boosted her now almost fully returned resolve. If Arabella thought she was going to get round her so easily with constant references to the happy old days, she had another thing coming. 'No thank you,' Eleanor declared.

The tone of her voice seemed to also bring Arabella back to the reality of present times. Gone was her carefree laughter and impish goading, and back was the uneasy smile. 'I promise not to get pissed,' she attempted to vouch, but Eleanor was back in angry mode.

'Language, please,' she admonished her with a stern whisper and a furtive nod in the direction of each of her sons. 'Kids on site.'

Oh Lord! 'Shit, sorry.'

'Ah,' Paris gasped, as springing up suddenly in their seats, both boys stared in horror at Arabella and then at their mother.

Eleanor rolled her eyes. 'Well done,' she jeered. 'And this is you sober.'

Arabella took instant offence. 'Billy goat gruff,' she huffed off the cuff, only to soon be cringing with embarrassment as the words rang out. It was hardly the most mature of comebacks and the rest seemed to think so too.

Within seconds of its utterance, the twins, followed by Eleanor, began to giggle. Arabella eyed them sheepishly. She wasn't too sure if they were laughing with or at her. There wasn't a trace of malice in any of their expressions. *Thank God!*

Temporary, as was her nature, Arabella relaxed instantly without further thought of why she'd snapped. Changing her position in her seat to match her now returned carefree state of mind, she took the opportunity to order herself a hamburger with a double portion of french fries. Food and drink had always been Arabella's chosen complement to all emotions. Sad or overjoyed, it made no difference. Once she was done ordering what she wanted, she turned to the twins. 'Boys,' she prompted them, and they too began to order.

Eleanor regarded Arabella fondly as she involved herself in Paris and Malachi's ordering with purrs of approval and dares to try side dishes that they would never otherwise have dreamed of considering. This was vintage Arabella: childlike in approach and nonchalant to possible repercussion. What did she care that between her and the boys, they were ordering far too much for six-year-old boys to eat, especially before their bedtime? And what if they threw up afterwards? So be it, life goes on!

Eleanor became pensive. Someone this short term-minded couldn't be spiteful, the two just didn't go. It would be like saying that Paris and Malachi had it in them to be evilly spiteful. No way. Spur of the moment, childish tit for tat kind of spite definitely, but nothing premeditated and heinous like Arabella's disclosure had previously seemed to Eleanor.

Maybe Max was right, Eleanor now reconsidered. Maybe Arabella hadn't wilfully tried to hurt her.

Eleanor watched her ex-friend some more. The Arabella she'd always known wasn't a spiteful person, let alone to be of the mindset to premeditate a mean act. The woman was too impulsive for that to be possible. Especially with her overly 'carpe diem' spirit that was all about instant gratification, without consideration for repercussion.

To premeditate, one needed to weigh up all the odds, which was something of a no-no for Arabella, beyond the realms of her consideration. She wouldn't know where to begin. And besides, she would see it as being too much hard work. The less thought the better was more her *modus operandi*.

With this in mind, Eleanor began to smile subconsciously. This spontaneity of character was Arabella's allure: it was her quintessence and what made her special. Still smiling, Eleanor recalled the dynamics of their friendship. Arielle, due to her sensibleness, was the one she would call whenever she needed a logical mind or someone to organise her. Whereas Arabella was the person for whims and naughtiness, the perfect partner in crime for that sneaky bottle of champagne down at Que Pasa when they were supposed to be having an early night because of an important meeting on the following day or supposed to be cutting back on expenditure in a particularly broke month.

Being of a character that erred more on the Arabella side of thinking meant that Eleanor did more things with her than she did with Arielle. And even though she loved them both dearly, she'd always had a slightly softer spot for Arabella because life with her around was always like being on an exciting adventure with an unpredictable ending.

The more she watched and thought of Arabella, the more Eleanor's resentment of the past couple of years ebbed and she began to realise just how much she missed her and their times together. It was time to talk about that night, two years ago, time to clear the air, but not in front of the boys.

'And for you?' the waiter asked, interrupting Eleanor's thoughts.

Ooh, she wasn't prepared. She looked at her sons.

'They're done now,' the waiter informed her.

'Okay.' *Um, what the hell!* 'I'll have double fries and a large hamburger with a fried egg and plenty of cheese on it, please. Ooh, and some barbecue sauce too.'

'Whoa,' her sons chorused with apparent surprise. 'Mummy, that's –'

'Lining your stomach,' Arabella proclaimed. She remembered those days well, as did Eleanor.

'Yup,' Eleanor agreed and reordered the contentious bottle of champagne. Seeing Arabella up close again had reminded her of how she used to be and feel. Of course, she couldn't be exactly the same as before, now that she had children and there was no T.J. with whom to manage their lives together, but it didn't mean that she and her sons had to go through life with metaphoric seatbelts fastened all the time.

Eleanor remembered the taxi driver and one of the many things he'd said on their journey back to the hotel. He was right: life was too short. T.J.'s death should have been her constant reminder of the fact. It wasn't living life to the fullest that had killed him, but a plane crash.

Had she stopped travelling by air? No, she hadn't. Yet she'd stopped living and had inflicted the same on Paris and Malachi by default.

Eleanor suddenly felt angry at herself for the way she'd allowed her grief and yearning for T.J. and their past life to stifle her and her sons' future. Were it not that she and T.J. had lived to the fullest when he was alive, there wouldn't be half as many great memories that she'd been trying to forget.

She regarded her sons again, this time with regret and remorse. Memories of happy times with T.J. that served no purpose being shut away came flooding back to her mind. It was time to start sharing and being a family again, time to start laughing again.

Chapter Twenty

Too much too soon

Picking up her freshly filled glass for a sip, Arabella spoke to Eleanor. 'I can't believe I never noticed when you first cut back on your drinking,' she told her.

'Yes, but as I said, you wouldn't, though, would you?' Eleanor replied as a matter of fact. 'Not when you're drinking heavily and I'm dashing back and forth after these two terrors.'

Paris' eyes lit up. 'Us terrors?' he asked his mother.

'Yes, you were worse than terrors,' she exaggerated with a faked look of despair on her face.

'Really?' Malachi interjected, wide-eyed with interest.

'Truly,' Eleanor riposted. 'You were like demons sent to punish your father and me, especially when you were around two.'

'The famous terrible twos, eh!' Arabella interposed.

Misunderstanding what she meant, the twins peered round at each other and sniggered.

'Famous, us?' Malachi gasped.

'All over the island,' his mother fibbed.

'Why, what did we used to do?' Paris enquired.

'Oh,' Eleanor sighed dramatically, to the further amusement of her sons. 'It'd be easier to ask what you didn't do,' she told them.

'Really?' the boys giggled together.

'Yes, you were way too naughty for words.'

'No,' Malachi smiled disbelievingly.

'You were,' Eleanor reiterated. 'There was no mischief that was out of your league and I really, really needed eyes in the back of my head to keep you from doing yourselves constant injury.'

Her sons held hands and shuddered with excitement. 'What sort of things did we do?' Malachi demanded.

'You mean apart from one of you ending up in a dustbin?'

The boys pulled a face.

'And nearly getting thrown into the rubbish truck?'

'No,' they squealed in unison.

'Yes,' Eleanor nodded. 'Don't you remember it?'

'No,' Malachi grimaced with delight. 'Was it me?'

'No,' Eleanor scowled playfully. 'It was Mister here,' she said, suddenly grabbing Paris, who lurched forward with a start.

'Me,' he beamed, clearly thrilled to have been the one. 'What did I do, what did I do?' he squealed with glee.

Tilting her head slightly to one side, Eleanor cupped her cheeks with her hands. 'I think you were about two-and-a-half,' she said with uncertainty then paused. 'Yes. No ... you had just turned two ... I remember because Aunty Arabella, Aunty Arielle and some other of Daddy's and my friends were due to be flying over to Tobago for the big party we used to have every year for your birthday and Daddy's and my anniversary –'

'I remember those,' Paris piped up. 'Why did we stop having them?'

Remembering what Max had said about being honest about her grief, Eleanor, for the first time since her husband's death, admitted to her sons just how hard carrying on without their father had been and still was for her.

'So as you can imagine,' she told them with tear-logged eyes, 'I've been finding it ever so hard to be fun like before and so there has been no way that I could possibly have pulled off our favourite parties since.' Eleanor looked at each of the boys with remorse. 'I'm so sorry for not having been strong enough,' she sobbed.

'Hey,' Paris whispered, beginning to rub his mother's back as she always did for them whenever they were sad. 'You're Supermom,' he told her as if he were the adult consoling a child.

'And lots of fun,' Malachi added.

'Oh,' Arabella whimpered, beginning to cry too. 'Bless you,' she whispered. 'You're all so brave.'

Eleanor eyed her. 'Don't you dare start,' she rebuked her immediately, beginning to laugh through her tears at a flashback of how the slightest sad thing would always get Arabella blubbering. Wiping away her tears, she looked around the table. As she did so, she pulled a face. 'Look at us,' she cried. 'Like a load of soggy cheese.'

'Soggy cheese?' Arabella now began to giggle.

'Yes, limp and minging.'

'Minging!' Arabella exclaimed. 'Since when did we start that lingo?'

Eleanor winked playfully. 'You know me, lady,' she quipped. 'I'm never one to be knowingly behind the times, be it in fashion or language. I picked it up the last time I was in London. Anyway,' she added suddenly, grabbing her sons as she did so and startling them. 'Do you want to hear about the dustbin story or not?' she reminded them.

'Yes, yes, yes,' the little boys replied with reignited excitement.

'So,' Eleanor resumed. 'Aunty Arielle had just arrived and you were playing hide and seek with her.'

'Aunty Arielle's always great fun,' Malachi enthused to Arabella.

'What about me?'

'You too, but we don't see you anymore.'

'Ssh,' Paris chided them.

'That's my boy,' Eleanor praised him in a fake American rap tone. 'You tell 'em. No interrupting when ma Momma's on the mike. So back to the story,' she interposed in her normal accent, which she hyped up with a tone that was loaded with drama and suspense. 'Aunty Arielle had found you where you'd been hiding,' Eleanor continued, directing her words at Malachi. 'So you decided to help Mister, here ...' she hugged Paris tighter. '... not to get caught.'

The boys peered round at each other and conspiratorially cackled with expectation as their mother carried on with her story.

'I don't know whose idea it was,' she told them, 'but you both sneaked down to the kitchen and somehow, between the pair of you, you got him into the big bin by the back door and put the lid on it.'

'So how did you find me?' Paris quizzed.

'I didn't. The cook and Aunty Arielle found you,' Eleanor explained. 'They were both wondering where you could be, when I called out to Cook to warn her to get the rubbish bags ready for the dust men who were just pulling up outside. As she opened the lid of the big bin, Aunty Arielle spotted you.'

'Was he covered in rubbish?' Malachi asked eagerly.

'Potato peels and everything,' Eleanor exaggerated.

'Gross,' the boys squirmed and began laughing.

'Yeah, you can laugh now,' Eleanor said, stretching out both arms to tickle them. 'You nearly didn't make it to your third birthday.'

'How come?' Paris asked, raising his head slightly above his body, which was curled up in defence against the tickling.

'Because you were so naughty that I almost murdered you both when your father was away on business.'

Squirming out of her reach, both boys came up for air at the same time. As they did so Arabella, who had been pensively taking it all in, spoke. 'The parties were great,' she said, 'but we also had a lot of fun in those days just hanging out. Didn't we?'

'We sure did,' Eleanor smiled wistfully.

'I miss the old days.'

'Me too, but that's life,' Eleanor shrugged and then fell silent. After a moment she spoke again. 'Arielle and some of the others still keep up those thrice-yearly visits.' She paused again. 'It helps having them around during those most difficult periods like birthdays, and so on, but it's not the same as before.'

Malachi slid back towards his mother and, wrapping his arms around her waist, snuggled into her side with a tight hug. Eleanor kissed him lightly on the forehead and then glanced over at Paris who had grown pensive on sensing his mother's continued expressions of loss.

Arabella sat sadly watching Eleanor and her sons as they sat in silent reflection. Then suddenly, out of the blue, she broke the gloomy silence. 'How's Arielle?' she chirped.

'She's great,' Eleanor nodded and then, pausing momentarily, added, 'she's happy …at last.' As she spoke, she became aware of someone walking towards them. The twins sprang up suddenly, as if in reflex action.

'Grandpa,' they cried aloud in unison, leaping off the sofa and running towards the approaching figure.

Oh no, Eleanor pouted. Arabella alone or Max on his own she could handle. But the two of them together, with the boys around? *Too much, too soon,* she frowned.

'I miss you both,' Arabella's voice broke in.

'What?' Eleanor glowered.

'You were more than friends to me,' Arabella continued.

'Sorry?' Eleanor snapped.

'You and Arielle.'

'Oh,' Eleanor relaxed. 'Yes, we were all pretty close.'

'More than pretty close, you were like the sisters I never had.'

Max and the boys were now almost at the table. Eleanor regarded them with agitation. As she did so, out of the corner of her eye, she spied the half full bottle of champagne. 'Pour me another glass,' she ordered before adding in a softer tone, 'please.'

Complying, Arabella refilled the empty glass and handed it to Eleanor. 'It hurt having you both dump me the way you did,' she resumed on the topic of their past friendship.

Eleanor eyed her. 'How did Max know where to find us?' she challenged.

'I told him. We were supposed to be going to dinner and –'

'You should have gone.'

Arabella looked greatly saddened. 'Maybe,' she agreed. 'But I needed to see you, to talk to you.' Her eyes began to well up with tears.

Eleanor looked away. 'I understand,' she relented. 'But I'm not ready yet to present you guys to the boys as a couple. And maybe not even to myself.'

Arabella appreciated her honesty. 'I'll ask him to go,' she volunteered.

'No, it's too late,' Eleanor replied with resignation and, making the sign of the cross, downed her glass of champagne.

Chapter Twenty-one

Hey, remember me?

Spotting what his daughter-in-law had done and also noticing the look on both women's faces, Max tensed up. *Oh man!* he groaned and quickened his step. Veering left at the table, he made his way to Arabella while the boys skipped gaily back to their places by their mother.

'So what's been happening?' Max asked with a tentative smile.

'We've been talking about the old days,' Malachi responded.

'Okay.' That was too generic a response. Gently squeezing Arabella on the shoulder, he stooped and gave her a peck on the top of her head. 'Are we all cool?' he whispered.

'Yes, great,' she chirped stiffly and ushered him along with a gentle push away.

So that's a 'no' from you, he decided and turned to Eleanor. 'How about you, kiddo, is it all good with you?' he checked.

'Fine, thanks,' came the equally ill at ease reply as Eleanor slid her empty champagne glass towards Arabella for another top up.

'Whoa, that good,' Max quipped playfully and, walking over to her, gave her a peck on the cheek. It was clear to him that he was interrupting something – *something good*, he hoped, *like reconciliation* – but it was hard to guess from their demeanour. Whatever it was, it had begun in his absence and Max knew that it needed to be concluded in his absence. He needed to find a pretext to leave them to it.

Using the excuse that he'd soon be leaving the house to move in full time into the place that Arabella had found for him and her, Max suggested that he'd like to spend the evening packing and hanging out with his grandsons.

Relieved at the prospect of a night off, Eleanor, who was already tipsy, readily consented to her sons' supper order being boxed up and sent up to their room where Max and the boys would be gathering other provisions needed for the impromptu sleep over.

The party of three – Max flanked by his two excited grandsons – looked natural together as they made their way through the restaurant in the direction of the bar and the couple of steps leading towards the main foyer of the hotel.

As she watched them, Arabella daydreamed of Max being Paris and Malachi's father, while she was their mother, proudly watching from the distance as her good-looking pretend family attracted admiring glances from strangers who, without a doubt, secretly envied her.

Wistfully she observed them: the little boys bobbing along without a care in the world and then occasionally breaking into a trot to keep up with Max's manly strides.

Suddenly Arabella felt an anxious and familiar twinge at the top of her stomach, right where she imagined her soul and the heart of her emotions to be. It was, she imagined, her biological clock again trying to remind her that time was very much of the essence. It seemed to be telling her that there wasn't even enough time for her to be sitting there day-dreaming about what she was missing out on.

Arabella's expression clouded and her content smile vanished. Yes, she was aware that time was slip-ping by too fast for daydreams, but what else could she do? Having already declared her feelings and desires on the matter to Max on the night of her arrival, all she could do for now was wait until he told her his.

She wondered if he had given their conversation any further thought. He had said at the time that they'd definitely have to talk about it again 'sooner rather than later.' *But when was that 'sooner' going to be?* she mused.

An unsettling thought sprang to mind. Had Max already come to his decision, and because it was a 'no', he'd decided to put off telling her until later?

Arabella began to pout sadly. That wouldn't be fair, she decided, especially if his decision was based on his misguided idea that he was too old to have a child.

Oh, Arabella groaned. If only Max could see him-self now with Paris and Malachi, he'd realise how natural and not-too-old he looked as the father of a young family.

Max had told her about how guilty he felt for being too busy working to spend quality time with his sons, particularly T.J., when they were growing up. Why couldn't he understand, she wondered, how having a child with her could be his second chance to be the amazing father that he hadn't been then.

With Max soon to be retired and definitely in no need of any more money than he already had, Arabella could imagine no better time for him to become a dad again. He'd have all the time in the world to spend with their child.

What a wonderful way to see out his life. Without regrets of what he should have done and brimming with pride for what he became: the best dad in the world.

'He's great with them, isn't he?' Eleanor's voice seeped into Arabella's thoughts. She'd noticed the look on Arabella's face and it made her feel sad for her. Arabella was the one person in the group who'd always wanted children and yet she was the only one who still hadn't had any.

'Yes,' came the absent-minded yet thoughtful reply. 'He'll make a great father.'

'He'll make a great father?' Eleanor cried. 'Is there something I should know?'

Suddenly aware of her slip of tongue, Arabella sat up abruptly. 'He and T.J. had a good relationship, didn't they?' she challenged, more defensively than she'd intended.

'Yes?'

'Well then, so he's made a great father.'

That wasn't what she'd said earlier and Eleanor knew it. 'Sorry, I misheard,' she fibbed with a sneaked curious look at Arabella who seemed to prefer not to make further eye contact.

Not wanting to push the issue, especially seeing how it was obviously making Arabella uncomfortable, Eleanor changed the subject to the disclosure that Arabella had made two years ago about T.J. and Belinda. Being a topic that they were now both comfortable discussing, it proved to be a well-chosen interlude.

Starting with the hurt that Eleanor had felt at Arabella not having told her from the very start about T.J.'s relationship with Belinda, to the most important question on Eleanor's mind – did T.J. ever cheat on her? – the newly reconciled friends talked it all through.

Arabella's position was that, as she had clearly stated on that evening of T.J.'s funeral, she had never told Eleanor because firstly she could see the promise in Eleanor and T.J.'s relationship, so didn't want to spoil things for them with what she deemed as meaningless scuttlebutt. Secondly, because it was irrelevant, seeing as how Eleanor was doing the same to Cort and both sets of relationships had ended within weeks, giving room for T.J. and Eleanor's to blossom, which it did.

Understanding the reasoning in her friends logic, Eleanor not only apologised for doubting the goodness of Arabella's intentions, but she also confessed that she'd forgotten so much about Cort that the fact that she'd been in a relationship with him at the time had completely slipped her mind.

Arabella smiled mischievously. 'So what would you do if you saw him again, here in this hotel today?'

Eleanor eyed her. It wasn't a good question to be asking her while she was inebriated, as she was after happily guzzling the last glass of the bottle. Just then a thought sprang to mind. 'He's not is he?' she demanded.

Arabella laughed. 'No, he isn't.'

Eleanor was becoming nervous. She knew Arabella well enough to know that there was a reason for that question. 'I don't believe you,' Eleanor told her.

'He isn't,' her friend began to giggle even more.

'Oh my God, he is ... where?' And with that Eleanor shrank down in her seat and began to surreptitiously survey the neighbouring tables to theirs. She'd barely begun her scanning of the joint when, on cue, Thorsten stood up to get something out of the back pocket of his trousers. Eleanor caught sight of him. 'Oh Jesus,' she exclaimed, ducking lower down. 'Why didn't you tell me before?' she hissed at Arabella.

'Because it isn't him.'

Eleanor, raising her head, took another look. She didn't recognise any of the other people at the table with him. She decided to sneak a proper look at Thorsten, but he turned suddenly and, catching her, their eyes met. He smiled at her like a friendly stranger. Eleanor turned to Arabella.

'He's acting like he doesn't know me,' she announced.

Arabella began to laugh again. 'That's probably because he doesn't know you.' She joined Eleanor for another look. 'I met this chap at the airport and his name's Thorsten.'

Thorsten was still watching when they looked back. This time he recognised Arabella. 'Hello again,' he waved, happy to have finally made contact and corroborating her story.

'Phew,' Eleanor sighed with apparent relief. 'I don't know what I'd have done if it was him.'

'Do you think you'd still like him?' Arabella asked.

Without hesitation, Eleanor admitted that 'His looks, yes, I'd go for, definitely. But his character and the type of person he is? No way.' And then, smiling impishly, she added, 'Once you've had the best, it's easy to leave the rest.' She was referring to T.J.

'Touché!' Arabella also smiled and changed the topic back to what they were discussing.

In their further discussions – during which Eleanor kept sneaking glances at Thorsten and he at her – both women agreed that they both had been wrong with how they'd handled their altercation on the night of T.J.'s funeral. With that said, they apologised for their part in the unnecessary estrangement of their relationship.

Finally, Arabella disclosed everything she'd known about T.J.'s feelings for his wife. He'd been as smitten with Eleanor as she was with him, and to the best of her knowledge, Arabella believed that he'd never been unfaithful to Eleanor and probably would never have, had he lived until old age.

Eleanor was beside herself with joy: what great news, what a great evening, what a great life. *Hm,* she purred, and how wonderful it felt to be sitting here with her best friend and both of them pissed and enjoying the moment. *Like the happy old days.* Another bottle was in order.

With their friendship completely back on track, the drunk and giggling Eleanor and Arabella awaited the fresh bottle of champagne they'd ordered to toast new and happy beginnings for them both. As they did so, Eleanor broached the topic of children.

'Here's to your pregnancy that you're trying to keep quiet,' she slurred, raising her half empty glass to toast the good news.

Arabella looked surprised. 'What pregnancy?' she asked.

'Yours.'

'But I'm not pregnant.'

'Aren't you?'

'No.'

'Oh,' Eleanor frowned. 'But you should be, you know,' she insisted. 'Because I think you'd make a great mother.'

'Me too,' Arabella concurred, raising her glass. 'And although it's not going to get me pregnant, I toast to me: the fab mother in waiting.'

'Hear, hear,' Eleanor seconded and clinked glasses with her friend. Suddenly out of the blue, she asked. 'Is that airport chap single?'

'Why, do you fancy him?'

'I might do, is he?'

'I could always find out.'

'Don't be so silly,' Eleanor chided Arabella and fell silent. Seconds later, she spoke again. 'I can't believe you're not pregnant,' she said, and they fell silent again.

In no time, Eleanor piped up again. 'IVF,' she declared.

Arabella pulled a face. 'For whom?'

'For you. You're not a Catholic, so you're allowed.'

Arabella looked bewildered. 'But I'm not infertile,' she announced. 'At least I don't think I am.'

'Oh, so what's the problem then?'

'The men I end up with.'

'Shame.' And then almost immediately, Eleanor added. 'Max can't be infertile, he's got three sons. Well, two live ones and one dead one ... who loves me.' She smiled; it felt good to be able to say that aloud with confidence. As her smile eclipsed her whole face, Eleanor's thoughts drifted back to what she'd been thinking. 'So Max can't be infertile,' she repeated. Pausing, she regarded Arabella. 'Maybe you just need a bit of a booster then.'

'I don't need a bloody booster,' Arabella snapped. 'I just need a man who wants to have a baby with me.'

'Alright, calm down.' Eleanor looked at her friend as if surprised about something. 'Is that all?' she demanded.

'Is what all?'

'Is all you need a man who wants to have a baby with you?'

'Yes.'

Eleanor smiled victoriously. 'Then ask Max,' she slurred gaily. 'He loves you loads, he'll say yes.'

'A fresh bottle, ladies,' the waiter interrupted.

'Thanks,' they chorused.

'And the bill?' Eleanor muttered with drunken lethargy.

'It's been settled …'

'Aw, bless Max,' she cooed. 'He's the best father-in-law in the world.'

'… By the blond gentleman over there,' the waiter corrected.

'The blond gentleman?' they cried in unison, looking towards Thorsten.

Thorsten and his friends were standing to leave.

'That gentleman,' the waiter confirmed.

'Ooh,' Eleanor thrilled. 'Stop him, call him over, now, please. We must thank him,' she added shyly as an afterthought excuse.

And with that the waiter rushed to intercept Thorsten's exit. He got there in time and, as the women watched on, Thorsten waved his friends ahead and followed the waiter back for the introduction he'd been wishing for all night.

With acquaintances established, he stayed with the women to finish the bottle and then the three of them went to join his friends at a nearby bar.

Chapter Twenty-two

What a bloody mess!

Eleanor awoke with a start. 'Shit, twelve o'clock,' she groaned as she caught a glimpse of the time on the radio clock that had fallen off the bedside table and was dangling off it, suspended in mid-air by its taut flex.

It must be Max, she thought and picked up the black cordless phone that was lying flat on its face beside where the radio clock was meant to have been standing. He was due back with Paris and Malachi round about now.

'Hello,' Eleanor managed to barely croak into the receiver. The dial tone burred back at her; there was no one on the other end. Sighing with relief, she returned the phone to its cradle.

It was time she arose anyway, so gingerly sitting up in her bed, Eleanor returned the radio clock to its rightful position and wondered what had woken her up. The bell rang again. It was someone at the door.

Oh Heavens, they're here, she concluded. With great care, but nevertheless still wincing with pain, she slid herself and most of the bed linen to the edge of the bed.

'Things can't go on like this,' she chided herself as, disentangling her body from between the untucked base sheet and the red and green patchwork eiderdown, she noticed that she was still dressed in the halter neck turquoise-coloured tie-dye maxi-dress that she'd worn out the night before.

Oh, she thought, steadying her head with both hands. Why did she push the boundaries of her drinking ability when she knew the consequences? Her body was unforgiving and always got its own back the following day.

Eleanor stood up. *Urgh,* she whimpered from the current of pain that suddenly and at once surged to and from every part of her throbbing head. *Argh* and a flashback of the night before didn't help either. The insides of her eyes were burning too. She shut them to a squint.

Oh Lord, take me now! Her hangover was too much to bear.

As far as Eleanor could remember, it was a great night out, but not worth such payback that her body was now meting out to her. Every muscle was getting its own back with every step she was taking towards the walk-in wardrobe. No one in the world could be worse off than her right now, she imagined.

On reaching her destination, she opened the closet door. Inside was dark. *Thank you, God* for the reprieve to her eyes, which she still kept half shut. She knew where to find T.J.'s old white kimono-style dressing gown with grey Japanese characters all over. It was always left hanging just on the inside, by the door, so that all she had to do was stretch her hand in to find it, like she just had.

Draping it over her dress, Eleanor pulled the slightly open bedroom door to her right wider open and slowly made her way towards the staircase.

It had been a month since her and Arabella had rekindled their friendship and she and Thorsten had become acquainted and for the third morning …

Afternoon, to be precise, she clarified.

Here she was rendered useless *again* by the after effects of too much alcohol and too little of the common sense that she should have used to control herself.

Why hadn't she listened to that little voice inside when it had gurgled *enough*? And more importantly, she frowned, when did she start doing shots? Eleanor had never drunk spirits in her life and for the past twelve years had stuck to drinking champagne or cava, sekt or prosecco. Nothing else.

That's it, she decided, *enough is enough.* It was bad drinking too much of what she enjoyed, but way out of order to inflict this sort of suffering on herself by over-indulging on shots that she hated with a passion.

Stubbing her toe, she came to a halt. 'Ouch.' It was Malachi's train that he'd wanted to take to his grandfather's but had said he couldn't find anywhere. So much for his, 'I've looked everywhere, Mummy, but I can't find it.' Eleanor toyed with the idea of hiding it now: *that'll teach him not to leave his toys lying around next time.* But the thought of bending to reach it made her queasy, so leaving it where it lay; she began to make her way down the stairs.

Eleanor had barely made it down the first lot of steps when the doorbell rang again. 'Oh for crying out loud,' she grumbled louder than her fragile head could bear. 'Ow!' It had to be Paris ringing like that. He was as impatient as she was, with her 'chop, chop' mentality.

Just then, the phone started to ring. 'What the ...' Eleanor snapped, but she stopped herself, it hurt too much. Whoever it was would have to either leave a message or call back, the choice was theirs.

And as for Paris, he'd have to wait until she finally made it to the back door to let him and his brother in.

As she neared the bottom step, Eleanor couldn't believe the sight before her. 'Oh Lord, no,' she complained loudly and covered her face with both hands. Why the hell had she allowed Arabella and Thorsten to talk her out of clearing the dinner things from the dining room table before they'd gone out? It wouldn't have taken long.

And so what if she had broken a plate or two while doing it. It would have been far better than all this mess that she was going to have to tackle with her presently intolerable headache and the kids now back. *Argh,* she wanted to scream, but she felt too weak. Getting to the back door was proving difficult enough as it was with the little strength she was somehow managing to muster up.

She'd now almost made it to the ground floor. Turning right at the last step, Eleanor skidded and almost ended up, bottom first, on the floorboards at the start of the dining area. The shake-up it gave her made her head throb even more. She'd have to take better care as she went along because she'd left the carpeted part of the house and was in stocking feet.

Gingerly looking down at her feet, Eleanor frowned. Why on earth was she wearing stockings? she wondered, but carried on regardless. Slipping and sliding with every step, she didn't get far and so stopped to get her feet bare. Just then she spied her high turquoise Jimmy Choo sandals peeping out from underneath the dining table, where she'd obviously kicked them off on her return.

'Oh no!' *Oh yes.* She must have worn the stockings out with her sandals. *How shameful,* especially as they were the horrible 15 dernier American tan-coloured ones that she only ever wore as a last resort in winter, with closed shoes when she knew she would have no cause to take off her shoes in public. No more alcohol ever, she decided.

And it gets worse, she cringed suddenly when, using the wall on her right for support, she reached out with her left hand to try to roll down a stocking and found it to be a pop sock. One of her mother's old ones, no less, and one that had grown bobbly from having been washed too many times. 'Oh Lord, shoot me now,' Eleanor cried at the discovery. With her maxi prone to rise whenever she crossed her legs, they must have been on full display all night wherever they went. And she'd spent the night feeling so cute and chi chi. *Shame!* What must Thorsten have thought? Oh God that she could die now!

Hurrying to rid herself of the contemptible pop socks, Eleanor teetered and almost toppled over a few times. Finally getting them off and stuffing them into one of the pockets of her dressing gown, she was good to go now, albeit with compounded pain.

Resuming her journey, Eleanor made her way through the white arch and on towards the back door. As she got to the kitchen area she stopped to gingerly crick out some of the tension in her neck tendons. As she did so she caught sight of the state of the room.

'No!' she cried out loud. 'It's even worse than the bloody dining room,' she moaned on noticing the extent of the mess in which her kitchen had been left.

Her usually immaculately clean cooker was splattered with Bolognese sauce. The sink was filled with practically all the pots she had in the house. And Heaven knows that since Max's time there were many pots, more than Eleanor cared to count now.

She became angry at herself. Why had she allowed Arabella to cook in the state she was in last night, especially with her knowledge that Arabella was a messy cook at the best of times? Eleanor craned her neck for a better look at the state of affairs.

Oh, and from what she could see, the stupid cow didn't even bother to scrape out the leftovers from the pots before partially filling them with water and then dumping them topsy-turvy in the sink.

Eleanor noticed the colander. 'Oh, bloody hell!' Why didn't Arabella leave it in the sink with the other stuff while she was at it? she grumbled. 'Now look at the mess.' There was pasta and slimy pasta water all over the counter.

Eleanor's eyes followed the gungy off-white trail of starchy water and pasta which had seeped out of the colander, dribbled all over the surface and then down the front of the cabinet below until it reached the floor and pooled in a stodgy puddle.

At this sight the insides of her stomach tightened and began to churn in loud grumbles as if in protest against the disorder. As her mouth began to well up with surplus amounts of overly salty-tasting spittle, Eleanor knew she was on the verge of vomiting and so made a dash for the back door.

This day could only get worse, she concluded, grimacing with a mixture of pain, anguish and disgust.

Eleanor quickly opened and headed out of the door, and almost collided with Max, who stood sad-faced and staring down at the grey wooden slat floor of the back deck. Rushing past him, she ran to the corner of the garden and threw up.

'Not you too,' he remarked as he waited for his daughter-in-law to recover enough to make her way back to the house.

She didn't take long and was soon returning past him without a glance. Her head was pounding, her stomach churning. As far as she was concerned, she could feel no worse than she was feeling and so neither wanted to hear, nor see, any signs of disapproval. With the frown on her face clearly communicating this, Eleanor walked past Max and back into the house.

A couple of steps later it hit her: something was missing. Eleanor stopped. *The boys!* And then, almost immediately, Max's demeanour from when she'd first opened the door suddenly registered in her consciousness. He looked awful, like something bad had happened. Eleanor's heart sank.

Oh my God. 'What's happened, where are they?' she demanded, looking around for her sons.

'They're not with me.'

'I can see that,' she snapped. And then for the first time since she'd opened the door to him, she properly looked at Max. There was an air of desperation in his eyes as they twitched with what looked like a mixture of anger and the anxiety of someone at their wit's end.

Oh God, no! she despaired. All life, her pain, everything, at once drained from Eleanor's body and soul, leaving her semi-catatonic. Frozen to the spot, Eleanor spoke again. 'Where are they?' she asked gingerly.

'Arabella's taken them for a day by the waters in Kirkland.'

'Kirkland?' she echoed, trying to make sense of what she'd heard.

'Yes, she left you a voicemail message earlier this morning.'

They're okay, Eleanor's mind at last deciphered. 'Oh thank God,' she sighed just as her headache returned with doubled ferocity. *Ooh!* But it was okay: her sons were fine and that was what mattered.

'Guess you didn't get it then,' Max interjected.

'I guess I didn't,' Eleanor replied, unsure of what he was talking about, but continued slowly on her way regardless, with resumed groans and whimpers of pains. At the threshold of the kitchen, the implications of Max's words dawned on her. Eleanor glanced back at him. 'Arabella got up much earlier than this to go to Kirkland with the boys, you said?'

'Mhm.'

'Why?'

'Because she wanted to.'

'Ha,' Eleanor laughed. 'There are many things I'd love to do today, but wanting to and being able to are two different things.' She cast Max another glance. His forced smile was now gone. It occurred to her that although her sons were okay, something awful still could have happened, but to Max instead. Pausing, Eleanor looked back at him. Max smiled. It seemed a forced smile to her.

Instantly Eleanor's mind began to process everything. Max had said that Arabella was throwing up earlier that morning, which meant that she too must have had a hangover. Arabella rarely got hangovers, and from what Eleanor recalled from the past, on those rare occasions when she did, they were worse than anybody's in intensity and duration. This meant that Arabella was in no fit state to be taking the boys to Kirkland, so why did she?

She and Max must have had a tiff, Eleanor concluded. She turned back to him. 'Is everything okay with you and Arabella?' she asked.

'Yes … thanks,' he nodded, but Eleanor wasn't convinced.

Eyes never lie.

On following his daughter-in-law into the house, Max spied the kitchen. 'Arabella, huh?' he asked, rolling his eyes knowingly.

'Who else?'

As Eleanor spoke, her dressing gown drooped open at the front as the belt became loosened. Max noticed her dress that was clearly in view. 'Just got back, huh?' he asked, signalling to it.

'Of course not,' she retorted defensively. 'Arabella and I left together.' Max was T.J.'s father and Eleanor wasn't comfortable with him knowing that there was anything going on between her and Thorsten. Arabella was sworn to secrecy and Eleanor hoped she would remain schtum until advised otherwise.

'Oh,' Max retorted to his daughter-in-law's dismay.

'What's that supposed to mean? she demanded.

'What?'

'Your "oh".'

Max stared at her in disbelief. *Oh, for Christ's sake! What is it with these girls today?* 'It's meaningless; a filler,' he snapped. 'What else can it possibly mean?'

He didn't sound like he knew anything, but she couldn't be sure of that. 'Alright,' Eleanor surrendered, eyeing Max suspiciously. He had her full attention for the fact he'd never been a man of irascible temperament, yet he was today. Something was definitely up, but what?

Noticing the look on Eleanor's face, Max flushed with embarrassment. 'I'm sorry, kiddo,' he apologised and then admitted, 'today's not a very good day for me.'

'Nor for me,' his daughter-in-law concurred. 'Hangover, messy house ... it makes me edgy. I'm sorry too.'

Casting a quick glance about, Max pulled an unimpressed face. 'I feel for you,' he sympathised because he knew that for him even without a hangover there was no way he could hang out anywhere in this state, especially here and today of all days.

Damn it, he cursed silently. And this was where he really wanted and needed to be. He'd have to sort it. Retrieving his mobile phone from his pocket, Max returned his attention to Eleanor. 'Why don't you go upstairs,' he suggested, 'take a shower and some painkillers and I'll get the mess sorted out.'

But lovely as it sounded, Eleanor didn't want that. 'I can't have you cleaning for me.'

'I don't intend to,' he laughed dryly. 'I'm calling in for help,' he explained.

'Not Arabella, I hope,' Eleanor joked.

'No way,' Max shook his head vehemently. He needed space from her to think through everything that had happened so far to him today.

Max paused for thought. It wasn't that he was angry with Arabella as such. *Hm,* he reconsidered. Yes, he was and very much so too. It was wrong of her to try to emotionally blackmail him like she had with a threat of suicide, which he most certainly didn't appreciate, especially today of all days. *What was she thinking?* he grizzled.

The reality of the matter was that Arabella wasn't thinking. Her hormones were raging, she was feeling particularly below par, like she had done on that day when she had taken an overdose of sleeping pills two years and some months earlier, and she was more or less wondering aloud.

Recounting the story of her alleged suicide attempt was her way of trying to fathom what was going on inside her mind then and today – what motivated her to do or not do things – like why on that day she felt like taking the pills and yet not today even though her emotions felt the same to her on both occasions.

Unfortunately due to the timing of her revelation, Max couldn't see it as anything other than a threat, as emotional blackmail. As far as he was concerned, Arabella must have guessed what the letter she handed to him contained and so decided to warn him that leaving her again wasn't going to be an option for them.

Just then Max noticed Eleanor watching him. Had he sounded as bitter as he was feeling? he wondered. Forcing a smile, he quickly tried to fool her. 'You've been friends for a while, and so you know that she just reallocates mess instead of cleaning it up.'

Hurt though it did, Eleanor burst into loud laughter. Yes, she did know that. For Arabella, cleaning meant transferring and hiding away clutter. As Eleanor thoughtfully recalled some of the many times when she'd seen her friend do this, Max, with his phone still in hand, overtook her and led the way down towards the front of the house. On arrival in the sitting room, he made his way to the first of the floor-to-ceiling windows on the left. There he took hold of the strings that were dangling from the drawn blind. 'Mind if I open them?' he asked.

'No, go ahead,' Eleanor replied on joining him in the sitting room. As Max untangled the strings in his hand, she made her way to the blind that was covering the window on the far right. On her way to it Eleanor took care to give a wide berth to her sons' new small plastic tent that Thorsten had set up for them in the middle of the room.

Without recollection of the weather outside from when she was out back vomiting, Eleanor yanked the blind up in one go. 'Ouch,' she recoiled almost immediately. The unrelenting brightness of the sun's rays was too much for her hurting eyes. 'Maybe we shouldn't open them completely,' she suggested and let the blind drop back shut. Taking hold of the stick control beside the strings that she'd just released, Eleanor manoeuvred open the slants to let in the sun in gentle strips.

Watching her with bemusement, Max did the same. 'It must have been one hell of a night last night,' he remarked.

'It was. Too hellish and never to be repeated.'

Max laughed. 'You said the same after the two previous times,' he reminded her.

'I know,' Eleanor admitted, 'but this time's different. I physically can't do it anymore.'

'Nor can Arabella judging by the state of her this morning.'

'Sounds like it,' Eleanor tittered and then winced almost instantly with pain. For Arabella to have thrown up, it must have been a 'larger' night than she remembered. And if that was the case, maybe she was not such a lightweight after all. Pausing, Eleanor thought of Arabella taking the boys out with as bad a hangover as she appeared to have. It beggared belief. 'The boys must have whined her into it,' she concluded aloud.

'No,' Max declared. 'The idea was Arabella's.'

'Ugh,' Eleanor grimaced. 'She's off her trolley.'

'Or made of sturdier stuff than the rest of us,' Max added.

'Sturdier than me, that's for sure,' Eleanor admitted, pulling another face. She was feeling sick again. Gripping tighter onto the stick with which she had operated the blinds; she eased herself to perch on a nearby low-set shelf. A surge of bile was on its way up. She made a dash to the downstairs toilet.

'Feeling sick again?' Max called after her.

She couldn't reply: her mouth was brimming. In the nick of time, Eleanor reached her destination, got the seat up, and threw up. *Never again, God,* she vowed as she began to convulse with retching.

Moments later it subsided. She waited. All but her throbbing head was still. Eleanor dared to stand. It made her feel giddy. She could bear that. Without further ado, she washed her hands and headed back to the sitting room.

'Go and get a shower, you'll feel better for it,' Max suggested on seeing the state of her.

'I think I will,' she conceded. 'Once I've caught my breath.' As she spoke, she noticed Max glance thoughtfully at the red wall. The expression on his face felt familiar.

He sensed her watching him. 'I'm sorry,' he began, 'I –'

'Need to be alone,' Eleanor interjected with a smile. 'I understand.' She too had days like this when she wanted nobody, not even her sons, around. Those were what she called her 'T.J. days'. They were times she wanted to spend alone with him in her thoughts. Interludes for reliving memories, as Max seemed to have been doing just then when he was surveying the wall.

With Eleanor now also casting a thoughtful glance about the room, Max spoke. 'Who'd have thought back then, when he and I were getting this place set up, that our lives would change so drastically in a matter of years?' he remarked.

Eleanor smiled sadly. 'Not me, that's for sure.'

'Me neither,' Max agreed, and then turning, regarded her with compassion. 'Goodbyes are never easy are they?' he commented, but before she could respond, he added quietly, 'not even when we instigate them.' And with that, he brought out from his back pocket the envelope which Arabella had earlier that day brought up from their mailbox and given to him. After regarding it momentarily, he handed it to Eleanor.

She cast him a questioning glance.

'It's the latest update,' he told her. 'I thought you'd like to know.'

Pulling out the paper inside, she scanned it quickly. 'Oh.'

'Yup! "Oh" indeed!'

Finishing off reading, Eleanor handed Max back the letter that confirmed his new status as a single man with the words 'Divorce Absolute'.

'So how do you feel?' she asked him.

He smiled sadly. 'How do I feel?'

'Mhm.'

'Let's try sad … and then we can add a shot of anger to that. A big shot,' he stressed, as if he were ordering a beverage of his own concoction. 'And then last, but most definitely not least, garnish it with lots of regret.'

'Regret?' *Hm!* Eleanor looked taken aback.

But Max didn't care. He wasn't interested in anyone's feelings about anything. Today was his day to wallow in self-pity and yes, regret. So the world and those nearest and dearest to him would have to take him as they found him. Bitter and angry, although with himself mostly.

'How come?' Eleanor's voice cut in.

Without speaking, Max stared at her. He so wanted to communicate what he was feeling to her or anybody, but he didn't have the words, couldn't find the ones that would accurately convey that, as far as he was concerned, things between him and Bianca would never have come to this if he hadn't let his reactionary spirit lead the way.

How could he explain that there were many times he should have talked to her about what he was feeling, about what he thought had happened to them, about everything, but he hadn't? How could he adequately express and explain the regret he now felt, knowing that things between him and Bianca needn't have ended like this? They needn't have ended at all!

Reflecting briefly about how things used to be between him and Bianca, Max sighed sadly. They'd always been a communicative couple. It was part of their success: the key to their happiness. No subject was taboo until he started getting so upset about her family and their hostility towards him. *Damn them, damn me.* It wasn't supposed to end like this. 'It's my entire fault,' he suddenly voiced. 'We were supposed to be together forever, but I dropped the ball. I never asked her why.'

'Okay.' Eleanor looked perplexed but brimming with sympathy for him. He wasn't making any sense to her. Instinctively she knew it wasn't because he didn't want to. Whatever he was feeling could only be communicated by thoughts to the wall he'd painted with T.J. and which now had his full attention again. It was time to give him space. 'I'll go take that shower now,' she decided out loud and left him to his thoughts.

Eleanor awoke to the sound of a vacuum cleaner in use. It seemed to be coming from the direction of her study, across the landing. Rolling over sleepily she realised that her headache was gone. The Advil she'd taken before her shower had done the trick.

Thank God, she sighed and squinted at the radio clock. It was three fifteen in the afternoon. 'Oh you lazy cow,' she chided her reflection that could barely be seen against the deep red background of the radio clock face, and then, with a lethargic yawn, she heaved herself up into a sitting position. She had fallen asleep after her shower and for much longer than she would have liked to and so was now feeling a tad groggy.

As there was no other sound apart from the buzz of the vacuum and a wafting of jazz music coming from downstairs, she assumed that the boys were still on their day trip with Arabella and Max was still downstairs.

Eleanor rose to her feet, and quickly discarding the dressing gown that she was wearing over her matching navy blue sporty Sloggi underwear set, she put on the maroon-coloured track suit that had fallen off the bed while she was sleeping. Her hair was too short to show whether it'd been brushed or not, so she left it as it was and made her way out of her bedroom.

Stepping onto the landing, Eleanor tripped over the extended flex of the vacuum cleaner, which had been plugged into the wall on the other side of her door. Max's cleaning lady, Imaculada, came out with the appliance in hand to see what had interrupted her progress.

'Buenos dias, señora,' she chirped to Eleanor, who looked mortified at having been caught surfacing at such a late hour in the day.

'Buenos dias, Imaculada,' Eleanor replied. Avoiding eye contact with the elderly woman in a belted-at-the-waist knee-length grey and white paisley dress, she pretended that she needed all her power of concentration for plugging the flex back into the wall. 'Siento haberla molestado,' Eleanor muttered just before the vacuum cleaner roared loudly back into operation.

'Sin problema,' Imaculada responded in a loud voice as she bent over the appliance and switched it off from the base. With the loud hum of the cleaner quelled, she lowered her voice. 'Mr Wilner is downstairs,' she told Eleanor who, smiling, thanked her for having kindly agreed to help her clean at such short notice and then began her descent to the ground floor.

To Eleanor's delight, on her arrival at the bottom step, she noticed that the dining room had been returned to better than its original glory without a dirty plate to be seen. Encouraged by this, she hastened to the kitchen, which was as spotless as she had found it on the day she had returned to the house after Max's departure to the rented accommodation that Arabella had chosen for him and her.

'Mm,' Eleanor purred with happiness, and then deeply inhaling the fresh citrus scent of the freshener that was still lingering in the air long after Imaculada had sprayed it, Eleanor purposely opened and banged a cupboard shut to warn Max of her imminent approach. There was no acknowledgement, so she headed towards the front of the house.

As she neared the stairs leading down into the sitting room, Eleanor, who couldn't see Max anywhere in sight, spied that the front door was open. She descended the steps and was disappointed to see that the tent had been dismantled and was lying in a neat pile by the wall beside the guest toilet door. Eleanor had intended to take it, fully assembled, into the garden for the boys to play in.

Never mind, she shrugged and continued towards the open door. As she got to the threshold, she spotted Max in the distance, on T.J.'s favourite slab, at the top of the slope in the park. It was hard to tell if he was feeling better than when she left him, but, all the same, Eleanor decided to fetch him a cheer-up drink. He spotted her before she could retreat and waved for her to join him.

'In a second,' she told him and rushed back to the kitchen.

With a bottle of Segura Viuda Cava and two flutes in hand she joined her father-in-law moments later.

'Feeling better, I see,' he smiled, signalling towards the bottle in her hand. He seemed in a cheerier frame of mind than before.

'I am, thanks, but it's not for me,' Eleanor replied. 'I thought you might like a pick me up.'

Max smiled again. 'I've already helped myself to several of those in the form of the scotch that I found in the drinks cabinet. Hope you don't mind.'

'Heavens no,' Eleanor smiled back. 'It's yours from when you were staying here.' She paused. 'Did it help?'

'A little.'

'Need any more help?' she asked, gently swaying the bottle temptingly in his direction.

Max's smile broadened. 'Hm,' he pretended to ponder. 'Maybe just a little bit more.'

Eleanor cast an eye towards the street to their left, where Max usually parked his car.

'Couldn't find my keys, so I got a cab instead,' he volunteered.

'Well, in that case …' she responded and handed him the drink to open.

As Max eased the cork out of the bottle with a soft pop, Eleanor, who was waiting with the two empty flutes, tried to think of something to say to get him to reveal why the regret. 'Was it all amicable in the end?' she ventured at last.

Max put the cork into the breast pocket of his green polo shirt and began pouring the sparkling wine into the glasses that his daughter-in-law was holding slightly tilted towards him. 'Was what amicable?'

'The divorce.'

'Mhm.'

'She could have taken you to the cleaners.'

'She wouldn't.'

'I'm surprised she didn't,' Eleanor admitted. It was the wrong thing to have said and she realised that once she spied the barely noticeable crow's feet at the corners of her father-in-law's eyes instantly crinkle into deep grooves of vexation.

Waiting for the fizz in the second glass to subside, Max fixed Eleanor with a disappointed stare. 'Goes to show how little you know Bianca, doesn't it?' he retorted. 'She's got a lot of class and she's not vindictive.' And with that he resumed filling the glass.

Eleanor felt bad for having upset him. 'I'm sorry,' she apologised. 'It's just that you seemed really upset earlier and I was worried th –'

'That she'd cleaned me out? I wish she had.' With both glasses filled to two-thirds of the way, he bent down and placed the bottle beside his feet, on the concrete slab.

Eleanor was baffled. 'You wanted the divorce and you've got it, so what's the problem?'

'It wasn't meant to end like this,' Max replied as he took one of the filled flutes from her. 'It wasn't supposed to end at all and wouldn't have, had I known.'

Eleanor's mind boggled with intrigue. *Had you known what?* she wondered.

'Bi-racial marriages weren't the done thing, you know,' he added.

'And they still aren't to some.'

'Their loss … or should I say my loss, no thanks to them,' Max laughed dryly. He paused for a sip of his drink.

'You met at a human rights march, didn't you?' Eleanor asked. It wasn't the question on her mind, but …

'Uh huh …' Max's expression softened. Suddenly his eyes began to sparkle with pride. 'You should have seen her that day, kiddo,' he quietly told Eleanor. Stopping briefly, he nodded, as if to himself, as the pride changed into nostalgia. One could almost see the images of that day begin to take centre stage in his mind's eye. 'Her energy, her passion …' He stopped speaking.

Suddenly the expression on Max's face clouded over with apparent anger and bitterness. 'Sons of bitches,' he cursed suddenly. 'They went crazy, started beating down on people like they weren't humans.' He paused and glanced at Eleanor. 'Real sons of bitches they were, those policemen,' he explained.

'Nothing's changed there, then.'

Max's smile returned. 'But Bianca didn't care what they did to her.' He momentarily paused again. 'You know, technically speaking, as a white person, it wasn't her fight. She could have stayed home, but she didn't. It was her fight, all our fight, as human beings.' Max's lips parted into a broader and more pensive smile. 'That's always been her take on racism and injustice, and she wanted people to recognise this fact. She was there to be heard and nobody and nothing was gonna stop her. No sir, not Bianca.'

'Did she get hit as well?'

'Of course. Everybody who made a stand or tried to resist being silenced got hit,' he replied without looking at his daughter-in-law. 'They even killed some people.' Glistening with a thickening film of tears, Max's gaze dropped sadly to the grass in front of his feet.

'In front of you?'

'Close to where I was, apparently, but I didn't see it happen. There was so much pandemonium once the police arrived. But I knew a couple of the guys who died.' Max's eyes flickered up at Eleanor with disquiet. They looked as if they didn't want to remember the worst of what they'd seen that day.

Quickly she shifted the conversation back to Bianca. 'So Bianca was quite a force to be reckoned with in those days?'

The mention of his ex-wife appeared to still the anxiety in Max's eyes that metamorphosed into a tranquil smile that took a while to reach his lips. 'She still is,' he declared, and the smile arrived with lashings of smugness. 'She didn't seem to care if they killed her or took her alive.'

'Wow!'

'Yup.' Max held his smile.

'Quite the freedom fighter, it seems.'

'A fighter for everything she believes in.' Pausing, he glanced briefly at Eleanor. 'She believed in us; in our marriage,' he told her. 'But I let her down, I gave up on us. Damn me,' he cried. Pausing, he downed the rest of his drink and poured himself some more. Returning the bottle to his feet, he began to speak again. 'She didn't want me hurting, so she didn't tell me what was happening behind the scenes.' Max let out a sardonic laugh as his eyes filled with tears. 'And now we're both hurting.'

None of this made any sense to Eleanor. 'What a mess!'

'You can say that again.'

'What a mess,' she repeated playfully.

Max eyed her and they both burst into laughter.

Putting his arm around her shoulder, Max gave his daughter-in-law a sideways hug. 'You're a great kid,' he told her. 'And thanks for always being there.'

'Ditto.' She said smiling sadly up at him. 'How did it all get to this?' she asked him.

After a moment's silence he replied. 'You could say through the same way it all started: race issues. Bianca's family thoroughly objected to her marrying me,' Max explained.

'Really?' Eleanor was clearly taken aback by this. It had never occurred to her to imagine the possibility. But on further reflection, it began to make sense. Bianca's family never really featured in the couple and their family's life. In fact, Eleanor recalled, they neither attended hers and T.J.'s wedding nor T.J.'s funeral. 'How awful!'

'People are people, kiddo, and we're all entitled to our feelings.'

'Yes, but not such bigoted ones and not in this day and age.'

Max regarded her kindly. 'They're older and from a different time.'

'Whatever,' his daughter-in-law rebuffed. She wasn't of such a charitable mindset that could make allowances for bigots and their issues.

'Anyways,' Max intercepted before she began to rant, as she was prone to about such things. 'Unbeknownst to me, they were keeping up the digs at her for supposedly "throwing her life and future success away" by marrying a black man with whom her life would never amount to much.'

'Bloody cheek!'

Max cast a knowing glance. 'You're very much like her, you know that, kiddo.'

'So what happened?'

'Bianca didn't want me hurting, so she never said and took them on herself. She and I were both doing well in each of our fields, so that was cool, but it wasn't enough. We all had to aim for perfection and be perfect in everything and every way. And if we couldn't be, we'd act like we were. She was gonna show them and the world that she'd done better than good by marrying me.'

'Aw, bless her!' Eleanor felt bad for the times when she and Bianca hadn't gotten on and the harsh things she thought and said about her. If only she'd known all this before, she'd have made a better effort to understand and like the woman. Anyway, she shrugged; at least things between them had changed since T.J.'s death. She and her mother-in-law could actually be called friends more often than not.

'Yes, bless her indeed,' Max interjected. 'And damn me for letting her down.' He turned to his daughter-in-law. 'But I didn't know all this.' Looking back towards the road below, he stared blankly into space. 'She shoulda talked to me –she shoulda told me,' he said quietly. Downing his drink, he placed the empty glass by the bottle. And then resuming his former position, he momentarily covered his face with his hands. 'If she had,' he began again, 'I coulda told her that they didn't matter, nobody else mattered but us. Yes, I did used to get upset with what she told me they were saying,' he confessed, 'but not for me –for her.' And then almost immediately after this, Max added, 'Perfection is a big ask for a guy like me, you know.'

Eleanor frowned; he'd lost her with that. 'What do you mean?' she asked him.

'I wasn't cut out to play act at being perfect,' he explained, 'not even to spite hateful people like Bianca's family.'

Immediately a realisation dawned on Eleanor. *That's what it was,* she cried silently. It wasn't, as she'd thought, that Max and Bianca's relationship was 'too grown up' for Max's playful character. 'It was too perfect for you.' It didn't allow for either of them to be who they are, to kick back like he and Arabella often did.

'Yes, exactly,' Max agreed. 'I'm the kinda guy who likes and enjoys journeys,' he confirmed. 'And so for me life has to be a journey. Bianca and I were supposed to carry on how we'd started, which was taking a few life steps, stopping to reflect together, laughing or crying together about where we'd got to on the journey so far, while making sure that we learned the reason why we were where we were, before we set off again, either on the same path that we were on or on a different one and so on.'

Max sighed heavily, almost as if he'd become angry. 'Perfection all the time is stressful, it makes life seem more like a mission than a journey and that's not enjoyable for a guy like me. I need to feel life.'

'By having affairs?'

'Yup!'

Oh dear God! How truly sad it all was. But Eleanor still couldn't understand his reasoning. 'If you knew all this and felt how you say you do, why did you continue with the divorce, why did you get back with Arabella?'

'I didn't know about Bianca's side of things until a few hours ago,' Max admitted. He'd called to see if she'd got her letter and how she was doing and they got talking. With their old honesty this time, after all, they had nothing else to lose. That was when he'd told her why it had all gone wrong for him and she explained why she'd changed. 'So that's why I'm so mad. I wish I'd known sooner.'

Bloody hell! 'So what now?' Eleanor asked him.

'We're divorced.'

'I know, but ...' She noticed Max pour himself a half glass of drink, which he downed immediately. 'You're going to get drunk,' Eleanor warned him.

'I sure hope so.'

Oh dear, she thought. 'And then what?'

'Life goes on.'

Yah, but with whom? she wondered. 'Would you ever go back to Bianca?' Eleanor heard herself ask.

Max replied with steely resignation. 'My journey is with Arabella now and I care a lot about her.'

'But you love Bianca.'

'That's life.'

Typical, Eleanor sighed sadly. Although his past affairs didn't suggest so, Max was fundamentally an honourable gentleman. And that's how he was going to remain. Eleanor shrugged. There was nothing to be said on the matter but fair enough, even though the situation was clearly not an ideal one for any of the three involved parties.

Eleanor tried to console herself with the idea that at least Arabella was none the wiser about all this and so could remain happy. But it was no consolation. Eleanor couldn't help feeling torn and like crying. Yes, Arabella was her friend and she'd hate for Max to ever hurt her again, but what about Max and Bianca? They truly loved each other and were a partnership for forty years. Didn't that count for something? Wasn't true love supposed to prevail; especially after all they'd been through together?

Eleanor was a romantic at heart, so for her love was supposed to conquer all and forever win through. Had T.J. survived the plane crash and something like this happened to them when they were older, she would have prayed for them to get back together and see the rest of their life through together, as they'd intended when they got married.

Eleanor looked at her father-in-law. He looked back at her. 'It's all good, kiddo,' he said, but it wasn't and they both knew it. Eleanor glanced up at the sky. *Oh God,* she cried silently. Only He could sort this out in such a way that no one got hurt and everyone lived happily-ever-after.

Chapter Twenty-three

If only you knew what I know

The sound of little feet running interrupted the silence of Eleanor and Max's thoughts. Looking round, they saw Paris and Malachi thundering towards them.

'Hey, it's my champs,' Max called out to them as, approaching their mother, the twins encircled her into a group hug by wrapping their arms around her waist.

'What's brought this on,' Eleanor smiled as, stooping down, she returned the kisses and hugs that were being lavished on her.

'We've missed you,' Paris replied.

'Ah, bless you,' his mother cooed. 'How was the beach?'

'Fab,' Malachi chirped in typical Arabella fashion.

Eleanor eyed her friend who was at a distance and slowly making her way up towards them. 'I hope that's all they've picked up from you, madam,' she called out with playful reproach.

'That and turning every occasion into a shopping trip,' Arabella called back.

'Oh dear,' Eleanor groaned and turned back to her sons. 'So what did you buy?' she enquired.

'Nothing yet,' Paris riposted with a smile that Eleanor recognised only too well. 'We saw a really cool pretend motorbike that'll be great for all three of us.'

Like father like son, Eleanor thought, recalling T.J.'s passion for motorbikes.

'Yeah,' Malachi chipped in. 'It's shaped like a tri-angle and was low like a Harley Davidson. But it wasn't a Harley,' he added quickly. 'And it's got one seat in the front and two at the back –'

'And it goes tut tut tut tut,' his brother demonstrated to complete the picture.

'You let them test drive it?' Eleanor asked, returning her gaze to the now nearing Arabella. She looked awful, not well at all. 'Oh my goodness what have they done to you?' she exclaimed.

Arabella had now reached the slab. 'Yes, I let them test drive it,' she confessed. 'It was all I could do to get peace.' She reached out to Max, who pulled her up the last step.

Eleanor shook her head in dismay. Now the boys had tried out the bike, she'd never hear the last of it. Soon, would come the whining for her to go and have a look at it and all in the hope of convincing her to buy it for them. 'Kids, who'd have them?' she pretended to complain.

'You,' her sons chorused, causing the adults to laugh.

As they did so, Eleanor noticed the flash of sadness briefly register on Arabella's face. 'You okay?' she enquired.

'Mhm.' The reply was lacklustre.

Eleanor responded with a questioning glance that was discreetly replied with a shrug.

Oh dear, Eleanor groaned silently. Something was definitely up. 'Okay, you two,' she decided, gathering her sons by an arm each. 'Bedtime.'

'Already?' they cried out together.

'Yup, come on.'

'But we haven't finished telling you about the bike,' Paris protested.

'Another time,' his mother riposted.

'But –'

'Be good and it's yours,' their grandfather negotiated.

The little boys' eyes lit up.

'Really?' Malachi checked.

'I promise.'

'Max,' their mother objected, but it was too late. A promise was a promise and his grandsons knew it. All they had to do was to continue being good and obedient, especially now.

'Goodnight,' they chorused and thundered back towards the house with their little rucksacks on their backs that made them look like two-legged tortoises from a distance.

With her sons now gone, Eleanor turned to Max. 'You spoil them too much,' she complained.

'They're great kids,' he replied.

'But not for much longer if you carry on spoiling them like this.' Sensing that her protests would change nothing, Eleanor resigned from further comment with the threat of 'Wait till you both have kids.'

At the utterance both Max and Arabella flinched secretly. Max because, although he'd begun to warm to the idea of him and Arabella possibly having children together, he'd changed his mind that morning after hearing about her past attempted suicide.

For him, mothers were supposed to be resilient and never give up, no matter how difficult things got, and he wasn't so sure now that Arabella was that kind of person. What if, even with all effort from him, things didn't work out between him and her, would she try again to kill herself? And if she did, what if she succeeded this time around? It wouldn't be fair to their children and he wouldn't be able to explain away such a 'quitting' mindset that made no sense to him.

On her part, Arabella had started at the mention of them having kids because, according to the home pregnancy test kit she'd used that morning, there was one on the way. It was what Arabella had been dreaming of for so long now, but with Max not having broached the topic since their initial discussion a month ago, she'd misconstrued his wanting to wait until when his divorce came through to give her the good news as being a sign that, just like her father had supposedly not wanted her to be born, Max didn't want to father any children with her and so wouldn't want this child she was carrying.

With these misconceptions, it was hard for Arabella to delight in the discovery that she was at last pregnant. How could she, when she believed that there was so much thinking to be done? And by herself in secret, so whatever decision she came to would be one that spared her child the lifetime of pain that she'd been forced to endure since learning the truth of her birth?

'On that note,' she interjected suddenly. 'Shall we?' It was the cue for them to be leaving.

'Sure.' Max couldn't have agreed more. It'd been a long day and the sooner he was asleep and getting it over and done with, the better.

A scream from the house attracted Eleanor's attention. 'Go to them,' Arabella suggested. 'We'll speak later.'

Eleanor recognised the tone. Arabella wanted to chat about something, *but what could it be?*

Chapter Twenty-four

Incidents and Accidents

'Free at last, free at last,' Eleanor chanted as she followed her sons through the open door beside which Arabella was standing. Having completed and sent her agent the fifth and what she hoped to be final revision of her latest novel, she and her sons were en route to the Cheesecake Factory to celebrate.

It was the first time they'd seen Arabella since the day Max's divorce papers came through. 'You're looking positively blooming,' Eleanor remarked as she stopped to give her friend a peck on the cheek.

'And you're in an exceptional mood, how come?'

'I've finished all my rewrites.'

'Well done.'

'Thanks. We're off to the Cheesecake Factory to celebrate –'

'Yay,' the twins thrilled from near by.

'And we've come to get you to join us.'

'Ew!' Arabella grimaced, ushering the boys towards the television at the other end of the flat with a nod in its direction.

'Ew?'

'Yah, I've gone right off them,' she explained as she returned her attention to Eleanor.

Arabella had always loved cheesecakes with a passion. This was news to Eleanor. 'Since when?'

'A few weeks now.'

'Hm!'

'But we could go for seafood,' Arabella counter suggested. 'The boys love it, as do you.'

'But you don't.'

'I do.'

This was also news to Eleanor, who recalled Arabella always meeting up with them after seafood because she hated 'the smell of the stuff', in her own words. 'Since when?' she quizzed.

'Oh, a few weeks.'

Eleanor became suspicious. 'You're not –'

'Yes, I am.'

'Pregnant?'

'Mhm,' her friend beamed back at her.

'OMG!'

'Can you believe it?'

'OMG!'

The twins perked up. 'What's happening? What's happening?' They too wanted to be in on all the excitement.

'Aunt Arabella –'

'Now likes seafood.'

'Yay.'

Eleanor eyed her. 'Is it a secret?' she mouthed.

'Yup.'

'Max doesn't know?'

'Nope.'

'What?' Eleanor exclaimed and then, spotting her sons' interested gazes, changed the topic. 'Where's Max?' she asked.

'At the golf club, why?'

'We need to talk – you and me – in the kitchen now.'

'No,' Paris protested. He knew what that meant whenever his mother said that to one of her friends. 'We're supposed to be having cheesecake, remember?'

'And we shall, poppet, seafood too,' she added as a bribe.

The boys nodded disagreeably and, ushered along by their mother, reluctantly shuffled their way towards the sitting room with its impressive taupe-coloured corner unit sofa that ran along the two perpendicular walls, just beneath the non-stop line of windows looking out to the rainy day and choppy grey waters beyond the front.

Once they were comfortably seated and the television had been put on, Eleanor returned to Arabella who, as instructed, had remained there, at the kitchen end of the open-plan luxury Bell town apartment that she shared with Max. Without further ado, the women branched into the kitchenette and took cover behind the large fridge.

'What's going on,' Eleanor immediately demanded in a whisper.

'I'm pregnant.'

'We've ascertained that bit. You and Max,' she clarified. 'What's up? How come he doesn't know? But before you answer …' Eleanor added. With her sentence uncompleted, she ran round the short counter that separated the almost non-existent dining room from the compact kitchen with its big American appliances and limited floor space. With one of the heavy dark wood dining chairs in hand, she returned to Arabella with a command to 'sit.'

'I feel better standing,' Arabella informed her and began to drag the chair back to its original place in the dinning room whose yellow walls tastefully showcased the still life pictures that had recently been acquired from a local gallery. The pictures by their simplicity accentuated the beauty of the eye-catching and stylish lemon and soft mint-coloured rug that lay graceful under the round dark wood dining table and its matching chairs.

'Wait, I'll do it,' Eleanor intervened.

'I can manage,' she was duly told and left waiting in the kitchenette. On her return, Arabella hoisted herself onto the counter that separated the dining and kitchen areas. 'So where were we?' she asked, but Eleanor had something else on her mind.

'You shouldn't be jumping around like that in your condition,' she chided her.

'Yes, Mother –'

'Talking of which,' Eleanor interjected, 'does she know?'

'Yes, as does my father. They're both flying in next week.'

Eleanor gulped. 'And you haven't told Max yet. Well, you better hurry, before they get here.'

'They'll be here for a day only. In a hotel. He won't see them.'

Eleanor suddenly looked worried. *Why all the secrecy?* 'You're not thinking of aborting the baby, are you?'

'God, no,' Arabella declared. 'That's the only thing in all this that I'm certain of.'

Eleanor looked unconvinced. 'So why the delay in sharing the news with Max?'

'I haven't decided if I'm going to stay with him or not.'

'What? How can you not stay with him, he's the baby's father, isn't he?'

'Of course he is.'

'So, why the –'

'Shush,' Arabella reproached her. 'That pair of yours never miss a trick and I don't want them breaking the news to Max before I'm ready,' she whispered.

'So you can scarper before he gets wind that you're carrying his baby,' Eleanor accused.

'I've told you, I haven't decided yet what I'm going to do,' Arabella reiterated.

Eleanor looked her friend straight in the eyes. 'You have to stay with him, Arabella. He's given up so much for you.' Eleanor wished that she could disclose just how much, but she and Max had chatted on the phone the day before and he'd made her promise that their conversation two days ago, regarding the divorce and so on, would be kept between them.

'I won't give my child up for him or any other man, ever again,' Arabella whispered angrily. 'And I won't stay with him either, if he doesn't want to be a father.'

'Which you won't know, until you tell him.' Eleanor paused. 'You owe him that much.'

Arabella nodded. 'Yah.'

Eleanor had other questions in mind. 'When did you get a chance to pop into the clinic for a test?'

'I did a home test that morning after our last night out and I got further confirmation today from that Swedish medical centre place.'

It all now made sense to Eleanor. 'You had morning sickness that day, not a hangover.' Suddenly Eleanor's expression perked up with a look of determination. 'You can't keep this from Max any longer. It'll all be fine. But you must tell him now.'

Arabella seemed to be losing her cool. She inhaled deeply, as if for patience. 'Max doesn't want any more kids,' she blurted out. 'Well, not with me anyway. He has as good as told me so.'

'What, when?'

'Yesterday, for instance, when he skilfully steered me from the topic.'

'But that doesn't mean anything.'

Arabella became angry. 'Look, Eleanor,' she began tersely. 'The man has more or less told me that he doesn't want to have kids with me and that's all I need to know.'

'He told you he wanted to think about it first.'

'That's just delaying tactics.'

'And you think the best response to that is to run off and have the baby without him?'

'In my experience, yes.'

'In your ... Hold that thought.' Eleanor had spied her sons watching them with concern. She forced a smile. 'Are you guys okay over there?' she called out to them. Without answering, the little boys looked away quickly. She turned back to Arabella. 'Have you got some fruit juice and biscuits?'

'Sure.' And with that she leapt off the counter and onto the dark wooden floor space between it and the trendy stainless steel sink unit against the wall opposite. 'Their devoted grandfather, who doesn't want any more kids of his own, makes sure we're always well stocked up on those malt biscuits that they like, plus apple juice and sparkling water.'

'Oh God,' Eleanor groaned. 'I'm going to kill Max one of these days. I've told him time and time again that those biscuits are full of hydrogenated fat and I don't like them eating things with all that inside.'

'Oh, chill out, Eleanor.'

'But it's bad for them, Arabella. Wait until you have your own.' The words echoed like a déjà vu of when they last saw each other. The irony wasn't lost on Eleanor, who instantly broke into a smile. 'It's mad, isn't it? Three days ago, it seemed light years away and now it's only nine month –'

'Eight months to go.'

'Not that you're counting.' She paused. 'Wow! What a life! One never knows what's coming round the corner: deaths, births. It's good, though.' And then, noticing the tray of biscuits and fizzy juice in Arabella's hand, she thanked her for them and hurried the provisions over to her sons in record time.

On her return, Eleanor resumed the conversation from where they'd left off before. 'You said "in my experience" when you were saying about running off and having the baby without his knowledge. What did you mean by that?' Eleanor asked.

Arabella, who was back sitting on the counter, jumped off it again. 'I was talking about my father,' she disclosed without looking at Eleanor. 'That's what my mother should have done to him. It would have saved us both a lot of bother.'

'Rewind, I'm lost.'

'He didn't want kids either,' Arabella explained. 'But Mummy thought he'd change his mind after I was born.' Arabella walked out of the kitchen and across to a door in the wall directly opposite the narrow kitchenette entrance. As if in a trance, Eleanor followed her.

'Did your mother get pregnant on purpose?' she asked, following her friend into the minute laundry room opposite.

'I believe so. And he made her pay for it.'

'How?'

'He left her. Well, both of us.'

'So that's why they broke up?'

'Yah.' Arabella's eyes brimmed over with tears.

'Oh, you poor baby,' Eleanor cried, leaning forward to embrace her friend.

'Poor Mummy, I'd say,' Arabella interjected, eluding Eleanor's hug. 'You'll only make me cry more if you do that,' she said, forcing a smile through her tears. 'I suppose he couldn't stay living with a woman who didn't respect his wishes and a child he didn't want around.'

'What an ass.'

'Is he, though?' Arabella wondered aloud without looking at her friend. 'Why should he or any man be forced to assume a responsibility that he'd clearly stated that he didn't want?' Arabella appeared to be getting angry. 'She had no right trying to force him into a family situation like that.'

'I suppose.'

'He did well to leave her.'

'Arabella!'

Looking lost in thought, Arabella smiled sadly. 'They've started talking again,' she divulged. She fell pensive. After a moment she burst out laughing. 'Wouldn't it be funny if they got back together again, now that I'm no longer an issue?'

'How are things between you and him now?'

'I love him, but he doesn't like me very much. I get upset about it, so he retreats. That's our cycle; always has been, always will be.' Quickly emptying the basket of dirty clothes on the tiled floor in the stuffy utility room, Arabella began stuffing the washing machine with whites only. 'So you see, that's why I'd rather have my child on my own. You cut out the middle man,' she said coldly. 'Daddy died before you were born – end of – no pain for the child. You can't miss what you don't know.'

Eleanor didn't know what to say, except 'I'm sorry, I never knew.'

Arabella regarded her with a sad smile. 'Life goes on, what ho!'

It was all bravado and Eleanor knew it. What a couple of days they were all having. *Well, Max and Arabella,* Eleanor thought. She sincerely hoped that no other crisis was still to come.

Just then, they heard a key turning in the latch on the main door into the flat.

'Max,' Arabella whispered.

'You have to tell him and give him a choice.'

'I'll try.'

'Not try, you must.'

The formerly muted voices of Paris and Malachi reporting their mother's conduct to their grandfather suddenly became audible as the dimly lit room filled with light that was streaming in from the main body of the flat through the door that Max was holding open.

'Hello, you,' Eleanor chirped. 'What are you doing back so soon?'

'Golf was rained off.'

'Ah, sorry to hear that,' she lied.

'I'm not,' Max smiled. 'I hear I'm just in time for cheesecake celebrations, once you two get out of there.'

'Yes,' Arabella chirped.

The twins linked hands and shuddered with glee. 'Can we go now?' Malachi chipped in.

'Yes, so come on, the pair of you. Chop, chop,' Eleanor commanded, ushering her sons into motion. Within seconds, the boys and their mother had rushed out of the flat and with the slamming of the door behind them made it clear to Max and Arabella that treats for today were going to be strictly for three.

As the door banged shut behind them, Arabella remembered that she'd forgotten to tell Eleanor about the good news she'd overheard. The day before, while out shopping, she'd spotted Thorsten. Wanting to surprise him, she sneaked up behind him and found him to be on the phone. He was speaking in German, but Arabella knew enough of the language to gather that he was talking to his ex-fiancée. They were discussing their break-up and who was getting what and moving where.

From the snippets of the conversation that she'd overheard, Arabella gathered that Thorsten's ex would be staying on in the apartment they used to share because he was going to be working abroad for the next few years. Seattle, Arabella assumed. *Fab news for Eleanor*. She could always stay on in Seattle and fly back to Tobago once a month or something to make sure all was going well with her affairs out there. Arabella couldn't wait to hear what Eleanor would decide to do.

Chapter Twenty-five

Mixed Blessings

As Arabella sat in her car in the airport car park, she began to cry. What a bittersweet day it had been. It had started badly with yet another argument with Max, before he left for the East Coast for the completion of the sale of his company, but had ended well with her parents, who were now on their way back to London, where her father had an important board meeting the day after next.

How ironic life can be, she smiled sadly.

As her past was beginning to take the shape she'd always wished for, her future, which two months or so earlier was looking like a dead cert for success, appeared to now be crumbling. She and Max were arguing like crazy these days and he was using that as an excuse for no babies.

He still didn't know that she was pregnant, but she knew now, for sure, his stance on the kid issue.

'Things aren't exactly running smoothly with us, are they, Arabella?' he'd begun that morning. And not without her noting that for the first time in as long as she could remember, he was calling her by her name. Max never did that. It was usually 'pumpkin', 'babe', 'hon', 'belle', or other things, but never 'Arabella.' Yet he'd called her that this morning, when he'd told her that 'I think we should focus more on figuring out where we're headed as a couple than on us having children.'

Well, that certainly told her: the baby she was carrying was a bad idea, in his books.

Juxtapose that with the situation with her and her parents. It turned out that their divorce had nothing to do with her father not loving her.

Her father, bless him, had almost passed out when she told him that she'd known all along that he'd left them because he hadn't wanted her and didn't know how to love her. 'Why didn't you ask me the truth, you silly sausage?' he'd demanded with tears in his eyes.

But how could she have? She thought she already knew the answer and that was bad enough. How did he think she would have coped if she had asked and he'd told her that she was right and left her no hope? No room for those wishful thoughts that she may be wrong and that he did love her as much as she loved him and wanted him to love her. Where would she have been then, without those daydreams that she used to doze off to with a smile in her heart? She would have rather died than to have been robbed of them.

She had questions for him too. Why had he never told her that he loved her?

'I did,' he'd smiled. 'Everyday without fail, but you won't remember.'

She did remember and the kisses too, especially on that last day at Kenwood House. The day he left.

'The last day at Kenwood House wasn't the day I left. I took you there one more time, a few months later, but you cried non-stop.'

Arabella had no recollection of that day, but her father did.

'I never forgot it,' he'd said. 'You told me you hated coming to Kenwood House, you hated me. I told you I loved you, but you called me a liar. You said if I did love you I wouldn't leave you. I tried to explain that it didn't work like that, but you wouldn't have it. You screamed, you shouted and tore at me. The more I told you I loved you, the louder you screamed.'

This was all news to Arabella because she had no memory of the incident or of others on the telephone when her father again tried to convince her that he did love her.

Sophia remembered the incidents on the phone. 'You got in such a state each time that he had to stop calling you for a little while.'

Now that Arabella did remember, but she thought he'd stopped calling because she'd merely cried about missing him so much.

'No,' her mother had rebuffed the claim. 'You did more than cry,' Sophia told her. 'You were literally convulsed with anger each time you spoke to him that I couldn't risk him calling in case you hurt yourself.'

'Fine,' Arabella conceded. But why didn't her father ever offer her more than money? Why didn't he ever take an interest in other areas of her life?

'I did,' he told her. 'But you didn't want me to. When you were growing up and I'd ask you questions about your life, you'd clam up and say you had to go. Money was the only thing you ever called to ask for. Everything I know about you is from your mother.'

That revelation had shocked Arabella. She hadn't realised until she moved to Seattle that her parents were on talking terms, let alone for how long and that her father had parented her by proxy, with the help of her mother.

'And then when you grew up,' her father had added, 'you stopped calling altogether and seldom returned my calls, so I gave you space and stopped calling too.'

How weird it had been for Arabella, hearing about her from her father's point of view and learning that all along they'd both wanted the same thing, a better relationship with each other, but neither daring to ask for it for fear of the other's rejection. How truly sad! But on the up side, at least now things would be better between them.

Arabella's thoughts ran to her mother. *What a woman!* she smiled. Good on her for insisting that they came together, in person, to tell their daughter that they were back together again.

As Arabella turned on the ignition, she remembered that with everything that had been happening to her over the past week, she'd forgotten to ring and tell Eleanor the good news about Thorsten. Switching off the engine she dialled her friend.

'Guess what?' she launched in as soon as her friend picked up.

'Max is thrilled about the baby?'

'No.'

'Oh, he's not?'

'It's nothing to do with Max or me, it's about Thorsten.'

Eleanor knew she would definitely not be able to guess, so she said so and didn't bother trying to hazard a guess.

The news was too good for Arabella to bear to hold in any longer. 'He's in the process of breaking up with his fiancée,' she shouted excitedly.

'And that's good news?'

Arabella could scarce believe her ears. Was it her imagination or did Eleanor sound unhappy by the news? 'El,' she called out. 'Did you hear me?'

'Yes,' her friend sighed. 'He's leaving his fiancée.'

'She's his ex, he's already left her.'

'I asked him not to.'

Arabella was now confused. 'How many ex-fiancées does he have?' she asked.

'One that I know of,' Eleanor replied.

'So how could you have asked him not to leave her, when he'd already left her before you met him?'

'But that can't be right.'

'It is,' Arabella confirmed. 'I overheard him on the phone. I overheard him telling her that he'd already couriered over the keys, as he'd moved all his stuff out to his brother's before he left for Seattle.'

'Oh,' Eleanor gulped. Thorsten had told her about his break-up with his fiancée, but she'd assumed that he was breaking up with her because of his relationship with Eleanor and so she'd told him that she didn't want to see him any more. 'Whoops!'

'What?'

'I finished with him.'

'What?' Arabella cried. 'Why?'

Eleanor began to squirm. 'I thought they were together when he started seeing me and was ending it with her because of me.'

'Oh, for goodness sake. What's wrong with you, woman? So that's that, is it?'

Eleanor now hoped not, but the decision was out of her hands. Thorsten had flown to Nigeria on business to report back to the private airline on whose behalf he had been negotiating a deal with Boeing. He wouldn't be back in Seattle for another couple of weeks and then he'd be leaving soon after for a year in Nigeria. He'd been very upset with Eleanor when he'd left. Would he take her call if she tried to ring him on his return? That she didn't know and could only try._

Chapter Twenty-six

Season's end

'Where is she?' Max demanded as soon as Eleanor opened the door.

What? she squinted. 'You're back in town. Where's who?'

'I'm not in the mood for games, okay, so where's Arabella?'

'Arabella? What do you mean where is she?' Eleanor couldn't hold back the yawn.

'Where is she?' her father-in-law shouted.

'Max, please,' she implored him 'Calm down.'

'No. I will not damn well calm down,' he bellowed.

From over Max's shoulder, Eleanor noticed the curtains at number 9152 twitching. It was Mrs. Schumann. *Oh no!* Eleanor groaned. Mrs. Schumann was the most difficult neighbour on the block, who didn't need an excuse to complain to the housing association.

She'd already complained twice about Paris and Malachi flying their kites too close to her house and leaving their bikes too far out in the road that she could barely drive by. It wasn't true, but that's what she'd said. Eleanor didn't need her issuing a third complaint. 'Please, let's take this inside,' she immediately suggested and almost dragged her father-

365

in-law over the threshold. 'I know you're upset and all that,' she told him once they were inside. 'But it's been a rough day for the boys and me, and now that they're finally asleep, I don't want them to be woken up.'

'What's happened? Are they okay?'

'Yes, they're fine.'

'Good.'

Eleanor had barely shut the door behind them when Max started up again.

'Why didn't you tell me she was pregnant?' he demanded.

'It wasn't for me to tell you, and besides, I found out less than an hour before you did.'

'Do you have any idea where she's gone?'

'What?'

'She's gone,' Max reiterated. 'Arabella's gone.'

Oh no, Eleanor gasped. She'd suspected that that was coming. *Oh God!* 'I'm so sorry.'

'You knew she was gonna leave, didn't you?'

Eleanor let her gaze drop to floor. 'No, I didn't, not for sure.'

'Not for sure,' Max blazed. 'So you had an inkling?'

Eleanor felt wracked with guilt. Yes, there was the inkling, but she didn't believe that Arabella would finally go through with it, not after what she'd found out about the truth about everything to do with her father. 'I'm so sorry.'

'So am I. I thought I could trust you.'

'You can, always.'

Max gave her a dirty look. After a moment's silence, he spoke. 'Could she have gone to stay with Thorsten?' he asked.

'No, he's left the country for good.'

Max was distraught. 'Come on, Eleanor, you've gotta know where she is. Another inkling, maybe?'

But she honestly didn't. Max refused to believe her. 'But you said you spoke to her an hour ago.'

'Yes, but she didn't say anything about going anywhere.'

'She must have.'

'Not to me,' Eleanor snapped and then, cooling down, lowered her voice to a sympathetic tone. 'Look, Max, she's probably checked into a hotel for the night … you know, to cool down.'

'Cool down from what?'

'About you not wanting the baby.'

'How the hell can she know what I want when this is the first time I'm fucking hearing anything about it?' With that he flung a piece of paper at her, which slowly floated down to the floor.

'Max, please,' Eleanor snapped. 'You're angry, I realise, but waking the boys isn't going to solve anything.' Bending down, she retrieved the paper he'd dropped and began reading it.

'But,' Eleanor gasped. 'She was going to tell you weeks ago, that day when your golf got rained off.'

'You knew then?'

'Yes.'

'So why didn't you tell me?'

'It wasn't for me to tell you.'

'What the hell are you talking about?' he raged.

'It had to come from Arabella.'

He took a few steps away. 'I don't fucking believe this,' he said, shaking his head, and then swinging round to face her, he glared at her. 'When has that ever stopped you, Eleanor? For two damned years now, you've been neck deep in my business and now is the time you choose to get picky about what you get involved in?'

'She was supposed to tell you.'

'Of course she was, but she didn't,' he hissed, snatching the paper from his daughter-in-law and stuffing it back into his trouser pocket.

'Do you want the baby?'

Max glared at her. 'What the hell kind of question is that?'

'It's the kind of question she's going to ask you if you find her.'

Just then, Eleanor's mobile phone began to ring. She took it out of her dressing gown pocket and inspected the screen. 'It's her.'

'Give it to me.'

'No, let me speak to her first, please.' And with that she started to walk towards the dining room. 'Hello.'

'Have you heard?' Arabella asked her.

'Yes, I just did.'

'I'm sorry, but I couldn't tell you, before,' Arabella said. 'You would have tried to talk me out of it.'

Eleanor sighed. 'So where are you?' she asked.

'On the way to the airport.'

'Oh, Arabella, this is such bad form.'

'Damn right it's bad form,' Max shouted and headed towards Eleanor. As he got to her, he snatched the phone from her hand. 'Arabe –' He looked sadly at Eleanor. 'Hello,' he said in a lower tone. Taking the phone away from his ear, he handed it back to Eleanor. 'She hung up. Where is she?'

'On her way to the airport.'

'The airport? What the …? Oh my God, no,' and with that Max dashed out of the back door and towards his car that was parked blocking the back gate.

As he drove towards the airport many thoughts raced through Max's mind, but none of them made any sense, not even this journey to the airport. When he got there what would he do? How would he find her? What would he say to change her mind? Did he want to change her mind? If so, why, and if not, why was he chasing after her?

He remembered the note she'd left him, that was 'bad form' as Eleanor had said. Max felt the hot flush of anger begin to rise from his chest. After all they'd been through, after all they'd claimed to feel for each other, and the best she could do was a note on a small sheet of paper. That hurt.

How could Arabella believe that he wouldn't want this baby? Yes, he'd rather that they'd worked things out between them first, but as the baby was already here, what could they do but muddle through somehow?

Why was she so keen to believe that he wouldn't want the baby? A thought occurred to Max.

'No,' he said out loud in an attempt to dispel it. Of all the negative things that Arabella could be accused of, a fake she wasn't. There was no way she could have been faking her feelings for him. No way this could be her revenge for him dumping her that evening at T.J.'s funeral when the news of the affair broke. His phone began to ring. He snatched it off the passenger seat and scanned the screen. It was Arabella.

'Hello.'

'I'm sorry.'

'What's going on, Arabella?'

'I'm scared.'

'What of?'

'Of you hating me.'

'Shit,' Max cursed and slammed his foot down on the brake. He'd narrowly missed crashing into a Mustang that had suddenly pulled out of the junction. 'Look where the hell you're going,' he shouted at the driver, who was already speeding on ahead.

As he watched the taillights meandering from lane to lane ahead, Max wondered if the driver was drunk or stoned. Whichever, it didn't matter; he'd have to keep an eye on the guy. Max put the phone back to his ear. 'Look, I really can't talk now,' he told Arabella, and before he could finish what he was saying, he noticed the taillights of the Mustang he'd intended to keep an eye on looming towards him. Having collided into the back of a car in front, the Mustang had been brought to a sudden stop without Max realising and now he was on collision course with it. 'Damn!' Max shouted as he slammed on his brakes and turned the steering wheel right.

Arabella heard his shout and then the screeching sound. 'Max!' she cried out, but he didn't answer. 'Oh my God, what have I done?' she despaired and began to panic. 'Max!' she shouted again anxiously. But he still didn't reply. He'd let the phone drop when he gripped the steering wheel tighter to try to swerve the car. 'God, please let him be safe, please,' Arabella prayed and wondered what to do.

Max let his head drop to the steering wheel. He'd managed to veer right in the nick of time. Any later and it would have been a bad accident. He shouldn't have been on the phone. *That Arabella,* he groaned silently. She thrived on too much drama for his liking.

Just then his phone began to ring. It was Arabella. Max considered ignoring the call, but he couldn't let her leave the country until they'd at least talked through the situation. He took the call.

'Hello.'

'Are you okay?'

'I'm fine,' Max's tired voice informed her from the other end of the line. Pausing, he took a deep breath. The Mustang driver and the driver of the car into which he'd careered were exchanging details. 'I can't do this, Arabella,' he told her.

'Can't do what?' she asked with increased tension in her voice.

'I'm too old for all this drama.'

'Don't say that, please, Max.'

'It's true ... I almost got myself into a serious collision just then.'

'Are you okay?'

'Yes,' he sighed. 'But I could have been killed.'

Arabella remained silent.

'And for what, Arabella, you, the baby, neither of which I'm gonna be seeing anymore, right?'

'That's why I'm calling.'

Max turned the key and started the engine. Looking over his shoulder, he checked for oncoming traffic. There wasn't any, so he put the car into gear and slowly pulled away from the hard shoulder.

'Max.'

'I'm listening.'

'What are you doing?'

'Trying to get my bearings to get back home.'

'Home? But Eleanor said –'

'I was on my way to come find you, but like I just said, I don't think I can do this anymore.'

'So I was right, you don't want the baby.'

Max shook his head and smiled to himself. 'Right now, I'm not sure what I want anymore, but one thing's for sure, becoming a father again seems the least of my problems.'

'So you're happy with the news?'

'I'm not happy with the way it was given to me.'

'But that was because –'

'You were scared … So you keep saying.'

'It's true.'

'I believe you.'

'Don't be like this, Max, please.'

'Arabella, I'm not trying to be anyhow. What you're hearing is a very tired man speaking. I am not and never have been set up for this kind of drama, so I apologise for not giving you the kind of response you were looking for.'

'Can I come home?'

Max swerved to avoid the taillights in front of him that seemed to have suddenly appeared out of nowhere. 'Oh man, I've got to get off the road.'

'I'll take that as a no, shall I?'

Arabella's voice reminded him of their conversation. 'What?'

'You don't care anymore, do you?'

'Not for dramas, no, and never have.'

'Don't you care about me anymore?' she specified.

Max smiled bitterly. 'That's not the issue.'

'What's the issue?'

'I'm not sure if I can handle any more of these ups and downs from the past coupla weeks.'

'You won't have to.'

'Who says?'

'I say,' Arabella eagerly vouched.

Max frowned. He wasn't convinced. 'I don't think you can help yourself.'

'I can.'

'So you've been acting up on purpose?'

'No.'

'Then how will you be able to stop it now?'

'Because if you really do want the baby and you still love me, then I have nothing to worry about and no need to get cranky and confused, right?'

'Right,' Max smiled.

'So can I come home?'

'You didn't ask me before you left, why are you asking me if you can come back?'

'Can I?'

Max wasn't going to make it that easy for her. 'If you want to.'

Arabella wasn't quite sure how to take that. 'Do you want me to?'

'I don't know, so it's up to you if you wanna chance it.'

'And if I decide to, will you come and pick me up from here?'

'Where are you?'

'The airport.'

'No, it's too far away,' Max retorted. 'Get a taxi.'

Arabella swallowed hard. She'd blown it.

'In fact, there's one in front of you as I speak,' Max added. 'But you've gotta be quick if you want it, before that guy in the tan sweater beats you to it.'

Arabella looked up and noticed the man in the tan sweater and chinos. How did Max know? A smile brightened her tear-sodden face. Behind the taxi that the man was rushing to get was a silver Mercedes. *Max*! He'd known her well enough to know that she'd never have made it past the entrance, she giggled. Arabella picked up the only suitcase she'd managed to pack and take with her. It suddenly felt very heavy. Her legs became unsteady. *Oh my God, I think I'm going to fai –*

She passed out.

Arabella came to in the hospital with Max by her bedside. The look on his face said it all. She began to cry: for the baby, for Max and for herself. Not feeling much like talking, she pretended to doze off again. Max was too tired to keep watch. He too dozed off.

As Arabella listened to the steady sound of his deep breathing, she thought back to the moment before she collapsed at the airport. For that split second, everything in her life was perfect and she had everything she'd ever wanted: parents who loved her and were back together again, Eleanor back in her life, a partner that loved her and their baby enough to chase after her to the airport, and a future that was looking like it could be rosy.

Arabella wondered how many people could ever say that they'd had that experience.

And now an important part of that dream had slipped away. Her baby was dead, miscarried. Opening her eyes a little, Arabella regarded Max. He looked tired, exhausted, to be specific. Arabella wandered if he was dreaming. And if he was, was it a happy dream about them. She doubted that very much, not after the past few weeks and all that they'd been through, everything she'd put him through. She should have trusted him, she should have known him well enough to know that he would have loved the baby regardless of whether he'd initially thought it was a good idea for them to have one or not. But she didn't.

Arabella's thoughts ran to Bianca. Had she been in her position, yes, she'd definitely have known Max well enough to know how he would have reacted to the news about the baby. Bianca wouldn't have put him through the drama of him having to chase after her. She wouldn't have needed to.

Arabella felt lacking. Her thoughts ran to the past few weeks and the conversations between Max and Bianca that she'd overheard. They were close – soul mates – something she and Max would never be. The trust between them wasn't there, on her part, anyway. She wanted it to be, but she couldn't help herself. It was hard breaking the habit of a lifetime.

Several of her inconsistencies came to Arabella's mind. For the first time in her life, Arabella saw herself exactly as she was: a damaged person who needed healing. No man was going to be able to heal her, not even her daddy. He was back and that was great and they were going to be making up for lost times, but that wasn't going to heal her. She needed a professional.

Arabella smiled. She couldn't believe what she was thinking. But it was good. It felt a little scary, but as Max would say: 'it's all good'. To Arabella, where she was at now, mentally and emotionally, showed that her healing had already begun and more could take place. Like the alcoholic who needed to hit rock bottom and say 'I am a drunk' in order for healing to begin, she was now able to see and say 'I need help'. And not in the playful manner that she and Eleanor would quip, when either of them did something silly.

So where did all this leave her and Max? Arabella wondered. Where they should have stayed before this last stint: apart. Yes, she loved him with all her heart and she now knew that he cared a great deal for her, but they didn't belong together.

Had never, Arabella admitted silently. Not like he and Bianca did. As this was her moment of complete honesty to herself, she readily admitted to herself that she'd known this fact since that night of T.J.'s funeral. The unbreakable bond between Bianca and Max had been plain to see even though Bianca was claiming that she was through with Max and his philandering ways.

So how was the break-up between her and Max going to be? Arabella mused.

She didn't have to wait long because just then Max opened his eyes. Seeing that she was awake and watching him, he smiled. 'Hey, kid,' he called her as he reached out to take her hand. That said it all.

Arabella smiled back. 'Hey, mister!'

Rising to his feet, Max came to the bed and hugged her. They both knew they'd come to the end of their road together. No one needed to put it in words. 'You okay?' he asked.

'Yup.'

'I'm sorry,' he told her.

'Yah, me too.'

'Maybe it's for the best.'

'I think so.' They were talking about the baby, but both knew that the same applied to them and their relationship.

There was no dramatic parting, no tears. Four days after she left hospital, Arabella moved into the house with Eleanor and her twins. Max came round as he usually did, and there was no awkwardness, not even a question from the boys. It seemed that even they knew that the relationship had run its course.

Eleanor wondered about this. She remembered what Max had once told her about her sons when they were bombarding him with questions about him and Arabella. Maybe he was right; maybe Paris and Malachi were smarter, more mature and more clued up about everything that was happening around them than she knew.

Eleanor smiled. Maybe they knew more about the year-long move she and they were going to be making to Nigeria than she'd given them credit for. She'd told them that they were moving there because she wanted them to learn more about that side of their heritage. She hadn't been lying, but there was the Thorsten factor too, which she'd failed to mention. Maybe they already knew that and were sparing her blushes.

Eleanor stared at the red wall. It was hard to believe that less than three months earlier, she could barely look at it without crying, that she couldn't think of T.J. without getting angry.

How life changes, she thought, _and so very quickly indeed!_ Take this house, for instance, she mused. First it was Max living there when she and the boys arrived, then it was she and Paris and Malachi. Now Arabella had joined them and soon there would be none of them living there. With Max moving back east to be with Bianca, and Arabella returning to London for a boat holiday with her parents and their friends before heading to Tobago to look after things for Eleanor during her stint in Nigeria, the house would go back to being empty.

But not for long, Eleanor hoped. She'd hate for the ghosts of their pasts to ever get lonely and forgotten in 9154. The house in which she had learned to laugh again.